DIGGING
FOR DESTINY

What Reviewers Say About Jenna Jarvis's Work

Digging For Heaven

"I was absolutely fascinated by this fantasy adventure. ...Great adventure with twists and turns to keep not just the characters guessing that I really enjoyed. Hope there will be future stories with Kella and Litz, as I am sure an exciting future now awaits."—*LESBIreviewed*

"...an absolutely amazing book. There's incredible depth to its characters and an amazingly deep and fleshed out world... I could hardly put it down. It had such a captivating way of tying the plot and characters together ...I can't honestly imagine how much better Jenna Jarvis's writing will get."—*To_hold_a_flower*

"There are times when a blurb holds more promise than the book but this was NOT one of those times! I love this story so much! ...Genius execution."—*The Stray Reader*

"This book had me hooked from the start! ...The story builds upon its worldbuilding...by expertly using its characters and their upbringing to show us...the political climate we are standing in... I highly recommend..."—*Bookterror*

"...a character-driven story. The writing was a blast to read."—*Double the Books Magazine*

"I was absolutely blown away by this book in every aspect. ...If you loved Eragon, or Fourth Wing...you'll love this one. The writing is fresh and fun, the characters interesting, and the world unique. What's not to love?! 5/5 stars."—*Grey Reads*

"Every character in the book was given such a full-bodied voice. ...I enjoyed this book IMMENSELY & I HIGHLY recommend it."—*ChristinaC Reads*

"A CONCEPT EXECUTED WITH ROARING PERFECTION... I was beyond entertained. ...I loved the plot, the characters, and the subtle romance."—*Nook Nerds*

"This was such a great book full of adventure, drama, excitement... I was hooked!"—*QueerAfictionado*

Ride With Me

"This was so much fun! From the first moment to the very last, Emma and Lucy shared a complicated adventure that was more than just a roadtrip. …I was smiling so much while reading this, unable to put it down…"
—*Lesbian Review*

"This story has humor, spice, romance and adventure…a beautiful journey about friendship, love, finding yourself, and starting over…a fun and wild ride that kept me hooked from page one! I loved the pining, the banter, the shenanigans, the intimacy, and literally everything about Emma and Lucy's connection."—*QueerAfictionado*

"…a fast-paced cross-country adventure with two dynamic main characters whose time together is as intense as it is amusing. While there's heartache and despair, at the core, this story is about the positivity surrounding change in order to move into the next phase of life. There's humor, sarcasm, tears, steam, and a lot of delicious food! I thoroughly enjoyed riding shotgun during Lucy and Emma's travels and plan to reread it in future."
—*Lesbian Review*

By the Author

Dragon Circle Series

Digging For Heaven

Digging For Destiny

Ride With Me

DIGGING FOR DESTINY

by

Jenna Jarvis

2024

ISBN 13: 978-1-63679-575-1

This Trade Paperback Original Is Published By
Bold Strokes Books, Inc.
P.O. Box 249
Valley Falls, NY 12185

First Edition: June 2024

CREDITS
Editor: Barbara Ann Wright
Production Design: Susan Ramundo
Cover Design By Inkspiral Design

Acknowledgments

This is my third novel, but my first time publishing a sequel. It's a whole new thing. Hearing feedback from people who took my debut novel and made mood-boards of it or listened to my playlists for it and tagged me in their reading updates for it, or who, bafflingly, took a chance on it after hearing me read from it at events has been thrilling. Friends or family have gotten invested in this series, many who don't read this kind of book, or even read at all. It all made actually putting pen to paper on a follow-up feel daunting. But it was always doable, because I'm lucky enough to be surrounded by people who are wonderful at chasing me out of my own head when I get stuck there.

To Cal and my family, thank you for accepting how unsociable I was all through our week's holiday last year, yes, that really was when a good fifth of this book got written. You've all been the most invaluable support system anyone could ever ask for, reading over passages and acknowledgement sections like it's the first time I've ever forced something under your noses. Cal especially for living with me when things inevitably got strange and manic in the deadline crunch time, and for forcing me to pause when the devil in my brain tells me I should just give up and send whatever I have.

To the wonderful colleagues at my day job who did everything to help get me away early or let me swap shifts with them in the aforementioned crunch time, thank you. Mark, you run the coolest of ships (if you're reading this and you like indie music you should check out Postcards from the Underground radio, hello) and everyone working with me then and now is a dream. I think I promised to shout out Jenni and Rachael specifically though for one specific undoable shift, so thanks, lads, you rock.

I have so many friends who were patient with my ranting about paleontology and sea monster ideas and love of big, stupid action films. Friends who accepted my total MIA status my last month of drafting, and my laptop being on my knee for basically all summer movie nights, some of them even having to briefly live with that constant presence. Jess, you get the saint award for at one point living *and* working with me through this and still talking to me after. Mairi, thank you for taking me outside to write; it's better out there. Katie, you are an angel for helping proofread while I was trying to balance multiple deadlines–other Katie (you all know who you are), Deep and Ismay: thank you for calling out my inspirations and keeping me humble even as you raised me up.

Once again, the team at Bold Strokes kept things so smooth through this whole process. Sandy, thank you so much for helping me figure out a series name. Barbara, you know exactly what a mess of repetition and slow action this book would be without you. I cannot thank you enough for all your support and humour that made the process of carving this monster up not only bearable but fun.

I've been lucky with online connections and support too. SJ, thank you so much for helping me launch the cover in far more style and fanfare than I would have managed alone. Alexia, you are a literal angel for giving your time to help me feel more confident about sections I was worried about.

It's a whole new thing writing a sequel, but this story has lived with me a long time. I hope that if you read the first book and sought this one out that it's for you in just the same way. Keep with it, I promise I'm going somewhere with all this.

Dedication

To Mairi, who read *Digging For Heaven* first
and asked me where the sequel was (here it is!)

CHAPTER ONE

L itz's family home was too large. That wasn't just her feelings either: her parents, Princess Minovita and her consort Geshid, were unfashionably monogamous for their station and neither had living parents of their own to care for or siblings sharing the same status. With all attempts at providing Litz with a sibling having long since been abandoned, this left their home always quiet, the four trees making up its corners rarely shaking with any noise or movement. Its upper quarters connected to the rest of town by stiff swinging bridges, and it even had a large stone entrance, merging forest and imported stone in a way that mirrored the palace. Her mother was very proud of that.

It wasn't quiet tonight. Her mother had paid for a bard to beat a few drums and play his long whistle in the corner in honour of Litz being home. She felt for him. This would be a long night. She left a few heavy coins in the colourful hat on the table beside him as she entered the room. He nodded at her with a knowing smile as he started to speed the tempo.

As though listening for her cue, her father turned, a rare smile bestowing youth to his whiskered face. He held out a hand in greeting, and when she took it, he squeezed her tightly before letting go.

"You look well," he said as he returned to leaning a foot on the dinner table. Unlike the tall meeting tables of Aelshia, this came only to their knees where they sat on cushions. Across from them, Litz's mother sniffed, no doubt offended by the lack of deference shown toward the staging area for their food. She got over it enough to turn her attention to Litz.

"Greetings to you, daughter," she said, her tone warmer than Litz expected. She took hold of her cushion and gestured for the others to do the same, sweeping her dress underneath her crossed legs as she sat in an almost grotesquely elegant gesture. Litz felt lumbering and awkward by comparison. Her mother seemed to agree and gave her a tight smile of disappointment as the scimitar on Litz's belt caught loudly on the tile.

"How was the campaign, Litzi?" Her father's smile was far more supportive but seemed a little drained. As Litz returned one, her mother observed them, mouthing his words.

"Hardly a campaign," Litz said, picking up her cutlery. "It was one small clan unhappy at being forced to move. Things were easily settled with little need for violence."

"For the new runway, yes?" Her father took a bite of his food, just a little of the sauce lingering on his moustache. "Wonderful news. It's a prime area down there. And with dragons setting up easier access, we may see development finally."

Litz's mother sniffed, her eyes on his moustache. "Yes, well. It'll be years until there's any real civilisation to be seen. Nothing to get excited for yet."

"Yes, but it's progress for dragons now," Litz's father corrected.

"I'm not sure I'd call any of it progress," Litz said quietly. "Just expansion. It's necessary, perhaps, but the people living there have a right to be upset about it."

"They can hardly be said to live anywhere," her mother said. "Don't they move around every other week?"

"I think it's every month."

"Every season," Litz corrected wearily.

Her mother sniffed again. It never took long in her company for Litz to remember how much she hated that sound. "In any case, it's not truly their home. They can move easily enough. They're simply being difficult because they hate dragons."

Reluctantly, Litz allowed her mind to wander back to the uprising she'd finished putting down that morning. The rage on the faces of those young fighters had almost been overwhelming. More than anything else, it had reminded her of Kella and the way Litz had recognised the righteousness of her anger long before she'd seen any evidence to concede the dragon killer had a point. It made her worry that there was something she was missing.

You're forcing them to move for frivolous reasons. And violently, even if you succeeded in hurting few.

Frivolous? For a runway you pushed for the planning of?

Frivolous for them.

In some annoyance at her dragon's input, Litz narrowed her eyes a little, and of course, her mother assumed that had been aimed at her and glowered back.

She's never noticed when you're speaking to me, has she?

Could you stop? Litz attempted a smile in her mother's direction. "In any case, I'm sure you don't want to hear about my day. How was yours?"

You're using your diplomat voice again.

Shut up.

"Your mother went to court today."

Her mother relaxed into a smile as though warmed by the memory. "I did. Xoia looks radiant, even in grief, gods bless her." She took another bite, almost furtively, her own grief for her dead sister apparently not relevant. "General Makiv has confirmed."

"I have heard."

"They're looking to line up a replacement for his retirement ceremony."

If there was one thing the army was dependable for, it was gossip. Litz had known this for months, and of course, knew exactly what her mother was angling toward. "It now seems to be between Genn, Kilmar, and myself," Litz confirmed.

Her father, who was not actively in the Aelshian army anymore, looked up in sleepy surprise. "Congratulations. They haven't made a dragon rider general in some years.

"Seventy, isn't it?" her mother put in, uncharacteristically knowing. "It might go easier were you to marry. That even if you spoke for dragon interests, you spoke for at least one other great family."

"Mother, you know I—"

"I'm not talking about a man." Carefully, she moved her cutlery around. "What of the second Annik daughter?"

Litz blinked. "You think I should marry *Nic?*"

"Does she not share your…preferences?"

Doesn't she just. Along with several all her own.

Litz fought to keep from choking. When she finally swallowed, she found both her parents' eyes on her, and their servant was refilling her glass. "Yes. I had heard that."

Same-sex marriage wasn't exactly encouraged in high society, but it wasn't much more of a puzzle than monogamy in general. It wasn't the Done Thing, but no one would stop her: like old river lords who died and left their total inheritance to their servants. It would bother his immediate family being slighted, but everyone else would find it, at worst, a benevolent oddity. It had never been out of the question for Litz but not an ambition her mother had ever settled for suggesting. Until now, when interest in seeing Litz rising in rank had increased her desperation.

"Did you hear she's been stationed back in Verassez? You should visit her. Perhaps even invite her to the family estate."

"She has her own estate." Litz took another bite. "But I might get in touch. It has been a while."

Oh, you mean that. And it has not. You tangled with her not a week ago.

Shut up. You like Nic.

For short bursts.

Litz finally had the chance to relax when her mother left the room after dinner, leaving her alone with her father and a room filled with woodblock books. It was an impressive private collection, embossed with a metal no longer found commonly. Litz had never been entirely clear on which of them was responsible for curating it, so she liked to think it was something they had chosen to build together.

"You seem different," he said, to the point as he often was when they had privacy. A common foreigner by birth and a soldier, the niceties associated with the speech of a man of his class had never come to him naturally.

Litz kept her attention on the shelves and let her hand run over the lingering dust. "How so?"

"I'm not sure yet. Is it your cousin's absence?"

She leaned lightly against the bookcase. "I am worried for her."

"That seems sensible. We have no idea where she is or what's happened."

Oh, we have ideas, just none we can prove.

Litz frowned. "I can't believe King Jevlyn had anything to do with it. I was as suspicious as anyone, but I found nothing to suspect there, not when it came to her. If anything, he seemed too careful and terrified of restarting war. He'd sacrificed so much for peace."

Her father put his head to one side. New lines creased his face, and they deepened as he smiled softly. "There's a lot that can go on in a marriage that's hard for an outsider to see."

"Ah, of course, I must cede to the expert."

"Do you think you might?"

She turned back to the bookcase, a little embarrassed to even look at him for long, "What, marry?"

"The Annik girl or someone else. Forgive me my curiosity in my old age."

"Hardly old age." She smiled back at him. "Truthfully, I don't think much on it. If Loren wasn't around to remind me of it, I'd forget the head on my shoulders."

"Now, that's not true." He moved to lean against the bookcase beside her. "If anything, you do too much thinking for your own benefit. I suspect it will make you a fine general. You can do as you please, of course, you always have. But don't leave following your heart too late."

Feeling a little uneasy at the rare poetic sincerity coming from a man who was happiest communicating in nods and shakes of his head, Litz awkwardly patted at his shoulder. "Not the advice I expected from you."

"No? Remember, your mother worries about securing you a fine place because the scandal that was our own courtship might have harmed your chances in life. We were young and daring and disgustingly in love. Indulge her sometimes. She only wants the best for you."

You never doubted that, Loren reminded her, *only that your idea of what was best connected at all.*

"Are you still disgustingly in love?"

Carefully, he looped his arm around hers and began to lead her to the next room where her mother would be waiting with sweet tea. "Oh, I've learned not to be so disgusted by it."

As they wandered, Litz registered that the musician had stopped playing. Perhaps her parents hadn't paid for them to be there all night. Her mother did suffer terribly from headaches. It could have been that the player had brought one on.

But it could have been something else.

You think something followed you home.

I came straight here from the campaign. And I did not hide that. As they were about to pass into the room, Litz held out her arm, doing her best to prevent her father moving any farther.

He met her eyes, the roughly applied veneer of a courtly gentleman falling away to expose the hardened soldier beneath. He unsheathed the knife at his belt slowly, the one that only appeared ceremonial.

With a quick nod, they burst into the room. Litz had ceased expecting her mother to be sitting incredulously. She was, just not in a position to admonish them. The bard's body splayed on the floor, bleeding over his broken instruments. Both he and one of the guards seemed to have been taken out by deep wounds on their necks. Her mother was still alive, gagged and tied to a chair. She stared frantically back at them.

Litz would not tolerate seeing her scared a moment longer, and apparently, her father felt the same. He gave his distinctive battle yell that resonated sharp and high from the top of his mouth and rushed toward the nearest intruder, his knife raised. He was knocked back with magic, shocking Litz, but not long enough to keep her from reacting. Assuming her father would think it was their attackers, Litz forced the door closed behind him with a flick of her wrist.

He bashed the door from the other side, but the thick red hardwood stood firm against his assault. Though she could hear him yelling, Litz kept her focus on the men in front of her.

"Hurt us, and you will never escape my dragon's wrath. You don't want to bring harm to your people like that," she said, trying to match their calm. She did not want to use magic in front of her mother, but if she wanted to get them both out of there safely, she needed to take some risks. Besides, her mother currently had a very limited field of vision.

One of them said something in Vidani, a language Litz knew only a few scant words in. Enough to yell "quiet," "listen," and "stop," all learned and put to use only a day before.

It is far too late for guilt to be of any use, Loren told her, not unkindly. *And I would be lying if I said I thought there was a chance I could reach you in time to help.*

Litz didn't tell her not to worry. Loren was both always going to worry and didn't believe Litz was in any real danger. These men were clearly exhausted and unlikely to have Litz's advantages. Her mother was a different matter.

"We're not here for safety," the other one said, keeping his voice low. "You have ended safety for us once more. We're here for vengeance."

Litz kept her eyes fixed on the knife in their hand. It was far too close to her mother's neck, even if by the looks of the corpses, they did not need knives to do damage. "I did as much as I could to see no harm came to your people," she said, trying to speak honestly.

She was met with expressions as inscrutable as the depths of the dark forest out the window behind them. "That's not how we understood events."

"You weren't there," Litz said, realising. She hadn't faced any magic users in the ambush, not trained ones, at least. But one kid had rushed at her, and she'd acted more harshly with him than with anyone because he'd tried to Push her. And he was a kid, and maybe she had some solidarity for people like her and didn't want to see him killed for making an attempt at the skills she was commanding. Or maybe she'd just dared to hope she'd imagined it.

People tended not to learn magic without an example to follow; she'd known that and had left without finding his teachers. Because as much as everyone wanted to praise her for her successes, she did not want to spend her time hunting down threats to the empire. And now the third and fourth mourners to that empire were in danger because of her inaction. But it still did not make her feel regret.

"Stop this runway," the one who spoke Aelshian said, his voice breaking a little.

"You know I can't," she said. Holding tight to her knife, she glanced carefully around the room for any more traps, anything she could use to help her now she'd forced her only ally out. Luckily, her mother's captors did not seem to have noticed that was her work. She might still have the advantage of surprise. "And I certainly won't be inclined to help you until you release my mother." Her mother's eyes flashed a little, probably incensed that Litz would consider negotiating with terrorists. "The Circle have made their decision, and we have done our best to carry out that decision in a way that works best for the most humans."

He spat on the ground. "Dragons don't belong in this forest. They stayed because your people forced a place for them, but it's killing the world." He sneered. "And still, you serve them. Still, you allow them into your minds, whispering their lies."

Ah. Warriors of the Earth. It's charming to meet humans who claim to follow a higher, selfless purpose.

I think he's sincere. But sincere or not, Litz wasn't about to let him keep the upper hand, not in her home. With a discreet flick of the wrist, she Pulled the ancient shield on the wall down on the non-Aelshian speaker's head, flooring him. Their shock gave her a moment to fling her knife into the other man's side. Her aim was poor, grazing him.

When he looked up, pained and enraged, Litz gathered the strength to Push her mother's chair away from the men standing up behind her. Her mother tried to scream through her gag but a third figure, no doubt hidden behind the furniture, grabbed her from behind. Able to keep her right arm free, Litz flipped a larger woman half over her back, yelling with the effort, and slashed at her thigh with her scimitar as she finished, feeling the blood splatter hot and satisfying over her shoulder and face as she hit an artery.

The woman hit the ground with a hard thump and a pitiful whimper. Litz stepped over her to meet the original attackers, who were back on their feet and moving again.

They'll be desperate now, Loren told her as the relentless noise of her father bashing at the door continued. *Finish this quickly.*

I'm trying. Litz knew she should summon rage, but every time she felt it rising, she remembered why these people were in her home and was left with only the facts: she needed to kill them. They wanted to hurt her and would not stop until they had done that, and they had seen what she could do. That could not be allowed to leave the room, however useful quizzing them on magic users within their clan might be. Besides, she suspected they would not tell her anything. And their very existence was proof that some tradition of magic existed among the Vidani.

Satisfied that her mother was turned out of sight, Litz became bolder. She Pulled at the legs of the Aelshian speaker, forcing him back to the ground. As she tried to rush at him to finish him with her scimitar, his partner held out a hand, and a force Pushed at her wrist.

Why hadn't he killed her yet?

This was all new. The only magical opponents she had ever faced were the Narani, whose powers had taken her by surprise; they had also taken her hostage in an attempt to bargain with the Aelshian throne for land rights. And again, despite her sympathy, Litz had known that nothing she could say in the matter would help them.

Unwilling to let go of the door, Litz released the man's knees and moved her other hand under her trapped wrist. She released the scimitar but was able to catch it with her other hand. She moved faster than her opponent, and her blade landed in his gut. As she'd hoped, his partner cried out, possibly yelling his name, and it was a long enough drop in attention to release her wrist, letting her move forward again. She let the door open as she Pulled the remaining Vidani's wrists back behind his back.

As she'd hoped, her father rushed into the room and twisted the blade in the stabbed man as Litz held the other man's wrists with her hands. His eyes were fixed on his friend, who slipped out of consciousness with a choking sound.

"Hold him still, Litz," her father said quietly as he took the knife out and plunged it back into the fallen man's breast. "Let's keep one alive if we can."

As much as it had not been Litz's intention to allow any of them to live, she was still shocked and gave a cry when the sobbing man forced a hand out of her grip and gestured at his neck. He spat out a few words of Vidani and then, using magic in the same awful way he must have already done with the musician and guard, he Pulled out his own throat and died surprisingly slowly, choking on his own tears and blood.

As her father let out a slow breath, Litz let go and inched away from the body.

I think I know what he said, Loren put in a little hesitantly.

Litz numbly watched her father remove the gag from her mother's mouth. *What?*

Stop trusting the dragons. They will be all our end.

I guess I'll just have to trust you on that, Litz replied as her mother started gasping, yelling. Even without trying to deliver the words aloud, they didn't sound like much of a joke.

CHAPTER TWO

The palace had undergone several changes since the last king's passing, but this wasn't surprising. Kings imposed their own style on where they lived, especially kings as successfully established as Narin had been. Xoia might have embraced her colours and makeup and wardrobe, but her approach to decorating was as drastically different to her mother's as her approach to romance.

Litz couldn't help looking up as she walked through the main hall. The lack of ceiling always drew the eye, and now the work being completed to install a living mural held it. Every branch was being shaped and coloured to reflect an image. It was a dragon because with Xoia, of course it was.

Nothing wrong with that, we are famously aesthetically pleasing. Those with taste will adore us.

Hush. You don't like it, either. If anyone is dragon-bent, or Circle-bent, it would be our new king.

Your new king. Dragons don't do kings.

As Litz marched, she was greeted by a hundred smiling faces, all content to be doing nothing but walk around the room admiring each other and the art around them, making spectacles out of what little was available. Though she politely inclined her head at the few who acknowledged her, Litz did her best to keep marching straight, as though on her way to a critical meeting.

Which she was. But since Xoia hadn't specified a time, Litz could keep whatever pace she chose. And slowing would encourage someone to tell her, once again, the news of the general's imminent retirement or congratulations for her brave quashing of the supposed uprising, or the few who might have the news of her dramatic night before might ask about that. She was doing so well at looking through people that she did not see who pushed a piece of paper into her hands. Unsure how else to react, her grip on it tightened.

Someone else wants your time and thoughts.

Since this would be very inefficient way of poisoning someone, I assume so. Carefully, she folded the paper smaller and tucked it into her belt pocket to review later. Even if the information was trivial, the last thing she wanted to be seen doing in full view of Verassez's court was receive private and urgent messages. In fact...

"Captain Litz?" Now there was someone a little harder to keep walking past. Stilling herself with regret, Litz turned to face Eisha's father as he emerged from around a statue of the River. He was a newly lost presence at court with his king and consort dead and his daughter missing. Though he was known for being the most charismatic and outrageous of Narin's consorts, and he still had a beautiful following of gaudily clad court hangers-on, it was clear he no longer fit here as he once had.

He still summoned a smile with ease when Litz turned. "Or is it still captain?"

She forced a smile of her own and inclined her head politely. "Greetings to you, Uncle."

His quick dark eyes were already moving. "Was that a note I saw? As a man living in grief and agony, indulge me, walk with me, and tell me of your admirers." His smile widened, a sight that Litz trusted as little as she would any other animal baring their teeth at her. To survive in this court as long and successfully as Reishann Sunblessed meant growing a thick skin and a vicious nature, even if his soft face and fine clothing did nothing to announce it. Behind him, an exceptionally pretty man Litz recognised as the second son of a Circle dragon's rider tittered into the back of his hand, amused by Reishann's trademark irrepressibleness.

"They say that not even King Narin could ever put anything past you," Litz said, keeping her tone light as she shook her head. "I had better wake earlier before attempting it myself."

A black curl of his short hair falling over his face, Reishann's expression became more indulgent. "I understand this is not usually your chosen battlefield, darling."

Itching to be moving, Litz held her hands lightly behind her back. "No. But after diplomacy in Jeenobi, I'm doing what I can to expand those battlefields."

"I'm sure you will do as magnificently here as with the ones following you home. How is your dear mother recovering?"

Litz took a breath. He would already know everything. "Thank you for your concern. She's doing well." She had almost fired the entirety of their remaining security and had tried to insist on the genocide of the entire Vidani people. Litz also had a lingering fear that she'd guessed that something about the way Litz had handled things was not entirely natural.

Litz herself was fine. It worried her a little just how fine she was. A few months ago, she had killed a fellow dragonrider using magic, and now she had killed a fellow magic user in the sanctuary of her childhood home. It was disquieting that neither of these events felt much more impactful than any of the hundreds she had carried out in an official capacity during war. They should feel different, should feel worse.

"The idea that the kingdom might have lost its king, second, and then, fourth and fifth mourner in under a year is a truly terrifying one. Or sorry, should I have said third and fourth?" Before Litz could answer, he continued, "And is it true? Did these savages use magic?"

Pausing as though to consider this, Litz did her best not to let her irritation show. "I believe so. They did not seem powerful, however, and were easily overcome."

"Yes, and how did you achieve that with only your weapons? Truly, it seems incredible."

"A successful career, perhaps." She nodded low again, sparing a brief look at his group behind them, who looked at the way she walked alone with questions in their eyes.

Reishann was laughing. "General material indeed!"

No one walked alone in the king's court. No one but dragonriders. When Litz walked away, she felt reminded of that anew.

It never used to bother you so much before.

After everything that happened, it feels uncomfortable to be so exposed. I know you're here with me, but I feel alone when I walk through here.

You feel lonely, Loren said with certainty so dizzying that when Litz reached the edge of the room, she almost stumbled as she looked to the nearby guard for permission to ascend the staircase. It might not be a battleground, but moving around the palace was always strenuous.

What?

The desert made you realise how lonely you are. And now Eisha is beyond reach, as is anyone you met along your journey. You are upset to return to a life you have only me to share with. With the link of soul and mind flowing sure between them, Loren's tone could not be misconstrued. She was not upset by this, only a little concerned.

Would it make you feel better if I went and found Nic for the sparring practice she asked for?

Not particularly.

To Litz's surprise, she was ushered through to her cousin's rooms quickly after climbing the steps. And to her personal rooms, implying that Litz had been summoned as family and not a subject. She didn't believe that for a moment, but she did what she could to keep her body language casual even as she bowed low when the door opened.

Over time, Xoia's commitment to embodying her mother's image had diminished, or perhaps Litz had just grown used to it. The same white makeup on her cheeks, wider than her mother's, that she'd shared with Eisha, painted orange lips parting briefly before curling up in fondness.

"My king," Litz said quickly, as always remembering a little late that Xoia's new status meant that she could never be expected to open a conversation.

"Litz," Xoia said as she leaned into the hand her consort Agsdon laid lightly on her shoulder as he stood.

He bowed politely. By most traditional rankings, he should bow when Litz entered a room; she was a cousin by blood to the king. But with Agsdon's position as Xoia's only consort and her intended First Mourner for herself and the Empire, the issue had become unusually blurred. Litz bowed her head lightly, compromising on the conflicted etiquette.

"Unfortunately, I must take my leave. The Circle riders have requested—"

Perhaps because Xoia had remembered what he was talking about or she didn't want him saying it in front of Litz or she truly didn't care, Xoia waved a gracious hand to cut him off. "Of course," she said.

When the door closed, Xoia ushered for Litz to take the small cushioned seat in front of her and took hold of both her hands. Litz marvelled for a moment at how soft they were. Xoia had never held a sword, been blistered by dragon fire, or held tools. She'd done her best to make her mind a weapon, even if, as Litz understood it, it had never been the sharpest one. She had none of her mother's political shrewdness or her sister's easy charisma. Litz had always sympathised with that, having felt similarly out of place as a child but had found an escape through Loren and had never needed to be groomed for a job unsuitable to her.

Careful now with the treasonous thinking.

Who are you going to tell?

"How is your mother faring?" Xoia asked with a little more sincerity than her stepfather had managed moments ago. "It's truly awful hearing what you had to suffer in your own home."

What had been worse had been the long night that had followed. Battle had been, if not easy, not preoccupying in a long time. Dealing with a hysterical mother with new distrust in her eyes over a success that was maybe too miraculous to be believed, blood and bodies covering the best room of the house, and still being nowhere near her dragon? *That* had been an endurance test. And still, Litz worried about the fate of the rest of the

Vidan clan. She did not want to have to lead another force against them into battle. She had killed their protectors. *Let that be the end of the bloodshed.*

"It's good to see you. I feel as though I haven't had a moment of peace for the last few days, bar your success with the clans."

"Thank you. Though truly, I would hesitate to call it a success."

"So modest, Litz. By all accounts, it was a smart and elegant piece of strategy that saved prolonged proceedings into bloodshed and humiliated its leadership."

As Litz winced, she felt Loren in her head. *Ah. The humiliation. You think that's why they came after you?*

I think they came after me because they were the strong ones, and they were not there when their people were attacked. I think they felt they had to do something. Doesn't that make sense?

"Is the runway really necessary there? What I mean is," Litz added as her brain began to catch up with her mouth. She wasn't used to the experience of offering political suggestions to the king of her land. "Surely, there were less contentious locations we could have found to ensure the dragons their new runway."

Xoia pulled her hands back and folded them neatly on her lap. "Sometimes, the contention is the point. It's a hard truth but a real one. To ensure the security and stability of the empire, we cannot allow civilisation to move at the influence of those who would see its destruction." She made a face, inviting Litz to sympathise with her difficult balancing act. "I'm sure your parents will be urging me not to give in to this kind of terrorism. I would have thought you would be saying the same."

Surely, they just don't want to see themselves destroyed, Litz almost said, but remembering herself, made a noise of acknowledgement. It was too late for arguments. She'd done the job; it had gone smoothly. The consequences had followed her home, as there was always a chance they would, and she'd dealt with those too. She hadn't offered any objections when objections would have counted for something.

She was suddenly grateful that she would almost certainly never see Kella Mabaki again. Kella, who had worked so hard to change the way she thought about the world and would have been utterly disappointed to see that Litz hadn't changed at all. After everything, Litz was still a soldier who went where she was told. Still a princess, a close mourner of the empire, who could wander casually into the royal court of Verassez and help decide the fate of a whole people, a whole nation.

"I want you to understand, Litz, because I want you beside me in this and in all things," Xoia continued. "You're the only one I can trust fully to care about Eisha as deeply as I do. I have no parents to support me, my brother is yet a child, and my allies are my mother's. And"—Xoia gave one of her mother's dangling earring of royal duty a self-conscious flick with the back of her hand—"I don't want to do things as she did. Not exactly, at least. I may not be eager to see us return to war, but I'll admit, I found her dismissal of the Circle's concerns in this disquieting."

Litz stayed quiet and nodded. She was still well-known as someone who was also unsatisfied by the way the war had come to a close, not least because it had seemed to put Eisha at the centre of it. It would make sense that she would still look favourably on any excuse to restart it.

But she couldn't unknow what she now knew. Worse, she wanted to explain her reasons, her thoughts, her concerns about acting as an empire that ultimately deferred to the Circle, her growing rage about fighting a war for her entire adult life that hadn't been what she'd thought it was.

Xoia said she wanted someone to trust. Litz desperately wanted that too. She wanted to tell her that the Jeenobian people deserved sympathy and not revulsion. She wanted to believe that Xoia could work to help change things for the better. To put the burden of knowledge on someone more qualified to do something with it.

But you don't trust her. And you're not a fool.

I guess not.

"You know all about the position I want to give you." Xoia gave a slight smile and leaned back in her chair. "You're family, you're popular with the troops, and by all accounts, you have a head for strategy most of your aging superiors have only read about. And from what I understand, it's unlikely you would find yourself with child. The Circle would appreciate another older dragon's rise within the army. And Loren herself is well regarded for her cool head. So, I'd like to make you general." She leaned her head to one side, giving Litz a formidable once-over. Again, Litz had to remind herself this was not her aunt looking at her. Her aunt was dead, and her peace would soon follow her. "But are you ready? Do you want it?"

"It would make my mother very happy," Litz admitted to a pretty laugh from Xoia.

"Wouldn't it just. You're young yet, but so am I. I think we could be a good new face of leadership together." She sighed and raised her painted fingers to her lips. "But I would want to know this was something you wanted and that Loren wanted, of course."

Of course, Loren put in, amused by Litz's rising anxiety.

What do I do?

Stall. You don't want this. And I feel no great urgency to return to the world of battle strategy. Though you should consider it. Much harder for

the Circle to have you assassinated if your position was this entrenched.
And I haven't even had my meeting yet.

For some reason, all Litz could think about was how Kella might say the word *general* as she mocked her, the way she'd once incessantly called her *Princess*.

Focus.

Litz cleared her throat. "I thank you, my King."

Xoia smiled. "We're alone. Xoia is always fine for you."

"Xoia. I will need to discuss further with Loren. She has her own priorities and ambitions, but she too is very flattered you thought of us."

"Of course. But I am of course considering other candidates. So tell me your thoughts soon."

"I will. And..." Litz paused, knowing there was no reason to expect an answer. "Has there been any news, any intelligence on Eisha's whereabouts?"

Xoia's face became grave. "I wish I did have something to tell you. Our attempts to reach out to the Jeenobians have been met with silence or accusations. They claim a dragon was involved in kidnapping her from their land." She smiled tightly. "Which sounds precisely what we'd expect as a response from a nation of dragon-haters."

"You could send me. I believe I established some rapport with King Jevlyn. It would be no great trouble. With Loren's help, we could spend a day or so in Malya and be home within a week of departure."

The Circle would not allow it.

Neither will she, I think. But I have to offer.

You don't really think you'd find her there.

No. But maybe at least some answers and a clearer idea of how close we are to war. And I may have allies there.

Who will have gone to ground if they have any sense. This isn't a real plan, Litz.

Xoia shook her head. "Thank you, Litz, for offering. But frankly, I've lost too much of my family lately. I refuse to risk more to the same man who took Eisha from me." She paused sharply. "I'm sorry. I know I shouldn't be making these assumptions."

No. She shouldn't.

"In any case," Xoia continued, "there is something I truly want your opinions on as a younger officer."

A little surprised and wondering if this was some kind of interview test, Litz cleared her throat. "Of course."

Xoia's manner became a little awkward as she seemed to find her next words difficult to choose. "As someone who has spent many years in and around our armies as they move," she began, "how essential…how do you believe our soldiers would react were we to ban their usual, uh…" She paused, recovered herself. "If we banned their pleasure caravan from following them, how would they take it?"

"Badly," Litz said before forcing herself to think. She was talking to her king, who at least didn't seem offended by her blunt response. "Is this about reducing disease within the ranks?"

"A little. It's also about the preservation of intelligence. Of eradicating weaknesses enemy spies may take advantage of before we move into a new era of war."

And it's about her wanting to make monogamy popular again, Litz finished for Loren's benefit.

Of course. More emulating dragons.

She wants her own life choices validated. She hates to be the odd one out at court and has resisted taking another consort.

Litz sighed. "I do not think it would be taken well. Not to mention, it would cause a great and sudden unemployment of the sex workers in question, who would only move back into the cities." She shook her head, giving the matter a moment of earnest thought. Some of the only level-headed people to be found in an army encampment were in those tents, and it would be a real blow to leadership, if nothing else, to lose them. "A pay rise for all soldiers would be expected as minimum compensation."

"That can be arranged," Xoia said thoughtfully.

Litz wondered again how she planned to change Aelshia under her reign. Surely, all rulers did, but King Narin had always given the appearance of changing nothing. Except ending the war. She had eventually done that. She'd sent Litz to Jeenobi with the instructions to safeguard both Eisha and her peacetime. Litz had failed on both quarters. If she didn't feel so bad for her own reasons, she might have had space to feel guilt and grief over her aunt's last command.

Happily, Xoia had few other questions, and Litz was permitted to take her leave not long after another quick discussion about the Vidan clan, who would have another force sent out to try to intimidate them and gather intelligence, but Litz, by her own request, would not lead them. Supposed palace experts in witch hunting would also be dispatched.

Litz was not squeamish about what she did, but she did not want to see that boy who had attacked her again. She would prefer not to learn what would happen there. Oh, and how Kella would condemn her for that too.

When Litz left the room, she let out a long breath, then started walking back down the steps, blissfully, for a moment, unobserved.

Now read your note.

Recognising Loren's wisdom, Litz carefully uncurled the paper as she moved downstairs. As she read the words, she received a groan from Loren in response.

Of course.

Deciding to follow the letter's instructions, Litz wandered farther down another flight of stairs, deeper into the tree, into the royal family's other private chambers. Briefly, when her father had been stationed abroad and her mother had been busy, she been allowed to spend a long summer sharing a room with Eisha. It was perhaps only her sixth or seventh summer and was one of the more cherished memories of her childhood. It was the time she and Eisha had truly become inseparable, despite their wildly different tastes and natures.

As she walked through the main corridor of the royal chamber, having been waved through by the guards posted at the doors, Litz was acknowledged by Glenash, the old king's most long-standing consort, who seemed to have very suddenly aged. Her kind, shrewd eyes blinked slowly from her seat reading in her room before standing to close the curtain to her room over, announcing clearly that whatever reason Litz might be here for, she did not care to learn it. She'd always kept to herself, a fact that had kept her as Narin's favourite confidante for so long.

It wasn't long until someone else noticed Litz. Her youngest cousin, Dessab, affectionately Sabi to his elders, yelled her name before she could reach her destination at the end of the corridor. Shaking her head, Litz obligingly crouched and held out her arms in readiness for the small child powering his stocky way toward her. "Collapsing" under the weight, Litz still successfully lifted him above her head before balancing him lightly on her hip as though he was still the infant she remembered so keenly. But soon, the soul earrings he wore would no longer need to be studs; they would soon start trusting him with earrings that dangled and proclaimed more about him.

"I got a new monkey," he babbled, sticky little fingers patting relentlessly at her cheek. "He pooed *everywhere*."

As Litz tried to figure out a response, Sabi's long-suffering father emerged behind him. "Your cousin doesn't want to hear about that."

"Will you tell me war stories, Litz?"

She smiled wide. She was famously a horrible storyteller, but children beneath the age of ten did not seem to understand this. "I'm not here for that, I'm afraid," she warned him, trying not to laugh as his face fell. He had Eisha's dimples, and his now dead mother's large ears. "But I'm sure I can tell you a quick one on my way back." She met his father's gaze. "If you're good," she added, framing the words as a question. She received a nod and a smile in response. The youngest and newest of Narin's consorts, Lexaniv seemed the least changed by her passing, but appearances were often deceptive around the royal household.

With a little regret, Litz carefully put Sabi back on his bare feet, unable to stop herself from pinching his round cheek. "Stop growing," she said because it seemed like the sort of thing a person said to children.

He puffed out his little chest. "Can't."

Despite herself, Litz laughed and gave him a little wave as she walked away, still watching him. Since she'd now effectively announced herself to most of the household, she had next to no idea of what the point to her next meeting was.

I suppose we'll find out.

Smiling wryly, Litz rapped her knuckles twice on the wooden door frame and stepped through the curtain when her uncle told her to.

Reishann was sitting in a wide chair strung together with wicker and heaped with colourful cushions on the far side of the room where the sun from the window streamed in. He was smoking a long cigar and nursing a large cup of what seemed to be tea. His sandals were off and his bare feet up on the table beside his teapot.

And his smile was gone.

As Litz moved closer, he gestured at the empty stool in front of him, sharp as a salute. Tired of sitting but driven by the need to know more, Litz took a seat. On the table in front of her, his feet stayed where they were.

For an audience like this, Reishann should speak first. But Litz was impatient, and a little irritated. "There hardly seems much point in secrecy when you lead me past everyone."

"I thought you were supposed to be a strategist, Litzi. It's the entire point. Privacy has been assured now we meet all but publicly."

Keeping her legs apart, Litz leaned back, rubbing at the fabric of the cushion beneath her. "I'm tired of games."

His face fell into its unbreakable stone state. "Don't you think I am too?"

"I don't know what to think," she told him honestly.

"Then let me enlighten you. You're the last person in this godsforsaken court to have seen my daughter, who trusted you above anyone. I trust that any concerns she may have had would have been confided in you. So I want to talk."

"Then talk."

His eyes sparkled with amusement, reducing the weight of the lines on his face. He still was the beautiful court dandy under these new anxieties. "This is why I like you. You speak as plainly as a Jeenobian. You have your commoner father's sensibilities perhaps. And you tire of society intrigue as much as I do."

More out of duty than any real outrage, Litz felt her hackles raise. "You give every appearance of enjoying yourself out there."

"Appearance being the key word." The amusement in his eyes dissipated as suddenly as it had arrived as he finally moved his feet and leaned forward on his knees to observe her more intently. "The king I served and loved almost three decades is dead. My daughter is missing. And I must now answer to a woman who has disliked me since childhood, until she finally puts me out of my misery and insists I leave."

There it is.

With no attempt to lower his voice, he kept speaking. "Do you think Xoia took her?"

"Took Eisha?"

Yes.

Do we?

If he suspects as well, that's becoming close to proof. Xoia wants her war, she said herself that dragons were involved, and there's been rumours of extra meals made for a palace room.

"What makes you say that?"

"I don't imagine you need me to spell that out for you. But here's my observation: Xoia treats all her mother's things as hers by right. She did not want the war to end, and her dragon-bent husband certainly didn't. No offense." He leaned back in his chair, the wicker beneath him creaking loudly. "She sees the war as not being her mother's to end, as an inheritance she missed out on. And as she's proving now, Eisha's life is a uniting one for people. Everyone loves her."

There was some pride in there that Litz could understand. Eisha had been who she was because of Reishann's training. She faultlessly remembered everyone's names, she led the way in fashion, and though she rarely shared gossip, she was not above making rumour her creature if she had a target to harm or build up. And in truth, Litz had barely considered how her absence, first through marriage and now by an unknown plot, would affect her father. Grief, anxiety and loneliness weren't expressions Reishann had ever been in the habit of showing. They didn't suit his face, as though he too couldn't quite remember how they should be affecting him.

"What do you plan to do about it?" she asked.

"She cuts to the heart of things yet again."

"You didn't call me here to ask if I agree with you."

"No." He leaned back. "Perhaps I asked you here to discuss a proposal of marriage. Together, we could be a formidable force at court."

"I don't think you mean that."

"No, but keep it in mind," he added, flashing a quick smile. "As general, you could have the power, I could have the connections…"

"And what would you want to do with power and connections?"

"Find Eisha, remove Xoia if she is, as she must be, the reason for it."

"You are talking about a coup a floor down from where she sits."

"Dastardly, aren't I?" He rubbed his forehead lightly, smoothing out the lines. Litz was distracted by the sigil on his ear that displayed his allegiance to his dead king. "I may not have appeared the most devoted parent, but I love my child more than my life and far more than my position. For that matter, I loved my king. I don't want to see everything she worked to build wrecked a matter of months after losing her."

"And you want my help."

He eyed her sharply. "You loved Eisha dearly. I expect I don't need to ask for it." He took a breath. "Have you ever considered taking the throne?"

"No."

"Sabi is still a child who adores you. Eisha is gone." His voice hesitated minimally. "And in any case, she's tied more to Jeenobi now. Xoia is dangerously unfit to rule. She may even have killed for it."

I can't hear this, Litz wanted to say, but she did not say it and did not move.

Your mother has considered it.

She has considered most things. That means nothing. She's also considering whether or not she raised a witch.

"I am not so certain Xoia has proven herself unfit. Not yet. And I have not seen any proof that she had anything to do with Eisha's disappearance," she added honestly, feeling she was failing Eisha by the admittance alone. "There is no reason for me to act. And no means. With what support would I take this on?"

"If she really does make you general, an army. And as I've said, connections."

"The Circle would not tolerate a human civil war. Especially not with a dragon involved, as Loren would have to be." Litz shook her head. "And a dragonriding general is strange enough. A dragonriding king, even as a regent, would be ridiculous."

Why?

It feels wrong. I don't think people would allow it.

I'm not sure whether to take offense at that.

"But the Circle might tolerate it more."

It's possible. They wouldn't like to be seen going against another dragon's decision.

Litz kept her face still. "I'm not interested in power. Or treason. Should you have any evidence, please, keep me informed. But do not contact me again in this way."

"Why did you come?" he asked as she stood.

"I miss her too. And she would want me to hear you out."

He spoke again as she reached the door. "Litz, think about it. For Sabi if no one else."

She nodded sharply to leave and only felt she could breathe again when she was out of the palace, leaving from its second-floor entrance out of the rope bridge high above the city that connected some of the oldest trees in the forest. *This is why I would make such a poor king. I hate that place.*

The two guards stationed at the first tree's crossroads saluted her as she marched by. She wondered if they assumed she'd just been promoted.

What would you have done if I hadn't joined the army? Would you have stayed involved in it yourself?

Sounding a little surprised by the question, Loren paused. *No. I don't think so. I'd done my bit. It's something I have a skill for but am not naturally drawn to.*

Would you have been a Circle dragon? An artist?

Perhaps I would have done nothing. The insidious human need for positions does wear on me. And you? Would you have ever been anything else?

There's not much I could have been, being who I am, Litz admitted, hating to think of it like that. She was incredibly blessed to have been born who she was. It felt ungrateful to wish for freedom to meet ambitions she couldn't have even put into words.

At the next tree, Litz took the old wooden staircase into the streets below. She would take the river walk back to Loren's rooms and wait for her to return from her own meeting. She felt the need to be near her.

Perhaps you would have taken after your uncle, Loren continued, understanding Litz's feelings without needing to acknowledge them. *Learned magic, escaped abroad to kinder shores and new adventures.*

Don't be ridiculous.

We still could, you know.

We can't leave our lives behind because we're not sure they personally fulfil us.

Why not?

Loren was, she suspected, half teasing, but her tone still frustrated Litz. *We need to find Eisha. We have importance here and people we're important* to. *We couldn't let everybody down. My mother almost died last night.*

Ah yes. All those people who always care so much about whether they let you *down.*

Where is this coming from?

You can't stop thinking about the clan rebellion.

Litz's breath hitched. *That's never bothered you before.*

Because it's never bothered you *before. Litz, you could raze whole cities, tear crying children from their mother's arms. It would not bother me so long as it satisfied you. But this does not, not anymore. It only follows us. And under Xoia's reign, these misgivings will likely grow, won't they?*

Litz said nothing, processing. *I like rebelling,* she admitted. *But I'm not brave enough to do it where people will know about it. I don't want to be Reishann's idea of a better king.*

With this new position dangling above you, whatever you do, people will see and take notice. And you let Kella see, didn't you? You let her see everything.

A squirm of shame that felt like the aftertaste of magic rushed through Litz as she looked at the river. The catfish migration was imminent now. The celebration that would inevitably come with it would likely be when Xoia chose to make her pronouncements. That gave Litz as much as a week to do her considering. *That was different. And it's not exactly a circumstance likely to be repeated.*

Not with that attitude.

Though Loren was clearly joking, Litz was a little alarmed. *Why does this matter so much to you? You didn't even like her, and you've never shown any interest in travel.*

Wherever Loren was, Litz could tell that she was shuffling her wings, doing what she could to become comfortable. *My time is far less precious than yours. I could sit back and do nothing for a century or travel the wide world. Whenever I chose to return, it would be unlikely I'd know anyone who still bore much of a grudge. Your time is limited and heightened in intensity for it. If there is someone or something that would bring you happiness, I want you to have it, Litz. It's why I never stopped you learning magic. I want you to have everything you want.*

Though she continued at the same pace, Litz had to wipe her eyes as discreetly as she was able to, not sure why she was crying. Loren loved her; that was a background certainty that could never leave her. But today she wanted Litz to know it.

Of course.

I love you too.

❖

With Litz being her third rider, Loren had a great deal of practice keeping secrets. Litz had always been less likely to notice that Loren was blocking her if she first flooded her with very real feelings to process. Humans might have felt time more keenly, but the depth of feelings only increased with time.

But it did not make dragons naturally kinder as they aged. Nothing seemed to do that. And the dragons who made an effort to maintain a position within the Circle had rarely been prone to kindness. Much like her rider, Loren had little time for those who chose to make a life for themselves in politics.

The position has been offered to her.

Yes.

And will you have her take it?

Loren paused, keeping her mind closed. The Circle was made up of eight dragons, four of whom were there today. One of them was Chernin, newly appointed after Loren had helped kill two Circle dragons out in the desert. Calino, whose rider Litz had killed in that same fight—and who dearly wanted Loren dead—was not present.

This was a civil meeting, where they would all politely not address that fact. Though Loren admired much about the way humans went about their diplomacy, she was frustrated that dragons had begun taking it on.

She wanted to insist that Litz would make her own decisions and that she would gladly partner with her in whatever that was. But this would get her nowhere. Only two of the dragons in the room had taken a rider in over a century.

We shall consider, she said, addressing all of them.

Is the hesitation due to hesitation over the war?

Fighting does take a toll, Loren said. Speaking with each other like this, dragons could not lie, not exactly, which made the exercise exhausting as well as infuriating. She hated being forced to pretend it made no difference to her that she'd helped kill thousands of humans in a war that now seemed almost meaningless. That her mate had died fighting in. She would have more gladly supported naked imperial ambition over false moral panic. Though she had little to fear from flying over a battlefield, her rider was human and fragile, and the idea that she could have lost her in a war manipulated to continue was intolerable. She had almost lost Litz the night before because the dragons in this room chose to act through humans instead of clearing the way for their infrastructure themselves.

But the game was not admitting that now.

The king will decide soon. And the war will begin again.

I understand.

Calino will soon take a position working on the new landing area you helped secure. We hope this will avoid any further altercations.

Altercations. As though they had engaged in a personal spat and Loren hadn't just survived an assassination attempt caused by a cry for help. *I'm sure it will.*

We encourage you to move your rider toward a decision that best serves her empire and its war effort. Your contributions as a team would be invaluable to the new king.

Understanding the conversation was finished, Loren adjusted her feet and flew straight up. Far above, the one entrance and exit to the Circle building, just large enough to let an older dragon like herself out, poured a sliver of sunlight down on them.

Loren resisted the human urge to look back. She knew they weren't going to attack her. Not today, at least.

❖

Litz's riverside walk was interrupted by a messenger. A little alarmed that her route from the palace had been so keenly observed, she stopped for the yelling soldier in uniform who ran toward her past the market stalls.

After a moment to catch his breath, he stood straight and saluted. "Captain Annik sent me. There's been an arrival by the Western Door, and they have been asking for you."

"An arrival?"

The messenger shook his head, apparently frustrated by his inability to find the right words. "From across the sea. The dragonrider doesn't even speak Aelshian." There was a flicker of interest, and Litz had a cynical burst of certainty that he had never wanted to learn any clan language local to him, but the idea of this foreign language tantalised him almost for a reason he couldn't explain. "But he has attendants who do, and they asked to see you by name."

Litz kept her face carefully blank. More politics. "Of course. I shall take a boat and be with them as soon as I'm able." She pressed a coin into his hands, enjoying more than she should his frustration at not learning anything about the most exciting news to reach Verassez since the old king's death and Eisha's disappearance.

Especially when Litz had absolutely no idea who could have asked for her. A *foreign* language. That couldn't mean Jeenobian and was unlikely to mean anywhere closer than that. Across the sea. Litz had visited some of those lands, but there was no need for them to have arrived through the forest's Western Door because they would have flown straight through the Eastern.

It didn't make sense, and clearly, Nic hadn't figured it out, or she wouldn't have sent for Litz. She hated asking for help unless she really needed to.

The river was quiet. Litz passed one sleeping dragon and only two other boats. All were readying for the arrival of the catfish and were apparently saving their energy. Litz felt safe to use magic to get her there a little faster, Pushing at the little fishing boat she'd commandeered. When Loren offered no reprimand for her recklessness, Litz had room in her head to worry about how the meeting with the Circle had gone. Loren hadn't spoken of it much, but it had been gnawing at her terribly. She wasn't used to a threat she wasn't able to intimidate.

And Litz wished she was coming home to talk it over, but instead, she was running around performing military duties on her day off, acting the good general without even having been appointed.

Ha.

Even on wide sections of the river, the tree canopy did its best to cover her. She'd never thought she would miss the wide sky. The stars were something she'd thought little of as a soldier. Until those endless and few desert nights alone with Kella, helping her sleep after nightmares. Now she never saw them, and she missed them.

Loren's offer to run haunted her. It felt like something that shouldn't have been expressed, even in the privacy of their shared minds. They'd manifested it as an option now, and whatever she did, it was just one more road she would never take, one more regret staring at her when she closed her eyes at night.

Maybe it was all the same one, she allowed as she reached a small dock close to the West Door barracks. Her one regret above all others would always be leaving Kella in the desert to fly home in the other direction. To play politics that she was bad at, to fight in a war she'd be better at but didn't believe in, and to fail at finding her cousin.

It was ridiculous that someone she'd known such a short time had made such an impact on her life, and she suspected she wouldn't like what she heard, but Litz would give a lot to hear what Kella would see her now.

For a moment, when Litz saw hair tied back in a braid, she almost convinced herself it *was* Kella. But only for a moment. Litz steadied herself and recognised her friend, Chelnic Annik, who smiled and turned at the sound of her gait. She wore her hair in the newly popular style, half-shaven, and it was still a little jarring to see a face she knew so well be framed so differently.

Her eyes smiling wickedly, Nic marched over and gave a salute with one hand while her other wound tight around Litz's wrist. "I heard a funny thing today."

"Oh yeah?" Litz said, realising there was no one around to see them and so resisted pulling away. She glanced up the hill, trying to get a better view of who might have asked for her but could see nothing through the trees. Taking a small step back, Litz kept their hands entwined. "What gossip have you been listening to?"

To Litz's relief and slight disappointment Nic let her hands hang more formally at her sides. "Oh, the usual. My mother's been talking to your mother. Who I hope is doing well."

"She's doing royally. She's promising to redesign the entire lounge after seeing it decorated red last night. And at over thirty years, I hope you have more impressive sources than your mother."

"So should you," Nic said with a sniff as she started wandering uphill, stroking the leaves on the trees she passed. "But I bet you don't, do you?"

Litz chose not to respond and followed her into the gloom.

"I'm sorry your little uprising followed you home. But you seem okay."

"It was hardly an uprising. They were protesting peacefully—"

"And you're in the lead now for the general position. *Especially* after all that. Fought off clan attackers alone in her own home and came out unscathed. No one will shut up about you."

Litz snorted. She wished she had something to say about that. She certainly hadn't decided how she felt about it yet, even after her strange morning of interviews. "What about Kilmar?"

"Dead a few miles south of the salt plains, didn't you hear?" Nic laid her hands lightly on Litz's shoulders this time, as if asking for a dance. "Happened a few days ago. Old cunt got sick and died with forty of his soldiers. Meaning you'd be leading that race if you weren't such an unknown. And you shouldn't be. You're the king's only first cousin, for fuck's sake."

Litz sighed and tried not to squirm, determined to deny Nic the satisfaction of making her uncomfortable. "Your point?"

"Make yourself less unknown. Partner with another great family." Now her smile split wide and bright, betraying the jest. "Litz Woskenna, we've been comrades and friends for a decade. The idea that I might have lost you to terrorist clan witches last night will haunt me forever. Would you do me the great honour—"

Litz rolled her eyes and pushed Nic's hands off her shoulders. *"Enough.* I'm not getting married for a job."

Nic pouted. "Not even—"

"No, not even to you. We'd be the end of each other within a month."

Nic straightened her back against the tree as though Litz was pinning her there. It had only been a few nights since Litz had pinned her to a bed, and their bodies seemed to remember the motions a little too well. It had always felt a little sad, this magnetism between them. If they were closer as friends, it would have bothered one of them, the casual way they could be so easily picked up and laid down. But that didn't mean that picking it up again wasn't always fun. "Is that a promise?"

Litz licked her lips but stayed where she was. Day off or not, they were both working, and eyes were everywhere. "Not yet. Who do we have? You're not supposed to working either, are you?"

"You weren't free to spar, and I heard we had strange invaders. When they turned out to ask for you by name, I was hardly about to excuse myself for a family dinner with my sister and her horrible little clan of a family."

"How long are they staying this time?" Litz asked dutifully as she craned her neck, trying to get a glimpse of the platform far up the steps.

"Oh, they say a few days, which means a month. My mother so misses having a daughter around to talk to."

"You being a terrible conversationalist."

"Exactly. I work very hard at remaining so."

It was difficult, forcing herself to keep pace with Nic and not charge up the creaking steps to face this great mystery alone. Who would ask for her? For *her?*

Rain patted lightly at her head as they reached the landing platform to the Western Door and found two dragons. One, a dark purple dragon with the shine of a beetle, she recognised but could not name as having territory nearby, making him a common natural lookout at this door. The other was younger, a bright orange flame colour Litz could only recall seeing once before. As they turned, yellow eyes fixing on her almost teasingly, and she became more confused. This couldn't be happening.

Nic was still speaking, telling her what time they'd arrived, that they hadn't moved or said much, but Litz couldn't concentrate on anything she was saying. She was too busy scanning under and behind the dragon where her attendants and rider were.

"This is the rider," Nic said, gesturing to the man in desert black who stood as they walked toward him, Litz's heart was in her throat. He turned, and Litz noted with great relief and disappointment that she didn't recognise him, though with the large gold helmet framing his face, it was difficult to be sure. He was paler than anyone native to the continent and beardless, probably some five or six years younger than her. It was an unusually young age to be striking out alone with only two attendants and one dragon. And he'd turned too quickly at Nic's words, so Litz didn't believe for a moment that he didn't understand them.

He nodded politely, holding her gaze. She still didn't know him, but he was making her feel like she should.

"You say it was the attendants who asked for me," Litz said, trying to keep her voice measured.

"Yes, they're just back here," Nic said, leading Litz after a polite nod at the dragonrider. "I think they're fixing her straps or something." She pointed up at the dragon's back, and the unmistakeable attendants obediently started making their way down.

The harness was obviously homemade, all painfully obvious, Litz thought with something between panic and glee as the two began to walk toward her.

Though there was only one of them Litz could look at.

Her hair and most of her face had been hidden by scarves, and her nose was considerably more broken, but her smile was unmistakable, and though her gaze purposefully wandered, when it found Litz, it was as though she was asking, "Do you see me? Do you get it?"

Litz got it. Nine months after Litz had tried to force her there, Kella Mabaki had come to Verassez.

CHAPTER THREE

Three Months Earlier

The bar was just about the right amount of busy. It wasn't quiet enough for anyone to stare as Kella walked in, but there was no loud Doshni sailor music to talk over, either. Not that she planned on talking much. Today, she was here to drink quietly. She managed this for half a glass before the man from the next table, who'd been squinting at her for some time, pushed at her arm and said, "Hey. You."

Maybe she hadn't wanted a quiet drink at all because now she'd been noticed, she wasn't particularly surprised or nervous. This was expected. Maybe even owed. But she didn't react because her mother had told her to never turn for any stranger who did not address her with respect.

"Hey. Aren't you the dragon slayer?"

She finished her drink with a loud gulp before looking over. "I must have one of those faces." She was angling for a fight, Ker would tell her. Maybe that was why she hadn't gone home to bring him out with her. But since she'd promised no more drawing attention to them, she dutifully stood, making to leave.

"My sister, my little sister, was burned alive with most of Kanceeni last week. D'you hear about that, slayer?"

The bar no longer seemed unobservant or busy. It had started to go quiet, waiting for the answer she hadn't come up with yet. She had heard about Kanceeni. An old village near the mountain passes, it had long been a prime target in dragon flight paths, and yet, people still lived there. They'd been celebrating the success of new crops when most of those and the people had been burned by a dragon. When she'd heard, she'd had a bottle of jhek to herself and tried to sleep as dreamlessly as she was able.

"I heard. Still not who you're looking for."

"You could have stopped that dragon. Put it down long before it got anyone."

Kella kept her gaze trained on the main door, more difficult as people began to gather, hovering in front of it, blocking her exit. "I'm sorry, I'm not her."

"Yeah, well, I'm gonna make sure of that."

The expressions of the people were hardening. She wasn't used to getting a crowd's attention without affection. And if she was honest, she wasn't all that used to fighting them, either. She had been trained to fight and kill extensively, but in the end, dragon slayers weren't made by training. They were people who dared to do the undoable, ignoring the pain, ignoring the torment that might follow, ignoring every instinct to do the smart thing. When what they were trying to fight was as big as a cramped street of homes and could see their thoughts, it was better not to dwell on their actions.

So, yeah. She could brawl. But taking out multiple thinking foes was not something she was likely to succeed at. She had two knives, but she didn't really want to use them. Not hurting anyone was supposed to be the point. Instead, she kept her hands at her side and eventually, not knowing what to do with them, placed them on her hips, feeling smaller than she ever had facing a dragon.

"Sounds like I'd better be leaving," she said, thinking it was better to be the villain than deliver a dull performance. And, oh, how she'd missed performing. "Were you planning on letting me out?"

❖

It had been practical but maybe a little sentimental too, to move beside the sea. Dragons tended to avoid it for the toxicity of the salt, and humans had little use for a rocky cove that spent most of the day flooded. Even if it did, at this time of the evening, make for a pretty view of the sunset. Luckily, it was a good few miles from Malya's docks, and the ragged cliff walls put off all but the most adventurous of young lovers.

Those walls, even though they currently cast no shadows, had never felt more like they were trapping Ker with the rocks and the anemones and the fucking gulls. *I hunted dragons once,* he wanted to tell the one-legged gull he'd been chasing around the beach with a spear for the better part of an hour. *You are nothing by comparison.*

Seemingly aware of his thoughts, the gull croaked from the barnacled boulder Ker was steadily approaching and held his stare, almost daring him to make his move. Taking a long breath, Ker concentrated on the way he held the spear, the angle his target required, the speed he would need to have a hope of hitting the bird before it could fly off.

The harsh sun was blazing behind the bird, judging Ker, obscuring his target. But he was committed. This time, he had it. He knew what he'd done wrong in his previous throws, and there would be none of the same issues. Kella would come home, and he'd be cooking a gull that he'd caught without magic.

He just needed to aim with his elbow and—

He launched his spear hard and true and almost didn't hear the splash of it hitting the sea over the mocking sound of the flying seagull's laughter.

Are you sure I can't just char it for you?

No! That'll attract too much attention.

Because this, of course, is not doing that.

Snarling, Ker Pulled and broke the seagull's neck. It flopped onto the stone beach. Letting out a long breath, hoping to expel his rage, he walked toward it, hearing the cackle of other gulls, as if they knew he was failing just like he continued to fail at fishing.

"It looks mangy," Sallvayn said, the gremlin suddenly at his side.

"Yeah, I know."

"We're sure your sister will be back soon."

"Ha. I'm not." Ker nodded toward the sea as he picked up the gull and bagged it in the sack at his side that contained his other meagre prizes of a handful of clams and edible seaweed. "The boats all came back in hours ago. There's a storm rolling in. She'd be back by now if she wanted to be."

She would come back; he was sure of that much. But without her actually talking to him, he was sure of little else. It would be better if she could be spitefully, resentfully silent, but no. She talked like she wasn't sure what deeper opinions were still acceptable to hold in his company. And when she was out, she did everything she could to keep pissing off the whole world, like if she got her nose broken enough times, she'd stop being recognised.

"We wish you luck with cooking, but we're going out."

"Again?"

"We have more business."

"*Business.*"

"In any case, your sister prefers it when we are not here."

Ker sighed. Having no connection to dragons, Kella couldn't understand anything gremlins said, and that made her ill at ease with Sallvayn and then guilty for feeling that way.

Sallvayn gave a long, froglike leap over the rockpool Ker passed to keep pace. "We'll be back before morning. As we're sure your sister will be."

"When did you get so comforting?"

"Still not now. We also wanted you to know there's a man watching you."

Ker stopped moving and looked up. He saw no sign of anyone on the cliff, but it was getting dark fast, and there were a hundred hiding places up there. Kella regularly abused them to test her stick throwing skills on him on her way home.

"What does he look like?" Ker asked before looking to see the gremlin had already gone. Off to tend to the "business" they'd been up to more and more these past few evenings. He only hoped that meant that Sallvayn didn't consider this guy a threat.

Deciding to appear casual, like he didn't know anyone was there, Ker continued toward the rough path up to Ellonya's new cave, where she was relaxing, resplendent with some of her treasure hoard finally transported back with her. Perhaps that was what someone was here for. If they'd noticed a dragon flying in and out of the area and they were desperate enough, they might be here for her gold.

There was no way Ker was leading them to her, so he stopped at the base of the rocky cove. Here, there weren't any angles for someone to look down without exposing themselves.

Should I come out and take a look?

No, wait for now.

He hated that this had become his constant line lately. His arrival in Ellonya's life had been so momentous to her, and for a while, every moment had been so joyous, so full of progression. It felt cruel to be constantly telling her and himself that they couldn't do anymore, that this was all they were allowed to be for now. No community, no achievements, no learning, only hiding and hunting seagulls, smelling like the sea and saltwater that would hurt her.

You know it's still what I would choose.

But you shouldn't have to. Leaning back against the cliff, Ker took a deep breath. Even without seeing whoever was up there, there was a chance he might be able to Pull them down, but that could result in their injury or even death, and without knowing their purpose, that wasn't something he was prepared to inflict just yet. *Could you be a distraction for me? Don't show yourself, just, I don't know, blow some fire?*

The warmth of her amusement heated him. *I can blow fire out of the cave if it helps. Only if that wouldn't draw too much attention.*

I think we might be past drawing attention.

Ker started running to the cove exit and was halfway up the rocky stairs by the time the wall of fire emerged from the cave, sure to draw all eyes in the area. Sure enough, when he reached the top, the watcher was leaning on his bow and looking at the cave mouth and not behind him.

Despite the longer hair tied back, Ker recognised him instantly, and that only confused him further on what he should do. Evlo would be familiar with an attempt made to keep him still with magic and might hurt himself fighting it. Though Ker wanted to believe he wasn't there to fight, he could probably physically beat Ker in one easily.

But his back was still turned, and there was only one way to find out.

Mindful of the sandy ledge, Ker ran and lunged, making Evlo squeal in surprise. He slipped out of Ker's original tackle and hold easily, but when he reached for one of the arrows at his side, he was thrown off by Ker pushing them off the ledge, where they clattered down the rocks to the beach below.

"*Hey!*"

"Good to see you," Ker said as he tried again to hold Evlo's wrists, even while he weathered the well-aimed use of Evlo's knee. Straddling him had seemed like the best plan, but now he felt exposed. "What are you doing here?"

To Ker's surprise, Evlo basically stopped struggling and glared at him with great contempt. "Zebenn taught me how to track. You're not exactly staying hidden wandering around with a fucking dragon." He paused. "And Kella's not difficult to follow home."

Ker tightened his grip. "Man, bad phrasing."

Evlo's face was clouded by sudden embarrassment. "Yeah, but you know what I meant."

Slowly, Ker released his hold and leaned back on his feet. Evlo started rubbing gratefully at his neck, and Ker realised he'd leaned an elbow on it a moment before. The fight felt ridiculous, but Ker couldn't bring himself to relax just yet.

"You've put on weight," Evlo muttered the moment Ker stood, as though pointing at the reason for his defeat.

Ker only shrugged and took a step back, then offered a hand.

Evlo ignored this and stood. "So you're keeping it in a cave?"

"Keeping what in a cave?"

Evlo's face fell into that pretentious sneer Ker had always disliked so greatly. "Your *master*. Your dragon." His voice softened. "I won't let it hold you like this, Keral. Let me help you."

Shaking his head, Ker felt Ellonya nudging at the back of it. *Should I come out?*

Not yet, I think. "How did you find us?" Ker asked, dropping the pretence. Kella would be back soon and provide some human context for the "us."

"Like I said, Kella's not careful enough coming back," he said with some satisfaction as his eyes skidded over the empty beach. "It must let you have some freedom?"

Ellonya said, *I'm not sure I like his tone.*

"Can you trust me enough to listen to me?"

Evlo kept the string of his short bow taut at his side. "Trust, heh? After what you pulled in the hills? Even if you didn't have a dragon in your brain, no. But I can listen. If you keep your distance," he added, his wavering tone confirming again that he seemed to be just as confused by Ker winning the fight as Ker had been. "And no more magic," he said firmly, brushing down his shirt and reaching for his bow. "It's just not fair."

He doesn't have the same disgust most do, Ellonya noted before retreating a little from Ker's mind, apparently no longer worried for him.

"Yeah, all right," Ker said, cheekily clasping his hands behind his back. Though he would still be able to exert unnatural control upon the world, it would be more difficult now, and in any case, this made him look less threatening. He knew Evlo had never liked having to look up at him.

It took a few moments, but Evlo slowly released the bowstring and let it hang more loosely at his side. "When did it happen?"

"What?"

"The dragon. When did it get you?" Evlo narrowed his eyes. "It had you when we met in the hills, didn't it? Did you make a deal with it to find Kella?" His gaze wandered again, looking frustrated that nothing had yet presented itself for him to hit. "What does she think about all this?" For a moment, his lower lip trembled. "Has it got to her too? Or is she just sticking this out for you?"

"Why are you here?" Ker asked again. "And how come you came alone?"

He made a dismissive *tsk* before almost smiling. "I guess I wanted to see this freakshow for myself. Didn't wanna involve anyone else in that decision. So, you gonna show me?"

Warily, Ker started to pace, circling Evlo, who stayed planted where he was. "If I do, how are you going to act?"

Evlo raised his arms, playfully balancing the bow in one hand. "I'll be the perfect houseguest. Sorry, *cave* guest." He narrowed his eyes as his smile widened. "What was your plan with all this? You can't have a job or a life. Not all the way out here."

Ker ignored this.

Ellonya didn't. *He's got a point.*

Stop agreeing with him. He's probably here to kill you.

They didn't say anything else on their awkward descent to the beach. At one point, Evlo struggled with balancing his bow over his torso, and Ker unthinkingly offered him a hand to help him safely to the next barnacled rock. The sun had almost completely set, and if Ker didn't know the way down so intimately, he'd have been struggling himself. Evlo took his hand briefly and firmly before releasing his grip in disdain. Ker tried not to react.

It was easier dealing with Evlo, who couldn't keep in his feelings about Ellonya and the changes she'd brought to Ker's life. Dealing with his da, or even Kella, was much more difficult.

As they entered the cave, Ker watched him carefully. He was trying to move casually, but his hands were unnaturally still, as though the only way he was keeping them that way was through unbreakable force of will.

"Is she...big?"

Ker almost laughed at what seemed like the strangest small talk he'd ever heard; it asked to be made into a joke. But he didn't have the heart to be cruel to someone who was so clearly afraid. "She's younger than most we hunted, so she's smaller. But she's an adult."

"Right." He stopped walking as Ellonya came into full view.

In dark of the cave, the sun struggled to reach them, but the campfire Ker had left burning silhouetted her spiked back in the gloom.

"She's sure not small."

"No."

Should I put on a show?

However you feel.

Gracefully, Ellonya raised her long neck, the scales falling into new positions as smoothly as feathers would. Her red feather crown framed her face magnificently as she rounded it on Evlo, whose breath caught.

As the archer on their team, it was rarely Evlo's job to get close to the dragons they hunted. He made his shots from hundreds of metres away. As far as Ker knew, this was the closest he'd ever been. But Ker also knew that Evlo had come from a land where dragons "were the gods," something not even the Aelshians would claim.

Seemingly mesmerised, Evlo slowly raised his arm as though to calm a horse. Obligingly, Ellonya pushed her nose toward him. For a moment, they made a lovely sight: the last of the setting sun behind them, Evlo's breath catching as Ellonya turned her head to better look him in the eye.

They noticed Evlo making his move at the same, alarm ringing between their heads in horrible tandem. Ellonya moved, and nauseatingly, Ker felt like it was his body, his tail that hit Evlo before the blade emerged from his sleeve, the one meant to pierce her eye. After flying through the air and hitting the cave wall with a choking gulp, Evlo slumped to the ground, his eyes closed.

Cautiously, Ker moved closer to him. *Oh gods, maybe we did kill him this time.*

CHAPTER FOUR

Kella was flung out of the bar with minimal ceremony. Considering she'd been attempting to fight her way to the door, that felt like a mercy, especially when no one followed her. She would have bruises the next day, and she'd landed in the gutter, but she'd be able to get herself home.

She wiped the back of her hand roughly over her bleeding lip as she realised someone else stood over her. The worn sandals were instantly recognisable.

"Hey, Dani," Kella said dully in welcome, briefly glancing up with the biggest smile she could manage, which wasn't very big. She saw what she expected to see. Findan was looking at her, exasperated, loving, frustrated, and holding all of that behind folded arms and a delicate mask of disappointment.

It was hard to look at, so Kella went back to staring at her newly broken sandal. She didn't really care to know how much Findan still cared about her because didn't that just make it all worse? If Findan didn't care, Kella wouldn't be disappointing her. And the fact that she'd left Kella for dead would at least make sense.

"I heard I might find you on this street."

Kella gestured limply at the pub. "My new favourite."

"You used to say it was too full of dockhands."

"Yeah, well, now I am a dockhand. It suits me fine," Kella said, pushing up the wall and wincing at the pain in her shoulder. They stood at about a height to each other, Kella never having grown into her mother's stature. Findan still had her arms clasped as though holding herself back from taking Kella in her arms. But she was not a natural hugger, and Kella did not want to be touched.

"You're hurt."

"Scratches."

Findan smiled. "Indulge me. Let me take a look at them and get liquids in you."

Kella wanted to say no. But the act of saying no to Findan wasn't something she had any practice at, and her mouth didn't seem to know how to form the word, even after all these months of distance. "All right," she said and let Findan's arm tentatively wrap around her bruised ribs, holding her up. The tenderness of the gesture made her want to cry, so she bit her lip and stared straight ahead as the wind whipped sharp at their backs, pushing them forward together.

"You cut your hair."

"It was annoying me."

"Did you see the new mural on Temple Street?"

"Ha. I watched that cunt paint it."

"Harsh language for a fan."

"Not a fan." With effort, Kella tried to put less weight on Findan's shoulders and stand a little straighter. "Y'know, I asked him what slayer it was meant to be because he's not that good, right? It could be me. It could be Mami. No distinctiveness to the sword she's holding."

"Did he recognise you?"

"Don't think so. Anyway, he shrugged and said it didn't matter. Didn't *matter*." Kella was still trying to look ahead but thought she saw Findan smile.

"Hmm. Perhaps it was meant to be metaphorical?"

"It's twenty fucking feet wide, I don't think he was aiming for subtle."

"They miss you out there."

Kella frowned. "They have you. And they even have a new me."

"Not even Gendi Goodsblade himself has tried to claim he's the new you." Findan sighed with obvious irritation over the odious task of saying the name of the newest dragon-slaying vigilante to spring up with a troop of his own. By all accounts, this young man, who was around Ker's age, hadn't planned on his new fame but had harnessed it after lucking out with a sleeping dragon. He and his tavern buddies had brought their wrath down upon it before it could wake. "They're just one more group of former army recruits who think luck and vengeful fury will be enough to keep them alive."

"Not dead yet. Or arrested."

Findan paused for a moment before answering, apparently worried by Kella's refusal to meet her gaze. "You have a right to be hurt that we didn't come after you, if that's what this is about. But nothing has changed out there. And we could really use your help."

"Well, things have changed for me," Kella said, injecting some false energy into her voice. "Found out that Aelshian dragons *talk*."

"They have a lot of strange differences on the other side of the desert. Their mind powers might be more formidable—"

"Sure, but they're people. And I don't kill people." Extricating herself from Findan's grip, Kella stumbled over the gutter and back toward the alley wall. "And I think you knew, right?" Findan said nothing, and Kella shook her head before leaning it back on the stone wall. "Yeah."

"There have been more younger ones that act differently," Findan offered cautiously.

"Different, heh?"

"They don't act as mindless as the generation before. They are not their parents." She risked another smile. "Children can be surprising like that. But they can't be trusted, Kella. Even if they can think more than we might have assumed."

"Yeah, like I said, they're *people*."

"And does your brother agree?"

"Haven't seen him in months, wouldn't know."

Findan paused but took a small step toward her. "You're still a horrible liar." Her eyes were full of concern. "If you didn't know what happened to your brother, you would not be here working. You would be looking everywhere."

"Maybe I did that already."

Findan crouched to her eye level. The gesture became more painfully patronising because Kella knew that was not how it was intended. "I'm worried about him."

Kella rolled her eyes, taking the opportunity to look away. Of course no one was worried about *her*. But she couldn't say that aloud, too terrified of finding it true, even now. Because she wanted to listen to Findan, wanted to be told what to do again, wanted to be looked after. And right now, it would be so easy. Ker and his new sensibilities were nowhere around; she had only her own to contend with. And right now, they were very tired. She could almost hear the cheering of the crowd that would make everything all right again. Injuries like the ones she currently bore would mean nothing if people loved her for them.

"I know about his dragon."

Despite herself, Kella stiffened. "What dragon?"

"I have no idea. But I think you know. And I think you know this is a dangerous path for him. He's let a dragon into his brain, hasn't he?" She shook her head as Kella met her eyes, and her voice became hoarse with emotion. Like she thought Kella wasn't enough to protect him. "Into his *soul*. The damage that could cause him—"

"Well, like I said, I've not seen him."

Findan tried to reach for Kella's hand, who let her, but looked away again. "Do you hate me? For not coming after you?"

Kella focused on not letting her voice catch. "I get why you couldn't."

"That's not what I asked."

I thought you loved me beyond sense, beyond reason, Kella wanted to say. *The way family is supposed to love. Love like that should be horrifying. You could have used magic to kill them all. It would have solved nothing and got you killed, but I would have been free.*

Kella hadn't realised her gaze had been drawn back until Findan's eyes slid away in defeat, as aggrieved as if Kella had spoken the words aloud.

Moments later, her hand slipped away. "Okay," she said quietly. "Well, if either of you want to find us, we'd love to see you. We're staying—"

"We won't."

Findan blinked and slowly straightened her legs to stand. "We're at the Gryphon's Head. Can I help you up?"

"I'm all right here."

Taking in a breath, Findan nodded. "Take care of yourself."

Kella slumped back. After a night full of disasters, watching Findan walk away turned out to be the hardest part. She could call out, and Findan would return, she knew that. But she forced the words down until she made herself sick holding them in, and holding her ribs, she pushed herself on. Ballian's shop wasn't far. Though she'd kept away from him since their return, now she was sore and tired and desperate for sympathy.

Going home was a strange concept for her. It would sound self-pitying to say that she'd never felt like she'd really had one, but there the feeling was anyway, slinking around at the back corners of her mind whenever her feet started walking her to the shop.

Ballian had done everything and more to make it a home for her long before he'd married her mother. But even, or maybe especially, as a small child, Kella had been certain that her clean bed, the kitchen with its spice cabinets, the musty books that had always felt friendly were not for her. None of it was Her Place. But it was a place she could lick her wounds for now.

She found the shop empty, its workers assumedly asleep upstairs somewhere, so she walked into his kitchen without waking them. Perhaps an hour went by before he wandered in and found her eating jam out of the jar. With only mild shame, she lowered the jar as he stared at her with painful fondness. Around his neck, his old mouser snake hissed sleepily. She'd always had a great love for Fin-Dani the snake, but today, she couldn't help feeling secondhand annoyance, thanks to her interaction with the reptile's namesake.

"Hello, stranger."

"Hey."

He approached her cautiously, like he was sure she'd sprint away, then kissed her forehead and threw a big arm around her shoulders so tightly that she winced. Instantly, he released her as though her skin burned him. "You're hurt."

She was getting too tired to put on an act. "Yeah, a bit."

He turned to face her, one hand lightly on her shoulder, the other gripping the head of his walking stick as he nodded solemnly. "All right, let's take a look." He had always been wonderful for not asking questions, and he did not break from that now. For this snatched hour of time, she could feel the familiar weight of the old family snake on her lap as Ballian bustled about, making her something hot to drink and finding a salve for her cuts. She could be his little girl again, even if she never had been.

In any case, he had a new child now, which was also her fault. "How's Darsin faring?" she asked, holding the drink gingerly between her newly bandaged hands.

He sat heavily across from her, making his little kitchen table wobble on its one good leg. "Good. He's been making friends. He has an eagerness that is difficult to deny." A little clumsily, he pinched her cheek. "Like some others I know."

"But he's happy, right?"

He withdrew his hand and seemed to think for a moment. It was the same expression Ker wore when he was speaking with Ellonya. "I have found him crying for home on occasion. But only once this month."

Kella swallowed. Great. One more life she'd fucked up beyond repair. "Do you think I should have left him where he was?"

"I couldn't say. But to be emotional in the night over changes made in the day, that's not so uncommon for any of us, is it?"

"I guess not."

It was a lovely, wise thing to say because he really was one of the most thoughtful, generous people that Kella had ever known. It was that wisdom that made what he could not, or would not, understand hurt all the more.

They'd come to see him not long after arriving home, and he'd cried tears of joy to see both his children alive and healthy after weeks of hearing nothing. He'd welcomed Darsin into his home and heart. His sign language was good, but he'd worked to reconnect with friends who could teach them both more. But introducing him to Ellonya, as expected, had not gone so well.

Ker had debated with her for most of their journey about whether or what they should tell him, with both of them changing their positions regularly. In the end, they couldn't come up with an alternative story about how they'd gotten home so quickly and didn't want to burden Darsin with holding secrets from the man who would hopefully become his new guardian.

Within an hour of returning home, Ker was leading Ballian to meet Ellonya near the cove that became a new place to stay. That had been the last time they'd tried.

Kella had always wanted to be like her mother, but Ballian had been the one to teach her right and wrong. Watching him recoil in disgust in the same shameful way that she had was hard to unsee. His brief rage over being contacted by Ellonya was especially familiar. It showed a fallibility that Kella had wanted to believe his good nature would overcome. It had felt so important that he was a better person than her.

He didn't pretend not to be worried, horrified, but he would say nothing to anyone. Above all, he loved and trusted his children, even if the limits of that weighed heavily on them now.

"So why the fight?"

She gave a one-shoulder shrug, her other arm still too sore to cooperate. "I'm not so good at blending in."

He smiled warmly. "No, you never have been."

"The burden of fame."

"And you've never been in the business of deescalating."

"Of what?"

He huffed out a laugh. "It hurts me sometimes, how much you remind me of those who are gone."

She felt something in her throat swell but tried to smile through it. "C'mon, Mami was never this annoying."

"No, less her. Though of course, you have her nerve, and you always have. No, more and more, I think of my sister when I listen to you."

"The dead one?" Kella cut herself off. She knew Ballian had only ever had the one; she wasn't sure what had made her speak that way. "Sorry."

He waved in dismissal. "Yes, Barra. Dead long before she could grow to your age. But I have no doubt that her mouth would have gotten her into fights, had she chosen to move to this city full of them."

Picking the hissing snake up and moving her onto the table with effort, Kella raised her foot to her chair and rested her head on her knee. "How old was she again? When she died?"

"Four and ten. And she had the most dazzling smile," Ballian said, settling into his easy, storytelling tone. "Even when she was being good, and that was rare, our mami suspected she was up to something. And she usually was." He reached for her hand that was still on the table, a silent plea for her to look at him. "I've missed that smile. But the moment you walked into my shop holding your mother's hand"—he sighed softly—"I saw her in you in an instant. I suppose that's part of why I took to you so quickly. You felt like mine, like family, long before you were."

Kella hugged her knees a little tighter as she slipped her hand from his. He didn't seem to notice.

"I think, well, I *know*, that she's most of why I can't listen to either of your new…experiences." He shifted in his seat that didn't quite fit him before continuing, even as Kella tried to find her voice to respond. "With your mother, you remember. I felt so much grief, I could barely function. But I did function because it didn't shock me. She was always going to die as she lived, and of course she would die for Ker. Even if, I know from what you've said, she may not have needed to. Nevertheless. It made sense."

Kella felt her lip tremble.

"But with my sister—"

It was a story Kella knew well, though it wasn't one Ballian had ever seemed fond of telling. He'd been nine and trapped under the remains of his parents' bed while he'd watched the dragon that had just burned down their home take his screaming sister in its jaws and carry her off. After that day, he'd never walked on his right leg again, and he'd never seen his sister again, either.

"She wasn't a fighter, though she would have liked to have been. She was just a child, even if in my mind, she'll always be my big sister. For me…" He paused. Though he cried often in his storytelling, specifically this story, his eyes were dry now. "That's what I'll never be able to reconcile. You can tell me this one dragon saved your life and is sharing my son's brain." His voice wavered slightly but didn't falter. "But I can't. I can't see a dragon and not see my sister and all she didn't deserve."

"Thinking and feeling aren't the same," Kella said, finding her voice. "That's what you always said."

He smiled brightly, but his eyes remained dull. "Yes, I did. And I do. Perhaps I should go easier on myself, heh? After all, my children have made me a parent again. I have a lot to think of in the morning." He leant back. "And you? Have you got your work in the morning?"

"No, and I should get home to Ker. Don't want him flying out to rescue me again." With reluctance, she pushed away the mug in front of her. The snake curled up next to it, tasting the air like it was trying to pick up the flavour she'd been drinking.

"You're still looking a little sore," Ballian continued lightly as she got to her feet. "And the mood outside has been growing uglier these past few months. Now the king is considering breaking the peace for his wife the way he would not for you."

"Heh. Hadn't thought of it that way," she lied.

"I am disappointed in that boy. I thought he'd learned enough watching Kira to remember himself better." How that would have hurt Jev to hear, Kella thought with some relish. And yet, she still didn't wish hearing it on him.

"Well, hopefully, we don't have to see it come to war again. She probably just ran off."

"I didn't realise you were such a defender of the king's peace," Ballian said with some amusement.

"Sure. Be weird to go around being pro-war, though." Laying her mug down with finality, she gave him a smile. "Thanks for the tea. And give Darsin a hug from me."

He leaned his weight down on his stick and stood. "I think the boy would prefer you see him yourself, but I'll give him your best."

After a beat longer than felt comfortable, she fell into a tight hug, relieved that her chin still fit in the same space above his collarbone as he kissed her head.

His thumb rubbed a circle over a vertebra as he said, "I'm always proud of you, baby. And that's true if you never perform another heroic deed or if you're known for a thousand more." Releasing her, he sniffed, and her eyes stung in sympathy. Tears would likely follow her exit for both of them. "Now, you get away, and make sure that dragon hasn't eaten your brother."

CHAPTER FIVE

It was a longer walk home from the shop than it would have been from the bar, but Kella didn't regret it. She had always loved wandering through the city alone, and now she only felt comfortable doing that at night. The full moon lit her way through the city and then the rocky beaches clinging to the edge of it. It was the farthest moon from Kella's. If her mami's superstitions were to be believed, it was not a lucky night for her.

Her aching ribs reminded her that maybe there was something in that.

The stars were out too. Litz had mentioned once that it was hard to see the stars in the Aelshian forest. Romantically—and pathetically, maybe—Kella wanted to believe they were looking at the same bright sky but doubted it. Had Ker not rescued her, they might have been looking up at nothing but trees together, doing what they could to spot stars through the leaves. To her surprise, when Kella entered, she found a bright fire and a full cave. Ellonya seemed to be sleeping, but Ker was pacing and looked up guiltily when she walked in. "It's Evlo," he said, like that was the answer she was looking for.

"Yeah. Got that part." She felt shaky and wished Ballian had given her something stronger to drink. "What's he doing here? Why is he on the ground?" She didn't bother adding her next question because it was clear from Ker's expression that he expected her to provide a solution. Of course.

"I didn't want to wake him up by nudging his mind. That felt wrong," he said when he'd finished explaining what had happened.

"You mean by Ellonya nudging his mind."

"Yeah, sure."

Too exhausted to eye him suspiciously, Kella crouched, happy to find Evlo had been laid on his side. Ker knew more about medical help than she did. Evlo seemed to be breathing. The problems would come when he woke up. And she wasn't one for waiting for her problems to arrive. "Couldn't think of a more human way to do this, heh?"

"Well—"

Taking her water horn off her belt, she poured the last of its contents on Evlo's face, ignoring Ker's noises of alarm. When Evlo gasped and splayed a hand out as though to stop himself from falling, she smirked.

"Hey, kid," she said as he rushed to sit up, panicking at the sight of Ellonya, who was taking a nap. Kella wished she could follow, but judging by the wild look in Evlo's eye, she suspected this might take a while. "Long time no see, heh?"

He took a few shallow breaths and grasped at his belt, but Ker had had the sense to remove his knife. "Yeah."

"How's the head?"

He grabbed his bow and slung it over his shoulder. "Been better."

"You here alone?"

Ker tried to meet her eye, but Kella kept her focus on Evlo. "I *told* you—"

"I'm asking him."

Evlo held her gaze before finally dropping his. "Yeah. I'm alone. So what now? You gonna kill me over a dragon?" He tried for a laugh that came out tragically like a sob. "Figures."

"Why?"

"Why what?"

"Why'd you come here alone?"

He snorted. "Findan didn't wanna hear what I had to say."

"I think you knew it would turn into a fight that could get someone hurt with more people. You wanted to see if you could sort this yourself." She tilted her head, doing her best to draw his eyes back. "What were you afraid of?"

"Do I really need to explain? You're shacked up with a dragon. He made a devil deal to save you, and now you've probably both lost your souls for it." He scanned her face, searching. "But you seem like you. Maybe it's not too late."

"Nobody's lost their soul," Ker snapped. "Meeting Ellonya meant I got Kella away, something no one else had any interest in doing."

Evlo craned his head, a snarl curling his thin lips. "Hey, I said I'd help, and what did I fucking get for it? Knocked out and left for—"

"It was too late by then."

"Yeah, 'cause it was already in your *brain*, right?"

"*What would you know of it, boy?*"

Kella and Evlo both stared at Ker. That had been him speaking, but it hadn't exactly been his voice.

"See," Evlo said, choked. "It already has him. It's speaking through him." He swallowed. "Might be nothing left of him to save."

For a moment, Ker looked boyishly uncertain before frowning. "I'm right here, idiot. That's just a…a dragonrider thing."

No, it's not, Kella thought with some panic. Because in all the time she'd spent with Litz, she'd never watched that happen. Litz had worried, hadn't she, knowing that this was Ker's second time bonded to a dragon. Maybe it was harming him in a way Kella couldn't even see.

"Would you prefer she talked directly to you? Didn't think so."

"I'd prefer you did what you were supposed to do, *Mabaki*, and let me make her stop talking altogether."

"Hey," Kella yelled, loud enough that Ellonya sleepily opened one eye before closing it again. "There's no need for all the shouting. I'm safe now, right? We all won the day, nobody's chewing peaches. Ker's fine. What did you mean by a deal with the devil?"

Evlo blinked, seemingly caught off guard. "What? Nothing."

"What is a devil deal? Like, in this context."

"Drop it, Kel," Ker intoned, rubbing his forehead.

"No, I wanna know what he's trying to say. What were you trying to say?"

Evlo sighed. "Look, a devil is just, like, a thing that grants wishes. You find it, and you kiss it, and it has to give you the thing you want most. But it's always trying to catch you out. It never ends well, even if you get what you want. The better a person you are, the more chance you'll get anything out of trying." He shook his head. "And, yeah, I tried to find one once. It didn't work out." With what looked like effort, he raised his arms in a theatrical shrug. "Nothing ever does for me."

"Tell us more about where you're from."

Over Evlo's head, Ker shot her a look of pure incomprehension.

"Like I've told you before, I don't wanna talk about it."

Kella crossed her legs, getting more comfortable. "I know why I hunted dragons. I know why I stopped. I found out they talk, that they're smart like people, and there's something wrong with the ones around Jeenobi. I wanna understand why you came here alone to rescue me and Ker from one that you know we've been living with for months."

"What do you want me to say?" He looked exhausted, but more, he looked disappointed. When he'd joined their group a little over a year ago, he'd looked at her with worship, had done anything to hear praise from her. She hoped enough of that regard remained for her to take advantage of now.

She leaned forward. "Anything. What are they like, your dragons?"

"Not *my* dragons."

She paused and waited.

"They're smaller.

"Like people?"

"Like young dragons?"

Evlo shook his head at them both. "Maybe half as large at their largest. I heard a Doshni guy say that island creatures get stranger-looking away from the mainland. I guess it's like that."

"So how else are they different?"

"Sometimes, they talk to people. If they choose to. And those people do what they can to keep on top of things. They're the ones in charge."

"Did you hunt dragons there like you said you did?"

He shot Ker a glare for the question. "No," he said eventually. "You couldn't hunt dragons there. Not successfully. But I tried. Once."

Kella forced herself to stay quiet, sure this would yield better results than pressing.

Sure enough, Evlo sighed. "Dragons are horrible beasts here, but it's better. People don't help them when they hurt people. People want to see them punished. At home—" He stopped, not obviously emotional but suspiciously quiet, his voice clipped and careful. "They had territories, and they were strict about them. Everything people did became about what the dragon of the area wanted for them, like they were the local god to be worshipped. They had spokespeople, they had attendants, they had palaces, and they had the final word on anything in the area. And because they were gods, they demanded sacrifices from time to time." He swallowed, and when he continued, his voice sounded hoarser. "Sometimes gems or shells from the sea. They all love trinkets." He paused, eyes flickering to the gold and marble scattered nearby. "Mostly, it was livestock. Sometimes it was—" He bit his lip so hard, Kella worried it might bleed.

"People."

"Yeah." His face moved through the motions of sneering, but it only made him look more like he wanted to cry. "Virgins, mostly."

"To eat?" Ker's voice was low and strange.

"They sure never came back. But sometimes as servants, for a while, at least. And those servants weren't right. Their souls were gone."

"Their souls?"

"Anything that had made them, them just wasn't there anymore. They were just bodies to be moved around and talked through. And like

I said, these dragons were smaller. There was no reason they couldn't..."
He trailed off, baring his teeth like he'd forgotten how to bite his food
mid-chew.

"But you didn't know."

"No. Not like I ever sat there and watched." His nostrils flared as his
gaze slid over the cave wall. "They took my little sister. She hadn't had
fifteen summers."

Slowly, Kella let a breath out.

"I say took, but he didn't need to take anything," Evlo continued,
speeding up. "We served her up, and she was happy to go." He shook his
head, lip quivering with rage. "She wore our mother's good dress, and they
let her wear her hair down like she always wanted." He took a breath, and
when he spoke again, his voice had dulled. "My parents had eight children.
Three died before they could talk. Two joined the service of our dragon to
fight, gaining new territory against other dragons' servants. One was still
alive by the time I left. And they're never seeing me again. So I guess they
don't have many kids left to 'em."

"How did you get out?"

He smiled like he wanted to laugh. "I tried to slay the dragon. Me and
my cousin. He wasn't long home from one of their wars, and I was the best
hunter our village had. We really thought we could do it. He'd gotten his
hands on explosives—powder more dangerous than dragon fire if its set
alight—and we thought we could smoke the thing out. But we never even
got close. We were just stupid kids."

"It heard you coming?" Kella guessed.

"Not even that close. Betrayal, arrest, sentenced to death." He smiled
grimly. Ker still hadn't moved from behind him, and Evlo seemed almost
too nervous to address them both at once. "You know the story."

"I guess so."

"Except, when I got away, I didn't hole up with a dragon."

Ker's mouth twitched, and Kella suspected Ellonya was talking to
him, much as she might be still feigning sleep.

"How did you get away?"

He inclined his head. "Why do you want to know?"

"Want to hear the end of the story, for a start."

His grin was bright and brief. "They whipped us in the town square
until Veni went down. War injuries. They killed him quick after that. But
they would have kept going with me as long as I could still walk. I was
rescued from our sorry little excuse for a jail cell the night they killed Veni,
recruited by a rebel group I'd had no idea was even running."

"Dragon slayers?"

He shook his head. "They would have wanted to be. But no." He leaned his head back as though to ask if he really had to keep going. When no one spoke, he groaned. "They had a *quest*. They were chasing down a rumour, a story. Everyone knew it. People said the dragons had conquered a devil, *the* devil, back when the island was new, and through their might, they'd made it bring them prosperity. The story went that if it ever got out, it would mean the end of dragon rule, even without more wishing." He pulled his mouth into a tight smile. "So, yeah. We were keen to find it if it existed."

"Did it?"

He blinked, apparently surprised by Ker's voice, but he recovered quickly. "An all-powerful, wish-granting creature? Not that we ever found."

"What did you find?"

Evlo raised three fingers and lowered them one by one. "Betrayal. Arrest. Sentenced to death."

"Some luck you got there."

"Like I said." He kept staring at Kella. "And then I came here when I heard about someone who wasn't afraid of them. Who killed dragons even bigger and deadlier than the ones I'd known and came back for more, whatever happened."

Kella felt her mouth twitch. "They sing about her all over, huh?"

"Not her." As his gaze continued, Kella finally dragged her eyes away. She didn't need to look at another person who she'd let down. "I couldn't save any of my family back home because they didn't want to be saved." He sniffed in disgust. "I guess it's the same story here too." He frowned, lower lip beginning to betray him. "And now you'll kill me. For trying to help."

"You tried—"

Kella silenced Ker with a raised hand. "No one's gonna kill you." She let out a breath. "No. We let you go. And we move, I guess." Doing her best not to think of Ballian, she gave Ker a grin. "We've done Malya, heh?" When he gave her nothing back, she shook her head, irritated. Bar Ballian, it would be all too easy to leave the city that had once meant everything to her. They had loved her here because she was someone she couldn't be anymore. And she had a bruised face and a side still throbbing to remind her of how much that love was conditional.

No, nothing tied her down. And if she couldn't protect her city, at least she could still look out for her little brother and safeguard his foolhardy choices. They were free to go wherever they wanted. But Kella didn't have anywhere she wanted to go. No, all she wished now…

Huh. Wished.

"…just gonna leave me here?"

"You walked here. You can walk back."

"You probably gave me a, how do you say it, a…"

"A concussion?"

"You gave me a *concussion*, Kerali."

"And whose fault is that?"

Kella interrupted the bickering before she really knew what she wanted to say. "Why do you think it doesn't exist?"

"What?"

"The devil. Why are you so sure?"

"Because it's just a children's story." Evlo got to his feet, one eye on Ellonya, who was curled up like a gigantic winged housecat. "When are they ever real?"

"All the time. There's a reason people tell the stories, right?"

"I guess."

Ker shook his head at her, his mouth open. Because he knew her. And Kella knew stories.

She was sure that if she ever tried, she wouldn't have the knack for magic, and that was fine. It was uncomfortable to think on and more, a little too cerebral, too unpredictable to ever be her style. They said that magic was wrong because it went against the story the world was trying to tell, that it interrupted the flow of it. That had always made sense to her; it was what made her such a good performer. If there was a local legend about monster-hunting, she made sure they played with that; if there was a natural end that suggested justice for her prey to die, she would try and deliver that; if the recent deaths could partly be blamed on inaction from local important figures, she would do nothing to pander to them. She could always tease out the edge of a story, feel for the groove of it, and help bring it to life.

This felt like the beginning of one.

And hadn't she always wanted to go on a quest? To have a mission beyond killing whatever was in front of her? This wouldn't be temporary; this wasn't about vengeance. If they succeeded, maybe no one would ever have to kill another dragon again or be killed by one.

Behind Ker, Ellonya opened both eyes.

"Guys, wait. What if we picked up your quest? What if we finished it? Fixed everything."

"*Kel.*"

Evlo looked worried, mostly like he worried she was laughing at him. "You couldn't do that. Even if it is real and you could find it, the wishes always go wrong."

"Yeah, but you said it sometimes went okay for a good person. Ker's a good person. He could wish."

Ker scrunched up his face.

"In the *stories*. But probably not even then in real life. Like, people wish their loved ones alive, and it turns horrific. People wish to be able to fly, and they're changed into a bird and eaten by a bigger bird the next day. If you wanted to wish for something big, the damage could be ridiculous."

"We'd just wish to cure the sick dragons."

"Oh, so you don't just live with dragons, you wanna run a dragon hospital?"

"We worked out there's something wrong with our ones. They can't talk. They can't reason. When they hurt people, they don't mean to."

"Yeah, and that's *good*." Evlo slowed his words as though he wasn't sure that Kella was understanding. "You get smart dragons, you get ones like mine. You get people like mine." His eyes became haunted, and for a moment, Kella was sure he was going to run for it. "You don't want that."

It was exactly what Kella was afraid of, but she didn't want to admit that. "You might be right. I've met dragons who have their minds, and they were even harder to fight than the ones we're used to. But." She glanced at Ellonya, who was still looking at her. "I've met more who've helped me. Who've saved my life. Just like people." She swallowed, reminding herself that she believed what she was saying. "They deserve a chance."

Evlo clenched his jaw. "I don't wanna be the one who helps give it to them, but that's how you wanna go out, be my guest." As he marched out, Ellonya lifted her head, watching him. Kella was impressed that this didn't seem to affect his sure pace.

"It's not a good idea," Ker confirmed, eyes also on Evlo.

"You know I don't really have any of those."

"But we want to try it."

She glanced at him, trying not to let the worry show. It was just like after their mother had died, leaving Ker traumatised in the ashes. She wanted to look after him, but she worried about the reason he was still alive to protect and where that would lead them. "We, huh?"

He met her eyes with only a little defensiveness. "Yeah, we. Ellonya wants to help the other dragons. Even if it gets us nowhere and it's a really, really dumb idea, we can't just hide forever. There has to be some sort of records we can consult to learn about this myth, to find out if there's any truth in it."

Kella smiled. Ker would always suggest consulting records. "We'll need him."

He nodded. "Gimme a minute," he said, sighing as he walked after Evlo.

Kella turned back to Ellonya, who had lowered her head again. "I think they need this," she said.

In response, Ellonya huffed smoke and closed her eyes again, giving every appearance that she had no worries. Even if her bond with Ker was concerning, Ellonya was more than capable of defending him against Evlo, so Kella sat to tend the fire, feeling more herself than she had in months. Maybe it was a dumb idea, but that was all dragon slaying ever was.

And she had a pretty good idea where she could find some good records. And that was giving her more dumb ideas. Gods, she was brimming with them. It felt as good as the rainy season come around again.

She was going on a quest like she'd always wanted. She was never going to be a mediocre dockhand ever again. Kella Kirasdaughter Mabaki, dragon slayer extraordinaire, might never return, but Kella Mabaki, hero and heartbreaker, still had everything going for her.

❖

"Hey," Ker called, not knowing how else to make Evlo stop. He suspected that if he ran to catch up, he wouldn't be so lucky in the fight it would inevitably inspire.

"You gonna beat me up again?" Evlo asked as he dutifully came to a halt, apparently having less faith in himself than Ker did.

"No."

Evlo didn't turn, but when Ker stood beside him, he didn't make to move, only stared out at the sea. Ker wondered if he was thinking about his homeland somewhere across it. Ker had seen the whipping scars on his back. Evlo wasn't lying about what he'd been through; at least, not about all of it. Ker had the strange urge to run his fingers over the light shirt to feel for them, to remind himself of their existence and to acknowledge that he understood how Evlo's experiences had clung to him. But he didn't move.

"She's going whatever I say," Ker started, as always finding it easiest to blame Kella. "And…and I don't think she's wrong. We can't stay how we are, letting things stay like they are. We can't do anything else. And I don't think you can, either."

Evlo snorted. "Watch me."

"You didn't tell Findan you were coming here. You wanted to save me more than you wanted to hurt Ellonya. So…thanks."

Ignoring this, Evlo frowned. "Who came up with *Ellonya* anyway?"

Maybe you should beat him up a little.

"It would really help to have you with us. You speak the language, for a start."

Evlo frowned. "Only two of six, seven, maybe. And I can't read any."

"And you're a foreigner. You look foreign, I mean. You could pretend—"

"Why are you talking like I'm coming with you?" Evlo asked, finally looking at him. "I'm walking away! I don't want *anything* to do with this." He poked a calloused finger at Ker's chest. "I don't want to help save dragons. I don't want to watch one of the only people I thought could never fall for their glamours lose their soul to one, and I refuse to travel with one."

Ker didn't move. "But you're still here."

Growling in frustration, Evlo started marching away again. "Not for long, Kerali."

Ker'd had enough of trying to be nice. "You gave up on them."

Evlo stopped again, the pebbles beneath his feet crunching with an ominous echo. "What?"

"Your family. You got out, and you left them there." Despite still having no audience, Ker threw his arms wide. "As you can see, *I'd* do anything to save mine, and I think I've fucking proved that."

Evlo spun just as Ker let his arms fall. "You don't know a thing about my family."

"Yeah?" Carried away by the catharsis of finally yelling at someone, Ker couldn't help but grin. All the frustration of living with Kella the last few months, who needed to be the centre of attention and of the three people she lived with, could only converse with Ker, and of living in fear that they might fight and say something unthinkable, was all pouring out now. Evlo just had the misfortune to be standing there.

And he'd tried to kill Ellonya. Ker wasn't going to forget that in a hurry. "Neither do you. They could be dead for all you know." He smiled. "You'll stay here and kill our dragons who can't help it because you're too scared to go home and face your own."

Evlo's short legs carried him with unnatural speed over a few feet, long knives in hand. Ker just had time to be impressed that he'd picked them back up without making a fuss. In an instant, Evlo had one knife across Ker's neck and the other pointed toward his gut.

Should I be concerned?

We need him. This is just...negotiation.

I think you need to get better at that.

Breathing heavily, his nostrils flaring, Evlo looked at Ker with pure hatred. "You don't know a godsdamned thing about me, Mabaki."

"You're right." Ker swallowed carefully, feeling his throat bob dangerously close to the knife. "You never told me. You hide most of it away. I get that."

Evlo scoffed, his eyes wide. "Why would *you* get that?"

Ker concentrated on keeping his breath steady. He needed to be believed. "Ellonya isn't my first dragon." The knife at his throat wavered and moved a little farther away.

"What?"

"This has been what I am for a long time before you met me. Only difference is that I'm happy now. Because she's alive and with me and not dead with my mother."

Evlo shook his head and backed away. "So it was always a lie. There was never a dream of dragon slayers worth looking up to." He sneered, seeming on the verge of tears. "Even the best of them have dragons in their heads and are ready to leave each other behind."

"Yeah, but there're still heroes." He pointed back at the cave. "That's what she is, and you know it. If she doesn't do this, it'll break her. And who knows, she might really do it. You told me yourself," he said, feeling a little desperation creep into his tone. "She's free. She's always going to do what she wants. And what she wants is to save as many people as she can. Don't you want to watch her try?"

When Evlo's face didn't soften an inch, Ker shook his head. "I don't care if you're scared of my dragon or if you're disgusted by me." Testing the waters now, Ker shoved lightly at Evlo's chest. He was a little surprised that he gave way. "I just need you to help me keep her safe. Because I want to keep the family I have left, just like you. So let us help."

"Nothing can fix that place." Turning away, Evlo bent to pick up a stone to throw. "Senice is dragon protected and devil cursed."

Ker took a seat on one of the boulders, happy to abandon the pretence of being tough. His legs had started to shake. "What, you think she'll care about that?"

Evlo looked back with a smile. "She really will go, huh?"

"Yup. But she'd do better with you. If you don't go, we'll just come up with a worse plan." Ker shrugged. "We want you with us."

Evlo's gaze became more pointed. "Do *you*?"

Though he couldn't have said why, something about being the focus of those eyes was making it hard to speak, even though he could barely see them in the dark. "I mean, you don't have to." When Evlo shook his head and turned away, Ker's panic rose, forcing him to come up with something else to say. "I...I liked it when you taught me songs before. I think you'd be a good teacher." Ker licked his dry lips, watching Evlo's shoulders shift and then relax. "And I figure you miss us, or you wouldn't have come to find us."

"You're doing a lot of figuring."

"Known for it."

Evlo sighed and pointed at the cave. "I can't be alone with that thing."

"Firstly, don't talk about her like that—"

"*And* I don't want to fly anywhere on it."

Ker nodded. "We'll see what we can do there, sure."

"And if I see it talking through you like that again, I might have to kill you to save your family the pain of watching it take you slowly."

"Thanks for warning me. I guess."

He almost received a smile for that. "And I promise not to tell anyone if you promise not to surprise me with any other dragons."

Deciding to save asking how Evlo felt about gremlins, Ker nodded and offered a hand, wordlessly asking to be lifted to his feet and to seal this strange deal all in one.

Evlo took it. The full moon watched, pouring her light over them without judgement. "You wanna help me look for my arrows?"

"Not really."

The rain started as their hands let go.

CHAPTER SIX

W hen the night began to clear a day after the storm began, Jev was sitting at the desk in his old room, flicking through the pages of one of his mother's notebooks. The new quiet helped him register the sounds of someone trying to break in through his window.

Many who'd known her had considered his mother somewhat contradictory. King Vikro had been a famously stern ruler who'd never wavered in her inherited enmity with the Aelshians. Yet, she had also kept a garden, and she had written books about plants. Even in mourning, Jev could not claim to find her writing inspiring, or even legible, but it was a comfort to hold her handwriting and more importantly, her delicate sketches. It was harder to believe she could be dead when he could read her voice on a page. It wasn't going to give him advice, but considering that most of her lectures had been delivered through gardening metaphors, it wasn't far off, either.

She might not have had a metaphor for his current predicament.

He'd gotten his peace, a wife, and the hope of stopping dragons out of it. A few short months later, he no longer had any of those things. His people despised him, his enemies accused him of killing his queen, and the dragons were as they always were, but the kingdom had one notable loss in its most famous dragon slayer.

Who was currently breaking into his chamber. Kella was undefeated when it came to killing dragons, and she was good at a lot of things. Stealth had never been one of them.

"I can hear you, Kel," he said, moving closer to the window.

"Might've been an assassin," a voice from below his childhood bedroom window said. It was sweet that she remembered how to navigate the maze and how to reach his bedroom the way she'd taught him. If he was honest, he'd been hoping she'd try something like this; it was why he'd been using the empty room so much lately.

He lowered an arm down and after a moment, his best friend clung to it to climb the last of the windowsill. He didn't hug her like he wanted to, but she let him hold her hand for a little longer than necessary. They were no doubt both thinking how much they'd missed each other, but neither was going to say it, Jev realised.

He let go first and said, "You lost your hair."

"You lost your wife."

He sighed as she walked past. She was unsmiling, sober, and likely planned on being mean, but she was clearly at ease. As he followed her out of his old bedroom, slinking around with the purpose of a housecat trying to pretend it wasn't lost, it occurred to him she might have also gotten lonely. "What are you doing here?" he asked as she reached a balcony identical to the one farther along, where he'd once stood on with Eisha and had watched Kella be taken from Malya for what should have been forever. But he'd never really believed that.

"Thought I should say good-bye," she said, pulling herself up on the balcony rail. To her back was a four-hundred-foot drop, but she did not seem concerned and even swung a leg out.

Carefully, he walked toward her and smiled. "Thought this was your town."

She craned her neck to look at the town in question as though expecting it to look back. Her profile was different now, with her nose looking markedly more crooked. "Not anymore. Did you even know I was home?"

He paused. "I knew you were alive. There were a lot of stories. I'm not sure if I knew you came back or just assumed you did." Where else would you go, he didn't say, deciding he had no right to be cruel.

"I tried getting you a message. You changed too many of the guards. Didn't trust these new ones."

"One of my servants helped kidnap my wife and then killed herself. You could say the whole thing has made me a little paranoid."

Shock widened her eyes. He could tell she wanted to reach for him. It was a peculiar tragedy, to have hurt the only person who could comfort him so deeply that she was no longer sure she wanted to provide it. Her hand quivered, then stilled as that famous willpower worked its way down to her fingertips.

Last time they'd met in these rooms, he'd wanted to fuck her more than he had in years, right in the bed he still hadn't slept with his wife in and perhaps never would. Anything to make himself forget how angry he was, and that whatever he did, there would be no going back. And he'd been right; he couldn't go back, so the want hadn't lingered.

"What do you think happened?" She flicked two fingers over her ear. She was not only listening but invested.

He shrugged, then tried to hide his fear at leaning too far over the edge. "The Aelshians. Maybe."

"I heard the rich gharifs were mad you kept raising their taxes. And the other theory is—"

"That she ran. She didn't do that, Kel."

"I believe you," she said too easily.

"Why?"

"Well, thanks to you, I got to know her cousin real well. And she didn't think she would."

"Real well, heh? Is it true you killed seven of my guard?"

"No."

"Is it true you talked a dragon into flying you home?"

"There's a lot of stories, huh?"

"You always inspire them." He paused, remembering. "Litz Woskenna arrived back in Verassez alone, claiming you were dead, and a third of the troop I sent with you returned full of wild tales that you had turned on them and were in league with dragons, demons, and witches."

"Huh."

"And guessing by the bruises you're sporting, at least some people in town believe those tales."

"Nah, my face always looks like this." She looked at her feet, teasing but without energy.

He sighed. "Why don't you hunt anymore?"

"What, are you saying you want me to go back to slaying dragons? Just don't get caught?"

"I don't see the reason you've stopped."

She turned her head up sharply, half smiling, "Excuse me, you threatened to throw me in the sword pit."

"Yeah, and usually, that would encourage you. So what's wrong?" When she didn't answer, his own theories weighed on his mind. "I sought Findan out the night you left."

"Braver guy than me."

"She told me to get lost. Called me a hypocrite."

"Fair."

"And said she wouldn't be coming after you. That I'd made that impossible."

Kella's face remained still, but her cheek twitched.

"They didn't come for you, did they?"

"Ker did."

He let that hang, waiting for her to explain. It didn't usually take long.
"Dragons aren't what we thought."
"What are they?"
"The Aelshian ones talk."
Jev blinked. He'd heard the same many times from Aelshians. But Kella, as well as being a lifelong hater of dragons, was as big a sceptic as he'd ever known. "It's true, then."
"At first I thought, oh, this is like a creepier, smarter version of our dragons."
"With the images."
"Yeah. But, no, they're just guys."
"Just *guys*?"
"Yeah. And there's something wrong with our guys."
"I'll say."
"I mean it, Jev, they're just sick." She shrugged. "That makes us murderers, I guess," she said flippantly, but he suspected the flippancy had taken practice.
"If they're sick, they've always been sick," he reminded her slowly. "Does it matter?"
"If we can cure them, it matters."
"Can we?" He didn't know how to feel about the use of we.
"I wanna try. That's why I'm leaving."
He was a little surprised by how sharp and strong his rising envy was. That had been *his* dream when they were kids. Kella had just wanted to kill dragons, but he'd wanted to travel, to see the world before he lost his chance. But he'd already lost it. "Where will you go?"
"They say the library in Aelshia is the greatest in the world. If the information I'm looking for is anywhere, it'll be there. Besides, I owe it to Litz to figure out if they treated her okay when she got back."
"From what I understand, she's still very involved in the army. So it's 'Litz'?"
Kella ignored this. "You really think it's gonna come to war?"
"It always seems to get back there."
She swayed and bumped his arm in a motion that could almost be mistaken for being accidental. "I think it matters that you tried to stop it. Even if it doesn't work out."
He gripped the balcony, wishing it would ground him. "Thanks."
"I'll keep an eye out for your wife."
Reluctantly feeling her sway away again, he raised his eyebrows. "Kind of you, thanks." He breathed out. "Well, they say their king is keeping someone well-guarded in the palace."

"Hmm. I'm good at getting into palaces."

"Don't get yourself killed."

"Oh, so *now* you don't want the Aelshians to kill me?"

"Oh, so now you want to stop killing dragons and travel to Aelshia?" She almost smiled. "Have you got my stuff?"

"What stuff?"

"Don't you dare play dumb with me, Jev."

"Anything we took off you when you were arrested will be down in the jail."

She narrowed her eyes as she leaned forward, her nails digging into the wall. Then, she straightened with a sniff and marched back into his rooms.

"Hey—"

"I'm getting them a cure, or I'm dying trying. Might even have to overthrow a foreign government. I need a fucking sword for all that, Jev."

He stood, shoulders slumping. He'd wanted so badly not to have her die a hero. But she didn't care what he wanted and never really had. Some things were always going to be more important. "Even you might struggle with toppling the Aelshian monarchy."

"I wasn't talking about Aelshia. A*ha.*" She wandered back into view with the golden helmet he'd once theatrically gifted her from a dragon's hoard and her sword swinging easily in front of her. "Knew you were lying."

He shook his head, but he couldn't help a smile. "Are you sure you want to cart around a dragon-bone-handled sword on your quest to save dragons? Bit insensitive, heh?"

She gave the handle a hard look, clearly considering this for the first time. Then, she swung it at his curtains lightly moving in the night breeze. "Nah. Fuck off, it's a good sword."

"You're really sure about this? You're really going?"

"Maybe never to return."

"Ker's going with you, right?"

She scoffed. "Yeah. Why?"

"Someone needs to look after you."

"And you think Ker knows how to do that?"

"Slow you down, then."

She snorted, not meeting his eyes. With much less hair on her head, the helmet slipped too far down her face. She looked like a child playing in their parent's uniform. "We'll be fine. Will you?"

He opened his arms. "Nothing bad ever happens to kings, remember?" He wanted to say, "You got my back?" because that was always what they had asked in the moments before a fight. But it would be ridiculous now he'd already proven he didn't have hers when it counted.

"Wrong again, pillock," she said, hopping on the windowsill she'd climbed through. "That's literally how we get new kings." She looked at the drop, tense. "Same way I got up, right?"

"Need me to toss you the helmet down so you can see where you're going?"

She glared before muttering, "Yes."

Unable to stop grinning, he sauntered over and liberated the gold helmet from her head.

"Thanks," she said, still sounding the sullen child.

"I'm sorry, what was that?"

The peck on his cheek was sudden and unexpected, but it was appreciated. "Thank you, all right? But I take that back if you drop the helmet on me. Or call your guards."

"Please. I'd never give you less than a ten minute head start. We're friends."

Her smile cut him deep. "Yeah. And I'm glad." She launched off the windowsill and disappeared into the night.

He wondered if he'd ever see her again. Even if she survived everything she was determined to keep throwing herself at, she might not be the same when she returned. She might—

"Hey! My helmet?"

CHAPTER SEVEN

Kella knew Evlo could not be happy about their situation. Not after reluctantly agreeing to their plan on the stipulation that he would not have to talk to anyone. But he should have known that just because they were all working with a dragon now, nothing had changed. Their plans never worked out.

She moved her shoulder forward so that she stood in front of Ker and a little closer to Litz. She'd had to be patient and quiet and really fucking nervous for a long time, and now she wanted the floor. "The Jeenobian king spoke highly of you as the one to trust here above any other." She remembered to nod back at Evlo, who stood stiff and unsmiling next to Ellonya in the makeshift uniform they'd created for him on the way. It was partially practical, if the leather shoulder Kella had been working on didn't slip when he pulled a bow over it. "Our master needs someone he can trust."

Litz blinked, seeming deeply unimpressed. Possibly by the story, more likely by the accent. Kella hadn't worked all that hard at it. She'd tried to copy the way Evlo said his vowels and had given up after that. Finally, Litz sighed. "Where does your party hail from?"

"Our master hails from Senice," Ker said. "Far across the sea, past the desert lands east of here. On a mission of grave importance." His accent was a little better, but Kella felt it confused things to have him speak immediately after her. Maybe they should have rehearsed.

"I see," said Litz, giving no indication of whether she'd heard of the place. "I am flattered King Jevlyn remembers my brief visit so fondly." She turned to the woman by her side who seemed to be an officer and had genuinely sounded charmed by them. Kella was wary of her. She kept wearing the same bright smile Kella tended to aim for when she was lying. "Has the king been informed yet?"

At the slow shake of the woman's head, implying an easy understanding between them, Kella felt an irrational burst of envy. For a moment, she felt as out of control as she had when leaping in the air from one dragon to another. Below, the ground waited. She was the only one who knew some of Litz's secrets, and that had felt like enough. But here was evidence she'd failed to imagine the mundane side of what she might find here because she hadn't envisaged Litz with friends.

Thinking of Litz on their way had been comforting. Ker had Ellonya and Sall to confide in and Evlo to bicker with, but Kella had spent a lot of time imagining. Imagining Litz in trouble, beset on all sides by more Circle assassins, with Kella getting there just in time to save her, or Litz longing for someone as changed by recent experiences as she had been. Or just Litz smiling with joy and shock to see her again, saying things like, "Somehow, I knew you'd find me."

The whole point of their arrival was keeping who they were a secret, but Kella was terrible at subterfuge and wanted Litz to smile at her. She could survive not getting a kiss, but she wasn't sure she could go on without at least a smile.

But when Litz led them toward a terrifyingly unstable-looking rope bridge, there was no smile, no wink, no reassurance. She walked beside Kella almost incidentally. Behind them, two guards brought up the rear. Ellonya was being shown to guest quarters farther in the city while her less-important humans were kept together for questions, and the gremlin stayed, for now, out of sight in Ker's bag. Though Kella was starting to see other gremlins around, these looked different. It was strange enough to see gremlins who felt confident moving through human spaces, but they barely looked like the same species. There were fewer reptilian features and more obviously amphibian ones. Their skin seemed glassy in ways that would have left them unprotected from the Jeenobian sun.

"No idea what possessed you to put everyone in danger like this," Litz said from the corner of her mouth, her voice lower and softer than Kella remembered, and she had tried so hard to remember it over these long months.

She smiled. "Maybe I just wanted to see you again, Princess. Didn't you want to see me?"

"I wanted you to stay safe."

"Have you met me?" Kella could feel Ker shooting daggers into the back of her head for briefly raising her voice. "Safe's not my style."

"Why are you here?" She didn't sound happy, and it was starting to wear on Kella. They'd parted after holding hands under a setting sun, after

Litz had admitted she wasn't ready to say good-bye. To go from the height of that to being treated like an inconvenience was jarring.

"I—*we're* here for reasons of grave importance. Like we said. This is Evlo, by the way. He really is from Senice. Heard of it?"

"Not really." Litz sighed, and now Kella felt uncomfortably sure that Ker was staring at her with sympathy.

Flying on a dragon, something she was still uncomfortable with, around a desert that had already had a few goes at trying to kill her, just to attempt a reunion in a kingdom filled with people who wanted her dead was the biggest gesture she'd ever made in her life. And that hadn't included anything she could call a real romance, but what she'd shared with Litz had felt different. It should have meant more to her too.

"You can't show your faces like this," Litz murmured. "Dragons have long memories. I'll find you net hats. We'll pretend you fear the bugs."

"Are you kidding? Of course we fear the bugs. I hear everything here can kill you with a bite. Sure, let's get hats."

"I don't think you're taking this seriously."

"And I think you missed me."

She got an almost smile and wanted to sing.

❖

This can't happen. Make them go.

As you know, I didn't plan this, Litz reminded Loren. *I can hardly stop them turning up.* And it was flattering just a little. Embarrassing to admit out loud, but it was clear that Kella had been wanting to see her, even if she was here for her own greater purpose.

You may not have planned it, but you like it. Make them leave.

What was all that about wanting me to be happy at any cost?

Happy, yes. Dead, no. The Circle leaves us be because they know us to be functionally with them and that we're not telling anyone what we know. Being seen with humans they want dead and a Jeenobian dragon will absolutely ruin any chances of a compromise. You know all this, Litz.

Well, they're here. There seems no point in not hearing them out. Sending them away before they have a chance to speak will look even worse.

Hmm. If they get Ellonya near me, I will speak with her. I doubt she knows how to conduct herself with other dragons.

Have you ever met a Senice dragon?

I'm not sure I've ever heard of the place. But human names for regions change with time, so perhaps I have.

Maybe it'll help if no one knows what she's supposed to act like. She can be seen acting strange.

The one acting as her rider isn't hers. That will come off as strange, whatever people expect.

The rope bridge wobbled a little as Kella took a step that was a little too hard and threw her arms out for balance. Without thinking, Litz grabbed her hand and clutched it before making herself let go. "Remember, you shouldn't have a problem with heights. You fly on dragons. Apparently."

Remember, you shouldn't be holding hands with foreign servants you've just been introduced to.

Hush. She's not found her feet yet.

I'll say. That accent was upsetting, and I don't usually notice them.

Kella gripped the sides of the bridge and nodded, breathing out. Behind her, Ker looked both annoyed and braced to catch her. Litz wondered how he felt with this other man, Evlo, pretending to be Ellonya's rider and being separated from her in a new land. He and Evlo stayed silent, though they remained strangely in sync, almost as though they really were sharing a dragon's consciousness.

Kella spoke loudly and constantly, certainly acting like all this was her plan. In contrast, the young men acted as though they were here to ensure her protection, probably from herself. When they reached the steps taking them down on the other side of the river, Evlo nodded for Ker to go ahead as they both turned their heads, watching the guards following them.

At the bottom of the stairs, Kella squealed. "What is this?"

Litz could see the guards beginning to notice how odd this visitor was. Fighting to keep her own expression blank, she followed Kella's pointing finger to the little amphibian that she was impressed Kella had even noticed. "It's a glass frog."

"I love it."

Litz could feel the guards looking at her, could feel Ker's tension, his fear. They were making too much of a scene. But it had been a very long day, and the last person she'd expected to see was Kella Mabaki, famed dragon slayer, in the heart of a dragonriding empire. And she'd forgotten how childlike Kella sounded when stumbling on something that amazed her; it was just like the day they'd tracked down the chimaeras, when she'd shown that she wasn't just someone who hunted monsters but admired them too.

Do you think they have frogs in Jeenobi? Litz asked Loren as Kella leaned down to go eye to eye with the camouflaged creature.

I have no idea, and I don't care. She is making a scene, and you need to gain some more self-preservation to make up for her lack, please.

"She was like this about camels a few weeks ago too," Ker muttered, keeping his eyes straight ahead as Kella hissed back at him.

"They shouldn't have more than one hump. They're too powerful with two." Things didn't get better when they passed a patch of mushrooms almost as high as their knees just off the plank path.

She's certainly convincing as someone new to Aelshia, Loren grumbled as Kella made them stop for a full minute to yell about purple spots and confirm that everyone else could see what she could. This time, Ker gave Evlo a look, who then said something stern in what Litz imagined was his own language. Though she doubted Kella understood it all, she was willing to shut up and start moving, looking almost chastened.

The look did not last. When they reached the busier areas of Verassez, Kella's eyes lit up like a dragon's open throat before it fired. "Market day. Reminds me of something."

Litz felt herself warm but tried not to react. "Mmm."

"Of when we met."

Litz nodded carefully.

"You weren't wearing a uniform. It was nice."

"I wasn't on duty. Here, I always am."

Kella stopped, her eyes wide. "Look at the *size* of those fish…I know, I know, I'm walking."

"You're not very good at hiding yourself, are you?" Litz said quietly, knowing fondness had crept its way into her tone and feeling helpless to stop it.

"I do okay. I got a job this year, y'know."

"A job?"

"Like, a real job. I turned up every day, and they gave me money at the end of it." As Litz tried not to laugh, Kella narrowed her eyes. "What?"

"I'm sorry, it's a little hard to envisage."

"Why?" Kella's nostrils flared. "You think I think I'm too good for it? Or not capable?"

"You don't strike me as someone who would reliably show up on time. Or take orders. Or who would enjoy being normal."

Kella pouted but seemed mollified. Litz suspected she was flattered to be so easily summarised. She continued to offer small expressions of amazement and delight as Litz led them farther into the floating city—the rope bridges and homes in the trees above, the busy passenger boats, the sewage boats, the carts designed to be lifted easily over bridges—but kept it quieter. She asked questions, none about where Litz was leading them or where Ellonya had been taken or how Litz's last few months had been or if war was truly imminent. Just all about the city. Did monkeys act like the gulls in Malya? How did people who used wheelchairs get around? Did the dragons always swim instead of fly through the city areas? Did dragons ever burn homes and businesses down by accident?

If nothing else, she sounds like a tourist, Loren put in. *Ellonya arrived in her quarters here. I'll keep my distance for now, but I'll try to find out if they send anyone to her.*

Let me know.

Of course.

And how was your meeting?

Litz caught a hint of uneasiness, possibly even evasiveness. Loren wanted to protect her from this, which was pointless but sweet. Digging for heaven, as Kella might have said. *Nothing of interest.*

They want me to take the job, don't they?

It would make them stop hovering, yes. And put an end to the barely disguised threats. And they're promising to send Calino away.

That would be good.

I'm not sure they will if you don't take on the job. It would prove we're with them and the king who loves them the way nothing else could.

I suppose.

Litz did not want her unexpected visitors in the palace. Instead, she asked nicely at a reputable inn, a building made up of several stories attached to a tree, for a room for them all. Everyone seemed briefly amazed by the floating building before following Litz, who ensured them a room through a mild amount of palace pressure. Showing up in military uniform wearing a dragonriding earring generally cleared the way without Litz needing to put much into words.

❖

Kella hadn't expected Litz to look different. That probably spoke to a lack of imagination in her more than anything else. Kella might have cut her hair off and started wearing silly disguises, but it was unthinkable that Litz, a woman she had known for only days, could have changed anything. She'd grown her hair out a little—it suited her—but the funny thing was that she wasn't dressed any different. The uniform was exactly the same, just not dragged through a desert trek and several battlefields.

She looked good. And worse—or also good—she looked at ease, comfortable in herself and her environment, displaying with every move an innate self-confidence and self-possession Kella could only dream of, that even Jev had only been able to imitate.

It was a little intimidating and extremely sexy. Especially when Litz was giving orders and pretending not to know her. It was horrifying, and Kella wished she would keep doing it. But, oh, how it felt special, even with the others there, for Litz to leave two soldiers at the bottom of the stairs of the inn and say, "A moment, please."

Kella could only hope they could get more than a moment, but it seemed that she too was at Litz's mercy, receiving as much as this powerful woman was prepared to give. This was different than breaking into Jev's quarters in the middle of the night, even if he was a king. She'd known him all his life, and he owed her that and another lifetime of apologies besides.

Litz owed her nothing. A thought that, fascinatingly, was just as attractive as it had been all those months ago.

Moments after they closed the door to their new room—spacious, but no palace, containing three slim beds and one long side table—Ker put the bag down, and Sallvayn popped their head out. Evlo turned away, disgusted by the sight. Apparently, where he came from, gremlins were more rodent-like but were always around, constantly spying for dragons and occasionally assisting in keeping people in line. Though he'd remained true to his word and hadn't attempted to hurt either Sallvayn or Ellonya, he hadn't grown much more at ease with either.

"It's Sallvayn, isn't it?"

Sallvayn didn't nod but did say something in their own language. Kella felt like she should make a joke about this before remembering Litz, as a dragonrider, could understand everything they were saying without needing to spend months working on sign language with them.

"It's good to see you again," Litz said respectfully, bending one knee. "Yes, that was also my concern."

Ker, who had surely been privy to their little conversation said, "I'm doing what I can to push down my connection to Ellonya while we're out, and we hope that as long as I stay close to Evlo, I shouldn't be noticed."

Litz hummed thoughtfully. "That'll have to do." She looked around, her eyes resting on Kella. "What are you doing here, really?"

For once, with those lovely eyes fixed on her as she'd worried they never would again, Kella found herself speechless.

Ker spoke for her. "We really are here about Senice. We've heard the Verassez library holds almost every book ever written, correct?"

"That's what the librarians and politicians like to say, yes."

"We think something there can cure the Jeenobian dragons if we know how to ask it nicely, and if it exists."

Litz shook her head as she turned back to him. Kella let out a slow breath, annoyed at herself for freezing like that. She could tell that Evlo was looking at her, wondering what had taken over her. "Does it? Where is Senice?"

"Like I said," Kella cut in, recovered. "Evlo's from there. It's an island. The Doshni sailors call it the Hidden Island because they've never been able to chart it. It's some ways northwest from the Nayonan ports."

"Sorry, you decided to fly east?"

Ker nodded. "For the library. It seemed foolish to make that trip without more information about what we're looking for."

"Forgive me, but this was barely less foolish." Litz rubbed an elegant hand over her forehead. Kella suspected she hadn't slept well the night before or had been forced up earlier than she'd have liked. "It's not a good climate for strangers right now, and there are still powerful dragons who want to see you and Ellonya dead."

"But not you?" Kella shouldn't have been disappointed that Litz wasn't in more danger, she reminded herself.

Litz shook her head. "No. They understand we're not going to tell anyone what we know. Disappearing us from the centre of the town is more trouble than it's worth right now."

"Right now," Kella repeated, emphasising the words carefully. "So if you're out on campaign, they still might?"

Litz looked uncomfortable. "It's unlikely. They're considering me, us, for promotion."

"Promotion? *Congratulations*, Princess."

On one of the beds, Ker looked exasperated. "Where are they taking Ellonya?"

"She'll be taken to the guest quarters on the northern side of the city. If one of you, especially her rider, wants to stay with her overnight, this will not seem strange. She will be largely left alone for tonight, from what Loren can tell, though there are many dragons curious about her and where she's from. But it's more likely you will go through more interrogation," she added, turning to Evlo. "You'll be seen as her spokesperson."

"We're not staying long," he said, probably as an attempt to remind Kella that he hadn't wanted this plan at all.

"Long enough that I'll need to present you at court. But the king is busy, so I can probably delay that until tomorrow." Litz sighed. "What are you claiming you're here for?"

Ker and Kella looked at each other and shrugged. "An alliance offer."

"Warning about a natural disaster."

Evlo turned. "What happened to the war machine we wanted to sell?"

Litz stared at them all, aghast. "You flew all the way here and didn't even agree on a story?"

"We had a lot of ideas," Ker offered.

"Besides," Kella said, "everyone wants to know more about Senice, right? They'll be interested in whatever we say we're here for."

"Being interesting in this court when you're wanted for killing a dragon isn't positive." She sighed. "Okay, work on making this as…as boring as you can. I'll present you tomorrow. I'll work on the how of that today."

"And the library?"

Litz hesitated. "Tomorrow. My uncle works there. He can help make it seem like part of a visitor's tour. But I might not be able to get you more than tomorrow there."

Begrudgingly, Kella could appreciate that even if Litz disapproved of their plan, she was helping. But she was also walking away.

"The inn will cover your meals," she was saying as she backed toward the door. "I'll try to send word tonight, but I'll come back tomorrow. I'll do what I can to keep any official eyes away, but I can't promise how normal people will react to you."

"Hey," Kella said, following her into the stairwell. The slim wooden staircase was empty, and mercifully, Litz stopped two stairs down, not forcing Kella to chase her. But the extremely close quarters made Kella want to be her most insufferable self and lean in for a kiss, and only the fear of rejection held her back. "Come with us when we go," she said, keeping her voice low.

Litz said nothing, but though she seemed exhausted, she couldn't hide the glimmer of interest in her eyes. She liked that Kella had asked and wanted her to keep talking, however stupid an idea she believed it to be. Feeling a little braver, Kella stepped forward, leaving no space between them. "Don't you want to fix everything?" Carefully, she laid one open palm on the wall behind Litz.

Litz gave a long glance down the stairs, but no one appeared to interrupt them. "I want to find my cousin."

Sobering fast, Kella retrieved her arm. "I'm sorry. Jev did ask me to keep an eye out. His spies think they're keeping someone—"

"In the palace?" Litz nodded. "I've heard similar, though I'd prefer not to believe it. Jevlyn, he wouldn't have—"

Kella shook her head sharply. "No way. He's really fucked-up about it." She braved a grin and hoped it was a charming one. "Okay, new plan. We find your cousin, fix all that, and then, we fly off and fix the dragons."

Litz sighed, but it was softer than before. "What is this cure you're looking for?"

"A magic devil guy who can make whatever you want happen."

Litz frowned, clearly sceptical. That was fair. Kella also had some scepticism that she was hoping would dissolve when she found some concrete information. But if not, maybe the library and being in Verassez would help them figure out what could be wrong with their dragons and if there was a way of helping them. They had backup plans. At least they were trying something.

"And I want our dragons to get well again. I want them to stop killing and destroying just because they don't know any better."

"It wore at you, not hunting them."

Kella took a step back. "I don't like people telling me I'm not doing my job."

"I thought you got a real job."

"You know what I mean."

Litz took another step down. "I can't stay longer, it won't look right," she murmured. She gave Kella a smile that made her insides flip worse than any of the harrowing flights had. "I don't think it sounds like you thought about any of this as much as you should. But it's good to see you again."

❖

"So not even your fellow dragon slave thinks this is a good idea," Evlo said as he continued pacing around the room Kella had left them alone in. Ker watched, thinking that the prospect of a real bed for at least a night or two, no matter what dangers they were risking for it, felt good. The fact that the beds were so low was odd, but it was a definite improvement from everything they'd had on their journey.

My quarters are beautiful too. Though I've yet to be spoken to by any dragon, I could get used to this. Ellonya sent Ker an image of her view: her room seemed spacious, and unlike their wooden quarters, hers was made of polished marble, with wide windows that caught the sun's glare.

"We never said it was a good idea."

"Well, she's right, we should have come up with one by now."

But that had been a hard thing to focus on, even with all the long travel time flying north around the mountains bordering the desert. It had, shamefully, been enjoyable. After all those secretive months of feeling trapped, with no one to talk to, escaping the coast with someone new, even if Evlo hardly wanted to speak most of the time, had felt wonderful. And since Evlo was far more likely to be convinced into conversation when they were making him forget what they were doing, their talk had often wandered to the trivial. In this way, Evlo had begun to relax a little with

Ellonya, and when Ker did report her words, it was in his own voice and usually with a joke or a question.

They'd all needed to believe they were doing something like the old days, on a normal quest to help, and when they got there, there'd be a fight. But since it had never arrived, they'd let themselves relax. But now they'd reached their destination, and all the issues they'd tried to put behind them were here looking at them.

"What are they like, these dragonriders, are they like you? I see the gremlins here aren't like any I've seen in Senice or Jeenobi." Evlo had asked similar many times before. From this, Ker took to mean: are they still themselves? Though Ker had wanted to dismiss Evlo's fear as ridiculous, he had begun to realise over time that Evlo had reasons to think differently about dragons than either Jeenobian or Aelshian sensibilities.

"Litz is the one Kella travelled with before. She seems to have her own mind and her own life. And Kella was won over to her dragon without being glamoured, as you'd say."

"As far as you know." Evlo huffed just as Kella slipped back into the room. "So did you sleep with her? On the road?"

"None of your business," Kella said, walking to the net-covered window that had become her new object of fascination.

"Why not?"

"What did I just say?"

Evlo made a face at Ker in a plea for solidarity that Ker, though amused, denied him. He suspected none of this was going how Kella had hoped so far, and though this didn't usually stop her from getting what she wanted, he didn't see the sense in aggravating her yet.

"She looks important. Is that going to help us?"

"It's going to get us into the library."

"And the court," Ker added. "Should we want to be in the court? Surely, we don't."

Kella shrugged as she sat at the foot of the middle bed, her short legs splaying over the floorboards. "Can't avoid it, I guess. Besides, might be a laugh. We might just find out where they're keeping Jev's wife and end the war before it starts."

"I doubt it."

"We can be efficient, who knows."

"And the dragons that are looking for you?" Evlo, still looking tense, didn't sit. "Do we kill them if they come for us?" His lip curled. "Your new principles wouldn't stretch that far, would they?"

"If they come find us, we'll give 'em hell," Kella said easily.

"Foolish," Sallvayn said at her feet. She glared at them, not understanding but suspicious.

"Though we probably wouldn't be able to. We are surrounded on all sides," Ker reminded them.

Kella flopped back on the bed. Though she'd gotten more used to flying, her relief to be back on solid ground was always palpable. "But that's when they'll least expect it. We'll be fine. Where are they keeping Ellonya, is it nice?"

I like it.

"She likes it," Ker said, ignoring Evlo's sidelong stare. His contempt he could deal with, but the worry in his eyes, like Ker was condemned to die a slow death but wasn't sane enough to realise it, continued to make Ker want to knock him out again.

Be nice. He's got better. And you know what he went through.

Yeah, and you're clearly nothing like the ones who hurt him.

To you. He's still afraid. And though he hates me, he has to feign devotion to me, something as grating on both of us, I'm sure.

Why are you so nice to him?

Because you want his approval very badly. Making him important to me too.

I don't—

Kella was clicking her fingers in his direction. "Ker, if you want to join us, we wanna go find our first free meal on the Aelshian Empire. You in?"

Focus on your now. I'll be fine.

Ker swallowed, worry for Ellonya and being surrounded in an unknown land still clawing at his insides, but since hunger had long since gotten there first, he nodded. "Sure," he said. "Let's go see if they ever catch any of those monster fish."

CHAPTER EIGHT

As things stood, there was no heir to the Jeenobian throne, and it showed just how many more immediate issues they had to deal with as a council that the fact had not been brought up in almost a year. This, for once, was more Jev's mother's fault than his own. She'd relentlessly prevented her uncle, Tashno, from taking a wife and bearing his own children. After quietly adopting Jev and raising him as her heir, she'd made sure he would never have siblings or rivals, wishing to avoid the bloody infighting that had preceded her own rise. It meant that growing up, Jev's every childhood illness, every battle injury from running around after the Mabakis, had been a source of not just maternal but professional and existential terror for her.

Though an understandable strategy then, it left him alone now. He felt it especially when the spiritual advisor to the throne, Sollon Astchin started speaking, their voice uncharacteristically sharp. But not so uncharacteristic since Kella's exile, when he had "picked a dragon's life over that of a human."

He couldn't blame them or any of the council who had trusted his mother and were trying to trust him. He'd promised a solution and hadn't delivered one.

"The dragons were meant to be a problem of the past with this peace," Astchin reminded the room. "But now we have no dragon slayers, no army fit to deal with them, and the fiends continue their destruction of the countryside unchecked."

"We have to find new ways of checking them," Jev said. "Ways that don't involve killing them."

General Vallso looked flabbergasted. "Who are we trying to appease by not killing them? The new Aelshian king makes no secret of warmongering. She blames us for her sister's death—"

"Disappearance," Jev corrected, ill with rage. "I wish to appeal to the normal Aelshian people who share our interests. I do not want us to seem like murderers to them."

"That's—"

"And I want us to think about who else might share interests with us," he continued. "My spies have people in some of the forest clans. They report that—"

"Well, they're worse than the Aelshians themselves."

Jev fought to keep his voice measured. "It doesn't make sense that we have not considered them as potential allies at any point in the last century. They are within the borders of an empire, subjugated by its might. We share a common enemy." Blank faces greeted Jev him. Only Professor Drallnock, the historian, seemed to seriously consider his words.

"We don't deal with witches," Sollon Astchin reminded him gently as they rested a hand on the empty chair beside them. Hallen Trailfeet should have been there, but no one had seen him in weeks. It would seem the tracker and former slayer had already had his fill of royal politics. Jev could sympathise with the lack of excitement the council offered after a life of dragon hunting—and would not miss the man's surly company—but he hated to lose his sole claim to anti-dragon credentials beyond his own past.

He would have to fix that. Along with so many other impending issues. Citing dragon defence, many gharifs had ceased to pay tithes, an obvious ploy that was difficult to move against with more and more of the local gharifs employing their own guard. Jev didn't have a prayer of fixing anything without funds.

"We don't know for a fact they still practice magic," Jev pointed out. They absolutely could and would deal with witches, as he knew better than anyone, but he wasn't about to bring that up yet.

"We knew enough," General Valsso insisted. Behind her, as though to agree, her new pet, a young anteater, snuffled. Jev chose to ignore this. It felt too cheap a joke to point out someone who wouldn't deal with possible human witches unapologetically brought a very real large beast into a council meeting. Especially when Valsso had been begging him privately to consult a real witch for months. Her problem wasn't with witches but with anything she didn't have on a leash.

"Forgive me, General, but if they lay siege to our walls once more, I will consider dealing with witches," Jev said, rubbing at his temples. Unseemly while stood before the people it was most important to seem calm and in control in front of, but he'd had a pounding headache for hours, and the hypocrisy around magic exhausted him. He didn't feel good about knowing people who used magic, but he certainly wouldn't avoid them anymore than he would seasoned generals keen to lead their armies into battle and death.

"But we already have more conflict than we can reasonably deal with," Astchin said gravely. "The dragon attacks have been increasing, according to the common folk. They're growing bolder, passing boundaries they avoided before. Yesterday, one was spotted down at the *harbour*." Their lip quivered. "So many children play down there as they wait for their parents. Are we just to accept that there is no safety for them because they were not born behind stone or salt walls?"

Jev glanced at the other faces. A couple—like Drallnock and Binjik, the treasurer—looked curious as to what he was going to say. Astchin still looked aggrieved. The rest did not look like they had considered factoring Malyan children into their arguments and were indifferent now that they had been. As always, Jev was being held to standards they would never trouble themselves with.

"Will you throw the dice for me?" he asked Astchin.

With a nod, they obligingly took their pouch off their belt. "What do you ask them?"

"The wisdom of using our connections to consult the Aelshian forest clans. I want to reach out to them." He raised a hand as a few of his council began to grumble. "But I will not if the advice reads otherwise."

A sollon's dice weren't so different than the usual six-sided variety Jev had gambled with in Malyan bars or against Kella out on the road. But instead of carved dots, there were symbols on each side: one for each god the sollons believed were worth consulting. Two would roll, and the sides landing on top represented the gods supporting the endeavour, though in private, the sollons asked more complex questions beyond permission. To receive two blank sides meant that no gods supported the motion.

Jev did not like depending on them, but it would soothe his council to be brought back to traditions. To ground them, united as they watched how the dice fell. To prove that through all his talk of tolerating witches and dragons, he remained his mother's child.

Astchin rubbed them softly together before letting them clatter to the table without ceremony. Jev shook his head, frustrated, as one turned up blank. The other took its time before settling on a face.

The room sighed as one, momentarily united as Astchin fingered the surfaces of carved bone. "The Moon, the supporter of doomed love affairs and great feeling." They looked up with eyes that were sorry. "You want this badly for romantic longings personal to you, and the Moon recognises this. She can do nothing but support such sincerity. You want to find a way into Aelshia that has not been tried, to find your wife without further bloodshed. But no other god believes this is worth pursuing." Carefully, they gathered the dice. Astchin believed Eisha had simply run away. Yes, there'd clearly been a plot to remove her from the palace, motivated by someone else, but who was to say the young queen, alone in a strange land, did not agree with them?

When Jev had refused to accept this possibility, their once close relationship had begun to sour. Though he did not doubt their good heart, they were influenced as always by their role as a spiritual leader, and it was not a spirituality with space in it for dragon-tolerance. "And therefore, I cannot advise for this," they concluded.

Jev nodded. "Thank you," he said, ignoring the stares. He wasn't even sure he would have said that what he felt for his missing wife was strong or romantic, but to have it described so, along with "doomed," was fast making him lose his appetite for dealing with other people. He found himself unable to focus, and when the meeting mercifully came to its end an hour later, he only nodded at his councillors left the room. He had another meeting scheduled with Binjik, a closer friend to him than most of them, who did not waste time on pleasantries. Astchin was at least kind and laid a hand briefly on his shoulder on their way out but did not offer more than that.

Drallnock was the last to leave, as always, even after Valsso's anteater had been led out. She spent some time gathering the reading materials she had brought. Most of the work she did with the university was through memory and recitation, but she liked to prove what a physical records keeper she was also. Especially when convincing them that things were not entirely as culturally remembered. She believed that human animosity with dragons was not inevitable and was a relatively new thing in Jeenobian history. Though Jev still wasn't sure he believed her theories, he respected her bravery to raise them.

She stopped, pausing above Jev's seat. Following her gaze, he smiled. "A battle wound," he explained as he flexed his stiff left hand. "Kella Mabaki is fast but not fast enough to stop dragon fire. At least that time."

"I knew them as children, though I don't think they remember," Drallnock said, leaning with surprising casualness on the edge of the table. Perhaps knowing more of his family's history than he did granted her less illusions disguising what he was.

"Oh?" Jev worried he'd failed to remember her too.

"My family used to trade with their father," she explained, her Malyan accent becoming more pronounced. "Or their mother's husband, is that right?"

He nodded.

"He would buy books from us on occasion, still does. His son reminds me of him. There's something about their bearing that is quite alike. It's kind."

Jev smiled vaguely. "You met them recently?"

"Well, I shouldn't say."

"Why not?"

"I don't want to get anyone in trouble. They only came to see me to enquire after a book."

Jev leaned his head to one side, a little amused. "What book?"

"Any books that I had on Senice and also folk tales about demons. But as it happened, I only had one to offer them."

"Senice?" Jev frowned. "Isn't that…"

Drallnock nodded. "Far across the sea. The Doshni avoid travelling there. They say it's cursed. They don't even like to put it on their maps."

"And we're at the mapmakers' mercy."

"Always. I've read the book in question myself: it's an old, poorly translated text. Though it claims to be a history, it seems more of an invention, saying more about the Doshni telling the tales than the people he told of."

"What do you mean?"

"They seem like stories to scare young travellers considering voyaging in that direction. If you believe the accounts, the land is run by soulless witches controlled by dragons who spend all their time raping young women."

Jev tried to find a funny side rather than worrying about Kella's last meeting with him. She'd said she might topple a government. Perhaps she'd heard of some land where she'd be able to kill dragons in good conscience and had shipped off there. Perhaps her search for a cure was an excuse.

"They never returned the book, of course."

"They are wanted fugitives."

"They still ought to have brought it back."

Jev smiled. "You might be waiting a while there. But if you see them again, let me know."

She smiled. "I doubt it. If they were looking into far-off lands we know little of, I imagine they'll be going there. And not be coming back for a time."

"A lot of that going on at the moment."

"Did…did you love her?"

He blinked. "I've always been close to the Mabaki family."

"No, sorry, I meant your wife."

Caught off guard, Jev tried to disguise his unease by leaning back. "I don't think we had the chance to find out." He was relieved that there seemed to be no agenda to her question. "Thank you for asking. I wish I knew she was safe."

"Anytime." She stood carefully, leaving her hand lingering. "I do mean that. If there's anything you need to talk through, whether about the history of dragons or anything else, I am here. And I am good at talking."

He forced a smile. "Do I seem so lonely?"

"Forgive me, my king."

"That's a yes, then?"

She nodded, her eyes smiling, though nothing else followed them in it. She had a very pretty face, he realised, her hair framing it like a cloud around the moon. "Everyone gets lonely. And as you say, you've had many people taken from you lately. But please forget the words I spoke if they offended you."

"No, I'll remember them." He smiled, not having to force it this time. "Thank you, Professor."

As she nodded respectfully and left, he sighed, newly aware of his own loneliness. He would have preferred to talk to someone, anyone, about who his next meeting was with, but he could not reveal the truth of their existence. Not yet.

And of course, if he told anyone else who he had locked in his maze, they probably wouldn't want to talk to him.

❖

Jev had tried not to lie to Eisha the first time she had asked him a question he wasn't sure how to answer. They'd been firmly in the small-talk phase, and he'd been permitted to take his prospective bride on a tour of Malya's walls: a way to remind her chaperones of the city's military strength while providing a convenient sunset view over the ocean. The sailors said that walking out with your betrothed when the sun was kissing the ocean would be a blessing on your romance. Though Jev wasn't sure he believed any of that, he'd been untried enough at relationships to be open to all recommendations.

He'd asked if she'd ever seen the ocean before—once, on a diplomatic excursion as a girl, though not the same ocean—and she'd asked, "And are these the walls your secret royal witch fended our dragons off from?"

Chuckling, he'd resisted the urge to awkwardly scratch the back of his head. "These are the walls our good Jeenobian soldiers fended off your dragon attacks from." He had first considered loving her when he'd noticed the disappointment in her eyes. But although scores of Jeenobian soldiers had indeed guarded those walls, that did not mean that there was no witch.

As he wandered the palace maze, he ran a fond hand over the bushes. It had been a long time since he'd tried to get deeper inside and not simply use it to leave the palace. But thanks to his mother's many exercises leaving him blindfolded within it, the dark didn't slow him, and he was soon standing before the unassuming hut at the centre of the maze. If he hadn't been encouraged to lick it as a child, he would find it hard to believe that it was made from salt; in the dark, it looked like an ordinary stone house.

The two guards stood to attention for no doubt the first time in their shift. They had a low light, but it was not bright enough for Jev to feel confident greeting them by name. Happily, they didn't seem to expect words. One stepped forward, brandished his key, and carefully opened the door.

A few months ago, a little before Kella had come to see him, someone had broken into the maze at the one time of night there was only one man guarding this place. His neck had been snapped and his body left slumped at the open door. Jev suspected the guards had given their prisoner a hard time when she'd refused to tell them anything, but Jev had been certain that this hadn't come from her. Someone had taken all that trouble to sneak in, even killing a man, all for an audience. There'd been no attempt to release her chains, and she had not moved when the other guards had returned.

Not knowing what else to do, Jev had made sure the family received a full army pension and had increased the guards. He nodded at those currently on duty and tried not to let his fear show as they shut him in the dimly lit room. The place was well supplied with candles, but its single occupant did not deign to use them.

"You look tired today, little king."

There seemed to be little point in entertaining formality. "You don't."

She laughed, moving enough that the iron chains on her ankle clanked. Part of him wanted her to sound unhinged, like the evil witches in the travelling plays, but it was a perfectly ordinary laugh: a little cynical, but that was all. As a child, Jev had always expected to find a terrifying old woman, or perhaps a young one, her beauty masking her ancient power. But there was only this woman—not particularly old-looking, not hideous, not savagely beautiful—who had a half-full mouth of teeth and often wore a softly sardonic smile worthy of his mother. She had a musical accent he'd never been able to place, who was perfectly well-kempt but seemed understandably tired of living with one ankle confined in an iron chain.

Once, Jev had heard his mother mutter to a guard that if the witch really wanted to, she could have gotten herself out of that chain, even with the iron in it. The salt in the building prevented her from using her magic but not her brain. Jev had wondered what that could possibly mean. He still wondered, especially after the guard's death and took a step back.

"Have you found your missing wife yet?"

"No."

The witch rolled her eyes and leaned on the wall behind her, reminding Jev of Kella as an opinionated teenager. "Sounds as though you're running out of options."

He exhaled carefully through his nose. "I need to know she's safe."

"Hmm. You bandy the word 'need' around very freely. But why should I need to do anything for you?"

"Why did you ever do anything for my mother?"

"Have you ever killed a dragon, boy?"

He wouldn't have tolerated anyone else calling him that. But he could not shake the knowledge of how old she might be, however she appeared. His mother had never been able to give him the witch's age; it was just one more thing they didn't know about her. "Yes." As part of a team, countless times, but only once had it been his sword bringing its end.

"And how did that make you feel?"

Noble? No, of course not. That was not what killing was, not if it was an enemy or a chicken for dinner. Brave? He had been afraid, but brave hadn't been the main thing he remembered. He had felt powerful. Not like when his mother had left him to hold court, or when she'd died in her bed and left him forever. A different kind of power. A real kind. The kind that had forced him to send Kella away because dragon slaying leant a person an undeniable authority. "So you do this to kill dragons? That's why you help?"

She stared at him with a snake's patience. "I help when I am asked. Because I want to beat the dragons. Have you ever had a problem with lice? Or perhaps some of your fields have become infested with locusts." She smiled, and Jev was reminded starkly of her age. There was no hiding the decrepit age of those few teeth. "Isn't it wonderful when you know they've all gone? I want to see them all gone. Do you?"

"I'm an enemy of dragons—"

"Yet you stopped fighting them."

He fought his impatience. He could deal with her taunts if it meant that he walked out with her help. "It wasn't easy," he admitted, possibly for the first time, "but I don't regret it. Now I need to stop them acting like they do."

She shook her head. "There's nothing that can be done to them that you'd be prepared for."

"Try me."

"There's nothing new I can offer you," she said meaningfully. "And I doubt you'd have the ability."

Alone with no one but guards who shared his frustration with her, Jev could have hurt her, would have probably lashed out if he'd thought it would have made any difference. Finally, he managed to spit, "Why would I need to learn magic?"

She looked at the ground, pleased. "How else would you trust I was doing it right?"

He stared her down, disgust turning his stomach as she looked back, smiling. Moments later, he walked back out into the comfort of the night air.

It was a last resort, he reminded himself. With any luck, he'd find Eisha safe and well without any reliance on dubious supernatural means, and he'd never need to walk back into the witch's prison again. But he'd told himself that after his last visit, and he had gone back.

CHAPTER NINE

Zebenn had worked with Findan a long time and knew when she was nervous, though she said nothing to suggest it. She might never have been the official leader before Kira's death, but Zebenn had always felt it and suspected their now scattered band of misfits had too.

Kella had inherited her mother's role, but neither of them had ever been able to do what Findan could, though Kira had come closer with her quiet, tactician manner. Her legend loomed larger now that she'd gone, and it was hard for Zebenn to trust their own memories. With Kella too, even if she'd been gone months and not years. The way people spoke longingly of wishing to see her again sliced at Zebenn's heart. Though Kira had been a force for change, her daughter had given people hope, remembered their names, drank with them, loved them.

That adoration was something Kira had been granted but had never sought; it was the air Kella had grown up breathing, and she'd never known how to leave it. Had it not been for the loving home she had to return to, perhaps she never would have. It was a home Zebenn appreciated, also, though today, they were no longer sure Ballian's characteristically warm welcome extended to themself.

Zebenn rarely felt uncomfortable with their size. Most of their roles in life required strength in environments that did not block them from the sky. Inside Ballian's small, crowded shop filled with precariously balanced books, burning incense too near to Nayonan scarves, and coloured crystals, it was difficult not to feel clumsy and lumbering, but Zebenn pulled their stomach in and followed Findan's sure steps.

Ballian was behind his counter, an unusual sight, but reading, a more expected one. As he noticed them, he sighed, and that felt like the worst indictment Zebenn could imagine. "I do not know where my children are," he said before sparing a brief glance at Zebenn. "Good to see you," he said in what felt more of a pointed comment to Findan.

"We're not here about them."

Though he didn't look convinced, he put down his pencil and flicked his ear. He might not be pleased they were there, but he would listen. "In that case, what can I do for a couple of dear friends? Salt arrows, is it?"

There was a clipped tone to his graciousness that Zebenn had never heard from him before. He was usually welcoming, ever the father the lost souls of Kira's group had never known, but then, usually, they could honestly prove they were looking out for his children. With all but one of them. Zebenn had rarely seen him interact with Findan, using proxies for that. Neither seemed at home in each other's spaces. By unspoken arrangement, each respected the other enough to stay out of each other's way. As though they'd both been Kira's widower, both parents to her children, but grief had separated instead of uniting them in grief.

In a bold move that felt like a threat, Findan leaned her sharp elbows on the counter. "A chat. With a dear friend."

Though Ballian was no slimmer than Zebenn and had only one real leg, he moved lightly through the shop. It was as much his environment as a fish in water; he seemed to dance around the ornaments as he navigated past to lock his door before turning with another sigh and gesture at his back room. "Shall we?"

Zebenn had found Kira and Ballian's relationship fascinating. There had been a romantic side to them, despite neither ever showing it openly, and had always been something painfully sweet about the rugged, silent warrior and the kind, one-legged man waiting at home, even if it was confusing. He seemed stern today, alone in his little kingdom, as he led them into a room more covered in books than the front, along with many illegal dragon materials. Bones and feathers hung from the ceiling in a good luck charm made to dangle for babies.

"A hot or cold drink?"

Findan glanced at Zebenn, who made it clear they weren't bothered. "Cold. Let me."

It was polite in Malya, and a necessity in the hill country north where Zebenn had grown up, for guests to be involved in making any food or drink their hosts provided. Though Ballian was usually more modern in his thinking, he nodded but looked as though he wanted to refuse. Though Zebenn doubted Findan would care, there would be no more calling each other "dear friend" after such an insult.

Zebenn couldn't remember ever seeing Findan in this kitchen before, but she moved as confidently as she would were it her own. Zebenn watched her, avoiding Ballian's gaze.

"How is your family, Zebenn?"

"I haven't visited in some time," they admitted, eager for a safe subject. "My brother's children have started helping him in his work transporting salt blocks." It was hot, tedious, slow work, but the towns valued it highly, salt being one of the only materials that dependably repelled dragons.

"They all stayed out there?"

"Yes, they like the hills. We're not city people." Habit almost had them asking after Ballian's family, but the grain of self-preservation they had left stopped them.

Luckily, Ballian had more to say. "Hmm. And they like that? Mining over farming?"

Zebenn smiled. "I think they like that it goes to helping people. And it pays better."

He looked thoughtful. "I've been thinking about what might suit my boy one day. He has issues communicating, and a lot of roles wouldn't work for him." He pulled out a chair to sit down opposite them. "I was always inspired by the way you started with Kira."

"Inspired?"

"She was always impressed that what you asked first was how you could help." His eyes skittered, in Findan's direction, likely not purposefully. "It struck me as a noble start. Better than how most found their way to it. You brought the skills you had to a team more learned than yourself." He grimaced. "You didn't find a sleeping one and attempt to make a career from your luck."

Zebenn looked at the table. The city had heard of the deaths of Goodsblade's five-person team the day before. They'd attempted to reenact their first lucky scenario and bring down a dragon while it slept, and all but one had been found dead the following day. The last had died of his burns after making it back to town, but his mouth had been too burned for speech, his face too disfigured to be sure of his identity.

Unsure how to reply, Zebenn rubbed their thumb over the rim of their cup when Findan set it in front of them. As she sat, Ballian's whole posture changed, tensing like a lioness low in the grass.

"How can I help?" he asked, a small smile creeping up under his moustache.

"Have you seen Hallen?"

"Not in a long time, though I heard he was called to the king's council, and he answered at least once." He tipped his head to one side. "Forgive me. Age fogs the mind, but I don't recall you having any more love for the man than I. Are things so dire you need to go recruiting the retired and maligned?" His gaze went between them, but Zebenn didn't assume for a second that anyone expected them to answer. They barely knew the reason Findan was looking for Hallen, suspecting without bitterness that she was holding something back as usual.

"Love for him?" Findan looked confused, as close to mocking as she ever got. "No, that's not grown with absence. But he does have certain skills that I am interested in recruiting, yes. I've never known his love for the cause to be inconsistent, whatever else about him might be."

"Hmm. The sollons do like to tell us inconsistency marks a healthy world." Finished with the pretence that he wasn't wholly focused on Findan, Ballian leaned back and crossed his arms over his stomach, using them to balance his own cup of cold tea. "As far as I know, he's not hunting. If he has been stocking up, it's not through me. Or he's found some other way of killing them." He smiled crookedly. "As you can imagine, we've not stayed close. Always more Kira's acquaintance than mine." His pause held carefully as Findan took a pointed sip of her drink. "What is this new venture, then?"

"We're going to put an end to dragons." It was as delivered as close as she ever came to a joke.

Ballian didn't laugh and kept his arms folded, waiting patiently for an explanation, not a punchline. Zebenn had expected some sign that he was uncomfortable. If Findan's estimations were correct, he knew where his kids were and about the dragon linked to Ker. But nothing in his face betrayed anything but mild amusement that was fast fading.

"We're going to make sure they never harm another human again. And I think Hallen can help with that."

"You certainly have me intrigued, as I'm sure was your intention."

"My only intention was to answer your question. I'm always more straightforward than you want to think."

"Then answer my question, Fin."

"We're leaving for Aelshia," she said after a moment. "There, I believe I can manufacture a way for the dragons to be the end of themselves."

Zebenn shifted, the old pains in their knees flaring up from being kept in one position too long. Ballian was right: they would always be here to help, but they hoped Findan was right too, and that soon, there would be no more need to provide that help. They were getting too tired, too pained, for an endless fight.

The kingdom felt tired too. It was losing Kella more than the laws changing that had so drastically changed that mood. Kella might not have been the best warrior, but she had the more important instincts about what people needed beyond killing dragons. If it wasn't a show, there was no meaning, no belief, no hope that followed.

"My new youngest," Ballian said slowly, "would be appalled to hear us speaking so. For whatever reason, he is completely enchanted by those creatures. But as you know, there is no love lost there for me. I don't believe you're telling me much about your endeavour, nor are you likely to, but I wish you well in it." He reached for his cane and pulled himself to his feet. "Now, if you'll excuse me, I have a business to run, and these tend to be my busy hours." He sighed. "Why do this now, Fin?"

"I lost them," she said after looking at her hands. "We cannot keep on as we are."

He held her gaze for a long moment, then turned away, leaning on his cane to direct himself.. "I haven't seen Trailfeet myself. But I have heard talk about someone fitting his description running a stall up Fisher Street every other afternoon. That might not be a bad place to start."

CHAPTER TEN

Litz was apparently an early riser. Ker and the rest of the travel-beleaguered former dragon slayers had just gotten changed when she arrived at the room holding a bulging bag and a small steaming basket. When this was unwrapped to reveal fresh dumplings, Ker forgave the early hour.

"Okay," Litz said around a mouthful as she started to pace, bag still in hand. "Since you're wanted for killing a Circle dragon, you need to keep your faces hidden." She sighed as she emptied the bag on Kella's bed. Monkey-like, Kella held up the netting masks and goofily made faces through them.

Litz sighed, though Ker suspected she wanted to smile. "It's more common for women to wear them, but Ker, I recommend you do so also. What you all need to keep in mind is that dragons talk."

"Kinda why we're here," Kella pointed out, dropping the mask.

"They're not sociable in the way humans are, but they share ideas, memories. If one dragon wants you dead and has trusted that to other dragons, then all those dragons know your face and want you dead. Dragon-scorned, we call it." Her face was grave, but Kella grinned because of course she did.

Ker was almost embarrassed for her. Usually, if she was ever this nakedly interested in a person, she'd already sculpted them into becoming whatever shape she wanted, like a child building a fort in the sand. But though Litz seemed to be loosening up, she was perhaps too dry to be shaped so easily.

"And they can skim the minds of humans."

"If they have a reason to look for us," Kella said, mouth full.

"If it seems too obvious that you're lying and that it's not him"—she nodded at Evlo—"but Ker who is Ellonya's rider, they will have great reason to be suspicious."

Ker nodded. They'd been expecting this. "Sallvayn and Ellonya, and Evlo, actually, have been worrying about this."

"Just try to keep any big emotions to a minimum. It's rude and difficult for a dragon to see a mind that does not wish to be seen. But a thought developed enthusiastically or with a lot of feeling will be a shout that's hard for them to ignore if it doesn't match what they expect."

If Findan had just taught me how to Push down feelings, we wouldn't need to worry about this so much.

But you're—

I'm... "We're working on it," he said aloud for everyone, then realised he had more attention from the room than that should warrant. *We're doing it again.* "We're just saying, we've thought of it, and we're trying," he added, irritated now in his own voice. And by it. Speaking alone, he sounded reedy.

Politely, Litz blinked and nodded, though she seemed curious. Kella looked embarrassed, like Ker was an old relative railing against a clan that hadn't attacked anything in decades. Evlo just looked moody.

"Okay," Litz continued more cautiously. "Well, today I expect us to be summoned to the king's hall. I will send updates of where we are to allow us to be found. Until then, I've expressed interest in showing you the city, particularly its jewel, the library." She gave a hopeful smile. It made her seem a lot sweeter than someone with her uniform should. "The king's judgement is hard to predict, and her court is a busy one. You may have a morning, or it may be a few days. Use your time well."

"Should we split?" Kella asked, brushing crumbs off her legs. "Evlo go see the king and someone else keep looking?"

"Sallvayn thought it might be worth someone staying with Ellonya in case something goes wrong on her end."

Litz nodded. "Of course, if they think that makes sense for them."

"I'll find them." Ker stood. He'd last seen Sallvayn outside, conversing with a local gremlin, so he headed out, glad to be away from Litz's explanation the dumplings were made from snail meat and the worry Kella was trying hard not to show.

When he found Sallvayn, they were alone, their froglike friend long since hopped away. Ker sat beside them to watch the water. It was a small river, as the waterways here went but still large enough to have plenty worth watching. Everywhere in Verassez was like that. It was undeniably a city, but the sound of nature followed in an almost deafening volume. And the water, while not an attraction in the way it would be at home, was a stage.

"Wait, boy," Sallvayn said quietly, their tiny, four-fingered hand pointing out a bubble in the river. Joyfully, a dragon head, feathers flattened from the water, emerged before splashing back down again.

"A baby," Ker said quietly, with some awe. He almost never saw a young one at home. Ellonya was almost the youngest dragon he had ever met, part of what had freed her from whatever had infected her parents' generation.

This one seemed even younger than the babies he'd helped kill the day he and Kella had been arrested. Guilt weighed on his shoulders, but ignoring that, he sat up straighter. "There's algae on their scales."

"Probably likes the water that much."

It had a snake that might have been even longer than itself between its front claws, and when it shouted, *Mine!* to the world, Ker felt such a bright happiness, he was almost overwhelmed. No wonder dragons were so loved here. Perhaps it had nothing to do with the power they held: people watched them grow up, and in doing so, shared what they felt. Of course they would value those feelings, even above their own.

"It's good to see them like this," Sallvayn said as it began to swim away. "We want to go home. But it's good to see this." Seeming a little emotional, they looked at Ker. "Why have you sought us out, are we moving?"

"We thought you should go to Ellonya."

"We can do that. A little description from the other rider should help us there."

Ker stood and through fond force of habit, offered an arm for Sallvayn to clamber up. They did so without comment and were brought upstairs on Ker's shoulder. "It will be good to see more of this city. The other gradachh we spoke to was telling us a little about life here."

"Does it sound better?"

"It sounds easier." They sighed. "And magic is easier for us when life is easier."

"How does that work? Isn't it just manipulating forces in the world?"

"No, that's human. We don't think about pushing and pulling."

"Then, it's Creating magic."

"I think you would say Chaos magic." They stretched their mouth in what Ker knew was a smile.

"You'll have to explain that sometime." A worker from the inn passed them on the stairs, and Ker instinctively raised his hand to shield Sallvayn, who didn't even move. When nothing happened, he breathed out slowly. "You're not so afraid of people here, heh?"

"They're not a threat here."

"Ellonya's still with struggling that."

They fear me in Jeenobi and want to hurt me there. It's odd not expecting the same.

But sometimes, they really are just here to brush your teeth for you. "And," Ker continued aloud, "I guess Evlo's trying to figure things out from the other direction."

It was nice to have a moment away from his loud companions to appreciate this place. But when he came back, they were exactly as they had been.

"Is it true you fought off thirteen witch warriors who were sent to kill you the night before we got here?" Kella asked.

"There were three," Litz said, looking more uncomfortable than amused by the teasing now. She was leaning against the loose sheet wall by the door and watching Kella with her arms crossed. "And only one seemed proficient in magic."

"Aw, c'mon, Princess, play it up a little." Apparently sensing Litz's reluctance to talk, Kella stood. "Okay, let's get going. I hear there's a lot of books to read around here."

❖

There was a temple on the southside of Malya where all the windows were made from green stained glass. Kella had never been able to forget the effect of walking into that great room, a temple to the Sun. Though she'd never really believed in it as anything but the hot thing in the sky and an occasionally cruel arbiter of justice in stories, she had felt love as the harshness of its rays were stripped sweetly from it, letting the light envelop her face and shoulders, kiss her all over, and welcome her in.

Now, walking under the great canopy of the Aelshian forest, she could better understand the artist's inspiration. The heavy stickiness of the air did not feel so oppressive under the light through the leaves, each wide piece of green lit up like a lantern. Especially now it had started raining. Though she suspected she'd be feeling otherwise soon, she was glad of the water cooling her off.

At home, there was singing and drinking in the streets when the rain came down. No one cared here. Just like the River didn't make it to any sollon's dice back home, here, he was honoured everywhere Kella looked.

"*Ow.*" But looking far above at the canopy now dripping the Sky's greeting to the Earth as she walked made it easier to trip over her own feet. "Sorry," she said, earning a glare from Ker, whose ankle she'd just grazed.

As they went up a few steps to cross a bridge, he put a little more distance between them. Kella was caught by movement below: crocodiles. Different by margins to any Kella had seen before—with shorter, thicker snouts—they seemed faster too. She suspected this was because they'd been prey to hungry dragons much more frequently than anywhere else, though in these denser forest areas with narrower waters, they were surely safe from all but the smallest and clumsiest of dragonkind. Dragons in Aelshia seemed to love the water, and though Kella remembered Litz mentioning it, she still found it a ridiculous sight. Back home, they were repelled by the sea, the only body of water large enough for them.

It was strange, really, how naturally at odds dragons and witches were and yet how alike in nature. Having travelled with dragonriding magic-users twice over, Kella wasn't sure how to wrap her head around any of it but was certain it had to mean something. Just as the children of cursed dragons were growing up and finding their voices, the disgust for using magic did not seem to have the same hold on people it once did.

Change was coming. And here she was, in a magic forest filled with supposed witch clans subdued for generations by an empire propped up by dragons and dragonriders. It made for an interesting puzzle. She hoped someone smarter than her was willing to assemble the pieces. She was just trying to enjoy Aelshia while she had it.

She'd wondered for months what life would have been like if Ker hadn't caught up with them, and she'd continued on to Litz's home country. Wondered what sort of person she might have become: abandoned, anonymous, and free. Unknown to anyone but Litz, who would have been forced to prioritise her.

Ridiculous, maybe, but it began to feel painfully real on the rest of their short walk to the library, a walk that Kella only made them take two stops on. The first was for a pair of what Litz called manatees close to the river's edge. Litz's voice had grown softer as she'd explained a little of the creatures' habits and the local respect for them. Kella hoped that the fond tone was a little about how Kella was looking at them, but she couldn't blame Litz if it was all for the creatures.

"Even dragons rarely hunt them," she explained. "They can hardly bear to. Look at them. How could anyone?" The next time they stopped, Litz had less patience. "No," she said, shaking her head so hard, her earrings bashed at her neck.

"Why not?" Kella wheedled quietly as she took a step closer to the crowd around the small puppet show. It was usually the Narani who ran shows like this. As travelling merchants, they were asked for stories anyway, and they did not share their songs. It might have been a show that would perform in Malya, though Kella suspected they would have to vastly change the material for such a different audience.

Or maybe not.

"Is that supposed to be me?" It would have been a disgustingly self-centred thing to ask for most people, but Kella wasn't most people, and she'd never been under any illusions that she was supposed to be. She had a lifetime of recognising herself and the people she loved become part of artwork and farces, so she didn't waste time doubting what her eyes had parsed already.

There was a dragon on stage and other people. All of them were taller than the Kella puppet that wore bright red, carried a sword almost the length of its little cloth body, and had wild eyes and locs spread long in different directions.

"Flee, dragon, or face my rage!" On the last screamed word, the puppet faced its moving mouth to the sky. The dragon turned to the audience, who giggled at its pointed silence. "You won't enjoy my rage. Though I be little, I am fierce as the sea that hates dragonkind and has sent me to destroy them one by one. Face me or die!"

The dragon shook its head and laid on its paws. This was a much larger puppet, possibly demanding two hands to keep it standing.

"Last chance!"

The dragon stared to snore, making the children at the front cackle.

"You were warned. Now I am in a rage!" With that, the little puppet leapt at the dragon, sword out, and bashed it some twenty times on the head, waking it up. They both sank beneath the view of the audience, but those near the show had what looked to be berry juice splattered on them as the comical sounds of fighting continued. With gasping breaths, the Kella puppet reemerged, sword held high, drenched in berry juice, and screamed her victory.

"Let's move on," Litz said.

"No, I wanna see."

"Don't you get enough of your own image at home?"

The puppet was swarmed by other larger puppets as it squawked that it was a hero who should be left alone.

Kella looked up at Litz. "Really?"

"As I say, we should get moving."

But Kella was strangely hypnotised. This more than anything felt like the answer she'd been craving as she'd taken her beatings over her many disastrous late nights back in Malya. It was that common insecurity to so many that had so rarely bothered her before she'd met Litz. The idea that someone somewhere was sharing a joke at her expense. There was a strange relief in having it confirmed.

And worst of all, the clapping and whistling of the people was closer to a crowd cheering her name than she'd had in almost a year. It made her miss the real feeling so violently, she felt ill. As puppet King Jev kissed her puppet self and made a secret plan to kill his wife, Kella giggled and clamped a fist into her mouth.

"What is wrong with you?" Ker mouthed as she laughed harder and wondered if she could give him an answer. That was her helping plan the supposed death of Litz's cousin. Litz, who she'd flown across the continent to impress. Litz, who was standing right beside her, listening to her laugh.

"Do you think they've got a you?" was all Kella could say. They stayed and watched another ten minutes.

They did not have a Ker or an Evlo. Now that the sad Eisha and evil Jev were left behind, this was the Kella and Litz show, or it was the Litz and Loren show, and the horrible creature they had to transport and then defeat. But the two were in luck. Kella was apparently a demon sent from the sea to destroy dragonkind, so her powers comically began slip away the farther into the desert they went. Away from the source, they dwindled.

"Have you seen enough yet?" Ker asked, his voice curt as Kella fell ridiculously out of sight again after her final failed attempt to kill Loren.

Kella shrugged one shoulder, still feeling a little strange. She wasn't recognisable to the children who'd been so transfixed. That made sense. The puppet no longer looked anything like her, and she wasn't slaying dragons. But she couldn't shake the feeling that they should know her anyway.

"Okay, onward," she allowed, walking away with a little regret. She'd wanted to see how it ended.

CHAPTER ELEVEN

Most things in Litz's life had changed since the first time she'd set foot in the Grand Verassez Library, the hidden jewel of the Aelshian Empire, but the reverence she felt as she descended into its depths had never faded. She hoped it never would.

There was a sense of national pride mingled in there too, and some guilt from helping enemies of and strangers to the empire mine its secrets. But it did warm her insides hearing the way Kella gasped when the lit stone staircase down into the earth became revealed. Kella might, as Loren had put it, have seen everything there was to see in Litz, and yet, this felt like a new level of intimacy. Litz had beds in several places, but here, where no bed waited for her, felt the most like home.

The looming brick ceilings were built to withstand flooding and keep the warmth out, and as they entered, the air changed. There were few structures like this throughout Aelshia; the pyramids were slate and stone, and most treetop structures used wood. This led to families sheltering in the pyramids when particularly brutal storms hit Verassez.

The rain reminded her that during the one truly terrible storm, her family had been one of the few invited to retreat in the library. The twenty-four hours underground was one of her most treasured times before Loren. She'd been left to wander the endless aisles of woodblocks and scrolls alone. The idea of ever having to leave had been unbearable, and it hadn't been long before she'd been back, begging to be left there whenever her father would leave for town. With her strict schedule with Loren, never wanting to be home, and with Eisha becoming busier, Litz had spent most of her free time underground, reading alone.

The ancient building represented an odd impasse in her mother's hopes for her; it was neutral ground. She could never be *against* academic learning, but dusty caverns hidden beneath the earth hardly fit within her designs for Litz. It meant she was safe and could be left alone in the quiet unsupervised, free and encouraged to read whatever she was able to.

The library curator was her great uncle, and he'd made it clear to his staff that she was to be assisted only when she required it. But it was usually his assistance she sought out, drawn to him in the same way that children always were to adults who had no time for them, suspecting that they must be hiding something unknowably interesting.

An only child, but never the centre of attention, Litz was always watchful and made a particular point of observing her Uncle Denone. A stout, fat man with an unfashionably large moustache and heavy-lidded eyes that always seemed to be considering something far in the distance, he was interesting for his strange accent and the fact that he was old and important but never needed to leave his library. He had travelled the whole world and since he rarely spoke of his travels, Litz took what he said as unquestionable truth. He wore no earrings, making his character and affiliations a mystery, but he had a ring for each finger. Sometimes, he wore bangles when he wrote in his scrolls, smudging them.

Litz had been thirteen when the library had changed her life. She was Loren's but still not formally. There were many more agreements needing to be made before that could be finalised. She'd been practicing silence like her sparring teacher had been drilling into her, and she'd watched her uncle knock over a pile of books on his desk. He'd glanced around, failed to notice her, and closed his eyes. As though pulled by invisible strings, the books had rearranged themselves on his desk.

Moments later, Litz was in front of him. "Teach me," she'd said.

For the first time, the old man had really looked at her. It amused her now to think on what he'd seen: a gawkish, gangly girl who'd already done most of her growing and seemed perpetually uncomfortable with fine royal silks hanging awkwardly off her shoulders. "Learn what? I already told you where the section on dragon warfare is, and I am not a tutor, child."

"I saw what you did to the books." It had been horrifying yet fascinating. Though she'd known it was wrong, she'd needed desperately to see it again, to be sure it had really happened.

"Read them?" he'd said, but his voice and eyes had sharpened.

"No." At thirteen, Litz was no political mastermind, but her whole childhood had been spent around the royal court. She'd known when a person was and wasn't supposed to explain what they knew. Discussing magic would be like describing how a person had relieved themselves. It just wouldn't be correct.

"Why teach you?"

Carefully, Litz had folded her hands and laid them on the desk. "Because I want to learn. And you wouldn't have to be lonely."

"*Lonely*? No, I am perfectly happy. And why would I teach a child? You could run home and tell your mother, have me killed."

"I wouldn't do that."

"You might tell your dragon."

Litz had no answer to that, so she simply said, "Please." This had never worked on any adult who wasn't a servant, but it had felt like an appropriate last ask.

He'd sighed heavily, causing the dust from his book pile to fly toward Litz's face. "If I tell you no, will that do me any good?"

She'd thought about this seriously and shaken her head. "I've seen it now. If you want to be happy, you should start smiling. And I want to do what you just did."

For the first time Litz could remember, she'd caused a smile to spread over the old man's face. It wasn't that he was imposing or stern, only that he had no time or interest to hear her speak. "Where did you hear a phrase like that, Princess Litz?"

She'd shrugged. "My nanny. The clan she's from says that. Will you teach me?"

Slumping, he'd shaken his head. "What a persistent little girl you are. I will teach you. But if we find that you do not have the knack, I will change you into a tree frog if you so much as breathe a word to anyone."

Already suspecting he did not have this power, Litz had nodded solemnly and thrust out her hand. Gingerly, as though expecting it to shatter, he'd given it one shake, his rings cutting at her fingers.

"Then, we have a deal."

He seemed to be napping today. Hating to be away from his tomes for long, he looked after himself poorly and rarely took days off, so this was not an uncommon sight for a man approaching his late seventies. With the library only open to the wealthy public, few of whom valued the wealth it held, there was rarely traffic for Denone to navigate.

Litz was tempted to leave him sleeping but was due at the palace soon and didn't have all day to wait. Not with the time-sensitive quest Kella had become gods-possessed over. When clearing her throat didn't have any effect, she leaned on the desk and said, "Uncle?"

To her relief, his eyes scrunched and opened without further prompting. She moved back again and took a careful seat on the edge of the desk, the eyes of her guests on her as she watched him take a deep breath.

"Hello, my dear," he said wearily. "What news have you for me today?" He noticed the others and sat up straighter. "Ah. Patrons. Has the king approved this visit?"

"She will. They're ambassadors from Senice," Litz said as she took out a letter she'd spent her evening writing and passed it to him while her guests stared. "This is my uncle, Denone Sandrez, the custodian of the library and museum here."

Leaning toward the paper, Denone narrowed his eyes. "Senice. Hmm," he said and fell silent. Since the paper contained a huge amount of information on everything Litz knew about the three people in front of them, why they were here, and the information they were discreetly looking for, it was going to be a lot for anyone to digest, though she had done her best to keep her script neat.

Hiding who they were from him had not occurred to her, though Loren, ever cautious, had suggested it. With one great secret between them, Litz felt comfortable telling her uncle anything, even knowing he would only care about specific parts. He had offered no more than polite sympathy over Litz's killing a fellow dragonrider, Eisha's disappearance, and the hole Kella Mabaki had left in her life. He'd cared little about the political ramifications of her run-ins with the Narani, though had asked a lot of questions about their culture and magic use. What she'd discovered about the Jeenobian dragons had caught his attention, making Litz sure that the unconventionality of Ker's story was sure to fascinate him.

When he'd arrived in Aelshia, as he'd often said, he'd been most interested in the dragons, and unlike many immigrants, was not broken-hearted when they felt no reciprocal interest in him. He knew his place, and it was as a researcher, someone who studied them and marked their differences from those he'd had a chance to observe abroad. Litz's story had brought him more differences to chart than he'd ever assumed there could be.

"Loren met with the eight yesterday," she said as he came to the end of the page, taking more weight off the table as he frowned.

"A general report? Or a reprimand?"

"Both, I think." She cast a casual eye around the room, but no one of any importance ever came here. Dragons kept few spies, and few others would care. "A warning, maybe."

"Has she met with the dragon who wants her dead?"

She shook her head. "No. And it's definitely on purpose." If it became common knowledge that one rider had killed another, the empire's very foundation would shake. And it would become common knowledge fast if that meeting between their dragons was encouraged.

Her guests seemed amusingly surprised she would speak so candidly, with Ker starting to smile in bemusement.

Her uncle acted as though he did not notice. "You would be the ambassador." After a slight glance around, he focused on Ker. "Please relay to your master how glad we are to have someone from Senice view the collection of scant information we have on his home. If you'd care to follow me, I'd be delighted to show you the way. And, Litz, why don't look into the writings you asked me about. You should find everything at these coordinates." With that, he picked up one of the chalk pieces that made his hands and face terribly dusty and scribbled on a slate for Litz. "If you need assistance, why don't you take one of…" He smiled at Evlo. "Apologies, your name was not noted."

Ker cleared his throat. "This is Evlo Lindin."

"Grand. Why don't you take one of Master Lindin's attendants, Litz. I'm sure he wouldn't begrudge you one after everything you've been doing to help him settle in here," he added, winking at her.

Smiling back, Litz took the slate, and tilted her head at Kella. It was ridiculous; they were still in public, and nothing about the stupidity or danger of the circumstances had changed, but she still couldn't help a rush of excitement at being allowed a moment alone with her. Though she seemed less excited, Kella's big eyes still widened hopefully.

I don't know what you think you're going to do. You are here to look at books together.

And we will. But as Litz had figured out in her youth, the library was filled with dark corners.

Stop that. I know I stated I would live a long time after you, but you seem determined to make worry for you be my end.

Some would say I am keeping you young.

Those sound like humans. And I've had enough of hearing what humans might say.

Then, I recommend you stop trying to listen when we reach our audience with the king later.

❖

It was one of their most well-worn dynamics. Kella had a problem with authority figures, so Ker tended to be overly reverent toward them to compensate for her actions. Though this library curator was no real authority any more than nice Professor Drallnock in Malya had been, Ker had the instinctive certainty that this man *should* command authority. This had only been solidified when Kella had mentioned him as the uncle who had taught Litz magic. Estranged from his only teacher for months, Ker hadn't realised just how much he missed the comfort of someone who knew more about those forbidden arts than he did. He might not delve much into altering the story of the world, but it was difficult not to gravitate toward someone who knew how to.

Besides, if they really were planning on surrounding themselves with enemy dragons, he wanted to believe he'd be able to help protect the people he loved. He couldn't fight well or speak any of the Senice languages, but he had to offer something.

Am I not a great enough something?

Of course you are. But you bring yourself.

No, you brought me here. You gained my involvement. There's nothing wrong with admitting that.

"The Senice section is this way," Denone told them as he led them up a staircase.

"What have you sent Litz to find?"

"The dragon diarist archives. I believe there are a few accounts there you may find useful. I've also directed them to the demonology section. But I believe there will be enough to keep us busy in Senice. It is a shockingly large section of knowledge, considering the little most know about your land."

Evlo did not seem as charmed by Denone and his funny accent, and whether due to that or a commitment to his role, he did not react to anything said.

I've just never seen this many books. I can't even imagine what my da would say.

As always, tinged with emotions Ker wasn't ready to identify when he brought up his da, Ellonya said, *Truly an achievement. This is a hoard. A treasure trove to bring any dragon considerable pride.*

I guess dragons have echoes rather than needing books.

I wouldn't know.

Ker winced. Ellonya was finding it difficult to connect with the dragons around her, tantalisingly close and full of the knowledge and companionship she'd always longed for. They all were staying out of reach through a mixture of self-absorption and her unwillingness to betray the lies her party had arrived under the cloak of.

I wish we were here under other circumstances, she agreed. *These make me worry that perhaps there isn't anything worth saving in us.*

Don't say that. He knew she was joking, or trying to, but there was real hurt in her voice that reverberated through his own chest. Her longing to find her people, to learn from them and be a part of them was quickly being replaced by resentment. She'd been abandoned and cast aside, and that was only was filling her with indignation. She was only so different because of their negligence and refusal to take responsibility for their own kind.

I think dragons are naturally selfish. And I think I hate that about us. He felt her breathe in, steadying herself. *But when I help bring the ones back home to themselves, things will be different.*

If you are their example, I'm sure they will be. But Ker was less hopeful seeing the size of the library and how much information they might find. Surely, if this was secret knowledge, it would not be out in plain sight and could take days of searching. And from what Litz had said, she couldn't even guarantee them one day. But at least Denone seemed to know the books in here just as Ker knew the few shelves of his da's shop.

It took ten minutes to reach the location, hidden in an upstairs corner. They passed other people, but Ker suspected they were all librarians. They wore the same simple dark clothes.

"Now," Denone said grandly as they arrived, gesturing at the full rows of shelves on either side: most of which were not filled with what Ker would call blocks of wood covered in metal to preserve them. He both longed to hold one and feared that the moment he did, he would damage it. "This is what we have on Senice."

"This shelf?"

He gave a low, kind laugh. "This aisle. It's far less than what we have for other known areas, but then, not much about Senice is known, is it?" He looked at Evlo. "If you were willing to give me an interview, I would appreciate the chance to jot down a few thoughts."

Evlo gave a grunt, staring at the shelf above him.

"We are supposed to be keeping his real past a secret," Ker reminded them.

"Oh, no one ever reads these things, especially not the exciting ones." He sighed. "No, the palace loves to be seen keeping knowledge in this way because it helps justify their empire's expansion, and it's what they've always done. But almost no one allowed to access it holds any real love for it."

"This truly is your kingdom, heh?"

"I do like to think so, yes." There was almost something melodic about his accent, far more any Aelshian voice. Ker found himself charmed listening to it. "Here," Denone said, deftly pulling out a book stack in the same careful way Ker sometimes watched his father pluck grapes from a new vine. "Take a look at this."

"Can I read it?"

Denone snorted, not turning as he continued to review the shelves. "I don't know, can you?"

Ker was expecting the answer to be no. He couldn't understand the few unfamiliar words at first or the difficult handwriting. But the alphabet was one he knew, even if some of the spelling was unexpected. He blinked rapidly at the page in surprise. "These are translated into Aelshian."

"Very good, dragonrider," Denone said lightly. "We make copies here, and we translate what we can't read. Not everything, at least, not yet. But perhaps one day."

"It's amazing," Ker assured him, carefully stroking the page. "The dedication to learning, to preserving knowledge."

"It's a worthy one for a building this impressive, is it not?" There was a slight twinkle in his eyes.

"Where are you from?" Ker found himself asking.

"Oh, I come from far to the south from this empire, but my brother's children grew up within the savannah edges of it. Down there, they tell stranger stories about how dragons and witches came to fall out." He gave Ker a meaningful glance.

"What kind of stories?" he asked as another block was passed down for him to carry, assumedly for perusal at one of the bench-tables scattered through the building.

"Well. Unlike Aelshian tales, this one does not depict dragons in a particularly favourable light, just as it does not vilify its witch. It says the first witch and the first dragon were the best of friends." As he continued along the aisle, Ker, captivated, kept close and heard Evlo do the same. "All respected and feared the joint power they shared whenever they walked or swam through the forest, for this was long before the dragons gained their wings."

"There's another tale of that?"

"Oh yes. But not this one. Now, the witch had a family who came to mean more to him than even his dear friend the dragon. And one day, his youngest child became deathly sick. The witch was skilled in using magic to soothe and coax at wrongs within a body, but neither this nor the medicines of his people could fight what ailed his child. In despair, the witch turned to his friend the dragon for help." Denone sighed theatrically. In this quiet library that Ker could not imagine him outside of, audiences were surely scarce, and Ker imagined he was enjoying this opportunity.

"But dragons are naturally selfish creatures, too consumed by their own beauty and power to care for much around them. And perhaps this dragon was jealous of the attention his friend showed to his child. So he told the witch that a mere scraping of his scale would cure the child of any ailment, but that he would never give this gift for any reason. The witch was hurt. 'Why not?' he asked.

"'Because they are a part of my body and may never grow back. I do not wish to risk looking less beautiful.' The dragon went to sleep that night, satisfied that this would be the end of the matter. But the witch was unable to leave it. That night, he used his magic for a darker purpose than he ever had before, forcing the dragon to stay immobile. When the dragon awoke to his friend hacking off his scale, he could do nothing to stop him."

I don't think dragon scales can do any healing.

Neither do I. I think it's just a story to teach about something else.

If it's meant to be teaching, it should be telling the truth.

"The sting of betrayal was a new feeling for the dragon, and he did not deal with it well. Ignoring his friend's apologies, the dragon swore that any human choosing to use magic would never be safe from his wrath. Witches had both the power to bind them as no other creature could and had shown they would not hesitate to use it, not even to preserve the greatest and dearest of friendships. He taught this same vow to his children and his children's children, so that the witches of the world would forever be considered enemies of dragonkind."

"But why do people hate witches?"

"I imagine that's another story again." He smiled. "And speaking of stories, I also hope to have an account of yours before you leave. A dragonrider to a Jeenobian dragon? Now there is a story. If your dragon would care to contribute, it would be much appreciated."

It would be nice to have someone curious about my life.

They still haven't spoken to you?

No. I'm beginning to think they're waiting to see what I'll do. They don't want to talk without anything to prompt them. But I'm not sure what I should be doing. I think they think I will do as I please, and if I need to explain myself, I will have my humans do it.

Has Loren seen you?

A little. She seems more disapproving of our being here than her rider.

"She would," Ker said, realising he hadn't answered Denone.

"Excellent. Now, let's see if we can't find you some maps."

"Dragons in Senice discourage map making," Evlo said, finally speaking up. "They call it seeing with dragon eyes. They don't think it's a view humans should have."

"Fuck off," Ker said, not thinking. "They just don't want you to know how to go anywhere."

"Pretty much."

"That would explain why we don't have many," Denone mused. "Oh, I would love to have you both here to dictate for me for a year, but I suspect you will not sit still for that, will you?"

"We're not really the sitting still kind," Evlo said, and Ker smiled.

❖

Litz couldn't have said what she wanted Kella to say now that they finally had a reason to be alone, but she was a little disappointed that the first topic she wanted to discuss was her brother.

"Do you think it's weird?" she asked, bringing them back to his speaking for Ellonya. "Do other dragonriders do that?"

"I don't think so."

Kella stayed focused as they started climbing the main staircase to the third floor. "You don't think so?"

"I don't. Loren doesn't push through me like that. I don't think I've seen it before. But I'm not close with many dragonriders."

"Why not?"

Litz made a face. "I've known and liked and learned from many. But it can get awkward if our dragons are close or if they don't like each other or if they've never interacted. It just changes the way we interact."

"Dragon gotta come first, heh?" To Litz's relief, Kella didn't sound as bitter at that as she once might have.

"Yes. And, look, if there's ever an issue in a dragon's bond to their rider, it's the dragon other dragons are concerned for. If there's something about the rider worth concern, no one will care more about resolving that issue than the dragon."

"Okay. And it's rare for a person to be rider to more than one dragon?"

"It's rare because humans aren't in the habit of outliving dragons. If a dragon was truly that old, they wouldn't take a rider."

"What if something kills them?"

Litz smiled. "We don't have dragon slayers here. That's not a common problem." At Kella's stare, she continued. "Yes, it has happened a handful of times. But historically, riders without their dragon don't live long enough to do something else. They wouldn't want to." Litz hadn't heard anyone's footsteps in some time. They seemed to be alone up here, and they were still talking about Ker. "It's amazing he survived as well as he did as a child. You should be proud for helping him through that."

Kella snorted, seemingly unconvinced.

"And with Ellonya growing up alone…clearly, they've both had no one to guide them in how they should be. It's a miracle they're as sane as they are separately, never mind now that their souls are joined."

"Will you help him?"

Litz turned, stopping. "Is that why you came to find me?"

Kella's breath seemed quicker, and Litz suspected that wasn't just because of the stairs. "No," she said, her voice low as she smiled. "I came for the books."

Stepping closer, Litz playfully dared to stand almost with her chin to Kella's forehead. They stood like that a few moments too long because Kella also didn't seem interested in moving. "Okay," Litz said quietly. "Let's look at some books, then."

When she turned away, she heard Kella take a heavy step, as though the effort of keeping herself still had been so great that without it, she was in danger of falling. Litz smiled to herself.

Stop tormenting her. This is insufferable.

You told me you wanted me to find more joy in life. I'm taking joy where I find it, thank you.

"So you didn't bring our small Narani friend with you? Adults sufficed on this adventure?"

"Oh, you do miss our child." Kella sounded delighted. "Darsin's good. He always asks how I think you're doing, but really, he just wants to know more about Loren and to get to see Ellonya."

Litz felt a strong aching fondness from Loren at this. *How sweet.*

"But you're looking after him?"

"Eh, better. He's with Ker's da."

"Does he know about everything?"

The delight seeped out of Kella's voice. "Yeah, he knows."

Though she was enjoying teasing Kella, Litz understood well enough when to stop.

As it turned out, Kella couldn't read well, but she was a quick study when it came to recognising symbols. "We want everything from the third shelf marked by this sign," Litz instructed her, drawing what she meant on the parchment she'd brought with her.

"So it's kind of like a crab?"

Litz turned it so she was looking from Kella's angle. "Hmm. I suppose."

"All the stacks from the crab shelf. Got it, Captain." With a smile, she disappeared, leaving Litz at the desk with her first haul of tomes. She suspected it might take Kella a while to locate the shelf. Hopefully by then, Litz would have found something. Her hopes weren't especially high.

She'd rarely ever heard of Senice. They had more ancient knowledge here than many other places, but it seemed that ultimately, to learn much about Senice, one had to go there.

Do you want to?

It sounds a horrifying place but fascinating all the same, Litz admitted. *I would like to see more of the world. But I suspect that's as much because I can't, at least not now.*

You're not tempted to run away with them?

Oh, you know I'm tempted.

By the time she had skimmed through the next stack and on to the second, Litz could feel her focus starting to drift. She hadn't rested much in her parents' home—she'd felt compelled to return there for the sake of her mother's nerves—and the archaic jargon was refusing to reveal anything helpful, sending her to sleep.

She didn't notice anything behind her until there was an arm firmly wrapped around her neck, an elbow she recognised pointing at the table in front of her. "You're dead, Woskenna."

"Nic."

The hold loosened, and a warm hand patted her shoulder. "Sleeping at your post makes for a terrible soldier, never mind an officer."

"Then it's a good thing it's still my day off."

Nic laughed, and despite her annoyance, Litz was, as always, charmed by the sound. Despite Loren's jabs, there were many people who noticed when Litz was in conversation with her dragon. Nic always wore an expression that suggested she could hear exactly what Litz was thinking even more than Loren and was highly amused by it.

"Day off, day on," she said, wandering around from where she'd "killed" Litz. Though her lack of patience had made her rise through the officer ranks slow, few were more formidable sparring partners, even if she was only playing. "Someone's out of practice either way."

"Or perhaps, someone wasn't expecting to be assaulted in a library."

Nic shrugged, her light beaded armour shrugging with her as she took a seat on the table. Apparently, she hadn't read the library signs forbidding exactly that, or more likely, she didn't care.

"You should expect attack from all quarters at all times," she said in a passable impression of their old sergeant. "Never forget that, Woskenna."

Litz leaned up, pulled unstoppably back into Nic's orbit to clasp her hands. "That's frightening, please stop that."

"Does stop mean stop today?" Nic asked, craning her neck, her face brightened by false innocence.

Litz glanced around. They really did seem to be the only souls venturing this deep into the northern corner of this library. Except Kella, who wouldn't want to see her with Nic. Whose lips were right there, just a little parted, like she wasn't shocked yet but was waiting to be. And Kella was going to leave in a day, and in any case, wasn't here right now.

Litz started sitting back but found herself held in place by Nic's hand clasping her wrist, reminding her of early mornings before their drills as young cadets. Nic had never gotten used to structured mornings after a childhood of being left to her own devices, and when the morning pipes had urged them up out of bed, her hand would emerge from the sheets to hold Litz's shoulder still. They'd felt inevitable back in their cramped barracks' room. There was only so much tension, so much loneliness that could be borne with another inviting body so close, just waiting to share, to be spilled into.

Litz was jolted uncomfortably back to the present by Kella standing behind Nic, her face blank and her arms laden with the blocks Litz had sent her looking for. Litz cleared her throat and took back her wrist. "Nic," she said, indicating behind her, "this is one of Master Lindin's attendants. I've been helping his party look into what knowledge we have about the land he comes from."

"Charming," Nic said, briefly glancing behind her. When Kella set her books down less than carefully, she kept her eyes trained on the ground. "The king, I'm sure, will allow you to continue with that after she gets her audience with him."

"Now?"

"Now. I got this from my guy, who got it from a palace guy. They've sent runners out, but looks like I found you first."

Litz sighed. She had hoped for more time. "He was keen to finish with what he was looking for today."

Hopping back to her feet, Nic shrugged. "Leave one of his people here. He only needs one translator, right?"

Kella met her eyes, and Litz nodded. "Go and find your master. The king wishes to meet with him. His other servant may stay here, should that be of use."

Kella gave a nod and hurried back the way she'd arrived.

"Funny expression on her for a servant, don't you think?"

Litz stood, smiling in a way she hoped projected innocence. "Who can say what a Senician traveller looks for in a servant?"

Giving a closer look at Kella's retreat, Nic frowned. "She's cute, I suppose." She spun around to continue her walk along the aisle backward, her scimitar hitting her leg as she moved. "Should we spar later?"

"I'm looking after the visitors today."

"And after?"

"I don't always like sparring on my off day, Nic."

"That's why you'll never beat me." She gave up on her backward walk and took up pace beside Litz, her tone becoming more solemn. "Do you think you'd make a good general?"

"I haven't thought on it much."

"You can hardly be worse than Makiv."

"He's always dependably—"

"Lazy. I mean, we'd have invaded Jeenobi ten times over if he knew what he was doing."

"And you think you could do it?"

"I would have managed to set Malya on fire by now, witch or no witch."

"I'm sure." Litz shot her a fond smile. "Maybe Sergeant Shappen would finally salute you with some respect."

"You know I saw him again last week? He's part of the new *royal guard* now. Little freak looked so pleased with his feathered hat."

Still smiling, Litz slowed as they reached the main stairs, scanning for Kella and Evlo. "I think I could be a general. But I'm not sure I want it. Announcing a new head of the army is all but a declaration of war."

"Thought you were dying to get back out in the field? When the war ended—"

"I know," Litz cut her off, painfully aware that Kella and Evlo were re-entering earshot. "I complained of little else. But now, we might start one over nothing."

Nic stopped, leaning in where Litz held the banister, her long eyelashes fluttering like birds confused off a breaking branch. "What about your cousin?"

"She wouldn't want to see a war start for no reason, either."

"She's hardly no reason, Litz. Kinda a big deal around here."

"I don't forget that."

Breathing out a small sigh of relief when Kella and Evlo finally appeared on the other side of the main library floor, Litz made herself smile at Evlo specifically. One of them was supposed to be an important guest of the empire, and it wasn't Kella.

CHAPTER TWELVE

The palace in Malya looked the way a palace was supposed to look, Kella decided as she walked into the main hall in the boughs of a tree. There was something less patronising about it; it didn't attempt to make a person forget that it was better than them. It was made of a different stone, had a moat of seawater, a giant fuck-off maze that might or might not be hiding something terrible, and it sat on a high rock, proud above the city to shout: The King Lives Here.

The Aelshian palace shouted the same message but insidiously, like an order from a dragon. They wouldn't come out and say it—the tree was part of everything, the throne was grown from the tree itself, everyone could walk in—but Kella only saw a certain type of person. A few like Litz and her friend, dressed in uniforms, but most wore one kind of outfit, losing all the charm and variety of the streets far below.

And because Kella was supposed to be a lowly servant, she did her best to keep her mouth shut and in a politely straight line. But it was hard. She wasn't exactly ignored, and with every interested glance from a wealthy, important person, Kella wanted so badly to react, to give them something to look at. But she kept herself from that for Evlo. He was frightened, though he was trying not to seem it, and Litz was on her other side. She had a whole life here still, even if it was precariously balanced. One wrong move from Kella could make it topple. She couldn't do that.

Oh, but she was tempted. It would be so easy. Litz was looking for an excuse to give in and throw it all away. But if Kella was here to prove that she was a good person, she shouldn't start by ruining Litz's life, even and especially if that life involved hot women throwing themselves at her in libraries. If Litz wanted to ruin her own life, that was different.

The king was on her throne seeing speakers, but everyone continued to mill around in their own conversations, as though this meant little to them. Kella supposed if all these fancy rich Aelshians came here every day and did nothing, it really would mean little. But the people seeing the king stepped forward one by one in a hard-to-discern queue. Litz jumped ahead a few spaces. Perhaps no one wanted to risk her ire, or maybe word of who they were had spread quickly enough for their petition to have become an anticipated show.

From what Litz had said, the king would greet them and hear their piece publicly before taking them into her private chambers, should she wish to continue with questions. They'd spent the night before figuring what they wanted to say and practicing. Though the attention would be on Evlo, Kella would be talking.

Evlo had originally planned to speak utter nonsense and have as much fun with it as he could, but Ker had talked him out of this, worried that a dragon could pick up on his surface thoughts. As much as possible, they should all attempt to mean what they claimed.

The king looked more like a king than those Kella was used to, but maybe she was biased. She'd been fucking Jev, and she'd known his mother mostly as his mother, who'd never let him have any fun. This king wore an inch of makeup that looked toxic to touch and clothes that had to be too hot, even if she was planning on sitting all day. She sat proudly, seeming distant and barely on the same plane as those below her, but her eyes darted around anxiously, betraying her as a mere human. Her shoulders were burdened with a heavy cape of crocodile skin that gave her an almost draconic appearance.

Kella knew she should look away when those eyes found hers, but she couldn't. Some people were hard to pass by and remain respectful of without feeling the mighty urge to bully, whatever their station. She finally let her eyes drop as Litz introduced Evlo.

He was doing his best to stand casually with his hands loosely clasped, but he wasn't fooling Kella, who was starting to feel a burst of protective energy. Those interests helped her set aside her less useful ones that sought Litz's approval and attention. She wasn't here to make Litz want her. If she didn't already, it was too late to worry about it now. She was here to be Evlo's voice and shield. And since she'd spent half the night working on her accent and story, she could do that.

The king looked at them more closely after Litz finished speaking, though surely nothing was a surprise to her. It was all a performance, as much as the puppet show had been. "Greetings to you, traveller," she said, addressing Evlo. "Our court has not seen a visitor from your land in my lifetime, and a dragon and rider are always a cause for celebration. What would inspire you to travel so far? Surely, crossing seawater with a dragon must have been a harrowing experience."

At a glance from Litz, Kella took a step forward, her moment at hand. She spoke a few song lyrics Evlo had taught her, quietly prompting him to launch into the language she had been calling Senician in her head, though he insisted this was wrong. His voice did not waver, and though it did not carry enough, he corrected himself with increasing volume as he continued.

Kella turned to the king after bowing low once more. "My master did not find his journey east easy, but he has been rewarded by the magnificent sight of your forest kingdom, and he would do anything his dragon, the Great Llonya, asks of him."

Litz's eyes narrowed as though saying, really? She'd just dropped a syllable?

"He used a Doshni barge that was able to accommodate her greatness, and this is also how he met me and my brother. We agreed to be within his service, translating for him while he moves through these lands, and he has promised to bring us with him when he leaves." Kella, who had a whole extended backstory ready, was a little disappointed to see no interest on the king's face at this excerpt.

They continued without incident through a few polite questions. How long would they be staying, were there any special accommodations that should be made for "Llonya," and other than the library, had they any interest in seeing the more exclusive sections of Verassez? Finally, she got around to asking what they were doing there.

Oh, it was phrased more politely than that, but there was no disguising it or the creeping hostility behind it. Though Litz's posture didn't change, her gaze intensified. It was harder this time to wait patiently for Evlo to finish and act like she was listening. More nerve-racking, but oh, more fun than the other questions. Kella almost felt the ears of the room turned to better hear. It felt like coming home.

"O King, my master is but a humble adventurer, eager to see the world, both known and unknown. The Great Llonya, however, does come here with purpose. She wishes to speak through her rider. She acts on behalf of a great dragon lineage by the southern Senice shore. They know better than to attempt trade with any of the wicked east coast of your continent that so infamously disrespects dragons. She wishes to investigate how likely an alliance of arms and flow of trade would be established. Perhaps even"—Kella licked her lips, even the lie feeling poisonous—"of labour. The dragons of Llonya's province are very interested in acquiring human labour for several upcoming projects of great importance." She swallowed and did her best to paste on a passive smile, aiming for servile over sarcastic.

There was a strange horror in watching the way the king considered this, as though Kella hadn't said anything newly interesting. Watching her sit quietly sickened Kella, especially when she didn't see Litz react. She knew they were only playing roles, but it was dawning on her that discussions like this were Litz's normal.

Kella didn't know her well. She'd met her removed from all contexts of where she came from. Now, Kella had come looking for her in the griffin's nest and had found one more griffin. She was doing her best to remember that this was disturbing and not just hot. Because imperial evil griffin metaphor though she might be, Litz was still helping her and still got flustered when Kella flirted.

Eventually, they were dismissed, but Litz seemed to know otherwise. After a few quiet words with one of the king's attendants, also dressed in crocodile and bird feathers to look like ridiculous little dragon babies, she motioned that they should linger. All seemed to include her friend Nic too.

What she'd seen back in the library shouldn't have bothered Kella. She wasn't, as a rule, a jealous person. But to claim she had rules and habits within relationships was to imply she'd been in them before, which was a lie. Though this certainly wasn't a relationship she was trying to stumble into, that didn't stop her from feeling violent when Nic leaned in to speak to Litz quietly, making her smile.

It might have been easier to bear had Kella been having a better year. But since returning to Jeenobi, she hadn't had fun with anyone, which wasn't like her, but that fit. This new version of herself who didn't slay dragons and did manual labour and sometimes remembered not to draw attention to herself didn't have much luck talking people into taking her home. Instead, she'd spent a disgusting amount of time thinking about Litz, missing her, wanting to tell her things. And the moment Kella had figured out a reason, she'd made her way straight back to Litz. Only to find she was not only not in danger but doing great.

Later, as they were led into a meeting room on the floor above, Kella couldn't help staring at Nic, feeling envy gnaw at her. She remembered walking like this into palaces and temples and other public spaces. And knowing she wouldn't ever have the right or clean conscience to walk in them again made her resent that anyone else was permitted to, even more that she resented Nic's hands on Litz earlier.

She did not envy the king. When they were reintroduced in a more private setting, she had clearly grown so frustrated by the heavy tightness of her attire that she ordered two servants to stand beside her chair with large fans. And yet, solving the issue by removing the crocodile skin apparently didn't occur to her.

She also seemed changed by now having her queen beside her. Or consort was what he was called here, even if there was only one. From what Kella understood, that—and his inclusion here—was considered odd. But it did not seem to surprise the man, Agsdon. He seemed a good amount older than the king, but that might have been his bearing giving that impression.

A thin-faced man with a joyless expression and thick hair bunched tightly in a bun, he seemed like someone who would understand the library's coding system and could engage at length in a conversation about trade tariffs. Kella also felt sure that, despite his king's obvious devotion to him, he did not have any worthwhile hidden sides he'd bring out in bed. Kella might not have gotten any herself in months, but she had good instincts for spotting and avoiding a lousy lay.

There was no table in the room, only simple wooden stools that servants moved to accommodate them before leaving. But guards still stood by the exit, which struck Kella as an interesting cultural difference. It was uncommon for Jeenobian royalty to allow guards to remain inside their private chambers. Perhaps Aelshians were less secretive. Or perhaps this new king was paranoid. Or perhaps this meeting was not a private one at all.

Paranoid or not, the king sounded casual when she said, "I wish to speak now of war."

Kella resisted the urge to exhale loudly while making a face. Things really were as bad as they liked to talk it up back home.

"As you've noted, the Jeenobians and most other clans and kingdoms to the east do not share our values. There are no dragonriders there, no respect nor even safety for dragons such as Llonya. We would be glad to enter into a trade relationship with her family in Senice, but we fear it would be a danger to both ourselves and any Senicians. Jeenobians want nothing more than to see the suffering of dragons and any who hold love for them."

Beginning to run dry of song lyrics, Kella did her best to make a show of saying something to Evlo. He looked appropriately grave as he gave his answer. "He says he understands there is a peace between Aelshia and Jeenobi."

"For now. However, we do not expect that to hold." She sighed. "They've been remilitarising previously abandoned forts and planting spies in my court."

Kella tried not to make another face. Surely, the spies were already there.

"This is all following the disappearance of my sister, who was living under their protection. If war was to break again, support for that would be greatly appreciated. Better to once and for all remove those with a hatred for dragons and clear the way for future trade and peace. Does Senice have a significant navy to call upon?"

The king continued on like that for nearly another hour, never finding Kella's answers helpful enough. Kella tried not to be too enthusiastic for her part; she wasn't, after all, actually representing Senice, and too much information could reveal her as a fraud.

She was starting to understand the appeal in making decisions that affected everyone as a king or person of importance. A person could surely become addicted to the feeling and forget they were speaking about real places, real lives.

Finally, the focus left her when a guard quietly entered, whispered something in the king's ear, and left. The king's smile was bright in response. "I have just been informed that the first catfish have been spotted on the Main River."

Wondering if catfish was code for something, Kella did her best to get comfortable on her stool and sit up straight.

"Is the party tomorrow?" Nic asked hopefully. When the king smiled her way, she beamed.

"I should think tonight. I believe that, if we're recognising something beginning, we should celebrate it tonight." Her smile became almost shy. "I know my mother's philosophy was always about taking as much time to plan as possible, but I feel that no one could be doing anything more important than this tonight. In any case, I hope to use the event to make a few announcements." She finished by fixing her gaze pointedly on Litz, who glanced questioningly at Kella.

"I have considered your proposal," Litz said, shifting in her seat. She was probably speaking to Loren, and Kella wondered what about. "And—"

The door swung open, and another message was relayed, this time between guards before passing to a fan holder, who passed the information to the king's ear. She sat up straighter. "Another terrorist attack," she said, and her voice started to shake. It was a careful shake, though. Kella was no longer under any illusions that the king thought of this as a private room. "This one not aimed at anyone as equipped to fight as you, Litz." A brief, unsettled smile flickered over her face as she raised her hands, clearly uncertain how to present them.

False as her reaction came off, Kella was certain this news did come as a surprise.

"The left bridge to the courthouse was destroyed. A witch must have Pulled it down from below and escaped into the crowd. Dozens of people have fallen to their deaths, many members of the court."

Litz looked almost fearful. "And this wasn't simply an issue with the bridge?"

The king's eyes turned cruel. "No." If she'd seemed like someone to bully before, that impression was leaving fast. "It would seem I need a new direction for our armed forces to take as a matter of urgency, to deal with internal struggles along with the external threats."

Kella found herself also unable to look away from Litz, who was clearly being forced to make a choice.

"I would be honoured to accept your offer to command them, my king."

The king relaxed as Litz continued to look miserable and far from ready to command anything. Beside her, Nic looked thrilled.

Kella felt like the air had been punched out of her. Litz was staying here, and if war came back to Malya, she would be the one to decide how it reached them. Kella let that humiliation and anger take her, but it was hard to focus when Litz still looked so small, sitting here without her dragon.

"Wonderful. I want you to start with the clan who attacked you. The troop we sent yesterday is expected to return tomorrow. I'm anxious to hear their thoughts. The Vidan clan clearly has a tradition of magic they've been concealing and a willingness to blame ordinary people for their misfortune."

Litz looked as though she wanted to argue but nodded. "Yes, my King."

"I just hope it will help your poor mother rest a little easier at night, if nothing else." She smiled as though giving Litz a gift she should be grateful for, then made it clear that, final as that had sounded, they were nowhere close to being released. "Now, we should be providing refreshments for our guests. Let us bring the good wine to celebrate my cousin, who will soon serve as my general." She beamed, and Kella wondered how long it would take to claw her face off and what that might feel like on the nails. "I'm sure Eisha would be happy knowing you were standing by my side for this, Litz."

❖

Litz had a lot to think about as they left the palace. They hadn't been able to leave after the meeting without engaging in a discussion with a pair of twin dragonriders she barely knew. Everyone wanted to be introduced to the Senice dragonrider, and Nic wouldn't stop talking about what she planned to wear that evening. And through it all, Litz could feel Kella seething.

It felt almost like when Loren was frustrated or hungry or particularly amused. Without even depending on their link, Litz could sense the feelings emanating from her like an aura. The aura of Kella's emotions was almost too large for her body, especially her abnormally small one. But Litz suspected that if she attempted to craft that thought into a joke, she might not live to regret it.

When Nic left, making Litz promise to wear shoes that would flatter her legs, Kella finally spoke, unprompted, as though the words had been ready on her tongue for hours. "Who are you?" she asked, and though her words confused Litz, they still cut. Because disdain threaded through her voice that Litz hadn't heard since the first time Kella had realised Loren was in her mind.

"Is this a trick?" Litz felt weary by the hours of court talk, of discerning what people meant behind what they were saying. Though rarely serious, Kella usually spoke plainly, and Litz badly wanted that familiar version of her back.

"I'm just trying to understand who you're supposed to be," Kella continued in that same low, bitter tone as she ignored Evlo's hand on her arm.

Her mind scattering, Litz kept leading them toward the nearest river. As she took a spare transport raft, they all stayed quiet until after she pushed off. Evlo, who had taken a seat cross-legged, said, "Kel," and the weariness in his voice distracted Litz from telling him off for not trying to look more important. A dragonrider shouldn't sit like a servant or a child in public, but he was foreign, wasn't he?

"Tell us about this rebellion you squashed," Kella said, fake cheer straining her face as she also sat, looking up at Litz with eyes wide like a child. Below, Litz could see catfish passing through. Sure enough, soon, the rivers would all be swarming with them bullying their way upriver to spawn. Litz often wondered whether they knew how dangerous the journey would be, if they knew it was likely a suicide mission, or if they just followed what their bodies insisted was destiny, unable to think against the great requirement of their species' survival.

"It was hardly a rebellion."

"Mm, but it was enough for them to promote you. Enough for the clan to send its witch protectors in vengeance." She sniffed. "Did you tell them they were witches?"

"I wasn't the only witness. Or the only one at risk." Litz kept her voice steady, determined to avoid an argument. She wasn't necessarily proud of her recent actions, but she wouldn't stand for being judged by someone who, for all their undeniable heroism, had spent most of their life turning murder into entertainment, even if they hadn't understood it as such. "What should I be, Kella?" She shook her head, repressing her own anger. "This is my job. And I'm good at it." She pushed the oar more aggressively, turning to avoid seeing Kella's expression.

But she was denied that as soon she felt the boat rocking. Kella had stood again. "Oh, okay. I get it," she said, in a tone that suggested she had no interest in getting it. "It's not like this is what you want to be doing."

"But even if it was, would that be so terrible?" Litz's teeth ached. She must have been clenching her jaw too tightly again.

The boat nearly toppled now, and Litz felt a hand on her shoulder, imploring her to turn. "Yes, it is," Kella yelled. "Of course it is." She gave a cutoff laugh. "You know what I wanted when I got home from the desert? I wanted to go do what I was good at, to go be with the people I loved, and be everything the kingdom I care about wanted me to be. But you come home, and you don't think what you do is doing any good, either, but you do it anyway because, hey, it's a job."

"I don't have the luxury of being hundreds of miles from the Circle *we* angered. And I'm here for Eisha."

"Oh, *sure*."

"Imagine if you'd got home, and Ker had been missing." Litz was matching Kella's pitch now. Evlo's expression and Loren's mild disapproval reminded her this was a terrible idea, even out on the wide and quiet river, but she found herself unable to calm down. Kella forced her to tap into a side of herself much harder to control.

"I can. And after I tore everything apart looking, I would have set the whole fucking city on fire if no one told me where he was."

"I'm sure that would have helped you find him alive. And how do you know I haven't been tearing everything apart?"

"You've been kept a bit busy tearing helpless villages apart, Princess." She smiled mirthlessly. "Sorry, should I say, General?" She sounded just as scathing as Litz had imagined she would saying the word. But while deriding her in person, Kella also crossed her arms and shook her head as if she'd been granted the wisdom of the earth mother. "I've been working for my food instead of being handed it. Crowds that would have cheered for me now beat me when they figure out who I am." She sneered, releasing Litz's arms to wave hers wildly. "Do you have any idea what I would give to go back to being who I was? It would have been so fucking easy. I wanted to come home and make a big, bad return from the dead. But y'know what I did instead? I hid in a cave with a dragon and came up with a plan to try to save them."

Litz shook her head. She was angry enough to want to say again that it was a bad plan, and Kella had clearly dragged everyone here to see her. But that felt far too dangerous to bring up. Instead she said, "I'm sorry we can't all live up to your standards of heroism."

The air released from Kella's chest so slowly, Litz half thought her nostrils would emit smoke. She said nothing, but her disappointment and bitterness felt just as loud as her anger. It was silly, but it was difficult not to think of the little puppet version of her they'd seen earlier being flung about the stage "in a rage."

Litz walked them back to their inn because she'd said she would. But when Kella, who seemed to have cooled off, and Evlo, who was avoiding looking at either of them, reached the door, she kept her face still. "I have to go," she said. "I need to get ready."

"For your party?" Kella sneered. "Are we supposed to go?"

"I don't think that's a good idea," Evlo and Litz said together.

Litz took a stiff bow. "I'll see you tomorrow," she said and walked away. She didn't look back.

When Kella had re-entered her life, she had been thrilled, even knowing that logistically, keeping them both safe would be a nightmare. She'd wanted to show her Verassez, just like they'd talked about all those months ago. But she could have done without hearing what Kella thought of her now. She'd chosen her path, and it was too late to change that, but she wished she didn't have to know beyond doubt that Kella hated her for it

CHAPTER THIRTEEN

K er didn't need to ask to know something had gone wrong: that much had felt inevitable long before they'd arrived. Kella was always going to be disappointed, even if things went exactly as planned. Ker, who had not had high hopes, especially not about Kella's visit to the palace as a polite servant, was happy they'd at least made it back to their room alive. He cleared his throat.

Evlo looked at him, chin half covered in the animal fat mix they'd been using to shave, but Kella was still focused on sharpening her knives. Ker felt a sharp stab of pity for Evlo. Though Kella had been the one to help him shave since he'd had any facial hair to grow, and she was technically very good at it, when she picked up her knives in a mood, it was unnerving to be on the other end of them.

"I found what we were looking for," Ker prompted, sensing that Kella at least might need a reminder of where he'd just been. Annoyingly, even this did not seem to rouse her from her focus.

Evlo did turn, putting his other cheek in imminent danger from a frustrated Kella. "What did you find? Did the old man know something?"

"Not much from him but a lot written down. There's even a map. It seems unlikely it'll lead anywhere real, but it confirms some of what you were saying."

Evlo turned completely, inspiring Kella to narrow her eyes. "It's in Nibralin?"

Ker shook his head. "No, but you said it was in the capital, right? Well, two different sources imply that the dragons captured this thing in Venxian—am I saying that right—that was at that time—"

"The capital." Evlo breathed out slowly. "They changed the capital, you're right. It wasn't in the ruins of the old."

Ker frowned. "Ruins?"

"There was a terrible flood after a battle between two dragons burned down most of the city. It was barely even a functional town when I left. Can I see?"

Ker handed the map over, keeping back the copy of the diary he'd also been allowed to hold on to.

Though she still looked annoyed, Kella at least put her knives down. She looked over Evlo's shoulder, frowning, then up at Ker. "So the devil's real?"

Ker lifted his arms to let them fall limply to his sides. "By all appearances. There's a lot of different stories saying what it is, but it seems certain there's something down there, and the dragons are afraid of it. A lot of the stories imply the dragons would never have gained power without it, and they fiercely protect it and have warred many times over the right to do so. Whether or not it grants wishes, they seem to think it does something, and they didn't like our tourist dragon asking about it." Ker waved the diary about and patted it. "There's a lot they didn't want them asking about."

He met Evlo's eye. If even half the stories were true, there couldn't be words. Evlo wouldn't like to hear it, but Ker could understand just how painful Evlo's story was because of Ellonya; she too had come from a cultural death, from believing that her people might not have be worth saving and would perhaps never understand her. "You really come from a terrible place," he said instead.

"Yes."

Kella's expression of dour irritation was brightening. "Then we were *right*." She was only growing energised but with an energy Ker had learned to be wary of.

"It's starting to look like it." Evlo still looked dazed.

"Okay. We've got what we came for. We can go. We can fix everything."

"That was the idea, yes."

"Can we wish for more wishes?"

Evlo turned to Kella like she was an idiot. She did not seem to notice this.

Shaking his head, Ker smiled, hoping she wasn't serious. "No, I think that would count as selfish." He grimaced. "No selfish wishes. Only one wish allowed from one person. And I don't think it even has to appear to everyone." He hoped this might start them on a calmer, longer discussion on what the wording of their theoretical wish should be, but neither of his companions seemed interested in indulging him.

"Let's leave tomorrow."

Ker blinked. "Do you think we're ready?"

"Quicker we're out of here, the safer we are, isn't that what you both keep saying?" Downright cheerful now, Kella stood, spinning a knife between two fingers, ignoring Evlo's half-finished face.

"What about Litz?"

The knife stopped spinning, and she rested it lightly on her bottom lip that curled up deviously. "Leave Litz to me."

❖

Litz's mother had always been insufferable before a party. Before a party where her daughter would be the guest of honour? Unseen heights of difficult. When Litz went upstairs to fetch her, she found the woman assigned to help with her mother's hair outside crying. Litz did her best to coax her back inside. Between a bloody attack and a nervous mistress, her family's servants had been going through a lot, and she would prefer her parents not lose them all in one way or another.

"I need a glass of something for my nerves," her mother said as Litz walked in.

Litz inclined her head toward the door at the previously crying servant, who gratefully took the out. "Let me help finish your hair, Mother."

"You still need to get ready."

"I am ready."

"Are you sure?"

Litz smiled and put down her mask and picked up the discarded comb on the table. "Surely, being the new general frees me from the need to look a lady."

"If you are someone important, you must be seen to succeed in all that you attempt. If you are trying to look good, you must succeed."

"Mmm."

"My sister said that often."

Litz found herself soothed by the familiar motions. After killing people, especially within these walls, it felt good to care for someone with her hands again, to remind herself they could be used for that too. "Do you miss her?"

Her mother said nothing for a moment, though her hand opened and closed around her ceremonial skirt. "She is everywhere, I am sure of it. The gods scatter her greatness through everything. I hear her in you sometimes," she added more quietly. "Whenever you judge me and the things I care for. You sound and look just like her."

"I've never wanted to make you feel judged."

Her mother gave no indication she'd heard. "You will make a good leader."

It was the first of many times someone would tell her this that night. That her resemblance to her aunt's spirit was clear, that the army loved her, that the dragons approved of her. Always unsure how to handle being the centre of attention, Litz felt deeply uncomfortable by the time the second dance began, especially when everywhere she turned, there Reishann seemed to be, smiling at her.

They were on a promenade platform hastily constructed that day to better allow the king's partygoers to view the river. So far, the spawning had not yielded much excitement. From Loren, Litz expected that the party was a little premature on Xoia's part, and most dragons would not stir for fishing until the morning.

After Litz's father took a seat, she remained ready to dance another group dance, thinking a little wistfully of badly and drunkenly teaching it to Kella by another, much smaller body of water. Litz turned to the water after her first partner spun away, seeing not even a splash yet, thinking how they would have appreciated a full-grown catfish out in that tiny oasis.

When she looked back, she was holding someone new in her arms. "Hello there, stranger," Kella said behind both a fish mask and netting hat.

"No. You—"

"Can't be here?" Kella asked, imitating Litz with what looked like a smirk on her netted face. At least she'd opted for that modicum of caution. "But here I am. Heard there was a party." She spun, perfectly keeping time with the other dancers. Litz, stunned, allowed her. "And if it's my last night in Verassez, I figure, how could I leave without making a night of it even once?"

Still unable to think, Litz spun Kella again, feeling more like she was the one being twirled till she was dizzy. "How do you even know these steps?"

"You taught me, remember?" Though the dance didn't call for it, Kella pulled in closer, lowering her voice to a soft murmur. "I remember everything, don't you?"

Litz looked around. They were surrounded by people she knew and loved, people she recognised but could not name, servants who saw and reported everything. There would be no way out without being noticed, and notice here would inevitably lead to talk. Though Kella had hardly made a smart decision with the way she'd intercepted Litz, the bold option in this case was likely the smart one. Hiding in plain sight was their only chance. "I can't go with you."

Kella leaned away, one eye on the dancer in front of her, who seemed rightly confused she wasn't moving on as she should. "But you want to."

"I need to find Eisha. Her brother is a child and likely to be used by others if I am not here for the politicians to focus on. And I need to try to stop this war escalating past what our nations can manage. I'm about to be put in the position where I can do both."

"I think you know that you can't do anything from inside the thing you're against." Beneath the veil, Kella smiled, but it seemed sad now. "It would have been like me going back to killing dragons and saying I was helping reduce damage."

"I can't abandon Eisha," Litz reminded her again, ignoring their abandonment of the group dimension of the dance and Kella's comments. She wanted to deny them, but they felt true. "We can't all be heroes, Kella." The words were strangely hard to say. Litz badly wanted to live in Kella's world, where if someone found out they'd been doing wrong, they changed their entire life to make it right again, no matter the consequence to themselves or the people they loved. Litz wasn't sure she was strong enough to live and fight in that world, but she wanted to be. Because Kella would be there.

"It's been nine months," Kella said, her face grave. "Don't you think you would have found her if you were going to?"

Litz fought to keep from showing her rage as Kella and the world kept spinning.

"Unless you, what, become general, launch a coup? I don't think you want to do that, either." With great care, Kella dipped her. Litz let her, no longer watching the other dancers to see if this would fit, if they were being observed.

"What do you know about what I want?" she asked, her words intended to sound biting but coming out more like a plea. Soon, Litz would answer to almost no one but her dragon, her king, and the Circle. For the last time, she wanted some moral authority in her life to tell her what to do.

Kella drew her back to her feet, her wide, pretty lips still turned down in a frown that suited her face oddly. "Heroes are just people," she said so softly that her voice was almost drowned out by the drumbeats that were growing louder and faster as the tune reached its climax. "And we can do this without you. But I think we make a pretty unbeatable team, right? Seems a shame to split that up with the world on the line."

With polite cheering, the song came to a close, and Kella, with a confirming glance at the other dancers, took a bow. Litz was dimly aware she should do the same but was incapable of doing anything but stare. "But if that's what you *want*, I'm gone." She moved in, holding both Litz's arms. "Ker found the information we need. We were right about everything, and we fly tomorrow night. You know where to find us."

Litz opened her mouth. Realistically, this was good-bye, and it really was unlikely she'd ever see Kella again. Why would she? This had been a fluke, the universe telling her this was her last shot at escape and maybe ever at being happy, at seeing the world as Loren had urged her to. And now, it was quite literally about to walk away from her. Before she could think of something else to say, Kella was smiling and releasing her grip slowly, like she was hoping Litz would tell her to stop.

"When did you get so casual about flying?"

Kella's smile was lopsided. "The worst happened, and you caught me, Princess."

Litz swallowed. "I'll come and see you tomorrow," she promised, compromising with herself.

Kella said nothing, her large eyes filled with understanding, and within a moment was lost in the crowd, now milling around congratulating each other on the dance and leaving to wander to the drinks' table.

"The next dance will be a traditional Asnam one," the caller announced as Litz continued to stand there, absently wondering if anyone who would call themselves Asnam was there to watch the high society of the Aelshian empire dance their little forest nation's dance in what had once been a sacred night for them and many other clans. The return of the catfish to their source meant the death of the old year and the beginning of the new one to many clans, but to the Aelshians, it was only a party. And an excuse to announce their new general, and soon, their new war.

Litz made one last attempt to look for Kella before someone tapped her shoulder. She turned, then had to smile. Nic's mask covered her face strangely; two blue dragon feathers stretched up over her head and behind her ears, taking up most of the bright red mask. Though most wore fish masks, many, like Nic, had veered away from tradition into fashion.

"Dead again," Nic said as she laughed quietly. "Were you looking for me?"

Litz tore her eyes away from their search. "Just looking."

"They're announcing it tonight?"

"Later, I think. Then, the ceremony tomorrow afternoon."

"They might as well get it over with," Nic said, wordlessly taking Litz's hands, then crossing their knees over as Litz began to join the dance. They fell easily into sync despite neither having a great sense of rhythm. "Everyone knows by now. And about the whore ban."

"Don't call it that."

"What do you want me to call it, General?" Nic's eyes lit up with a wicked smile as she pulled away and started to clap, inviting Litz farther in. "Oh, and did you hear they've put you in another little puppet play?"

"I was forced to see some of it, yes."

"It seems some people love to see you in the centre of things, even if you hate to put yourself there." She grinned. "But don't worry, General, we'll get you better at that."

❖

Kella got a drink. Because this was a party of rich people, and it was unseemly to make them actually pay for anything on a night they were supposed to be enjoying themselves, all the drinks were free. Free but bitter, as though the wealthy did not want to admit they were enjoying what they had.

When she had her drink, she stood back and watched, wishing the netting over her face was a little easier to see out of, but she wasn't quite self-destructive enough to take it off yet. She passed her drink under her veil and took her sips discreetly. Like a fine lady.

Litz looked happy. She was almost laughing after Nic had surprised her, and she was keeping the beat as the band played its next tune, relentlessly demanding more from the dancers. She looked untroubled.

Kella wished she wanted that for Litz without feeling something bitter and tight clench around her insides. Litz deserved to be happy. And she was right. Not everyone could be a hero. Not everyone deserved to die like one.

That was maudlin and pathetic perhaps. But after turning up in disguise to a royal party like she was living in a story, what had Kella expected? She'd wanted to drag Litz down or along with her because that would have been validating, it would have been hot, and it would have given this whole attempt the veneer of a quest and not just whatever it was.

When they'd arrived, Litz hadn't looked happy, and had said it was because she'd wanted Kella to be safe. Back in the desert, Loren had warned without words that Kella would hurt Litz, whatever her intentions. Kella wanted Litz along because she didn't want to fly away from her again. Just like they'd pulled Evlo along. Just like she'd always dragged Ker behind her. Always. The longest time she'd gone without him at her heels, she'd been in a cage.

Her mother hadn't needed anyone. Oh, people had always clung to her, surrounded her, followed her wherever she went, but she'd began what she did all on her own. She'd been the real kind of hero, the kind Kella wasn't bold enough, or perhaps cruel enough, to be. But maybe it wasn't too late to be a good person or to work on it. Maybe she could wish peace and contentment on Litz. That seemed like the good person thing to want.

Not selfishly demanding someone she cared about upend her entire life to spend time with her.

She'd wanted to believe back in the desert that, even as they'd said good-bye, they'd only ever be doing it once. She could see now how delusional that had been. Kella might not want to leave her behind, but being rejected, she could just about deal with. Ruining Litz's life now that she was on the precipice of something important felt cruel and pointless, just like it had when she'd ruined Ker's and ended her mother's. Though horribly melodramatic, it didn't feel like the worst way to look at it. She'd seen Litz's eyes lingering on her. There'd been regret there, true, but there was still possibility. Kella hadn't been shut down yet.

She kept expecting the feelings that Litz had left her with when they'd been alone in the world together to leave her soon. But they'd stayed as strong, like heat lingering on stones after the sun went down. Kella had known the warmth of her affection, had basked in the feeling of knowing she was so wanted, and had been desperate to get that shine back.

But maybe it was time to start letting it go.

As she started to back away, she watched Litz smile and hold tight to her friend's hand as she unsuccessfully scanned the crowd for Kella. That made the decision easier. They would leave in the afternoon. If Litz arrived to say good-bye, she'd find them already gone and would not be tempted. Loren, when she learned of it, would thank her for it.

Her slow retreat became a rapid one when, moments later, she saw the woman whose clothes she'd stolen at knifepoint emerge down the steps. She looked confused, but since that generally sat uneasily on the face of someone this important, that confusion was quickly becoming anger.

Feeling kind, Kella slipped off the bangles and anklets to leave on the wall beside her, keeping only one that she planned to use for buying provisions the next day. Maybe she was trying to be more selfless, but there was no need to be *that* kind.

CHAPTER FOURTEEN

By Ker's estimation, Kella hadn't slept. When he'd woken in the night, she'd been gone, and though she'd briefly been in bed again when Ker had left to fill their water flasks that morning, a task charmingly easier than it was at home, when he returned, she was gone again.

"I didn't even see her leave," Evlo admitted. "I came back from taking a piss, and the bed was already empty, I swear it."

"She's avoiding me," Ker muttered, not sure why he was so certain. They were due to leave that evening. Had Kella's ill-advised late excursion put her off that? Much as he wanted to believe that she hadn't been quite that bold, or stupid, he suspected she'd been trying to convince Litz to come with them. As he started walking toward the market, he could come up with nowhere else she might have gone alone at night. He passed a pair of old ladies, one wheeling the other, who held their bags, and felt that their giggles were somehow at his expense, as if everyone in the world knew where his sister was but him.

He'd instructed Evlo to wait in the room in case Kella returned, but he didn't have much belief that would work. No, this was familiar. They needed Kella before an expedition, so she was be nowhere to be found, and they sent Ker out looking. Zebenn had called them the twins, and in some respects, it was how everyone at home seemed to think of them. If Kella, the action side, had gone somewhere, then Ker, her thoughtful shadow, would magically sense where she'd gone. Despite the fact that he usually succeeded, it felt insulting.

And now you're aware things have changed and want her to acknowledge that, but it makes you uncomfortable.

Change is always weird. The point is, I don't know where she is.

And you feel like an earlier version of you would have found her by now, yes?

Are they still watching you?

Yes, Ellonya said, allowing for the subject change. *I will fly off the moment I have the opportunity. This may mean you'll have to move your schedules ahead.*

We can do that.

When you find her.

Ker gritted his teeth, looking around at the riverbank path that was only becoming more packed as the stalls began to thin out. *When I find her.* Though some people in the growing crowd appeared to have fishing equipment, they hugged the shore tightly, a few venturing into boats. Ker had been around enough crowds waiting for a dragon slayer to arrive and provide a show to feel anticipation in the air. The crowd was waiting.

To her credit, Kella hadn't gone far. But she was easy to spot because she'd forgotten her fucking net hat. Forgotten or had blatantly left without it.

He found her maybe a straight mile down the river, surrounded by others all pushed up against the rope separating them from a muddy drop covered in tree roots that led to the river. There were too many people for Ker to push forward, especially since he didn't tower as much among Aelshians as he did at home.

But it wasn't just Aelshians around for this busiest of days. He'd gotten better at spotting the forest clan people, though he didn't know the names of those nations and had little ability to tell them apart. They were shorter, and they wore no earrings. Many did wear jewellery, particularly dangling from the nose and lip and ankles, and they dressed far less conservatively than even the most common Aelshian people. There were far more clan folk out today than he'd noticed since his arrival, all thoughtlessly rubbing shoulders with Aelshians of every class. There were even fine members of Aelshian nobility out in bug masks that matched their parasols, all in outfits that suggested they wanted to be seen, with servants helping them onto high seats constructed on a wooden landing above the riverbank.

He heard it begin before he saw anything: shouts from children way down the river to his right, the few who'd ventured out on their boats hugging the shore even tighter.

The water began to move as though the wide river had become the sea and was beset by fierce tides moving back against the river's direction. But they weren't waves, Ker fast came to realise. They were fish.

Catfish, Ker could see as a few more passed by. He'd seen plenty at home in fish markets, but these were larger than he'd believed any freshwater fish could possibly grow, and they moved with all the smooth grace of a dolphin.

But they weren't the show, not alone. A few had begun to be picked off by crocodiles bold enough to move against the wall of them, but that too wasn't what the crowd held its breath for.

"Look, look!" It was a large, older man standing near Kella who made the first shout this time, his wrinkled old finger pointing straight and sure at the sky. At the dragons. They were amassed like Ker had never seen before, like old soldiers swore they'd seen on battlefields that none of their friends had returned from. There were so many that with the help of the tree canopy, they really did block the sun's light. The day became dark but still bright enough to see the terrible, awe-inspiring way the first red dragon swooped down and easily scooped up three fish, all easily as heavy as Ker, into its mouth. He gave Ellonya the feeling of envy she should be experiencing.

No one mentioned this to me.

Maybe it's not too late. They look like a good free meal to travel on.

I don't want to draw attention to myself any further today, she said, a little defeated. *I'm giving up on Aelshian dragons for now.* She paused. *Except Loren. Loren's nice.*

Even if she doesn't approve of us.

Even if.

With that, Ker sensed some opportunity and moved forward a little, almost in touching distance of Kella. He was certain that had he entered this throng with any valuables, they would not be on his person by the time he left.

The people gasped as one as a dragon with the changing look of a chameleon caught everyone's attention. A fish flung itself from its mouth in a desperate bid for freedom from fifty feet in the air. As it hit the water, it caused a great splash that hit people in the face. Kella burst out laughing, then started to cheer and clap. A little shocked at first, several people around her followed, including a few of the wealthy on their podiums. The loudest came from the clan people, who seemed genuinely gleeful at the unexpected win.

Ker gritted his teeth as Kella continued clapping. Of course she would cheer for the catfish, ever the contrarian rooting for an underdog.

The crowd shifted again as the migrating fish moved on, and Ker was able to grab Kella's arm. Her uncovered face changed from shock to joy to annoyance as he started pulling her away and held up her forgotten mosquito hat. "I was in a hurry," she offered in explanation as she started to move away.

Ker kept pace. "To see the fish?"

"No, I didn't know about that until I got here. Y'know the fish do that every year? I wanted to get supplies," she continued before he could reply.

"We don't leave until the evening."

"I figured afternoon works better."

He huffed. He'd hoped to have a little more time with Denone. Even Findan had never spoken about magic so freely. "Better if you tell us that's what we're doing and don't just disappear without a word and without your hat."

She shrugged, starting to walk with a little more space between them. "Don't see you wearing one. You're just as wanted a guy as me."

"I'm wearing the headscarf, and it's only the women who wear them here."

"Sounds like someone who didn't like wearing it, either."

"Hey," Ker said, stopping them with a hold on her shoulder. She seemed to have a full bag of provisions already, and they'd been exposed long enough. "This isn't a joke."

"Yeah, and I'm not trying to joke around. We leave today as soon as we can."

"Did she reject you outright? Is that what this is?" He stared. "This really is Jev becoming king all over again, isn't it? You figured she'd still be yours to call on."

Kella shook her head, not meeting his eyes. "Fuck off. Look, I still need a few things, but I'll come back."

"No." Ker hated the whining, incredulous tone to his voice, but he couldn't help it. It was ridiculous that she still wasn't getting his very simple point. "No! C'mon, Kel, put on the fucking veil, and let's get out of sight already, heh?"

"Yeah, well, I wanna see the end of the fish thing. I'm being cultural, making your da proud. And I'm fucking sick of hiding. Thanks to you, I've been doing a lot of it lately."

Ker blinked. "Thanks to—"

"Shut up, y'know I didn't mean it like that."

But since she wouldn't meet his eyes, he didn't know. "The only reason that me and Ellonya—"

"I know, I know," she snapped, raising up her hands. "Give me a fucking break here. And like, an hour."

"What, so you can keep drawing attention to yourself out here? So you can come back with another kidnapped child?"

Really, Ellonya put in, *what's drawing attention is your yelling.*

"We need to…"

You should—

"*Get back.*"

As his and Ellonya's voices merged on a single thought, Kella flinched and stepped back, the surprise, fear, and disgust she no longer thought worth hiding plain on her face. It broke his heart almost as much as it made him want to slap her.

How dare she, he thought before even realising that was how he felt. He could feel Ellonya trying to soothe him, but it wasn't helping. She was right. They'd been hiding a lot lately: from the world, from each other. Something was finally giving. *I can't have her look at me like that,* he amended. *She went nearly my whole life thinking there was something wrong with me, I know she did, but until now, she's never let me see it.*

A lot has changed for her too, Ellonya reminded him. *You've seen her vulnerable. She can't hide her fear from you completely, not anymore. And wouldn't you prefer she was honest?*

Ker breathed out slowly. "Look, I'm sorry, but it's nothing to freak out about."

"You sure?" Kella's voice had risen to unnatural heights. "Because Evlo sure thought there was. And this isn't something Litz does. She's never even seen it before." She gave a bitter laugh and took a step back. "I know I don't know anything, believe me, I'm well fucking aware, but something's not right here. And I don't want to lose you, especially not to something you only did *for* me."

"Ellonya's not a *something.*"

Kella clenched her fingers around empty air like she wished they were the necks of her enemies. "I know! I know that! I'm not saying she's some evil monster that's eating your soul."

"Then what are you saying?"

"I'm saying, it's not healthy." She was yelling now.

You both are.

"It's not healthy," she continued, "it's not right. And I've never given a fuck that you don't want to be anyone's husband or whatever, and believe me, I never will. But if you wanna make friends, or hells, keep your family, you're gonna need to remember how to talk like a human being every once in a while."

"We're literally talking like humans now!"

Ellonya's voice came through as a sigh. *No, but you're both still yelling like humans. And you're making a scene.*

Ker shook his head as he made a real effort to lower his voice. "Ellonya's right. We need to go."

"Oh, is Ellonya right, is she?" Though Kella still sounded a little delirious, she followed pliantly enough when Ker grabbed her arm and started to march them in the direction of their rooms.

"Yes, she is. And when we get back, we can call her and get out of here as soon as she's able to."

Kella was letting him lead her now, but she sounded like she would never forgive him for it. "I'm thrilled to hear you've got it all worked out."

"Someone had to. You've not exactly been stepping up."

Don't be cruel for the sake of it. Ellonya sounded exhausted now. *You'll only regret it later.*

Though Ker knew she was right, later hadn't arrived yet, and it felt incredible to let out some of his fears and frustrations at someone who deserved it at least a little bit.

❖

Kella was calmed to some extent by the time they reached the inn, but she still couldn't bring herself to look at Ker. Gods, she'd spent years telling him to be less of a pushover and to start standing up for himself. Considering she made up most of the human people he talked to, it figured that would be directed at her when he finally pushed back.

She should have been better than the anger she felt, but apparently, she wasn't. She'd endured whining, mockery, complaints from Ker, sure. But yelling at her like that? True, she was new to leading an expedition, but who else was going to rise to that challenge? Evlo, who hadn't wanted to come? Ker, whom no one had ever looked to lead anything?

Except now, he had a gremlin and dragon hanging on *his* words, not Kella's, and who wouldn't or couldn't even speak to her. So maybe that had started to get to him after all these months in isolation.

They'd always had times when they'd got mean with each other. But kicking her while she was down like this over someone he knew she liked? That was cruel and not like him. And it made her worry how she could have missed that venom in him. She'd been paying too much attention to the obvious changes in his life and not enough to the subtle internal ones. It was arrogance probably, but she'd always felt she knew her brother inside and out, as well as she would any extension of herself.

"Evlo should be here," he said, forcing Kella out of her spiralling thoughts for long enough to notice that he was right. The room was empty.

"Maybe he went to get Ellonya."

Ker shook his head. "He still doesn't like being around her on his own." He frowned. "Maybe he went to find us. But I didn't take long."

"Still not sure why either of you needed to come looking."

Some horrible piece of her crowed in delight when he glared in contempt. However annoyed he might be, he still wasn't able to ignore her.

"Ellonya says they're acting strange around her."

"Define strange."

He ignored her, remaining oddly still. "Somehow, they know, they know it's us." His lip curled. "What did you do last night, Kel? Who did you tell?"

"Who did I what?" Vaguely aware this was becoming serious, Kella found herself unable to get past the accusation and made a face, hands lightly resting on her hips as she leant back and shook her head. "How fucking dare you? This is my godsdamn quest."

"Quest? Okay, sure. Shut up and help me pack. We need to get out of here and find Evlo."

"Quit telling me what to do."

"Start acting like you want to live, please!"

Kella heard the door behind her creak open and closed her eyes.

"Oh, there's no need for that at this point," the voice from the door said quietly.

Turning, Kella quickly counted the guards, all wearing light armour in colours she hadn't noticed before, as they entered the room single file. As she'd been reminded so often recently, having an unpredictable fighting style only got her so far when she was outnumbered almost ten to one. So it was comforting when Ker inched closer, but when he stepped in front of her, she took her sword from her bed and sidestepped the protection he never would have considered giving her a year ago. Wildly, she glanced around the room as the guards, or soldiers maybe, began to fill it. They might make it to the roof, but she doubted they'd make it down safely from there. They were two floors up, and there were crocodiles in that water and dragons who could be sent after them up high.

As though watching her come to these conclusions, the first man through the door, the officer maybe, smiled, sincere as the crocodiles Kella was still considering taking her chances with. "Nowhere to run," he said quietly.

Annoyed into action, Kella ran right at him, her sword high. She almost landed the hit on his neck before he had a chance to block, but some barrier of her own making held her back, lasting long enough for someone to grab her wrist and twist. Her sword fell to the ground with a dull thunk. Someone pulled her arms behind her back so tightly, her shoulders nearly left their sockets, but the humiliation was worse to endure.

Now she was facing Ker, she could guess that he was speaking to Ellonya. That either meant rescue was imminent, or things were worse than they seemed.

As a knife was against her throat, she stared him down, wanting to tell him to move, to use magic, to grab his sword, to do *something*. But she could tell he wouldn't, not with her neck on the line, not like this. The violent, obvious, stupid way of proceeding just wasn't Ker's style.

Holding Kella's gaze grimly, he pulled out his short sword and dropped it. If she wasn't worried about grazing her neck, she would have shaken her head. She hoped he was planning on saving his magic for the moment the knife moved away. He looked as though he wanted to say something sarcastic but maybe judged it was too dangerous. Or maybe he couldn't think of anything else to say.

The blade at her neck dropped, but still no magical rescue arrived.

It was probably a good thing Kella didn't have the knack. She was certain that however much caution a situation demanded or how ashamed it made her feel, it wouldn't stop her. "Anytime now," she muttered as they were shoved briefly into each other on the stairs.

"You hesitated," he said instead of responding as he was pushed out front. He didn't look back at her as they walked downstairs, but it was sweet in a way to know he was still annoyed at her, like the last few minutes had changed nothing.

Chapter Fifteen

Kella had spent so much time almost losing her life because of dragons and had more than enough scars and burns to prove it, but being captured by dragons was new. Burned alive by one, sure, dropped from a great height, trampled, torn apart, all of these she'd considered. But never in any of her nightmares had a group of old gleaming dragons, grown to serpentine lengths with age, looked down at her to decide whether she should live or die.

A year ago, she wouldn't have believed dragons could speak or reason, never mind have political interests. For the second time in a year, she was facing the likelihood of execution, and this time, her fate would not be in the hands of her oldest friend. Only that kept her from laughing.

And once again, Ker was beside her, ready to be forced down with her. "Look at the ceiling," he said, nudging her with his elbow.

"We're about to die, and you want to stare at ceilings?" Kella said, looking up despite herself. It was like nothing she'd seen before. She wasn't even sure it counted as a ceiling, considering the giant hole in the centre, assumedly for the dragons to leave through. Some of the dragons seated on gigantic rocky ledges above would scarcely fit through it. Many were far larger, older than any she'd ever seen, and she'd taken down some truly large beasts. Some took up almost a whole level by themselves. She wondered if they took up whole rivers, bending with the water as it meandered. But one of the shortest she recognised, even if she hadn't seen her in almost a year. She nudged Ker in the ribs when she noticed Loren at the centre looking very small. She was two hundred and fifty years old, Kella remembered. How old did that make some of the dragons flanking her? Three hundred? Four? Seven? It was maybe a silly place to let her mind wander to when the real worry was that Loren was being flanked.

Maybe this wasn't all that different from Jev sentencing her after all. She wasn't sure how much Litz and Loren shared thoughts. It seemed like less than with Ker and Ellonya, but she'd had less opportunity to observe them. And Litz had once been able to block Loren from her mind entirely. Kella suspected Loren would not be above doing the same if it meant keeping Litz from information that would hurt her.

Though something about the dragon's body language looked almost apologetic, it was hard to tell how she would act. Maybe it was Litz looking out of those eyes and making the hard choice that Jev had already been forced to make. Because Kella liked to think she'd done some growing over the past year, she tried to forgive Litz in anticipation of the worst. But because Ker was probably in even more danger, she couldn't manage it. She would not watch him die.

"What if you Pulled the ceiling down on them?"

He made a face. "Don't think so. Can hold them back from us, though."

"Can you keep fire away from us?"

"Might be able to misdirect it. For a minute." He frowned. "Probably not."

"How lucky I am to have such a formidable witch beside me. Tremble, O enemies."

As he glared, she began to realise that the discussion had begun already. They simply weren't worth including in it yet; no human was. This did not faze the guards. She'd been right in her original assumptions: they weren't in service to Aelshia or its crown but to this dragon Circle. And she now understood the name a little better. This place was shaped in continuous circles that forced the dragons to look down on the humans. One unconcernedly had a human cleaning their teeth while being kept neatly between their mouth and tail.

This Circle moved seldomly, but tails twitching and eyes blinking reminded Kella of cats more than anything and made her certain that discussions were becoming heated. Only two remained still: Loren, who Kella felt would reach out to her if she could—or had anything to say—and another dragon who stared at them with yellow eyes cold as Kella's old mouser's when cornering unsuspecting prey. This dragon did not have to do anything else to convey their hatred. And though Kella would be lying if she claimed she recognised it, she knew it had to be the dragon of the rider Litz had killed in the desert, the one that had gotten away.

Perhaps this was the reason they'd been spotted. This dragon had been fishing for the catfish and remembered them, even if Kella and Ker had failed to do so after a lifetime of killing dragons no matter what they looked like. No, instead they'd yelled at each other like a couple of territorial fish merchants and drawn attention, and now surely—

Oh, Litz. Litz had killed that dragonrider with magic. Even if politics had saved her before, perhaps it couldn't now. Unless she could prove she wasn't associated with them. If Loren could do that for her, maybe she still had a chance.

The reason Loren looked so apologetic became even clearer.

Every sound echoed in this room: every swipe of the guards' spears against the stone, every time one of the dragons' tails whacked at the ledges on. One of the guards moved from their position with a nod, and every step rang loud. Loud and wrong. This wasn't a place for humans and their heavy steps and spoken words. This air didn't feel designed for speech. It was shaded and cooler than anything outside, but Kella felt more aware of the sticky closeness of the air. Breathing had become more difficult too, like her body understood that she didn't have many more breaths left to take and was making her savour them all.

The guard was carrying a bundle of weapons, and as he came closer, Kella recognised them. Without ceremony he put them at their feet and stood back from them. He spoke low and in a heavy accent, and for a moment, Kella couldn't understand him as he said, "You've been condemned to die." She was much more aware of his breath, rancid, with a spicy smell she didn't recognise that rose sharply above the smell of the dragon's smoke and found herself briefly fixated on. Eventually, she processed what he'd said and remembered she had a voice, that even if she wasn't going to kill dragons, she wasn't about to be judged by a group of aging politicians of whatever species.

"Yeah, we get that. Quit dragon it out." The joke did not seem to break the mild language and accent barrier, or maybe this guy just didn't have much of a sense of humour. But Ker groaned like he'd just opened a cupboard door and found that an animal had crawled in there to die.

Since that had been the point of saying anything, Kella was able to smile. Loren was looking out for Litz, and with a little luck, Ellonya and Evlo had made it out already, and Ker had her. And even if she couldn't save him like their mother had, she damned sure wasn't going to let him worry about it in his last moments, and she was going to pick up the sword they were so kindly letting her die with. Probably a neater disposal of evidence this way.

It was a funny kind of thought: after everything they'd both done to never harm a dragon again, they were still doomed to die, condemned as dragon slayers, even if no one would ever sing songs about it.

She wanted to reach for Ker's hand but worried he might see it as her giving up, so she stretched her fingers into the empty air instead.

❖

Litz had been torn on what to wear that morning. It felt like letting Eisha down—and certainly letting *her mother* down—if she didn't dress up, anticipating walking into a surprise high-society function held in her honour after a flattering promotion granted personally by her king. But it was a promotion within the army, and it felt bizarre to consider wearing anything but her uniform.

Taking Loren's advice to work toward a compromise, Litz wore some paint and more jewellery than normal, so she maybe looked, if not a lady, then someone whose appointment was ceremonially calling for war. By taking this position, she was signalling the army's continued alignment with both the king and the Circle, and she was admitting to herself that she was here to mitigate damage rather than stop the war Xoia was so determined to have.

She was giving up.

Kella was leaving that evening, she wanted Litz with her, and Litz was struggling to remember why she hadn't said yes. It was easier when Kella was next to her, holding her in a dance. There was no way to forget just how dangerous she was while Litz was looking right at her, in the same way that people liked to daydream about petting tigers before meeting one. Away from her, it was harder to think about her spending her last day hoping that Litz was going to show.

Kella had said she wished the world was kinder, that they could make it kinder. And here she was, offering Litz a chance to make it so. And Litz was going to, what? Continue to pick on small clans who had the bad luck to learn magic in circumstances that would force them to find something to do with it? To make new war against Jeenobi, a land cursed with a problem Litz would do nothing to help with or speak the truth of in the hope she could mitigate that damage as it came up?

But for once, her parents would both be proud of her. She could continue searching for Eisha where she was most likely to find her. And if she truly couldn't suffer under the weight of being Xoia's attack dog, she could always listen to her uncle and overthrow her. She didn't want to do it and certainly didn't want to actually take charge of Aelshia, but she was beginning to understand just how easy it would be. Frighteningly easy. Xoia had a personal guard she paid well, but she didn't understand the army, and unless the Circle specifically chose to take that moment to take revenge on Loren, they wouldn't go against her. Litz spoke for a dragon, and dragons, to dragons, would always take precedence over kings.

Though Litz had seen the main hall of the court during a ceremony many times, it still felt eerie walking in with no fine people there to watch, only rows and rows of empty cushions and a heightened awareness of a room with neither true ceiling nor walls. It was too open to feel trapped in, and yet, Litz found it stifling. After today, one way or another, she would never really get away from it.

If I didn't know flying above it all remained an option, I'd truly be upset by that thought, she admitted to Loren and was a little dismayed to receive no answer, especially when she had the strong sense that Loren was awake, just distracted and possibly not too close by.

Happily, she only had to make it halfway up the room before she saw someone less distant to complain to. Nic walked in from the other side with a few other uniformed friends, all apparently planning on being there early, but she broke away to speak to Litz. She didn't seem concerned by the fact that Litz had turned down going home with her the night before, and looking at her easy smile, Litz felt foolish for worrying. Nic was frequently sparked into anger, but she didn't hold on to her bad moods. It was part of what had kept them such good friends for so long.

"General," she said, her voice deeper than usual.

Litz continued walking as Nic kept pace with her. "Not yet."

"Might as well begin good habits early. I wouldn't want to forget myself and start calling you by some other name."

Litz shook her head, smiling despite herself. "If you made a habit of that, I'd simply ship you off to some faraway fort to prevent you ruining my reputation."

"No, you wouldn't," Nic stated confidently, a spring in her step as she kept pace with Litz's march to the top of the room. "You'd miss me. Besides, if it's reputation you care for, you're not doing much to safeguard it. Dancing with mysterious masked women at balls practically held in your honour? Who *was* that last night?"

"A mysterious masked woman. I never got the name."

Nic frowned and looked almost troubled. "You're a poor liar, Litzi. Is she the reason you wouldn't come home with me?"

"What? No. She was…" Litz grazed her teeth over her bottom lip. "Look, if you must know, she was the servant of the Senician dragonrider. I noticed her, and she begged me not to tell her master." For someone who truly was bad at lying, Litz was quite proud of her little half-true tale.

"Hmm. I can imagine he'd be a mean one. The quiet ones usually are."

"He's not quiet. He just can't speak Aelshian."

"I'm not so sure of that," Nic said, slowing her words. "He reacts too often to things he shouldn't understand. A canny trick, to fake being the helpless foreigner. Are they invited tonight?"

"I have no idea." They'd be gone soon, and a good thing too, with Nic so close to having them figured out. Much as Litz loved her, this was not a secret she would trust her with.

Is being general what you want? Loren asked her without warning and with great insistence.

Litz frowned, vaguely aware that Nic was explaining something about the order of ceremonies to come but not having the state of mind to focus on two voices. *It's the path I've found myself walking.*

I don't want to hear metaphor from you, Litz, I want to know if you want this. You turned Kella's proposition down last night. Why?

Nic was gesturing at cushions she was promising to reserve for Litz's parents.

I...I can't just run away.

Yes, you could. Do you think you'll find Eisha here? Do you think Xoia will let you find her?

I don't know.

Kella will probably get herself killed without you. Would you prefer knowing that or being unsure of when you will next see your parents again?

Why are you asking me this?

Visibly irritated now, Nic was waving a hand over Litz's face, who tried to make it move into a more apologetic expression.

I want you to be happy. You know this. Now, will this bring you happiness or a life you do not want?

I... Litz tried to smile. "Sorry, Loren's trying to get me to decide something for her."

"Can't she do that for herself?"

Can you decide for me? What should I do?

Litz felt the force of Loren's full-body weariness as she considered what she was about to do and just how old Loren was. Because Loren was very old. She held more grief and pain in her than Litz even had the capacity to understand. Usually, she wasted no thoughts on that terrifyingly deep well of feeling, but whatever she was deciding, she was thinking on it now.

What is it you say? If you want to be happy...

...start smiling. I'll smile for you if you think it right.

Be ready, Loren ordered eventually. *I will be by the palace in moments.*

Loren—

But before Litz could say anything else she was given a view of what Loren was looking at. She was in the Circle, a room Litz had never entered, and she was flanked by dragons looking down on guards holding Ker and Kella. Ker looked wary, like he was probably conversing with his own dragon, but Kella looked almost delighted, as if daring them to try it. As though, even about to meet a fiery death, she doubted the dragons looking down on her would have the ability, or possibly, the nerve, to finish her off. Her arm was stretched over Ker, who towered behind her, both of them seeming unaware of this apparently thoughtless gesture.

Get them out of there, Litz thought, feeling a wave of nausea crest through her body. *I'll be ready.*

❖

It would have been easier if she hated them in a more general way. But they weren't the mindless beasts sent by the Sky and Sun to wreak evil upon the world, the inevitable force of nature that had robbed her of her mother, not anymore. As she'd told Jev all those months ago, they were "just guys." And these were doing what they were about to do because of vengeance or politics or because they were too cowardly to do anything else. They were villains she should have been sharp enough to outwit.

"What's Ellonya saying?" she murmured, not turning away from the dragons who still hadn't killed them. She squeezed at the sword she ached to use on something.

"They tried coming for her in her quarters, but Evlo got to her first."

"That's where he went."

"He saw the guards coming toward the inn and got out of there to get help. He's with her now, but they won't reach us in time."

"How mad will they be if we die, and they end up stuck with each other, heh?"

Ker glared at her. Feeling panic clutch at her that she would never hear him say anything again, she grasped to find the right words. She should apologise for yelling at him and saying the things she wasn't supposed to. She should tell him she loved him. She should—

Loren moved without warning. Usually, when dragons took flight, they needed a runup or at least some prancing from foot to foot, but Loren launched herself at them almost eerily, showcasing her innate magic. There was something not quite natural about dragons, and sometimes, it showed, like the brief shimmer of a mirage. As she landed beside them, Kella felt a snarling voice in her mind ask, *What are you waiting for?*

The dragons of the Circle roared out their fury so loudly, it shook stones loose from the cave's rafters, and Kella grabbed Ker's wrist and started running toward Loren's tail, not needing to be told twice. That was good because Loren did not wait for them to reach her saddle before taking off.

They struggled to make their way to her saddle as she flew up in circles, approaching the exit above. They secured themselves in the two available harnesses rapidly, with Ker having to help Kella with the buckle as Loren launched through the ceiling of the Circle room.

Kella expected to hear sounds of pursuit, but there was nothing. Perhaps these Circle dragons were so shocked to be defied, they would do nothing, or they were too important to dream of doing anything themselves. She screamed as images and commands assaulted her mind, coming from multiple voices, multiple dragons. The reason they'd been left unpursued was becoming nakedly clear.

She saw herself with her hand in front of Ker. She saw Loren's tail disappearing through the ceiling. She saw Loren as she'd allowed them to jump on her back. And she saw Litz on a different day in her usual armour and maybe a little younger. It had been a hot day, and beads of sweat had formed a crown around her forehead.

THEY CANNOT LEAVE THIS FOREST. DO NOT LET THEM LEAVE. DEATH TO TRAITORS.

Bile rose in Kella's throat, and she clutched harder at the reins, letting her fingernails dig into her palms. The blinding certainty that what she should do was jump and die before she allowed herself to leave the forest filled her. She was a traitor; they all were. She should push Ker to his death. She should take Loren down the way she had countless dragons throughout her life and take away their ability to escape.

Even knowing it was a false truth that had only just arrived in her brain did no good. It was like knowing scratching an itch would only make it worse but being unable to stop putting nails to skin. She only realised she was trying to unbuckle her harness when Ker put his large hands over hers, stopping her.

"Don't," he said. She could hear the effort in his own voice, and that made it easier, to know he was struggling too. Having Ellonya with him had to help.

Just as the commands in her brain became easier to fight, Kella realised they hadn't been the only target. The screech of birds, monkeys, and scores of animals she couldn't identify began to follow them wherever Loren moved next. And though Kella had thought she'd gotten a handle on her fear of flying, those fears became far more rational now that they were whipping through dragon lanes and into forest ways not large enough to hold them.

When they came down low over the river, still busy with scores of dragons sated from catfish hunting, one leapt from the water like an awful sea monster, going right for Loren's neck before she sharply turned upward on her side. The people too. Anyone holding a weapon flung it at them, uncaring who else they might hit in the attempt. There was a great roar of anger wherever they moved, and there were dragons on their tail now, literally snapping at Loren until she whipped her tail sharply at the dragon behind her, who let out a great wall of flame they only just dodged. The fire took out a few trees, their singed trunks leaning low over the water.

Kella was busy trying to pat down her hair that felt singed when a dart launched itself into it, managing to go through her fingers without a hit. Turning sharply just as Loren's changed direction, she saw one of the Aelshian gremlins holding a blowgun and hanging on to the reins of a large, colourful, bird. Together, gremlin and bird shrieked before being left behind.

As Loren turned again, Kella was forced to stare at the river beneath them that seemed to be coming alive with dragons and other creatures swarming in their direction. They might have dodged the weight of this great command for now, but how much longer could they possibly keep in all the gods' graces?

❖

"Do you remember we used to joke about hoping we'd make war on some beautiful land to the east so we could see it for ourselves?"

"Sure."

As they approached the edge, Litz thought it strange again that no safety barriers had ever been erected around the edges. Safety consciousness was simply not in style, and if the palace was about anything, it was about style, and invincibility.

I do not want to hear about invincibility today.

Are you all right?

Loren's pause went on for a worryingly long time, and Litz could feel her fear rumbling its way back to her. *Yes. Be ready.*

Litz swallowed. "Does it seem odd to you that we never just considered going for ourselves?"

Nic put her head to one side. "What did Loren say? She's okay, isn't she?" she asked before smiling as though realising what a ridiculous question it was.

"Loren's fine." Moving slowly now that she was so near the side, Litz eyed the edge. Heights never bothered her usually. But it was a very long way down. Was there screeching in the distance? A sign that something large was moving faster than it should through a forest that couldn't accommodate her at normal speeds? "I think Eisha's here," she heard herself say.

"Like, spiritually?"

"In Verassez. Maybe in the palace. But I don't think I'm brave enough to do what it takes to find her, and I'm not even sure she'd want me to do what it would take. But if you find her, if you see her, would you look after her?"

Nic eyed her very carefully before eventually saying, "This isn't General Woskenna talking, is it?"

"No, this is just Litz talking." She took another step. They were between two large tree branches, and she imagined it would not take any effort to jump unimpeded into the green oblivion below. Other people might be alarmed to see her stepping so close to the edge, but Nic knew her too well for that. She knew she wasn't about to take any real risks.

"Tell my parents…" Litz started before realising there was nothing to say. What could she say about abandoning her entire life and them with it?

"Litzi, what the fuck are you on about?"

Litz did her best to smile. If there was a way she wanted Nic to remember her, it was unafraid. Out of the corner of her eye, she could see Loren speeding into the more open water beneath the palace, her tail bleeding and surrounded by scores of small birds and at least three dragons. Jumping would definitely put Litz at risk of being set on fire, never the way Litz assumed her end would come.

Forcefully, she sent an image of herself to Loren as she heard Nic say, "Hey, is that…"

"Good-bye, Nic," she said and jumped.

As the wind rushed by and panic swept through her, she thought, *Good-bye, Verassez.*

She shut her eyes, then realised that was ridiculous and wouldn't help anything, so she opened them in time to see that the world was not passing her by nearly as quickly as it had been. In fact, as she let her arms spread, she almost felt close to floating. As she looked at Loren and her passengers rapidly approaching, she saw Ker with his hand out and realised he was Pushing the air up against her, slowing her a little.

It meant that if it hadn't been for the fire coming narrowly close to her left leg, she might have had a painless landing on Loren. As it was, scorching agony made her forget she was even falling.

Kella had to catch her. "The burn salve, Ker, you got it?"

"It's somewhere, give me a second."

Kella was looking at her frantically and arranging her into the saddle better so that she actually sit up and strap in. It made Litz the only human who had a good view of the dragon coming down at her, passing through Loren's warning fire, and she screamed an unintelligible warning just as she saw the dragon's neck swerve, broken.

Ellonya grasped the neck firmly, sinking her serrated teeth down to the bone before shaking like a dog with a rat and letting go, releasing the blue dragon to drop to the water far beneath.

Her rider, Evlo, wearing that ridiculous gold helmet again, had his bow outstretched to take a shot at something behind them as soon as Ellonya let go of her prey. He gave them a slow mocking salute before hanging tightly to Ellonya's reins as they both took off vertically.

"Heads down," Litz remembered to shout through the pain just as the branches started hitting her face, finally drowning out the sounds of screeching behind them. Terrifyingly fast, she felt the trees cut her, felt her face break through spiderwebs. Moments before they broke through, Litz remembered she had some ability to provide them relief and Pushed the canopy ahead of them toward the sky.

There was no one watching, but even if they were, she was free. Whether her decision to leave had been a good or bad one, she would never need to worry about her magic being observed again. For now, that felt worth the ache in her chest and the pain in her leg. The way Kella's hands clung to her waist in protection didn't hurt, either. They were scratched, bruised, and burned, but they had made it to the sky, and the world awaited.

CHAPTER SIXTEEN

Loren had considered killing Kella quietly, but the feeling of Litz's soul rising so high now that they'd left the forest made it impossible to regret her decision. All her life, Litz had longed to escape the trappings she'd been born into, carving out little hidden pieces of difference, of escape. Whether through Loren or the army or magic, she'd made herself a person who wasn't the princess people expected her to be. But now, finally, she had relinquished her royal personhood and responsibilities entirely.

Eisha would be a point of regret, but there was nothing that could be done about that for now, and hopefully, that would be enough for Litz.

"Why are you so godsdamn happy?" Kella was asking. With the salve from Ker's bag, Litz's leg was feeling much better, though Loren still longed to fly back and ensure that the dragon who had attempted to kill her died horribly.

"It's been a long time since I've flown in the open air." She raised her arms, childishly delighted as she often was when flying and had been since Loren had first taken her up this high. Loren ached with fondness thinking on it now.

She would miss the comforts of ever-present attendants and the cool waters of home to bathe and fish in as she pleased, but it had been a long time since she had gotten any kind of excitement. Though that wasn't something she characteristically sought, she was thrilled to finally escape the stifling range of the Circle's influence. Spending her life keeping them happy out of fear for Litz's life was no way to live. And neither was lying to her rider, as the humans' new conversation was beginning to remind her.

The archer boy was explaining that unlike the others, he had seen something like that chase display before. "Only there, they can do it with humans too," he said.

Ah, because he was the one from Senice. Conceptually, the place felt upsetting to consider. Dragons were naturally the most powerful creatures in whatever environments they found themselves in. To seek more seemed greedy at best and grotesquely overreaching at worst.

"I think it was easier to control humans there. They expected and wanted to be controlled. It gets seared into everyone's heads that dragons are the authority on everything, and that going against them is like going against God. Who is also a dragon there." He moodily curled in on himself as he smiled a little cynically at Ellonya's new saddle. Litz looked a little closer at the padding for Loren, who couldn't help but be interested. It had been a gift, commissioned by the king herself the day before. "That's why I don't like getting okay with these 'friendly' dragons. Feels like I'm slipping back into that mindset. Every time I helped kill a dragon, I felt like I was doing something evil. I had to learn to live for that, to like how wrong it felt."

"That's how I feel using magic," said Ker. "It's always felt wrong, but…"

"But like it could still be used for something good," Litz finished for him thoughtfully.

They were so close to understanding it all as the same thing. Especially now they'd left Verassez, Loren was running out of reasons not to say anything. Litz might have no choice but to understand Loren's reasons, but the last thing Loren wanted was to hurt her. That might be unavoidable now. How could she say that the only reason she felt an instinctual disgust toward magic was because dragons had long ago made the decision that every human should feel that way?

"I've never understood that," Evlo said. "Back home, magic gets used for everything. For transport, food production, fishing. I've never gotten why it's such a big deal here. It's not even something your sollons care about."

"Yes, it is."

"Well, sure, but they're not supposed to. I got one to talk about it once. They don't have a reason to be against it. They just are because they don't like it."

Did you speak to him? Loren asked Ellonya. *To get him to come to you?*

No, he came to me when the soldiers arrived, luckily before my guards reached me. He spoke verbally to me. I did not think he would accept hearing me in his head.

Loren spared a glance at Evlo, who secured his bow and arrows on his back. *I expect so.*

Do you think more will follow us?

Loren suspected that more than wanting answers, Ellonya was thrilled to have an opportunity to speak to her at all. She could not imagine the depth of loneliness she must have endured over the years. Some of that feeling slipped through while Loren said, *Not yet. They'll regroup first. A panic implies there is something to panic about. They will not want to present that way.*

Do not pity me, Ellonya said, full of youthful fire. *I would rather grow up as I did than around dragons like those. I hoped that what had happened in the desert was a fluke and did not represent Aelshian dragons. But that was evil.*

We are not interested in human markers of morality, Loren said mildly. *They were just trying to stop us leaving. It made sense.* Just as it had made sense to kill those trying to prevent it. Even if knowing them did sting.

I'm surprised you won't defend them more.

They did just try to kill me, Loren reminded her.

But they're yours.

I think I've proven that's not how I consider them. Tell me, do you think you'd feel such a burden of responsibility to safeguard all your own if you were linked to anyone other than a hero?

Yes, it's the right thing to do for them.

What is this "right thing" you're so sure exists? I cannot believe that is your own thought, your own impulse.

What does it matter where it came from? We are stronger together. Perhaps a very human anxiety took over Loren, or perhaps Ellonya had grown remarkably adept at mind-skimming without acquiring any manners because as they began to cross into the savannah north of the forest, with the salt plains gleaming in sight, Ellonya spoke up, some judgement in her tone. *I could never hide anything from Ker.*

You should be able to. Keep yourself a person without him. Loren did not say that humans did not live as long. Ellonya would discover just what that meant the hard way. But why would she have to? Even if she had been without community her whole life, perhaps Loren could offer some to her now. *Let me share an echo with you.*

Of course, Ellonya said, all eagerness, her earlier judgement evaporated.

It will hurt, Loren felt the need to caution.

I am strong.

Loren started quietly. She wasn't sure if Ellonya had experienced an echo before, and she didn't want to shock her too much. First, she sent the deep feelings of love and early attraction she'd felt toward her mate, then the very different feelings when she'd met her first rider, before she'd known that he would become so important to her. She emphasised the different way she felt for them both before echoing the moment she'd watched her mate die in the war, then skipping ahead to the moment her first rider had taken a mate of their own. She'd had to move back to give them space, feeling great love when his first child had been born while never feeling it was her child, and then the pain of his death and the unbearable loneliness that followed.

And then, I took another rider and another. And there have always been some things necessary to bear alone. Some joyous, some heartbreaking, but not everything will be yours to share.

Filled with emotion—not the least anger—Ellonya pushed Loren out of her mind. Loren took this as a positive. At least the young dragon knew how to hold herself back in some cases. But even if Loren had diverted their conversation away from Ellonya's judgement, she was still considering it. She should talk to Litz today.

❖

One of Kella's earliest memories was Findan telling her off for licking the salt on her mami's arrow tip: both because she shouldn't have been putting things in her mouth and because the weapon could seriously injure her. Ever since, she'd found comfort in licking salt off weapons. It looked obscene, and it usually got her a reaction of some kind, and it tasted exciting.

After landing at the edge of the salt flats, Kella wanted to go out and pick a up a piece of the ground and lay it on her tongue. But it wasn't the moment for fishing for reactions. And the flavour was a bit sad with no food to chase it. They were going to have to figure out their next move. Her stomach was still in the air, but come another hour, it would return and howl its complaints for being so long ignored. It had been a long time since she'd been wandering through the market watching catfish and sampling snacks. A long time since Ker had interrupted what she'd almost convinced herself was a nice morning.

She still wasn't sure she'd forgiven him enough to talk to him, but she wouldn't let him go hungry over her fuckup. All that planning and they'd left without food. But at least they'd gotten what they'd come to Aelshia for, however they'd had to leave.

The annoying part was that this time, Kella had actually remembered to bring a pouch of seasoning she liked but had nothing to use it on. So why did she feel like her control of the situation was falling through her hands like sand?

It wasn't supposed to go like this. She'd changed her mind, and the earth should have listened. It owed her that much. Litz had picked her. That was still too big a thought to process. Litz, now obviously arguing with Loren about something, even as Ker attempted to tend her wounds. Kella wondered if Loren too, was shocked at how willing Litz had been to throw her life away for Kella.

There was a dragon skeleton somewhere out there that she could make out if she shielded her eyes from the sun. Out in the desert or savannah, dragons could be made a meal of for years, something that had seemed wonderfully grotesque when Rall had first explained it to her. But not much of anything could live in the salt flats, or at least, nothing magical could, and anything of any great appetite would need food and water the area could not supply. Perhaps vultures had flown in and claimed the body, Kella thought to comfort herself. The idea of a body being broken down by nothing but the sun felt awful in an existential way that living animals devouring it didn't.

Salt dampened magic, making it toxic to dragons. Kella assumed Loren had chosen their landing spot because other dragons would naturally avoid it. Though Kella had never seen it actually end one, she knew that an arrow coated in salt would do more damage than one without, and that some elephant herds even coated their tusks in it to make dragons leave them alone. Her kingdom had done foolish and terrible things to claim or hold the salt plains over the years. And now, no one seemed to be here. At least, not at this corner of it.

Litz's private argument with Loren seemed to have spread to the rest of the camp. Everyone was now involved, apart from Ellonya, who was licking a wound on her front paw and seemed, if anything, smug.

"For how long?" Ker sounded about as shaken as he had the first time she and Jev had broken up as teenagers. He'd been rooting for them.

"As long as the Jeenobian dragons have been afflicted. It was the Circle dragons' vengeance on the witches they think caused the sickness." Litz's tone turned icy, and Kella felt relieved it wasn't directed at her. "Or that's what Loren believes. But she's neither told me nor investigated more about it since learning this months ago."

Evlo huffed a smirk and pulled his scarf over his eyes. "Figures," he said and leant back on Ellonya. It was unclear if their coordinated rescue attempt had finally bonded them as months of journeying together hadn't, or if he was simply too tired to notice what he was leaning on.

"Wait, what?" Kella asked Ker quietly, and Litz went back into a furious internal conversation with Loren that made her eyes blaze.

He leant toward where she stood. "Centuries ago, dragons made us all think using magic was bad. That's why nobody does it."

"Oh. Like their command thing?"

"Yeah. Loren knew. Litz is upset."

"Got it."

"Makes sense," Evlo said, his voice muffled by his scarf. "If a witch really did curse the dragons and fuck up their heads, that proves the dragons can't control witches. And magic's the only real threat anyone can pose to them. They make people take it away themselves."

"That's what the Narani were trying to say," Kella mused. "Litz, remember—"

But Litz was in no mood to be coaxed into reminiscing. There wasn't a lot of talking from anyone that evening, and with no food, the conversations that did follow were cheerless. Kella tried to point out to Ker that at least his da would have one less thing to be disappointed in when they told him, but he didn't seem to see the funny side.

Eventually, as they all huddled by the dragons for warmth and watched the sun go down, Evlo asked if they had a destination planned before reaching Senice

Worry in his eye, Ker glanced at Kella. "I figured, since we'll need to fly into eastern Nayona soon, we could try making Mictan tomorrow." He gulped, correctly concerned about her reaction. "We do know someone there who might help us."

She was not impressed. "Oh, do we know anyone in Mictan? Do we know anyone, or have we just heard about someone who might be there?"

For a few long moments, he held her gaze, annoyed, before finally dropping his. "Fine. But you don't have any better ideas, and you know it."

"He might hate dragons!"

"But he's not afraid of them."

"Because he's famously an idiot."

"By famously, you mean according to Findan. And we don't need to tell him about the dragons, why would we? We just need bed and board and food for the road, and none of us have money or a good trade to win that."

"We can survive on dragon leftovers."

"Not happily. Not without water."

Litz turned to Evlo, who had taken over helping clean her wound, help Kella should have offered if she could have even looked at the wound on Litz only bore because of Kella. "Do they always act like they hate each other?"

"It's worse when they're friendly, trust me."

Behind him, Ellonya rumbled something that sounded suspiciously like agreement.

Feeling some of her anger pulled from her by the ridiculousness of the situation, Kella breathed out. "Fine. We'll try the town he's supposed to be in. If he's there, go for it."

"Kel—"

"You want to take charge, dragonrider, you be my guest and take charge."

There was silence again before Litz spoke up, sounding surly. "Loren has pointed out that two or more dragons who are highly skilled could make us believe they weren't there until they were on top of us."

"You saying we should leave a lookout?"

"There's no point. With enough dragons, they can make us believe whatever they want."

Kella wanted to cheer her up, but everything she could think of sounded too flippant too much of a joke. What was there to say other than thanking her forever?

Since now didn't seem the moment for that—and Kella wasn't even sure how ready she was to say that sincerely—she did her best to sleep.

Chapter Seventeen

Nic was someone who always acted first and thought about it later. Perhaps to her detriment, she hadn't lost that no matter how high she'd climbed. And though she had survived battles beaten, heartsick, and exhausted to her core, she'd never suffered regrets. She didn't lie awake at night thinking about a move she'd never made or a friend she could have saved.

But now, every time she closed her eyes, there Litz was, looking both terrified and happier than Nic had ever seen her: jumping again and again. Nic woke from dreaming of it still reaching for her too late.

Her morning did not improve from there. After listening to her sister explain exactly why the new king was going to destroy the kingdom, Nic made a decision that whatever happened with the rest of her day, she liked the new king. She hadn't expected to, having understood that she was a prude, besotted with her own consort, and markedly more insecure than her little sister. But meeting her had been different. That insecurity was still there but buried far down where few would notice. She wasn't letting it stop her doing as she wanted. Nic admired that. And from what else she'd heard, this king would be good for business, even if the whore ban was a shitty start.

Of course, if King Xoia had her killed today, Nic wouldn't live to find out how enforceable that ended up.

She wasn't despairing for herself. It might be a death sentence she was marching to, but it could be something positive. Xoia would be looking for a new general to promote, and Nic wanted to make sure she was seen as an option. She might have been associated with Litz, had done her best to grab for her wrist and stop her from jumping, but she wasn't Litz. She wouldn't accept she'd lost her best friend and her best chance at a career all in one.

It was strange. Though she had never considered marrying Litz, and she despised being told what to do, since having put it to her as an option, she'd found herself unable to think of anything else. It had been a solid thing in its own way, what they'd had. They'd depended on each other in a lot of their strangest and darkest moments: for distraction, comfort, validation, solidarity. She'd known who Litz was, but it turned out that Litz was still able to surprise her. It made her question everything she knew and made her want to look at Litz differently. But she wasn't around, so Nic kissed her sister's children good-bye and left to see King Xoia as she'd been asked.

She could have taken a boat the whole way there, but it always felt so exposed, travelling the water alone, and she was going to have enough of that in the palace. Instead, she walked and did her best to disappear into the crowds over the high bridges, thinking about how easy it had been for a witch to bring one down and whether any warning had been given to the people walking on it.

She hadn't spent much time in the palace. Her father was the nephew of a former king consort, so they were a formidable force as a family, but with so many more important family members—and Nic's chronic inability to sit still or say the right thing—they'd spent little time wasting their efforts on including her. But here she was again, not to escort Litz, not as part of a military honour, and not as her family's scion. As herself, for herself, and if it turned out she was going to finish the day tortured into revealing whatever she didn't know about Litz's treachery, that still mattered. There was something solid and real to grasp, even if it burned her hands while she did. She was still indisputably making something of her own life.

And as she walked through the court, aware of the eyes glued to her instead of Litz, she wouldn't let it go, no matter the cost. It was nice to be recognised and led past the waiting petitioners by the empty throne to stairs she'd never ascended. She was being escorted to the King's private quarters. At least for now, she wasn't being taken to jail.

When the guards wearing the colourful feathered uniform of the king's personal guard knocked on a door, Nic had no idea how she was supposed to feel. She decided to relax and take the king as she found her. She was supposed to be good at that.

The king and her consort gave the appearance of a united, if a scattered, front. They were standing as if waiting to greet her but in mid-conversation as Nic entered. Curious. Though she was sure all important people had a false level of propriety, Nic had half suspected King Xoia never did. This was surely her in crisis mode.

"You claim to have no idea what drove Loren and Litz into conspiring with the Jeenobian dragon-killing spies," Agsdon said. "Do you still stand by that?"

Shocked to be spoken to so directly by someone who ranked far above her, Nic nodded hesitantly. "I do. Though I believed us friends, I never had the slightest suspicion." Summoning her courage, she swallowed and adjusted her stance so her hands were clasped behind her back, and her legs were a little more apart. "Forgive me, but it makes no sense. The woman I knew would never align herself with dragon-killers." But she had spoken about stopping the war. Nic wondered what had changed her mind on that too.

Xoia nodded, seeming calmer, as though Nic had confirmed her thoughts. "Our investigation will continue, as will our attempt to follow them. But this is not why we…" She caught herself. "It's not why I called you here." Whatever she was about to say, Agsdon looked more begrudging about it than she did.

Politely, Nic waited. With the amount of nervous exhilaration surging through her, she felt naked not carrying some kind of weapon, and she was happy to keep her fidgeting hands hidden.

"Litz should have become the next general," Xoia said simply. "Though it is critical we find her, it is even more imperative to solve the immediate issue of her absence. Despite your close connection, I like you best for it."

Nic's lips parted. "Your Majesty—"

Xoia raised a hand. "I didn't say the role was yours yet. Your family, I know. Your military victories, I am aware of. But why should I give it to you specifically?"

Thoughts swirling, Nic was determined to keep her face calm. Was she supposed to sound politically shrewd or military and uncaring? "I have victories on the field to be proud of," she said slowly, "but more crucially, I can fight."

"Why crucially? Some of the most capable officers in the Empire's history have been unable to walk at pace with a common man." Her almost smile encouraged Nic to continue.

"You should be seen as raising the best and fiercest to stand by your side and sit on your councils. Not the old advisors your mother might have chosen but the unbeatable forces who have faith in you and the more modern, united direction you have chosen to take the empire." Growing in courage, Nic took a step, keeping her hands behind her back. "If there is to be another war, it should be seen as your war for your purposes, not a slipping back into something stale and unfinished. I can fight, so though I may have inferiors who can out-plan me, they could never knock me down." Now, Nic really wanted a weapon, if only to demonstrate something. "You don't want someone beside you who people remember more as Reishann

Sunblessed's old drinking companion, someone promoted to keep them out of a war that injured them." She smiled. "I am not so arrogant to claim the enemy will never harm me, but any future injuries I sustain will be in your name." Overcome by a burst of theatricality that might have embarrassed Litz, Nic knelt, putting all her weight and both hands on one knee.

A small smile that Nic found curiously charming twitched up the corner of Xoia's mouth. "Rise, future General."

Dazed, Nic slowly rose. It seemed that, for now, her life was not in danger.

"The ceremony to induct you will not be as grand as the aborted one for my cousin. We simply don't wish to give anyone anything more to gossip about."

Though Nic nodded dutifully, she felt selfishly that a still larger celebration might be a better way to show they didn't care a whit about gossip. But it seemed a little early to be offering input, even if she wanted to.

"And since you're here, we are discussing how we mean to handle the rumours of her disappearance," Xoia continued in a more muted tone as she moved to take a seat.

Agsdon's eyes never left her face. "She's your only blood cousin. It looks bad that she would stand against you so dramatically. Better to support Minovita's theory: perhaps the terrorist clan enchanted her, turning her against her own people."

Enchanted her? Xoia seemed to consider how ridiculous this sounded. It sounded like something a mother desperate to secure her child's return might suggest. But Litz had been oddly cagey about her victory against the witch assassins sent after her. Perhaps something ridiculous had happened.

"We stick to the line that she's been kidnapped. Those who posed as diplomats were villains sent from King Jevlyn's court to sabotage what matters most to me."

"I don't know that we should run with both," he said, almost sounding like he was trying to chastise his king. "It's either the witches or the Jeenobians. Blaming both may incite a panic that we have found ourselves surrounded."

"All respect," Nic said quietly, tentatively wondering if a general-in-waiting might be more useful than a king consort in these matters. "People think Litz has made a stand against you. What you need to get ahead of is controlling the story. She was travelling home, completely unaccounted for, at the same time Princess Eisha disappeared. Perhaps she orchestrated that."

Xoia pouted, apparently considering this, inviting Nic to continue.

Strange and cruel as it felt, Nic was starting to enjoy herself. "The dragons are against her. They sent the whole forest after her." Growing in confidence, Nic delicately took a seat. "People don't usually require more than knowing that to dislike a person." Smiling even as she remembered hundreds of planning arguments around dragon strategy, she asked, "When are dragons ever wrong?"

Xoia smiled, then looked her slowly up and down as though seeing her for the first time. "Will you give us a moment, Nic?"

"Of course."

A little bemused, she watched Agsdon's frustration turn to real annoyance as she realised it was her expected to leave the room. "Oh." She offered a bow. "Of course," she said before making her retreat out the heavy carved doors. Out in the corridors with only one guard, Nic was briefly seized by strange madness. Should she look for Eisha herself? Succeed where Litz had failed?

But Nic remained still and watched the closed doors. Who did she think she was? And what would that even gain her? An absent friend's respect? A friend who had never respected her enough to be honest with her?

It was a relief when the doors opened again. Now, at least whatever happened was already decided and by someone else. She would no longer be left unobserved.

The royal couple were seated when she walked in, so she had to kneel to bow lower than them. Xoia looked a little awkward but satisfied. Agsdon looked murderous, an interesting combination for those so often of one mind.

"Rise, Nic," Xoia said before asking, "Now that you have accepted your new position, how would you like to double your devotion to the crown by joining Agsdon as my consort?"

Unable to help herself, Nic's eyes flicked to Agsdon. He still looked at her like she was dirt. But Xoia wasn't asking her to be his consort. And a little competition helped make life fun, didn't it? That this was a decision that would not only delight her mother but incense Litz's helped decide her too.

"Your Majesty, I can think of no greater honour."

CHAPTER EIGHTEEN

Nayona was the Jeenobian word for the region, but it didn't really have borders. The area was roamed and farmed by several large nomadic clans with a shared language and mostly shared religious practices, but these clans were all quite different. Some had kings; others were run by councils. Some farmed; some warred with each other. But most, in this newly modern age of peace, had a region they returned to. It didn't matter if a neighbouring kingdom wanted to call that land theirs so long as they were out of it by the time someone else needed it again. This area, far from the slopes of the desert mountains, didn't look like somewhere that could hold a more permanent settlements until the dragons began to fly lower, and Litz better understood how it worked.

Most of the buildings seemed to have been constructed underground, just like the library, and above were large huts expected to last seasons. In the centre of the town was a large building Litz assumed to be a temple, made from the same salt as the flats they'd finally left behind. The way it sparkled in the midday light made it almost difficult to look at.

They hadn't decided how far from town the dragons should land. Though most Nayonan clans weren't known for being explicitly hostile to dragons, they weren't known for making connections with them, either. Besides, if anyone from Aelshia was attempting to follow their trail, it would become far easier if a whole town saw them dismount from dragons with Aelshian saddles.

But landing too far away would give them a hot and potentially dangerous distance to travel. Ker and Kella especially had bitter experiences travelling far from people to meet Ellonya and were both passionate about the dragons not being too far away. But they were also circling each other oddly and sniping at every opportunity. Litz suspected something had happened before they'd left, possibly even before their capture. After being on the receiving end of one of Kella's outraged tirades, she sympathised with Ker.

And such a temper is attractive?

Though Loren could feel how Litz felt without having to ask, even from miles down a dirt path from the town, Litz did not reply. There was plenty they didn't tell each other, mostly because it wasn't important or interesting. But Litz understood. She just needed a little more time to stop her anger from rising up at the indignity of Loren lying to her.

With Litz limping and annoyed, and Kella and Ker not speaking, to Litz's surprise, Evlo began filling in the silence. Though he was usually in conversation with himself, he still managed to come up with enough to keep them going almost to their destination. But it was his jibe that Kella hadn't managed to kill any of the dragons he'd been left to fight that had Ker snapping that he shouldn't be wasting his water ration by drying his mouth out, plunging them back into silence.

Maybe he is picking up something draconic from her, Loren mused.

By the time they reached the town, they all seemed in a worse mood than when they'd set off, but the town certainly sounded in high spirits. There was a loud chanted song with a boisterous drumbeat egging on the singing.

Kella's face became annoyed, but Litz was beginning to think that a mask for nerves.

"Let me check," Ker said quietly, and though Kella still frowned, she nodded, and he went on ahead and got drinks from a pineapple juice stand. As he picked up a couple of bottles, he spoke to the person behind the stall. At first, it seemed like they couldn't understand, then the man laughed and mimed being stabbed. Ker looked alarmed and quick to dissuade this impression, but the man only laughed, mimed playing the drums, and pointed in the direction of the music.

Quietly, Kella gave a groan that sounded as low and dangerous as a growl while they watched Ker confirm where he was going. As he joined them again, he put one drink in Evlo's hand and opened the other for himself.

"The singer? Really?"

Ker shrugged his shoulders to his ears. "Always a bard, I guess."

Though Kella looked as though she wanted to find something else to say or do that might delay their walking to the player, she said nothing, and slowly, they began following the music.

It was a song about their mother, Litz realised. Pieces of the chorus were in Jeenobian, but the rest of the tune was in Nayonan. It had elongated vowels and less grit, well suited to singing. The singer hardly had the best voice, but he sang with energy, and his hands slapped so fast and confidently at the trio of drums fastened to his waist that she could barely see them. He wore nothing on his top half, a common wrap skirt and sandals, and a bright smile that reminded Litz of Kella at her most performatively charming. As his wide mouth raised at the corners, his eyes widened, eyebrows up toward his receding hairline in delight. This was a song he loved especially, or so he would have his small audience believe.

"Kira, Kira, dragon slaying he-rah, save us now, save us, from the pain and fear ah-ve; Dragonfire! Dragonfire!"

Though the rhymes seemed poor, and as far as Litz knew, there wasn't much of a dragon-slaying tradition in Nayona, the children nearest to him joyfully took up the chant and danced to it.

Litz was about to ask Kella what she thought of the rhyme when she noticed Ker's face warning her from it. Kella looked nauseated. "Maybe we should move on. Or interrupt," Litz added, as they continued to stand a few metres back from the group of mostly children. This wasn't like the puppet show, and Litz wondered if that was because of the performer or subject.

"Kel?" Ker asked.

Litz checked over her shoulder to confirm that Evlo looked just as confused as she felt.

Kella swallowed. "Yeah, I can't do this," she said, starting to walk away, ignoring Ker's attempt to catch her arm.

"I'm going to talk to him."

She laughed cruelly. "Hey, far be it for me to stop you doing what you want. I'll get the big girls some lunch." Litz was about to ask if she wanted company, but Kella was getting too far ahead, and it seemed pathetic to chase her.

Ker shook his head bitterly as he watched Kella's retreat. He muttered some words in too thick a Malyan accent for Litz to understand, but she suspected the sentiment was not kind, and the words were meant to be in imitation of his sister.

"What," Evlo started as behind them, the player came to the end of his set.

He kept his smile fixed as a few of the children began throwing coins and held one woman's hand charmingly, as though that was gift enough. When she moved away with some reluctance, Ker moved in.

"Hello," he said in uncertain Nayonan. The musician laughed and jiggled his hat. Frowning, Ker put in a coin as the man said, "Relax, kid, my Jeenobian's rusty, but it's better than my singing. You needing directions?"

"I'm looking for Ijnocius denFalian."

His face brightened. "Ijnocius denFali*ahn*."

"Okay," Ker said, his face relaxing an inch, but if possible, looking more nervous. "I think you knew my mother."

DenFalian seemed uncomfortable and ready to run. "I knew a lot of people's mothers during my time in Jeenobi."

"You'd remember this one," Ker insisted coldly. "You were just singing about her."

The man's eyes skittered over them, landing briefly on Litz. "Not her," he said cautiously, looking to Ker for confirmation. "The other girl who was with you."

Ker nodded as denFalian gave a sigh that rattled his whole body, making him look very small and skinny. It would be Kella's frame, Litz realised, had she not spent her entire life honing herself into a weapon.

"Is she ashamed of me?" He was probably trying to phrase it as a joke, but that made it fall still flatter.

"I've no idea," Ker said without sympathy. "But we need help. Some food, a bed for the night, someplace they won't remember our faces. One of us is injured."

He nodded, still rattled but not apparently overwhelmed. "Okay, all right, I can get you those. Anything for…" He gave a furtive glance up, as though worried Ker was about to hit him. "For family."

"Thank you," Ker told him and shook his hand over the drum set. The man's smile this close flashed a few gold teeth. "It wasn't my sister's idea to come here," he added.

The man still looked distracted, staring behind Ker's shoulder where Kella had walked away. "Of course, of course."

"I'm Ker. This is Litz and Evlo."

"Good to meet you. Family, and that'll be you, can call me Noshi. Anything you need or need to know about my town, you ask me." The way his tone, now much recovered, proudly pronounced "my town" made Litz vividly remember meeting Kella for the first time. When she'd shown her around Malya as though it was a tamed animal on a leash performing tricks because she asked.

Do dragons take from their parents?

Less than humans. Look at Ellonya. She doesn't remember hers and had no elders to help her through life. But everyone steals little pieces from the people they love, even if they don't keep pieces of their soul in the same way.

But Kella didn't grow up knowing him.

Loren mentally shrugged. *But she grew up with those who did. Absence can craft a role to fill often better than willing imitation.*

I suppose.

"My sister's husband runs most things around here. I'm sure she'd be happy saying what's hers is yours," he said.

Having been catered to for most of her life, Litz had no place for judgement, but she suspected this claim came from a person assuming the hard work of hosting would be handled by someone else.

"Let me take you to her." He gave a nervous glance at the horizon Kella had disappeared into before looking at Ker. "And…"

Ker kept his voice calm. "When we get settled, I'll find her. I'm sure she's anxious to meet you."

❖

It was amazing. Even far from home, where she couldn't speak the language, Kella found herself in a crowd. In the same way that Ker's da could have a good conversation with someone he met at the market and know about their crumbling marriage within an hour, Kella had a sort of magnetism. It was less that people interested her, but that she knew how to make herself interesting. Though she might not draw stories from people, they expected her to make a story of the world. Sensing spectacle would follow wherever she walked, their eyes followed her, often in spite of themselves.

For Ker, it wasn't hard to work out what today's spectacle involved. The underground bar, the stare Kella was giving the man across the table, the satisfied way she slammed her empty glass upside down. She was locked in a drinking game, and unless she'd dropped wildly in tolerance, she was winning.

She leaned back, brimming with kingly overconfidence. "What haven't we had yet?" she asked, surely knowing her words wouldn't be understood by her audience.

Her opponent leaned forward and grabbed her chin, pointing it toward the top corner of the bar where a smaller clay bottle shaped like a skull sat at the end.

Kella nodded. "Get me some of that, I guess." And she threw up her hands as if trying to indicate willingness, deftly throwing off the hand.

It was hard to tell what the rules were. The crowd seemed interested in getting Kella drunk for one purpose or another. She seemed mostly interested in working her way through every exotic drink behind the bar. Ker was only sure they were competing because Kella had that look in her eye: she had no intention of losing.

Someone came over with four small cups. Finally, Kella seemed to notice Ker but did nothing more than narrow her eyes before picking up a little cup in each hand and raising one higher. "This first?"

The man who'd provided the drinks pointed at the other. Shrugging, Kella downed that before coughing briefly and trying to do the same to the other, but it didn't seem to be liquid.

They were strange about gender separation in Nayona, Ker knew. Women were held up as important in their society, but their skills seemingly lay elsewhere than the pre-decided masculine arts. This, Ker suspected, was what was making Kella such a spectacle today. And perhaps what had made their mami so appealing to a young bard from the area travelling far from home for the first time. She'd not only been a hero with a story but a woman unlike any he had ever gotten to know before.

And they were all men in this bar, from what Ker could see. Men who seemed charmed by Kella as an exotic curiosity, like a bird that had flown in, but the moment it made a noise or a mess, their goodwill would end. The display of her biting the worm in the second cup with glee only inspired mild support. Ker felt like this ought to be the moment he pulled her away. Her novelty was beginning to twist into a threat and an oddity. But he'd be godsdamned before he pulled her away himself. Not after their argument in Verassez.

There were just five years between them, and they'd spent their entire lives working beside each other and shared little in common in their approach to life. They'd fought before. They'd fought often, and through several periods of their lives, viciously.

But he'd never spoken to her like that before. They'd finally toppled off the precipice they'd been tiptoeing around since he'd rescued her, and only sheer distraction was keeping either from screaming about it.

Speak to her. Make it right.

What can I say? I don't want to apologise.

Perhaps say that. But saying nothing is eating our minds from the inside, and I suspect she fares no better. Worse, there is no one to share that burden.

Is she right? Ker asked, annoyed at himself for thinking it but unable, as always, to hide anything from Ellonya. The little that had once stood between their minds was barely there anymore, and there were no secrets left in him. He felt Ellonya looking at Kella using his eyes, an active participation she rarely took.

I don't think so, she said, *though she cares about you, and that's still where her concerns come from. She worries to see you changing. She worries that she can't protect you anymore.*

She doesn't need to.

Yes, and that probably scares her even more.

Lips curling, Ker made his decision to meet recklessness with recklessness and Pushed all the cups off the table.

Kella's opponent gripped his chair sides. "*Verhnani*," he said with great certainty. Thanks to Zebenn, Ker knew the word meant ghost or demon.

Kella looked at Ker before sighing heavily. "It's not a ghost. It's a wet table." To emphasise her point, she moved a finger through the spilled liquid between their cups.

He looked murderous. "Verhnani," he repeated as he got to his feet.

Ker rolled his eyes and flicked his wrist within his pocket. He focused his Push against the table tipping over. Drinking and unexpected movements weren't ever good mixes, and when the table clattered to the floor, it soon became clear that no one was willing to risk seeing things escalate. Within minutes, only Ker and Kella were left staring at each other with an older man a few tables over who appeared to be blind.

"Drink?" Ker asked her.

She crossed one leg at a wide angle over her knee and raised her hands to sign, "Sure," apparently still too annoyed to use her voice. Though her mouth quirked up as it would when she was teasing, her eyes were oddly flat. He'd never seen her look so shutdown, at least not toward him.

Remember, she's changed too.

And that was the problem, wasn't it? Here he was, bringing them to Noshi and forcing her to change again, but he didn't want her to. He went to the bar and ordered two more drinks. Though they cost him much more than seemed fair, he wasn't about to stretch his grip on the language enough to haggle when the bartender was willing to take the coins he had. When he got back, Kella had wandered, and he had to chase her to another table.

He wanted to bring up Ijnocius and address why Kella was hiding from him, but when he opened his mouth, what came out instead was, "I'm sorry I yelled at you."

He hadn't intended to give an apology and hadn't felt like she was waiting on one. But when she didn't respond, he tapped his ear with two fingers in annoyance. They might never have done apologies since growing past the size where his da could threaten to bash their heads together until they did, but surely, she had something to be sorry for too?

"It was good yelling," she said, forgiving him instead. "Did you yell at him for me?"

"What would you want me to yell?"

"I don't know. He knows I'm here, right?"

"In town, sure. I played the family card."

"That's only good if it gets us somewhere."

"He had a few people throwing him coins. He's tolerated around here. Apparently, his sister's important. He put us up with her."

Kella snorted. "Y'know, the only reason Findan told me who he was was so I wouldn't think it was Hallen—"

"Trailfeet, yeah, I know." Ker tried cautiously for a smile. "I'm sorry I made you do this."

"It was the smart thing to do."

Funny how that still meant something. "Did you ever wanna see him?"

Carefully, she slid her cup across the table between her hands. Ker worried that with one more drink in her, she might start tossing it back and forth like a child with a ball. "Sure," she said eventually. "I thought about it. I sort of always…" She trailed off. "I always assumed he'd come find me. Like, not in a looking for his kid way, but in a, oh, my whole deal is making up songs and stories about heroes. I don't know this big hero over there, but she sounds cool. I should go find out her story."

"But then you stopped killing dragons."

"I stopped being a hero, and I'll never know if he thought I was worth coming to look for," she said, taking another long drink. "It was stupid."

"Maybe. But now you're here, and you should—"

She laughed. "I've not got anything impressive left to show or tell. Litz gave up her whole life for me, and I can't even look her in the eye."

"Maybe he doesn't need you to be impressive."

"Yeah, but I needed me to be that," she mumbled into her cup before biting the rim.

"Why can't you talk to Litz? You made us go and get her—"

Kella's loud groan cut him off. "I know, I know."

"You don't normally hesitate about this kinda stuff. Did Jev just really fuck you up, or is Litz different?"

"She's not," Kella said before pausing. "And not everything's about Jev, all right? I don't know. We had a whole moment, a whole series of moments back there in the desert. Then, she goes back to her nice life and probably fucking her hot ex or friend or colleague or whatever and getting promoted and dealing with her own shit. And not in danger."

"Well, sure, but she gave all that up for you."

"And that's fucking terrifying, thank you for reminding me again." She drained her drink, impressing him, who hadn't been able to touch his after the first sip. "She was staying where she was to find her cousin.

She picked my life and my dumb plan over her cousin's life. How am I supposed to look at her after that?"

"I don't think it's dumb."

"Don't lie."

"I don't. Well."

"You do," she insisted, the drunkenness becoming plainer.

"I don't think it's sensible. But sensible is not gonna fix anything."

"Huh."

"Yeah," he said, warming to his thought.

"When did you get so wise?"

"Are you saying I wasn't before?"

"Uh-uh, no trapping me like that," she warned, turning to face him better and making him worry she was going to topple. No, she definitely wouldn't be talking this easily if she hadn't drunk so much, probably half of why she'd done so. "When did you get start giving out life advice? You haven't even noticed Evlo's into you yet."

"Don't be stupid."

"See? Not noticed yet."

He scoffed and shook his head, not wanting to show his hesitance to dismiss her words. It wouldn't be the first time she'd been forced to point out someone had taken an interest in him without his awareness. "He's not."

"I'm not saying I know for sure," she said, already sounding happier to have moved away from her own life. "He looks to you, he always has since you brought him home."

"He's always hated me."

"Same difference. He's looking, isn't he?"

"Ha."

"What I can't work out is what you feel. You don't do the voice blend thing around him, have you noticed?"

He frowned. "You sure?"

"Pretty sure. I wondered if it was cause you and Ellonya don't think about him the same."

Almost afraid to check, Ker found no clearer an idea of this from Ellonya, so he decided to continue ignoring the possibility for now. Besides, it was ridiculous. Evlo could have anyone, regularly enjoyed making it clear he did, and surely was aware that Ker wasn't interested in anyone. Surely. "Are you ready to stop hiding now?"

Blowing air out of the side of her mouth, Kella got unsteadily to her feet. "Sure. I could be drunk enough to meet my da."

"So that was what this was about."

"It's a heroic deed to report. I might not slay dragons, but I can still beat all the men in his village at drinking."

He smiled and followed her lead. They weren't back to normal yet, and maybe normal was gone. But when Kella stumbled up the steps out of the bar, she gripped Ker's sleeve tight and didn't try to pull away when he supported her. "You didn't, by the way," he admitted, despite the fact that he'd promised himself that he wouldn't be the first to say something nice when she still hadn't bothered to apologise back, but he could feel Ellonya wanting him to.

"Didn't what?"

"Didn't stop being a hero."

Her response was obnoxious as it was immediate. "Aw," she said loudly, reaching one hand that couldn't quite reach to ruffle his hair. "You care about me. I'm your hero."

"Gods, your breath stinks."

"That's a hero's breath you're insulting, kid."

CHAPTER NINETEEN

K ella hadn't been lying: she hadn't thought much about meeting her father in an ordinary sense. But she had hoped it might last a little longer than an awkward shoulder tap, bobbed head, and him running away the moment he could find an opportunity.

But if she hadn't thought much about meeting Noshi, she'd barely spared any thoughts for his wider family. There were a few stilted introductions, too few of them spoken in a common language, but there were tight, firm embraces, and a stern, fond review of her. Drunk and starving as she was, it was more than a little overwhelming. There seemed to be a lot of pointing out features she shared with Noshi and with all of them: she had their ears, when she was nervous, she jutted her chin out, and that seemed familiar and amusing to them. But what upset them most was not that she had been kept from them all these years, or that she was "skinny as a fishbone," but that her hair had been tightly coiled in a protective style they now felt the need to unwind. After they'd ushered her outside to see to the food with them, she'd taken off her headscarf, feeling it too tight around her spinning head, and they'd caught a glimpse of her hair. They all had long, thick hair kept fairly straight, despite its firmness, in long plaits, and the short, coiled nubs of hair she'd been carefully and then not so carefully growing since she'd shaved her head seemed particularly offensive to them. Together, they mimed a promise to make it grow long and beautiful for her. She suspected they were also trying to tell her this would help catch her a good husband, and her smile became a little strained, but she continued to indulge them. It was nice to be looked after for a moment.

Ballian had always done her hair. It wasn't that Kella didn't think her mami wasn't able, more that she was always busy, always needed somewhere else. Findan was more likely. Having multiple female hands attending to her like this was too much, and she had to fight to keep her expression neutral, unsure of the most appropriate to have on show. They couldn't speak to her, but they shared pieces of her face. They didn't seem concerned with where she'd come from or where she was going, only that while she was under their care, she was treated as family. And family meant fixing what they deemed wrong with her.

One of them—her oldest cousin by this aunt whose home it was, she was pretty sure—had a little Jeenobian. She clicked her tongue as she was oiling and twirling Kella's hair and said, "He always comes back." She could only assume she was talking about Noshi. Other than Ker, Evlo, and a handful of children, Kella hadn't noticed any other men here. If this town was assumed to belong to her aunt's husband, this house was for her and other women she chose to keep beside her.

He always comes back. Did they mean today, after he'd basically fled from her? Or in general? From what Kella understand of most Nayonan clans, homecoming was critically important. If a person was not put to rest where their family was, their soul would be forever unmoored. Kella remembered finding it a funny idea when Zebenn had explained it to her. Surely, the earth remained the earth wherever someone wandered. And though women weren't necessarily seen as equal to men here, they were seen as the centre of family and home. Noshi was able to wander, never keeping his own home because his mother and oldest sister's home, and there were other sisters here, was where he would return, like a juvenile lion still sheltering with his mother's pride.

She should get to Ker's hair and beard; he'd never had much ability to do his own. They were probably ready to be normal around each other again. But since he'd fetched her back, she hadn't seen much of him or Evlo.

She caught Litz smiling at her from the door, but Kella looked away, preferring to feel the smoke in her eyes rather than look at her. Eisha had been the one to help with Litz's hair, with her style. Kella had forced Litz to give up on her, and for what? To watch Kella be tended to by the wider family she'd never even wondered about? It made her want to wriggle out of the careful grip of the women towering over her, but since she didn't think she'd be allowed to, she kept her eyes averted and watering as the smoke from the roasting calf began to sting.

An hour or two of this and the calf still wasn't finished cooking, and Noshi still wasn't home. But Kella had at least finally been released to occasionally run her fingers over her newly braided softened and oiled hair. And she was given a new task that someone placed in her arms without even attempting an explanation or introduction that made her feel less guilty about not helping with the cooking at all.

She hadn't ever had much to do with babies, though she had vague memories of Ker being one and helping with him. Still not entirely sober, the smallness of this baby terrified her, and she suspected that showed on her face. But either she didn't look like someone who would drop a baby, or they didn't care if she did. She held tight. This was her cousin. She'd never had a cousin before. Or maybe they wouldn't say cousin, considering this was her cousin's child. There was probably a word for that.

Her baby second cousin, who couldn't be six months old yet, seemed to scream less when Kella was moving.

"It likes you," Litz remarked.

Kella grunted. She hadn't realised Litz was watching. "It's she. And she likes being moved. Here," she added, spitefully sensing from the "it" that Litz had even less experience with babies than she did. She might be important in Aelshia, but it wasn't likely anyone would treat her as a good luck bringer and ask her to kiss their babies.

Litz took the baby but looked utterly perplexed about what to do next.

"Bounce her," Kella ordered with a smile, as if she knew what she was talking about.

Though she narrowed her eyes as if seeing right through her, Litz obliged and kept moving. Now that she had shed her uniform, her breasts bounced along with her, and Kella had to look away lest she catch herself staring.

She looked at the sunset instead, her hands on her hips, and felt homesick for watching the sun kiss the sea, the correct way to end the day. But she'd see that again if they didn't delay here. Part of her could admit that she wanted to. Or more, she wanted to want to stay. Knowing her cousins and family felt like something to want.

Litz seemed to sense her thoughts and moved with her. "Where next? The port?" Because she was putting that on Kella. The almost commander of the Aelshian army had chosen to leave her own family and life and career to follow some nobody Jeenobian exile, so Kella had to have the answer.

She shook her head. "Too busy. And too legal. If anyone's going to help us with the dragons, never mind two of them, we're going to need big ships that don't care about what they carry so long as they're paid." She smiled, unable to keep her excitement in. "Pirates. We're going to need pirates."

Litz did not seem suitably impressed. "But we don't have money to pay them. We might be able to barter the jewellery I was wearing, I suppose."

"What about the dragon scales or nails or something like that," Kella finished weakly, her suggestion rapidly losing steam under the force of Litz's horrified glare. "Hey, if I had any hair left to sell or toenails I thought anyone would pay for, they'd be gone already."

Litz looked unconvinced. "I suppose we could ask. Ellonya's fine with it?"

"Extremely fine."

"You've done this before?"

"A couple of times." A month. Ellonya far preferred it to them reducing her treasure, and she was charitable, as talking dragons went.

Litz continued bouncing the baby but looked suspiciously like she could understand exactly what Kella wasn't saying. Kella was trying not to let the judgement of a woman who'd grown up in a palace get to her. "I don't see why we couldn't just take a ship," Litz said with a shrug as she continued to move for the baby.

"What, you want to steal a pirate ship?"

Litz seemed unfazed. "Isn't that what they're always doing to other people's things? We have two dragons, like you say. If we wanted, I imagine we could hold a port town to ransom."

And again, Kella remembered she was talking to not just a soldier but a high-ranking officer of the Aelshian army, whose years of service had mostly been about burning armies alive. "Great, the military option again. Innocent scale reuse, bad. Maiming and killing innocent people, fine."

"Well, pirates. And I didn't say killing. I said threaten," Litz said, her voice drifting into a slower, more pronounced tone for the baby's sake, who seemed to have just realised someone new was holding her. "No one said anything about maiming and killing. Did we? No, we didn't."

Despite herself, Kella was helplessly charmed. She huffed, doing her best to cover that. "I suppose I should have realised you'd treat my fun adventure to save the world like any other campaign."

Litz dragged her eyes away from the baby. "Your mother was military too, wasn't she?"

Startled by the change, Kella retreated to the wall behind Litz for stability. "She was," she said slowly. "People don't tend to remember."

Picking up on the question in her voice, Litz nodded. "Ker mentioned it."

"She deserted before she killed her first dragon. Findan was there for that. That's how they met."

"Who was Findan?" Litz pouted, pretty as she always was when thinking and not just talking with Loren. They were very different expressions. "Your mother's wife? I know you have your stepfather, but—"

Kella shook her head, feeling uncomfortable with the direction of this discussion but not inclined to end it. Much as she might have been avoiding it, it felt good to talk to Litz casually, the way she'd been longing to for so long. If it wasn't for the painful subject matter and the fact that Litz was there at all, Kella would have been having a lovely time. "Findan wasn't her wife." She frowned. "I'm not sure what they were. But they did what they did together from the start."

"And she's the one who taught Ker magic?"

"He's been chatty, heh?" It was ridiculous to feel jealousy spike in her at that. It was nice that everyone was getting along. If she wanted to pretend she was leading this little group, she should be encouraging that. "Yeah, that's her. She probably never thought I'd have the knack."

Litz looked thoughtful. "Or that you'd be too hard to control."

"What?"

"Well, she was the leader, wasn't she? She had to have been thinking all the time about how to maximise everyone's skills and dynamics. And you're as obstinate as you are impulsive."

"Wow, thanks."

Litz smiled at the baby, and there was so much bright fondness emanating from her face, Kella found it odd the baby wasn't lit by it. "You're also brave, principled, and decisive, and you do whatever you do to help people, and it doesn't matter to you if that's the decision that best suits someone else's plan. If I were her, I would not want to see you with any abilities that ultimately come from willpower."

Unexpectedly moved, Kella bowed her head farther into the shade. "Joke's on her. Ker turned out to be the real rebel."

"None of us are what anyone expected us to be. I think that makes us all rebels."

Kella snorted. "Sure. We ran away from your family to hide behind my da."

"I wonder how he'd feel to hear you call him that."

"Don't tell him."

Litz smiled, and the knowingness of it was so sharp, Kella wanted to squirm away, but she kept her gaze steady. Luckily, distraction arrived that kept Kella from having to think about the father Litz might never see again because of her.

Her own father walked toward the home in loud conversation with someone who seemed to be another man, but as they came closer, Kella became less sure of that. Their grubby appearance was of a traveller who'd been on the road for days but who still managed to be clean-shaven, and they looked to be around Noshi's age. She would wait for them speak before making a guess.

Litz also turned at the sound of Noshi clapping a hand loudly on his friend's back and laughing. "He makes friends easily. Like you," she noted.

Kella, who had no friends waiting for her in Malya except maybe Jev, wrinkled her nose and moved toward them, letting her arms hang loose and awkward at her sides.

"Wallin, meet my only daughter," Noshi said generously in Jeenobian as he gestured at her. There was none of his earlier awkwardness. Kella suspected he was several drinks in.

His friend smiled. "Not only, surely," they said in Jeenobian with less of an accent. "Give it time for them all to track you down. What's your name, zebu?"

Unsure about receiving pet names from strangers, especially ones calling her cattle, Kella did her best not to become overly defensive. "Kella," she said. "Well met, Wallin."

They nodded. They seemed to notice how her gaze wandered from their smooth neck, free of a buried peach, and the outfit that seemed masculine. Her guess was Wallin was a man, whether by birth or preference or convenience, but she wouldn't risk using pronouns yet. They seemed to enjoy her hesitation. "You're the ones from Jeenobi?" They glanced at Litz, who was at least a head taller than everyone and still wearing her earrings.

"I'm not," she confirmed, still rocking the baby.

"Well, I have news of the kingdom that should be interesting to at least some of you." They smiled wryly at Noshi. "If I put it to song and drum, would your sister take it as an exchange for bed and board?"

"My sister has a famously giving nature and will grant you those for nothing," Noshi boasted.

Kella crossed her arms. "What's happening in Jeenobi?" She'd spent so long thinking of Aelshian politics and warmongering, she had scarcely spared a thought for her home country's politics and warmongering.

Wallin smiled roguishly. "Since I suspect that will be what secures my place to sleep tonight, you'll have to hear about it later, lass. But I can tell you that your king is up to something his mother would not have been happy with."

The baby started wailing. Litz must have finally stopped moving, but Kella was too engrossed to check. "The king?" Her mouth felt dry. *I have your back,* was what she'd wanted to say before she'd left him, but she hadn't. Because she was still mad at him, and because functionally, she didn't. She'd been about to leave him behind, alone in his palace, for however long it took to get the mission she'd set herself done.

"*He's listenin' to witches*," the chorus line went, drummed out over a dinner far more begrudgingly shared than Noshi had advertised. It was too unbelievable a tale to make a good song, but Kella was gripped anyway and could not look away from Wallin's hands patting lightly at the centre of the taut skin. To solve the dragon problem, Jev was going to use a witch to help take down the dragons or train them into submission. He was gathering them somehow, and he planned to fix them, to turn them into weapons. But what witches did Jev know? Findan? She had implied she wanted to try something different and drastic.

Maybe it didn't matter.

Jev was in danger, Kella was sure of that much. And it was his own fault, but it was very much hers too for abandoning him and not just him. This could put so many people in danger. And somehow, this felt more barbaric than killing dragons. This was enslaving them; if it worked and didn't just get Malya set on fire. Was it a show of strength for the Aelshians? Was this about to lead to war, the thing he'd done everything to avoid, even almost have Kella killed? Peace had to be a principle he stood by because if it wasn't, what was she?

Startling her assembled new family, Kella stood. "I'm sorry," was what she meant to say, but, "I'm sick of our lives being songs," was what she heard herself mutter as she walked out.

And didn't it sting? Jev couldn't trust that she was going away to fix everything. He had to have a crisis of conscience and faith and put his whole city at risk because he couldn't stand that everyone hated him now. But Kella could sympathise. Hadn't she also just run away instead of handling that feeling he'd had to bear alone for near on a year?

And if it wasn't Findan helping him, then who? He'd told her about his adoption, supposedly his biggest secret, but he'd also insisted so many times that there was no hidden superpowerful witch in the maze like all the songs said there was.

Songs again. Obviously, that was what she'd get more of in a bard's house.

It had always sounded romantic but felt grotesque knowing that the man who'd written all the most famous, grandiose, overly simplified anthems about her mother had helped create her. Truly, she was a child of myth and song, something that wasn't supposed to exist outside of the heroic actions she was no longer involved in. But even thinking something so self-pitying made her want to slap herself.

"Kella?"

Turning, expecting to see Ker out of sheer lifetime habit, Kella released a long breath when she saw Litz, who was putting a rough hand on her shoulder like it was meant to fit there and as if that would fix anything. She was outside and not breathing right, and Litz had followed to make sure she was okay because that was most of what Litz did nowadays. Kella had come crashing into her life and left her with no other choice.

"You're worried about him," Litz said, listing one more fact that had slipped in importance since her arrival outside.

"Well reasoned, Princess."

"Don't do that."

"What?"

"I'm checking on you. Don't be annoyed at me."

"Who said I was?"

"You call me princess when you're annoyed."

Or flirting, Kella finished in her head but didn't say. "Oh, I get it," she said instead. "You ruined your life to save mine, and now I'm not allowed to stop smiling at you ever."

"You know I was thinking of leaving, even if everything hadn't happened like it did," Litz said, having the gall to sound surprised as she tipped her head the way Kella wished she didn't adore. "You didn't ruin my life. If it's ruined, I did that. And I don't think it is."

Kella gritted her teeth. "We weren't going to give you the option. We were just going to leave. You weren't supposed to come with us. I tried to leave without you." She didn't realise she was shouting until a chicken in the background squawked and fluttered loudly away from her.

She took another deep breath, refusing to look at Litz and any hurt that might be etched on her lovely features, the rage that should have been there. Then, she walked away again, and this time, Litz let her go. She wasn't sure where she was going. She didn't know this place, so didn't want to wander too far, especially since she had the impression her aunt's husband wasn't supposed to know they were there. Storming away from friends and family wasn't who she was. Her place was in the middle, holding everyone together in as good spirits as she could keep them. But something about the events of the last year and Litz specifically had her thrown off her normal rhythms, her normal personality.

Where would moody, ungrateful people go to sulk?

In the end, she found herself by the chicken coop. There was a rooster stalking around, waiting for one of the hens to take notice of him, so far to no avail. Kella sat on the stone edge of the well and watched, remembering a simpler time she'd made Jev laugh by calling a dragon they'd been fighting a "chicken-brain." He'd been hard to get laughing until she'd gotten the knack down. She wondered if there was anyone left around him who was managing that or even trying to. They'd both tried so hard to fight their way out of their mothers' shadows, but it had only succeeded in pushing away the person who was, functionally, their only good friend. Though, had she? He'd ended his mother's war and nearly been the end of her life because she was so determined to uphold her mother's legacy to the end.

It took a moment to realise Noshi was approaching. He moved quietly without his instruments. He sat beside her silently too. Kella wondered if Nayona had any strangeness about conversation like Aelshians did. Maybe she was supposed to speak first when addressing her elders, or maybe it was flipped.

He broke the silence by clicking his tongue, sounding for a moment like one of the chickens. "Can I sing you something?" When Kella didn't answer, he looked apologetic. "I always used to do that for the nieces and nephews when they were upset."

Unable to argue that she wasn't upset, Kella said, "I'm not interested in hearing another song about my mami."

"I do other songs. Plenty of other songs."

"Hmm."

"I write a lot of fun ones for the kids to play. I got older and mostly wanted to make people smile."

"Tired of chasing fame by proxy, huh?"

"Yes," he said simply. "I've enjoyed my life, but I'm not sure I found what I was looking for in all that. I felt a stronger sense of pride knowing I had songs being imitated than in knowing I had a child out there worth singing about."

Kella was surprised to feel a stab of hurt at that.

"Her death really gutted me," he continued, apparently not noticing this was not in the least comforting. "There was no more possibility I could wheedle my way back into her life."

"Except me."

He dismissed this with the shake of raised, skinny hand. "Oh, I never could have presumed you mine."

"But you did know."

"I made assumptions. Never could imagine her a mother, though. Insane, ridiculous woman. I always told her she'd make a terrifying mother."

Slowly, Kella began to pull her knife from her belt.

"Was I wrong? Honestly, even the notion of her carrying life inside her unnerved me. There was always something too hard about her. But when I heard about her death, I could see it clearly for the first time: a lioness defending her injured cub."

Kella slid the knife back into its little sheathe, even if the excited look in his eye at the idea of the grand story made her want to use it still. "She wasn't like that," she said gruffly, not really knowing what she meant but incapable of staying silent any longer.

He smiled, a little surprised. "Oh, I know. That was part of why I didn't want to meet you, or, sorry, why I was afraid to meet you one day."

"Afraid?"

"I didn't want to hear stories about what she went on to become, whether or not that was good or bad. And every girl hates their mother a little, don't they?"

Kella had no answer to that, having never internalised that as an option.

"So my sisters would have me believe. And our mother could have been one of your Jeenobian sollons, she was so good." He smiled sadly and watched the chickens. "I wanted to keep loving and worshipping the woman I remembered, the hero I remembered. We get so fond of certainties, don't we?" he added, speaking quicker as he warmed to his topic. "Your mother used to throw a shoe at me every time I started playing a song about her, and she had damn near-perfect aim, but I used to play anyway, even knowing she would hit me."

"Maybe she wanted you to play something else."

"Maybe. Did she ever throw shoes at Ker's father?"

"Not that I saw. He never did anything to deserve it."

He cawed a laugh. "Wonderful. She always did have good taste in men. Less so in women. Whatever happened to Findan?"

"She still does what she does."

"How was she with you? Did she worry you would turn out like me, or did she love you for being Kira's?"

Kella decided not to dwell much on this question. "Little of both, I guess."

"That sounds like her. A complicated woman," he said with the tone of someone cleaning up after one of the crying babies they'd left indoors. Kella smiled, understanding how well they wouldn't have gotten along. "Is it her involved in all this, do you think?"

"Why? You want to write a song about her too?"

"Not for all the beasts of the earth, no," he said with an easy laugh. "Fin, if she is still as I remember her, is not the kind songs are written about. I have to assume she likes it that way."

Smiling, Kella felt pride and a little homesickness warm and nauseate her. "She's family."

"Like the king?" He looked painfully awkward but like he was enjoying himself a little more. "Aren't you supposed to be his secret mistress?"

"Ha. He wishes."

His voice softened, becoming almost fatherly. "So why does learning about his new decision hurt you?"

"Because he is family. And he's supposed to be my friend," she said slowly. "And because we used to think the same way about everything. And I'm not sure we can anymore," she said, realising it was more honest than all her worries for the dragons and Malya's population. She didn't like that Jev was making decisions that were incomprehensible to her. Even when he'd gotten married and sent her off to die, she hadn't been confused.

"But I'm assuming you don't have a problem with witches. Not if you grew up with Fin. So this is about his attempt to control the dragons. You don't think it can work? You want all dragons to die?" His tone was shifting in a manner Kella couldn't stand. He was too interested in what the story was. She felt as though she was being interviewed.

It made her want to do something really stupid, like upend his expectations completely. "Actually," she said, "I'm good with dragons now. Ker and Litz are both dragonriders. That's how we got here. Their dragons are about a half mile outside of town." She smiled unkindly. "Would you like to meet them before we leave?"

She had a perverse hope that this would be the end of it. That Noshi's affable face would turn cruel and disgusted, that he would tell her how much her mother would be too distraught by her actions to ever make a return to earth as someone else. That he wanted nothing to do with her as a daughter or someone worth writing songs about.

But apparently, Noshi also had no interest in conforming to her expectations. "Can I?" he asked, excited as a child at his first festival.

Kella didn't have the heart to deny him.

❖

Litz wasn't sure how to act walking back from speaking to Kella. She passed Noshi, and uncertain whether to warn him or wish him well, she did nothing but nod. Perhaps he wasn't even aiming to comfort Kella at all.

She found Ker outside the house. He was speaking to Ellonya, she suspected, but when he saw her approach, he smiled faintly. "Wallin's in there trying to get Evlo to teach him some Senician songs and tales. He hates doing that, so this could get interesting."

"And Sallvayn?"

Ker's lips turned comically down. He hadn't noticed they were gone. "They like to wander," he said eventually. "They'll be back." He leaned against the wall as Kella had just a few hours ago, with one foot up. "They don't like talking about a lot, either. But I think they go looking for gremlins. At first, I thought they just liked to hide at home, but now, I'm not sure there're many left. They think if we can bring the dragons back, it will save the gremlins."

Gently, Litz nudged at Loren with her mind.

Nayona is an unknown area for gremlins, Loren told her. *They mirror us, depend on us. It would make sense those here have declined as the dragons have, but I'm not sure.*

How long do gremlins live?

I'm not sure. Longer than humans, shorter than dragons.

That's a wide margin.

Why don't you ask a gremlin?

"It would be interesting to speak to a gremlin from around here. Or a dragon," Litz mused, finally remembering to speak aloud.

Ker looked distracted, likely still involved in his own internal conversation. "Hmm."

"Is it true? The king of Jeenobi keeps a witch in the walls?"

"Not that he ever said."

That must be why Kella is so upset and worried.

But not why she has to take that upset out on you, who left much greater worries at home.

"I don't know what he's trying to do," Ker said slowly. She suspected he was trying to address Ellonya simultaneously. "But I don't think he should have to figure it out alone. He's fucked up a lot, but he doesn't deserve that, and neither does the kingdom if it all goes wrong." Carefully, he tapped his fingers against the wall, more of a tremor than a tic. "We're out here, Ellonya especially, to help the dragons in Jeenobi. Something much stranger is about to start happening to them, and we're only moving farther away from them."

Litz crossed her arms and took a step toward him. "You want to go back," she realised.

He nodded hesitantly, looking very young. "It feels wrong to run away from it. Those are the people we're trying to help, and he was my friend. Kella wants to, but she won't. She'll just get grumpy and resentful and drunk. But if I go, she'll be so mad."

"It sounds like it would help some things," Litz said slowly, leaning next to him.

He looked pained but also like he'd found her words amusing. "Yeah, but we've never done anything apart."

She looked meaningfully at him.

He twitched, dismissing this. "Not willingly. We just, we don't do well on our own. I don't think she'd let me."

Softer than she'd planned, Litz said, "You're an adult, Ker. She could hardly stop you. And with Ellonya beside you, you're not defenceless." But looking at him now, she could understand more than ever why Kella might feel he was. His lower lip was quivering, and he really did look as lost as a child. As though sensing this assessment, he turned almost angrily, his chin up just like Kella's. "How'd you do it?" he asked. "I know you can do what Findan does, Push your feelings away or do it for other people."

"You mean with magic? Ah." Litz smiled. "I've never tried using the trick on myself. It's just the least noticeable way I can help others manage their own feelings." She frowned, thinking. "Pain is useful so much of the time, and I'm lucky in that I've almost never gone through more than I can bear." She had used it on a few occasions to help panic enemies, but she didn't mention that. "Fear is the main emotion people try to pretend isn't there, and again, it's useful. It has kept me alive more than once." She put her head to one side, happy to see he looked a little less upset now. "I can probably teach you, but I don't think it's a skill I'd recommend. My uncle told me some awful tales about the things people can justify to themselves when they've Pushed down everything vulnerable. I think that's where so many of the horror stories about witches come from."

He smiled faintly. "Maybe Findan was right not to teach me. But it'd be good to know how to Push fear down, to make bringing this up with Kella easier." He swallowed. "And to leave her, if I'm really doing that."

"I'll look after her," Litz said, even as she thought of the disgust Kella had looked at her with as she'd walked away. *I wanted to leave without you.*

Litz suspected this was Kella's guilt talking and not her rage over Litz's military actions, but what if the one person she'd given up everything for really did grow to resent having her around?

You would still look after her, Loren said simply, without judgement. *And you would still believe her plan was worth following.*

"You will, heh?" Ker said at the same time. "She's good at making people love her. Do you?"

"Will you change what you'll do depending on what I say?" Measured, Litz met his eyes. If she really felt that, she would say it to Kella before anyone else.

I think he knows already. You did leave Aelshia for her.

"No. I guess not."

Litz found she enjoyed the way he was looking at her, and she again felt she understood a little better how Kella worked. How bolstering, how frightening to be turned to for advice like this.

Interesting, Loren mused.

What?

I had never realised it before. But every rider I've ever taken has been an only child. Almost as if I found people looking for something they never could find for themselves in their home.

❖

Ker watched Kella avoided Litz. It was hard to tell how she was taking the news of a further betrayal from Jev as her aunt put her to work clearing dinner. She seemed calm, but chores always seemed to calm her. Much as she would chafe at the idea that women were destined for a domestic role, she liked being useful, and she was desperate to be liked. Despite her rebel image, she tended to do what was expected of her. Disturbingly, had she grown up with her father's family, she could have been a wife and mother by now.

There have always been rumours about the kings of Jeenobi keeping a witch to deal with parts of the war too unsavoury to manage, Ker explained to Ellonya later, when he went to bathe. *I think this is something Jev would only do if he was desperate.*

But he is *talking to dragons. Working with dragons and witches to find peace, like we are.*

Or controlling them.

Do you think you could control me? Ellonya asked, curious. *If you hadn't bonded to me, would you have been desperate enough to try that?*

I wouldn't have thought it possible, he admitted. *I'm still not sure I do.*

Ellonya was thoughtful. *I believe in what we're doing. I think its correct. But if I'm trying to save them and they're in danger right now, and we're abandoning them...*

It feels wrong.

They are sick, they are confused, and they have been abandoned so many times. To use them as a weapon in a war they don't even comprehend is awful. I do not respect any friend of yours who could do that.

We can't. But I can't abandon him, either, I think.

We are decided then, aren't we?

He found Kella extremely still on a bench outside the men's quarters, clearly waiting for him to get back from his turn bathing. She'd wrapped her hair for bed and was wearing soft clothing her family had provided her with, all of which made her look wiser and more composed than she usually did. "You want a walk?" she asked. Findan had always done that, taken them for walks when she wanted to speak in private. Something about being in motion did tend to encourage honesty.

"Noshi said to be careful about cattle wandering close in the dark."

"We'll be careful. And some dragon slayers we'd be if cattle worried us."

Too tired to consider correcting her, Ker smiled faintly and followed, taking hold of her arm so as not to lose her in the dark. The moon was still slim in the sky—Zebenn's moon, for the sweet and the cautious—so away from the campfires, the night became almost completely dark, but the stars were a brightly jewelled carpet that sparkled so dazzlingly, they seemed to be within touching distance. Earlier in the day, a light smog had covered the sky, but it seemed all gone now.

Ker wondered how high they'd have to fly for the stars to be within reach. It was impossible, according to the scientists at the university, but sky worshippers believed dragons came from the sun and stars and had the ability to return when they chose. The Narani thought something similar.

I don't think so. They look very far-off to me.

"Stupid putting any trust in kings," Kella said.

"Hmm. Sure."

"Do you think he loved her?"

Ker suspected that more than the walk, the dark was helping Kella speak more openly. "He seems to be doing a lot. But he would be like this even if he didn't like her at all, right? He would be offended that people thought he couldn't look after her or that he'd done something to her."

"Yeah, can't have his precious honour questioned," she said moodily, and Ker could hear her sandals scuffing the ground. "Do you think it's definitely a bad idea? Using witches to make dragons easier to live with?"

"I think we need to be there to know anything."

"And you're going to go, aren't you?"

Ker didn't answer at first, shocked that she didn't sound mean or even emotional. She was simply anticipating what he would do next. "I don't think Findan or Zebenn would do anything, and they were never close to him anyway, and he's only really got his uncle, and he doesn't even like his uncle, and I know he almost got you killed, but—"

"Ker," she cut him off and found his hands. "It's okay for us to do different things." It was such an obvious lie that for a moment, both were stunned into silence. "I know Senice is scary. I can't force you to come on this dangerous journey with me."

"Hey—"

"The adventurous life," she said with a sigh, "it's not for everyone, is it?"

"If I go, are you gonna let the others look after you?"

"Are you going to be careful? With Ellonya?" She didn't need to specify what she meant. "There'll be no one around for you. I'll have to take Evlo with me, though I suspect he'd prefer to travel with you."

"Because of your little theory."

"No, because he doesn't want to see Senice again." Kella started slowly turning so that their feet led them back to camp.

"How would..." Ker kicked the ground. "How do you know when you like someone? Like that."

"I'll let you know if I figure it out."

"If you're trying to say you don't know if you like the woman you made us travel hundreds of miles for—to a place that wanted us dead—I'm gonna have to hit you, Kel." When she didn't reply, he sighed. "Look, you were right before. Not everything's about Jev. But I know he made it hard to trust people."

"Not just him."

"Findan?"

"I get why it was you alone." The "but" hung in the air without needing spoken.

"If I see her when I get back, I'll yell at her for you if you like."

She snorted softly. "Better steering clear. She knows about Ellonya. She was trying to track you down back in Malya."

"When?"

"Just before we left."

"And you didn't share that with me?" Though he made no real attempt to imitate her, he thought it was clear enough he was refencing Litz's fight.

"Heh. Happily, I'm not sharing your mind. You already have enough going on in there."

CHAPTER TWENTY

Evlo made different noises than Litz would expect to indicate yes and no. His voice inflected upward as he hummed over the fruit stall they passed, his long fingers hovering thoughtfully for a moment, but she'd been travelling with him long enough now to know that meant no.

She did not, however, know all that much else.

He had experienced terrible things under dragon rule. She did know that, and yet, the fact did not stick in her mind. It was like seeing injuries left by fierce bush babies. They might not have been amusing when they were still bleeding, but it was still hard to picture the attack.

Most of the dragons Litz had ever known were uninterested in governing anybody. Eight rotating dragons of the Circle were all she could point to with any patience for it, and Litz had always assumed that eight was the maximum number that could be pushed into it. They just didn't care about human affairs. Though previous Circles had gone through phases of being aggressively minded toward dragon supremacy, this current one was far more moderate and tolerant of humans managing their own affairs without owing anything to them.

Of course, it was easier when they had already handled the only threat humans in their area could ever pose to them, leaving witches in the cruel and capable hands of other humans.

Loren was quiet in Litz's mind as they wandered the little town centre. Though the area did not seem explicitly against dragons, much of its infrastructure seemed to be about avoiding them. Loren was giving her space. The few times they had upset each other, it had almost always started with Litz doing something with magic, and that made this sting all the more.

"Hey, you wanted to find somewhere to sell your jewellery?"

Litz blinked against the bright glare of the afternoon sun and focused on where Evlo was pointing. "Yes," she said, and wandered over with him, their arms full of provisions they'd been trusted to pick up after selling pieces of Ellonya's newly shed skin. But it would be good to think about having money before moving on to the next town.

"Hello," Litz said. Even as she didn't expect to be understood, it felt foolish to say nothing. "How much for this?" As she ended her question, she took the necklace she intended to sell from her pocket and held it carefully before digging about for her anklet. It really was a good thing she'd been adorned with trinkets on her last day in Verassez. She might have left with no more than what she'd been wearing, but at least some of that was valuable. The necklace in question had been her grandmother's, with jewels plucked fresh from the riverbed and gold mined from Jeenobi in a brief summer of her youth when a temporary peace had encouraged her to visit. It was awkward and heavy to wear, the jewels meant to be displayed as raindrops from collarbone to collarbone.

But the shopkeeper pointed to the bangle she wore. A far denser piece of gold, it shone in the light.

"Oh," she said, clasping her hand over it. "No," she said, shaking her head for emphasis, making it easier for Evlo's now curious eyes to meet hers.

It did feel hypocritical to abandon Eisha but be unable to part with her gifts.

Through a mixture of mime and the handful of words the three of them shared, Litz was able to sell all her jewellery for two small pouches of wealth. They could have probably gotten more had they waited to reach the larger port towns, but this felt less conspicuous, and in any case, they had no money. Perhaps if the man continued travelling with his wares, he would one day resell the pieces to Litz's family. She wondered what they'd think of that.

After her aunt's death, her parents had seemed so much more mortal, so when she'd first come home, she'd had every intention of prioritising spending time with them. But now she'd removed her ability to spend any more time with them, possibly forever. As an only child to a monogamous couple, she was painfully aware she had left them with little, if any, family to support them.

Abandoning them should have felt worse.

"Why didn't you want to sell?" Evlo asked eventually on the walk back to Kella's aunt's home. Knowing that they were her guests seemed to have bought them a little goodwill, or at least more politeness than would usually be shown to a couple of visitors unable to speak their language.

"My cousin bought me the bracelet when she first left for Jeenobi," Litz explained. She hardly ever wore jewellery, but her wrist felt too easy to swing in step with the rest of her now.

"Ah." By his tone, Litz found herself struggling again with guessing how he meant this noise. She wanted to think it sounded understanding. "Do you think she's dead?"

Litz was a little shocked. But she wasn't in Aelshia anymore; people were more direct elsewhere. "No," she said, finding it still true. "Her corpse is a far more powerful and dangerous symbol than most things she could say or do alive."

"And you still think she's in Aelshia?"

Litz breathed out. "I do. I think I left her. I didn't look hard enough, didn't try hard enough."

"But she's alive. And it sounds like you already figured she's likely to stay that way." He scuffed the stone underfoot. "I let my sister die."

It was feeling less and less like a bush baby attack now. "I'm sure you didn't—" Litz started, but he waved a hand, dismissing her.

"I did." He swallowed and chin set hard, continued walking with his head facing the ground. "I knew it wasn't right. I even figured that if I could just get her away long enough from that place, that dragon, she'd be able to get better. But I didn't."

His shorter stature made him seem young, and he still couldn't be older than her. Since he had known Kella and Ker for at least a year, she doubted he would have been called an adult whenever his sister had been killed.

"A dragon killed her. And slowly, they'll kill everyone else I care about there. And instead of cursing that dragon, they'll be cursing me." His gaze was harder when he looked at her. "I'm sorry if I still can't relax around them. Or you."

Litz nodded slowly and focused on keeping her footsteps in time with his. That seemed important for some reason. "I imagine it must be hard to see them as friendly."

"Your dragon lied to you," he reminded her quietly.

"And you've never lied to the people you cared about to keep them safe?" Instead of meeting her slight smile, he looked at his feet. In the midday sun, looking down was easier on both of them. In her mind and soul, Litz could feel something in Loren relax a little.

"I tried to help Keral find Kella back when everything happened with you," Evlo continued a few moments later. "He wouldn't let me. I just…" He made a noise from his teeth like the tearing of fabric. "I wanted to help him. It felt stupid he wouldn't let me. And I needed to know why, to see what he'd gotten himself into. And now, I guess I know."

He wanted to help someone save their sister.

Loren was grateful Litz was reaching her but didn't miss a beat in responding. *And he still came looking for them both again. Even after Ker rejected his help. And he didn't leave even after learning about Ellonya. And somehow, they've convinced him to go back home.*

"You always do that," Litz said after a few moments of strangely companionable silence. "Call him Kerali, Keral."

"It's his name." A small smile quirked one side of his lips. "Well, Kerali's just for teasing. But where I'm from, shortening any name is insulting."

Though what he'd said about his past and his sister had been horrible, this tugged at Litz more. "He thinks you're mocking him. But you're honouring him."

He looked away. "Kerali brought me into the group at first. He saw me win an archery contest, drunk on a beach one day after I arrived. I told him to get lost. Then, I shot an arrow at the wrong man's boat, and he stood up for me. That's when I realised he was one of the people I'd been looking for. And even though I'd been nothing but a, what would you say, a pest, he brought me back to meet the others."

"He didn't give up on you."

"I guess."

Litz smiled. "You say that a lot too."

"Hmph." It was another noise Litz had to make assumptions about due to the tone, but it didn't feel like a fuck-off yet.

"Well, thank you for coming. Even if it doesn't work," Litz licked her lips. It was frightening to follow no orders, to do the right thing because she believed it should be done and not because she had to or because she thought she would win. "I think it's good that we're trying."

He smiled again, and this time, it seemed almost sleazy. "You're here for Kella."

Litz refused to be flustered or baited but took a moment to think of a retort. "I'm here because it's right." She paused. "Partly. But I am here for Kella. And for me. I think I've never needed to do anything really difficult before. That seemed like something to fix."

"I think Kerali's here because he's bored."

"Many a soldier is the same."

❖

Ker wasn't used to seeing anyone excited by dragons. In Jeenobi, they were met by fear, and though people seemed generally happy to see them in Aelshia, they were not a surprise. Sometimes, children would point them out, but adults would smile politely, as though passing their employer in the street.

Noshi was acting like a child who'd never heard of dragons when they introduced him to Ellonya, and less to Loren, who seemed embarrassed and irritated by the attention. Ellonya however, preened.

This is a little much, surely.

Oh, hush. And stop avoiding your sister.

It was too much, but it was what Ker would have loved to see from his own da when he'd introduced him to Ellonya. Openhearted, joyous, accepting. "Oh, I hoped I might come with you," Noshi said, still staring at Ellonya.

"Why?" Ker asked before he could stop himself.

Noshi laughed, briefly looking away before letting his eyes be drawn back to the scales under his hand. "I have one last journey in me before I settle down forever as the family babysitter. It sounds like whatever is going on in Jeenobi, I can make a better song out of it than Wallin." His new laugh was meaner. "And if you were planning on flying…" He pouted hopefully, still staring at Ellonya, "Well, that sounds like a faster way of getting there than me walking my old bones all the way."

Kella looked over at him and shrugged, amused.

"Fine," Ker told him, which inspired Noshi to move closer to Ellonya and start stroking her nose. She leaned in, docile as a house cat.

"You'd never think he followed the most famous dragon-slaying troop around for years of his life."

Kella smiled. "He just followed the story around. You're the new story."

"I'd have thought that was you."

"I'm a dangerous story, and he's getting old. And we don't really want to talk to each other much yet." She shoved his side lightly. "But keep him alive for me, would ya? Wouldn't mind talking to him someday. He's not so bad."

"Magnificent," Noshi continued to sigh in reverence, ignoring them.

"Who is this man?" Sallvayn asked, appearing from behind Ellonya's leg. "He's acting like a newly enchanted gremlin."

Kella nodded, not understanding. "Look after yourself, Sall. And you." She swallowed and looked annoyed at herself as she turned to Ker. "You'll be fine?"

He was sure she hadn't meant to phrase it as a question, but since it came out like one, he nodded. "Yeah. You too. And if the devil lets you have a second wish, see if he can't make you taller."

"Fuck off."

He smiled, terrified this could be his last chance to get a smile out of her. "And let them look after you, okay?"

"Don't. And hit Jev hard for me for fucking up my quest."

"I think I'll save the treason for when he really deserves it." He hugged her tight, feeling her bitten fingernails dig sharply into the back of his shirt.

"And tell your da I'm sorry."

"Tell him yourself when you get home." There could be no question she was making it home. Under the harsh light of the sun's gaze, Ker was terrified of inviting a new fate he hadn't yet considered, so as he slowly released her, he tried not to add anything else.

He moved away from Kella, who looked like she might be reconsidering letting him leave and turned to Litz, who, to his surprise, also hugged him. Her embrace felt almost as tight as Kella's, though it lasted for less time.

"You'll be fine," she said. "Between Ellonya and your magic to protect you, you shouldn't have anything to worry about, even from kings and armies."

"But they have a witch, apparently. And their own dragons, maybe."

She smiled. "Yes, but you're very resourceful. You find solutions, that's your talent. If war is truly imminent, there is no other voice I would be gladder to know is flying toward your king's ear."

Touched if not reassured, Ker smiled. "Thank you. And you'll be fine too."

Her smile widened, even though her attempt to make Kella join her in it did not work. "We will."

"Just let her think she's in charge, and things should go easily."

Evlo snorted, and Ker turned to him next. Awkwardly, they stood in front of each other, swaying a little. They had never hugged before.

"Well," Ker started. "I got you the diary. I got you the map. Now, you get to follow your world-famous dragon slayer around some more. Ideal, heh?" Evlo didn't react much, but behind him, Kella had finally met Litz's eye to be embarrassed for him. A horrible feeling squirming in his guts, Ker tried to keep his focus on Evlo. Kella couldn't be right, could she?

We did nearly kill him. Twice.

I know that.

And you yelled at him. And he still hates dragons, but he's still here going back to a land and people that terrify him because you asked him to.

Evlo was holding out a hand, his face frozen in an odd expression. It looked fond. "I guess so," he said as Ker took his hand and held it gently before eventually remembering to shake it.

You've always been clear you don't have sexual feelings toward others. Does that mean you don't have romantic ones?

I'm not sure, Ker admitted, meeting Evlo's eyes and realising it was the first time in a long time he'd put the question to himself. He'd always assumed no, but maybe he would if he gave himself time. Or a chance.

Evlo was leaving. He was about to miss this chance, if this was even what it was.

It was better, easier that way. *Look at the knots Kella's tied herself in. We don't want that. He needs to go there, or they won't survive in a place like that. And I have to go back, or we lose all hope in Jev and maybe in all the dragons too.*

Are you asking for confirmation? Perhaps you simply value him as a friend more than either of you have acknowledged yet.

"You'll be okay too," he said to Evlo, still not sure if he was looking for or expecting a response. "But you come back home when you're through." Finally, he had the courage to give Evlo a hug, which he seemed to allow. Ker had always been much taller, but he'd never been so aware of it before he wrapped Evlo in his arms. "You're a regular Malyan idiot through and through now. You're supposed to go, but you have to come back, heh?"

Over Evlo's shoulder, Kella met his eye. She wasn't crying, but from the look on her face, he suspected she'd be thinking on this later when she finally did.

❖

On Nic's wedding night, when the king's personal servants summoned her from her new bed into the king's room, she was ready. Before the ceremony, a genius, excessive distraction from royal treason and rampant terrorism, she hadn't been sure what Xoia wanted from her, but after being guided so sweetly to her feet by Xoia's fingers after her crowning and feeling her eyes follow Nic curiously throughout the night of dancing, she knew she had her attention if nothing else. Unwilling to be caught unprepared, she had covered herself in musk and brought a bottle of fine oil and her best toy with her.

If she missed anything about Litz, it was the chance to tease about how good she was going to fuck her cousin now. Though Xoia hadn't been the cousin Litz had been talking about before. "Eisha's here," she'd said. And Litz didn't jump to conclusions. She was logical to a fault, Nic could still trust that much about her, even if her stunt seemed to belie that.

Nic wanted to believe Litz was wrong with her conspiracy theories. It would make it easier to put her own guilt aside at not doing anything about them. She didn't care about rounding up terrorists she'd never met, but she'd gone to classes and parties with Eisha on occasion. And there was no doubt she was likeable, to an almost annoying degree. It almost made Nic want to honour her new wife even more out of spite. She knew all about having more likeable siblings.

Xoia looked ready when Nic was directed to her private bedchamber. To Nic's relief, she was alone. Nic suspected Agsdon was just as glad that sharing a night with both the king's consorts was not something Xoia planned on enforcing yet. And though Nic understood all the practicalities of Xoia keeping the head of the army close, looking at how Xoia waited for her made her sure that couldn't be all she wanted.

Xoia was clad in a light gauzy robe of bright orange and sat on the centre of her large raised bed-mat with her legs crossed in a casually suggestive manner over the layers of animal skins. Attendants covered her hair in silk as others remained kneeling, fanning the warm room. Nic wondered if they would be staying. She had spent the night in the beds of many important people in Verassez and had never seen that, but that didn't mean a king would think anything of it. Every moment of Xoia's life since her first breath must have been watched and tended to. She surely found it odd to be alone.

Xoia opened her eyes. Without her mother's makeup, they were striking. Her face was lovely, round and a little anxious, but those eyes bore into Nic with the ferocity of darts, leaving her almost breathless. Xoia made a swift slicing motion with both hands, and her attendants ceased their work, even those doing the fanning, and left the room.

Though Nic was a little relieved, she did have a moment of regret that the air would now warm. But maybe the servants would come back. Hell, there were worse jobs for a servant, and if Nic was going to dive into royalty, she might as well start embracing the lifestyle.

Xoia kept her eyes fixed on Nic, who couldn't tell if this was meant in warning or invitation. Or perhaps this was the only expression she was confident holding. Nic bowed. "Your Majesty."

Xoia nodded hesitantly, making Nic wonder if she was on the verge of asking Nic to call her by her first name within these private rooms.

But the invite did not follow. One to rise did however, and Nic gratefully stirred, her bad knee clicking as she moved.

"How may I be of service?" she asked, remembering herself enough to speak first.

Xoia leaned back, the bangles up her bare arms jangling loudly. "Do you find me attractive, Nic?"

The stray from title usage felt like a good sign. Even so, Nic could feel the weight of this new test pressing against her chest with frightening urgency. She had plenty of flattering answers on the tip of her tongue, but Xoia seemed to want honesty and perhaps deserved it too. "At first, I thought you looked like your mother," she said slowly. "And you have some of her looks, her eyes, I think. I'm always attracted to what looks powerful. I don't think that's unusual."

Xoia's eyes remained fixed on her, urging her to continue.

"And now, I have been honoured to see you without your royal face. I still recognise power, but your face speaks of an earnest well of feeling anyone should be grateful to receive." Nic thought about it, swallowed. "And your body demands worship."

"Because it's the body of a king or because it is mine?"

"Do I have to choose?" Nic wasn't sure how to take the tight little smile. She wasn't a poet, and she suspected Xoia didn't want one. "I think you're the sexiest thing I've ever seen." Even if she died for her forwardness, it might be worth it to see how Xoia's composure broke at her half-true words.

"I don't, ah…" As Xoia fought to put back her mask of self-assurance, Nic dared to take a step. Perhaps she was pushing too far too fast, but for now, Xoia seemed happy to be pushed.

Nic swallowed, a little worried even as she continued to move. "Of course, if you would prefer to rely on me only in a military capacity, I am happy to oblige, Your Highness."

"And what made you assume I have no interest in you physically?" Xoia quirked an eyebrow. This was still a front, but Nic suspected she was starting to enjoy herself. "Strip for me."

Nic hesitated but only for a second. She wasn't wearing many layers, and her sandals had been off from the door. Her robes slipped off easily, and she placed the little bag she'd brought on top of them. Though she didn't feel rushed, she hardly wanted to keep the king waiting.

When she was finished, she stayed still as Xoia's eyes ran up and down her body, evaluating cryptically. This, Nic was sure, would be the first time she'd been with a woman, if that was even what this led to, and she wasn't simply playing games.

What would she expect? Nic wanted to believe she had enough willingness and practice to outperform her co-consort. Bolstered by that thought, she met Xoia's eyes coolly. For herself, Nic enjoyed being taken. She liked someone she could trust putting her against the wall and having their way with her. It wasn't hard to find on campaign; the officer ranks were filled with frustrated women who had joined the army to get away from the possibility of being made to marry a man.

But she didn't see Xoia pushing her against anything. In the same way she'd been expected to speak first, she suspected Xoia was also used to others acting first. It might not be what Nic usually looked for, but as she'd said, power was always attractive. The idea that she had been granted some over the empire was more intoxicating than any drug.

With that haze filling her head, Nic found the courage to kneel between the king's legs. "You deserve worship," Nic said, her voice lowering as she realised she meant it. "Let me worship you, Your Majesty."

❖

Zebenn had worked with Hallen Trailfeet on one hunt before, and it hadn't gone well. They'd been new to dragon hunting, and new to their pronouns, and had still been deciding how they wanted to present themselves. Though Hallen had been more thoughtless than specifically cruel about it, spending time with him now felt like putting themselves back in that awkward, fragile headspace.

Though many things had changed since the last time, some had remained the same. Hallen still took too much pleasure in killing for Zebenn's liking and was still an awful team player in setting camp. He'd spent a lot of time in Nayona and seemed to believe it was women who ought to be doing the work of looking after the men.

For these purposes, he seemed to have assigned Zebenn to this category. With the eventual sharp word from Findan, however, he began to get more involved, redoing how they were pitching their tent. Apparently, the way Zebenn set up camp or planned to cook the griffin meat wasn't satisfactory. They missed Kella in this especially. She would have brought her little spice bag and ensured that their meal tasted like something.

"You'd think a real witch could make this happen instantly," Hallen grumbled as they sat to eat. Griffin meat was a little gamey, but the breast was dependably soft.

Considering that they were over a week into their journey along the Nayona mountains on their way east, it was a surprise that this was the most pointed jab he'd launched so far.

Though Zebenn took a sharp breath, Findan slowly finished chewing her food, then put the leg bone down. Her use of magic was part of why Hallen had walked away in the first place. It angered Zebenn to hear others, especially this other, judging Findan for it, even if it wasn't something they were comfortable with either. How dared this failed dragon hunter, who still wore a necklace of dragon teeth around his neck like some kind of sick prize, pass judgement on someone who'd helped kill more dragons than he'd even seen and had sacrificed far more of herself than he could ever understand?

But for now, Findan only smiled. "And you think a real witch is here with us?"

He almost looked uncomfortable, like he was afraid of truly knowing the answer, but manfully held her gaze. He was smart enough to see she was daring him to continue but not smart enough to have any self-preservation. Or perhaps he didn't know her very well.

Zebenn smiled, happy to see Findan clearly had a handle on this mutiny and had even expected it.

"Are you saying you're not one?"

"Lie to such a preeminent expert as yourself? I wouldn't dare." Her tone didn't change, but Zebenn could see she was laughing. She leaned back, putting all her weight on one wiry arm. "I can do a few tricks, and I feel no great guilt at being able to do so, considering what I use them in service of. Does that bother you?"

Braver than Zebenn had taken him for, Hallen belligerently met her eyes. "As much as it always has," he said with a grunt, eventually looking down in defeat. "I don't like you, and I think what you are is disgusting. But I would work alongside worse if I was sure that would bring an end to the plague of dragons."

"But you're not really sure, are you, Hallen?"

Zebenn was a little surprised by how lightly Findan seemed to be taking all this. Something was coming, and polite banter would not hide it much longer.

"I want to hear all of the plan," he said. "I liked the general pitch. I want the specifics now." He'd gotten that pitch when they'd found him sitting on an old crate selling leather:

"Wants to put together the most correct table of dragon experts the world's never seen," he'd grumbled about the king's council. "Most of 'em wouldn't know a dragon if it burned their house down."

"Why'd you go in the first place?"

He'd shrugged. His body language had been odd. Zebenn had suspected he had an equal wariness and fondness for Findan; he didn't like or trust her, but he missed talking about himself amongst people who would understand him, who wouldn't fear or be in awe of him or disbelieve his stories. Huffing a sigh, he'd leaned his arms casually over his knees. The forearm of his left had glistened horribly under the sun. "Couldn't really say. Sort of wanted a look at this kid who was Kira's project, who'd grown up to exile her daughter and be king." His eyes had flicked between them, alight with something cruel. "Lotta changes these days."

"All days are famous for it."

"Been hearing about your new competition."

"Then you'll also have been hearing what happened to them."

"And there used to be more of you. What happened to Kira's kids, they dead? Turncoats? Wandered away to hero elsewhere? I've been hearing a lot of tales."

"Do you remember how we used to talk about finding an end to all of it?" Findan had said as she'd picked up a leather poncho he had displayed and fingered it carefully. Zebenn, who needed new shoes, had wondered if he would offer any discounts. He didn't.

"Ending it all?"

"You know what I mean. Ending the need to kill dragons."

He'd huffed again. "You sound like our new king."

"I suspect we're approaching things from slightly different angles," she'd said. "He's looking for a way to control them, and it feels past time to try that. I know I can control them. But I need help." Her eyes had flicked gratefully toward Zebenn. "Zebenn is coming with me. We're going to leave Malya on a perilous expedition through the mountains. Our destination is Aelshia. Would you like you to come with us?" Though Findan had never been a leader who made motivational speeches, it was not one of her best. Zebenn had watched Hallen carefully as his good eye had searched for the joke.

He'd leaned forward. "You didn't do this while Kira or her brats were still with you. Making this something you knew they wouldn't like. Something even you consider unsavoury, you, who flaunt your witchcraft near openly."

Findan had said nothing and continued to smile absently.

"And you come to me. And you don't like me. You never liked to let the kids talk to me, even the one who did like me. Hmm. The Aelshian dragons, they don't hoard gold over there, do they?"

"Not commonly. They don't need to. And you don't need them to," Findan had continued, surprising them all. "You don't do this for wealth, though you like to have it. You do this because you hate dragons."

Just like with Evlo, Zebenn had suspected that Hallen had a story buried deep and painful that Findan knew every detail of and understood exactly why it was of use.

He'd sneered. "I'm retired." For a moment, Zebenn again dared to hope he would refuse out of spite alone. "When do you leave?" he'd asked instead, and Zebenn had felt their heart sink.

But now, he was asking questions again. Unable to help it, Zebenn sat forward. They too longed to know specifics, though they'd done their best to try not to care, being the last loyal friend by Findan's side. They were so desperately sick of drama. They just wanted to get back to doing what they did best with a team they liked and trusted. But it was good they had a proxy to ask their burning questions. Traitorously, they wondered what else they could push him into asking.

"Have you ever had a dragon try to talk to you?" she asked, and it took Zebenn a moment to realise she was addressing them both.

Hallen laughed. "Talk? Hardly. Why, can witches talk to dragons?"

Findan smiled faintly, pointedly looking at Zebenn as though understanding this had also been on their mind. "Dragons can speak with whoever they wish, but since they believe themselves higher beings, they don't do so often. The dragons we're used to, luckily, aren't like that. They're exactly the beasts they seem to be." She paused. "But I think the children of those beasts are becoming something more like Aelshian dragons, capable of making plans, of talking."

"Of taking revenge," Zebenn said slowly.

Findan nodded. "And perhaps we'll deserve it too."

"So the dragons are smart in Aelshia. Why in the godsdamned Earth are we travelling there?"

"Let me teach you a little of how magic works," Findan said, primly getting to her feet and walking toward a small bush at the edge of the cliff they'd made camp on.

Hallen tried to meet Zebenn's eyes, but they refused. Even if they shared a general fear of whatever Findan might do next, Zebenn planned on doing nothing that might make him believe he had an ally here.

"Magic," Findan explained, "is about Push." The tree bent away from them as though pushed by an invisible wind, and Zebenn felt disgust curl hard in their stomach. "And Pull." It bent back toward them, it's branches wide like a hand in invitation.

Far more alarmed, Hallen scrambled to his feet. "Hey," he said sternly. "Enough with this." But there was a quiver in his tone suggesting he knew that he had no ability to command her and no reason to believe she would take suggestions.

And indeed, she acted as though she had not even heard him. "Witches can Push and Pull at anything," she said almost dreamily as the tree continued to move in a terrible rhythm, speeding up with time.

Zebenn realised it was the first time they'd ever heard her call herself a witch. Also, she wasn't moving her hands. They had vaguely understood that was critical.

"I have also said it's about control or creating magic, but the truth is, it's all control. All that limits it is imagination." The tree bent all the way back. "And willpower." The bush snapped, and Hallen echoed Zebenn's shocked gasp.

"Dragons," Findan said as she turned, "don't require either of those things. They simply exist, with tails too heavy to lift, flying and breathing fire, and in some places, speaking. And they do that by magic, by getting into people's heads and changing what they know or think. Witches can change what people know too," she said, speaking even slower as she moved to sit. "I think a witch could change what a dragon knows. So what should we use that for?"

CHAPTER TWENTY-ONE

"D id you kill your mother?"
They were lying in the fine, thin sheets of Xoia's bed, and Nic had finally gathered the courage to wind her fingers around a loose coil of Xoia's thick hair and ask this. She hadn't intended to, having mostly decided she didn't believe it anyway, and it wasn't worth it, but there was probably never a correct time to ask.

To her relief, Xoia did not move away from her. "No," she said eventually, continuing to stare at the ceiling, every inch of which was beautifully carved in an image of dragons in the river. "Do you believe me?"

There seemed only one correct answer. "I believe you."

Xoia stretched her arms, moving out of reach, but she seemed satisfied. "I know many at court and among the people think I did. And though the idea grieves me, I have not tried to prove it false. I want them to believe my will is worth fearing."

Nic smiled, impressed. She kept thinking she had an idea of who Xoia was, and she still managed to surprise her.

"But the truth is far simpler, as deaths often are," she said, sounding detached, as though this had happened a lifetime ago. "She did not want to worry Eisha when she left, but she knew she was not long for the earth's surface. It was part of what made her so determined to end the war and be far more attentive with Sabi than she had ever been in either of our childhoods."

"She was more concerned with him?" Nic asked, sensing that as the more immediate sore spot and ignoring her own curiosity about the end of the war.

"I'm sure you can understand," Xoia said, looking at her with a smile more educated than truly knowing. "You have siblings. Did your mother treat you all the same?"

"Not exactly." Unsure what compelled her, Nic boldly took Xoia's hand. "I had a twin when I was born."

"I had no idea."

"My mother doesn't talk about it much. But they run in her family. It wasn't unexpected."

"How lucky."

"She died when I wasn't yet one, so I have no memories. The fever that went around so terribly that year. And I'm usually grateful," Nic added. Maybe being honest would inspire Xoia to be the same, and she badly wanted to know her king's secrets. "Because I don't think I would have become who I am if I'd had her with me. Perhaps I would have been happier or better liked by my mother, but I doubt I'd be here in this bed with you." She bounced their entwined hands, getting a thoughtful smile from Xoia. It was so delightfully simple to touch her now after hours of her shaking thighs draped around Nic's neck, her skin that shone bright umber in the low light of the pine torches. Her skin wasn't chafed by rough clothes or scarred by battle like the scores of other battle-worn women Nic usually took to bed but smooth and perfect. Rich. She felt special to hold in Nic's hands, like a new satin scarf commissioned for an older sister.

"Do you miss your sister?" And do you have her hidden away somewhere? But though she'd already asked about murder, she wasn't brave enough to ask about kidnap.

Xoia's face stayed extraordinarily still. "Yes. I have my little brother, but—"

"He's a child. And you didn't grow up with him." Nic turned on her side and stroked a careful finger over Xoia's lovely curves and folds.

At the ceremony, Sabi had been dressed in the outfit of the king's personal guard. It was the biggest party he'd been allowed at since his mother's funeral, and though funerals were always more significant events, this one was less bittersweet, and he'd seemed an irrepressible force. When he'd asked Nic why no one would talk about Litz anymore, she'd done her best to hold her smile. "She needed to go away for a bit," she'd said.

"Where?"

"I don't know. But Loren knows. You met Loren?"

He'd smiled wide like he had a secret. "She let me sit on her back."

"Aw, man, that's so cool, you must be so important."

The delighted secretiveness had continued. "I'm a prince," he'd whispered loudly.

Nic had obligingly gasped so loud, she'd nearly made herself fall out of her crouch, making Sabi giggle like a little hyena.

"I'm not sure Eisha and I really grew up together either. But I'll only ever have one sister," Xoia conceded, as though that was significant. "And we both cared deeply about each other's happiness and safety."

Nic's hand strayed lower over Xoia's thigh. She wondered if she could find a reason for them to stay awake a little later, surprised to find she wanted that. Xoia might have been cautious, with a lot to learn, but Nic might have fun teaching her.

And leading people. Watching her king give in to all of her soft commands had given her a taste for that too. Having not officially assumed her duties yet, she hadn't had much of a chance to think of that side of her new role. There were a few older officers she'd beaten to the position who would undoubtedly find grievance with a relatively young woman from a high family taking charge, not to mention the friend of a traitor. Perhaps her rumour-making had worked a little too well there. But she was eager to start throwing her weight around. She might not have Litz's skill as a strategist—or rather, Loren in her head providing strategy—but as she'd boasted, she was confident no one would successfully stand against her in a one-on-one challenge.

Interrupting her from a satisfying little scenario where she able to disarm the old captain who had taken a dislike to her, there was a low rap on the door.

"Come in," Xoia said airily, forcing Nic to hurriedly cover herself up.

When Agsdon entered the room, he glanced at more of her than she liked, but that faded when she realised his gaze was not lecherous. He seemed like the owner of a bird in a fighting ring who'd locked eyes with one far larger and stronger than his. Nic met his gaze with a satisfied smile before he turned to Xoia.

"Sorry to disturb, Xoi." It felt pointed to call her that. Yes, they were in the privacy of the king's chambers, but Nic sensed he wanted her to know there were privileges she hadn't earned yet.

Bold, considering they'd just spent all this time alone, but it was a correct gamble. Nic tightened her grip on Xoia's hand and raised them both so he was able to see how prettily their fingers fit together.

"I only meant to alert you," he continued, eyes not leaving their hands. "We have found a spy at court. He's confessed his allegiance with terrorists."

Xoia sat up straighter and took her hand back. To Nic's annoyance, the tiniest of smirks flickered over Agsdon's face before leaving just as smoothly as it had appeared. Nic wondered if the former king's consorts had considered themselves rivals or if they were the big, supportive happy family they'd always appeared to be. Maybe they'd all had separate relationships together, some as siblings or friends or lovers without the king's involvement.

"Cage them," Xoia ordered, her voice sharp but still lazy from the rest. "I will see them in the morning. Only one?"

Agsdon took a deep breath. His face seemed regretful, but Nic suspected he was enjoying himself. "One who is unfortunately worth your personal involvement."

Apparently needing no further information, Xoia nodded and stood into her house sandals. "Nic," she prompted quietly. Remembering herself, Nic hurried herself to find clothes for them both, hating that Agsdon was watching her flap.

A few minutes later, they were clothed and following Agsdon down many flights of stairs to the prison. Nic was amazed at the trust Xoia seemed to have in her cretin of a First Mourner. If someone had saved the reason they'd gotten her out of bed for the sake of effect, she would not have been acting so agreeable. But at least Xoia hadn't tried to leave her behind, and Nic wasn't sure which new position had secured her that dubious invite.

But who could be down here? Perhaps Litz truly had been living a double life and had left a conspirator here. Perhaps hiding in plain sight as a courtier but carrying the blood and sympathies of a forest clan. Perhaps they'd stumbled upon more witches taking out more infrastructure, even in what should have been these sacred halls.

When Nic walked into the airless prison at the bottom of the tree, she gasped when she saw who sat behind bars, beleaguered in his fine robes.

Xoia seemed satisfied and moved toward the bars without missing a beat. "Reishann Sunblessed. Did you truly think me stupid?"

Nic supposed that should answer her earlier wondering if the consorts preceding her had all gotten along. It was less surprising to see Reishann seem as unbothered as he ever did. "Xoia, darling, you have no idea how stupid I think you."

If anything, Xoia seemed as delighted by this confirmation as a child receiving the pet she'd spent months begging for. She might have been sincere about wanting Eisha protected, but that did not apparently extend to Eisha's father. "Did you kill my father?"

"Did you kill my king?"

"I am your king."

Nic watched the two stone faces. Her mother had not the wealth nor family connections to afford more consorts, but her father kept two more. She had at least one stepmother she would very happily never sit through an event with again. So she was not here to judge Xoia. As a soldier, it had never made sense to take much interest in politics. She might need to concern herself with this as a general later, but for now, she was a consort, and she could empathise with the need to bring a petty enemy low.

Or perhaps not so petty.

"Where is my daughter, Xoia?"

"I don't know. And you will never know." She turned to Agsdon with as bright a smile as Nic had ever seen. "I want him dead. He and all his witch conspirators."

"Witches?" Reishann crept closer to the bars. He moved like a much older man. Nic wondered if one of her enthusiastic colleagues had been beating his back. "There were no magic users. Only a few citizens of the empire rightly concerned that the Tree would not honour their land rights in the interests of their dragon backers." He spat viciously. "The big difference between you and your mother, Xoia—oh, and there are myriad differences—the one I respected her most for, was that she would not bend. And certainly not to dragons."

"She bent to Jeenobi," Xoia said, her tone icy. "And don't act as though you care about those you worked with. You have killed them as surely as if you'd held the blade to their necks." She paused as if fighting back her anger. "Litz met with you in the days before she left. Did you mean for her to take the throne in my place? Was her dramatic exit also part of your plans?"

He smiled, cheeks tight, as though he concealed some treat he was thrilled to finally be tasting. "Her dramatic exit, I can assure you, was nothing to do with me. I have no idea where she might have gone or why. Reports indicated they travelled north beyond the Salt Plains? I have not one idea what would take her there."

Xoia sniffed. "Though you have still much to tell my guard, I no longer have an interest in you. Good night, Reishann. I do hope you rest well."

"My king," Agsdon murmured, stopping her gently. "Perhaps this would be the time to consider the Circle's other suggestion."

Xoia's chin twitched as though she was trying to avoid a fly, and she waited a moment, staring at him. Nic thought she could feel some of the trust she had in him chip a little more. "No," she said eventually, her lip curling in a way that made her pretty face ugly. "I want him dead. I want them all dead." She met her guards' eyes. "I don't want to see pity for these monsters who've killed kin of mine. The families of the culprits, no matter how young and blameless, should not live through this." She walked out, and this time, Agsdon did not try to stop her. "I want every guard around the consorts questioned," Xoia said without turning.

No guards followed them, though perhaps Nic was expected to be bodyguard along with lady's maid, consort, and general. Truly, Xoia had gotten a deal with her. It would be interesting to find out where that would put her in the Mourner rankings with Sabi a child, Litz exiled, and her mother naturally out of favour.

"Someone knows something, and it may be another guard, it may even be another of my stepparents."

"Of course, my king." Though Xoia was not tall and did not usually hurry, preferring to float with an ethereal, royal gait, tonight, Nic was fighting to keep pace on the stairs. "And this other solution that Agsdon suggested?"

"Agh." Xoia scowled. "That."

Nic waited, hoping she'd done enough to be included.

"The Circle has informed him that to secure my new reign, they would be prepared to change the minds of a few of my dissenters."

"Change minds?"

Xoia clicked her tongue as if she didn't have the vocabulary to discuss this. "Dragons send speech, pictures, memories all through the mind."

"Yes, my king."

"Some of them can hone this into conveying orders, as we saw when Loren was attempting her escape."

Nic nodded. She hadn't experienced it before, but she understood the theory, and from her limited experience of touching minds with dragons, knew it was possible. They could not be argued with. And Xoia's reluctance to take their offer made sense. It must have seemed frightening to a king to consider a power that could command even them.

"This can be used by old, skilled dragons to write over what a mind should know. A dragon could make Reishann believe he has always supported my reign and is eager to name anyone we are not aware of." Xoia's face twitched. "But I'd far rather see him suffer than live in happy stupidity."

"Do you think dragons ever do it to their riders?" Nic wondered.

"Why, do you think that's what happened to Litz?" Xoia asked sharply, fully focused on her. "Is there a rebel contingent of dragons trying to take down the crown?"

Nic didn't know what to say, unsure what was the more likely option: the king was crazy, or the king was right, and there was a whole wing of dragon politics she'd never taken the time to suspect until now. "No, it's fine." She risked a smile. "Just Reishann, right?"

Slowly, Xoia turned and started walking, and Nic could breathe again. "Not for long."

❖

There was a Doshni island, or islands, maybe, as Kella understood. But where they took their name from originally never felt all that relevant: the Doshni people were all over the north and west of the continent, wherever there was coast to sail. They weren't exactly a clan or a nation. The ones she'd met recognised no kings beyond the captains they sailed under. Their similarity in appearance—generally a few shades paler than most on the continent, smooth-haired and broad-shouldered—was far from uniform but recognisable. But people called themselves Doshni after marrying or spending more than one term on more than one boat. What remained the same was their heavily tattooed skin and the fact that they would rarely call anywhere home.

Crathmere was the Doshni homeland not on the continent, and Kella had been dying to see it since she'd first heard of it. Because there were the Doshni sailors everywhere, and then the Doshni buccaneers, employed by the king to patrol in large boats with nice jackets and fancy buckles. But the Doshni pirates were who Kella had spent her whole life dreaming about, and the best of them berthed in Crathmere. And the very best, they had heard since arriving, was actually in town and leaving soon.

"What makes her the best?" Litz foolishly asked as they wandered down the old brick streets toward the inn Kella had confirmed the crew were staying at. "And if she is the best at piracy, do we want to be getting involved in that?"

Kella and Evlo answered together, talking over each other:

"She once killed a kraken using only her ship anchor."

"They call her Sailback because she killed a sailback fish with one hand, and now she wears the spines on her jacket sleeves."

"She bluffed her way into making the crown prince of Trehnon surrender half his treasury."

"They say she's sailed the entire world, and she did it with only two crew members and a broken arm."

"King Narin sent out a fleet to stop her after she stole her gift of jewels from…I don't know, some other guy. Then, when they couldn't catch her after a year, Sailback brought half of it to her as a gift."

"And the king thought it was so funny that she made her an honorary gharif."

"Gharif of the depths," Kella whispered. "The King's Buccaneer."

"They say they built her a palace south of Malya, but she told them—" Evlo started before Litz finally broke in, sounding sceptical.

"Who's they?"

"Her followers."

"Her conquered enemies."

"Y'know. People."

"Anyway, she doesn't even use it now. She says her only palace is her ship."

"The fastest ship that's ever sailed."

"Apart from the *Water Comet*."

"Yeah, but it's not like they ever could have a race to find out. *Serpent's Bane* was built later and must be better for it."

"Well, they say the craftsmanship of—"

Litz shook her head, looking like she was torn between laughter and concern for their sanity. "Why do you both know so much about pirates?"

"Why don't you?"

"I spent three months on a boat trying to learn their language after they rescued me from certain death."

Processing what he'd just said, Kella turned to Evlo. "Hey, do you want to try to find the people who rescued you instead?"

"When we berthed, they tried to sell me to a gang of Aelshian slavers, so, no."

Kella shook her head, always worried whenever Evlo revealed anything more about his past but enjoying Litz's look of bafflement. "Pirates, man."

"Pirates."

"And we can't just hire normal sailors why?"

Smiling at the slim view of the setting sun on the water and the masts rising from it, Kella started to skip. "We talked about that already. Besides, we're not going to find any this far north. Definitely none that'll take us anywhere far or with a dragon on board. Even if that's not what they would call it, everyone's doing something sketchy."

"Noted." Litz's nose wrinkled over the smell that had long ceased to bother Kella after a few months unloading fish off the Malyan docks. Finally, she might get to set sail instead of just staring at boats, wishing she was brave enough to leave. Now Ker had left her, and she was still waiting for it to feel worse. It was easier to forget how she did or didn't feel when she was living her fantasies of hunting down Captain Sailback to recruit her for a quest. She was even doing it with Litz by her side.

But on that front, Evlo was the far more comfortable presence. She might love that Litz had stuck around after blowing up her life, but she wasn't ready to be alone with her yet. She'd never gotten to find out for sure what Litz would have done if Kella hadn't been captured. Litz could have chosen to stay behind, whatever she claimed. And for some reason, that small distinction mattered.

"Loren says several people have spotted her but don't seem overly afraid or angry."

Kella shrugged. "That makes sense. They don't really think too badly of them here."

"They think they're what humans come back as," Evlo said. "That if they're not good enough to be whales or sharks, this is what they become after they die."

"Loren finds that...amusing."

Evlo shook his head, not bothering to hide his disdain for amusing a dragon as he stepped over an overturned waste bin that seemed to have been flung from a bar. It was smoking. Kella smiled. However the people here felt about dragons, it seemed most of them would be too inebriated to notice one among them.

"What if the ship isn't big enough for the dragon?" Evlo asked.

"*Serpent's Bane* is big enough," Kella said, confidence rising. They'd made it all the way here. She had to believe they'd gotten through the worst of it. "It's made for bringing home monsters. We'll make it work."

"If she lets us, and I really don't think she's going to, Kel."

Attention briefly taken by the loud singing from one of the taverns as the streets were becoming more cramped, Litz blinked. "You know we can always just *take* a boat. We do not need to waste days bargaining with criminals."

Kella glared open-mouthed at Litz, knowing that Evlo shared her sentiments, even if Litz had entirely foreign ones. "We couldn't take Sailback's ship. We wouldn't live to try."

"We have a dragon, and they have a wooden city and wooden boats. I think we'd be fine."

"We couldn't sail the ship with only three of us."

"We could have more than that. Again, we have a dragon. We could figure out an agreement from there."

Evlo stopped walking, apparently just as bowled over as Kella. Litz had a wilful ignorance about stories, refusing to listen to their call. It was fascinating. Kella nudged Evlo's ribs. "They were going to make her a general."

"A general what? Villain?"

Watching Litz's face transition from annoyance to amusement to almost flattered wasn't something Kella was going to tire of easily. And she let herself wonder if Ker hadn't been right about some things. Maybe she was overcomplicating everything. "I don't see how it's immoral to talk about threatening and stealing from people who spend their whole lives doing exactly that," she said primly as she started their downhill march again.

"She doesn't see how it's immoral."

"This is why you can't trust foreigners," Evlo agreed, loyally committing to her bit in the interest of winding Litz up. He'd seemed almost as conflicted as Kella when they'd parted ways with Ker. It was good seeing him joking around again.

❖

"There she is," Kella breathed almost reverently, but Litz didn't need her obvious pointing to know the woman she meant.

Sailback was unmistakeable, even after only hearing of her that afternoon. She was around Litz's height but wore heeled boots that rose to her knee and made her appear taller, and she carried herself like she knew she was the most important person in the room. It was knowledge that seemed to rest easily on her wide shoulders, that were spiked by the spines rising from her signature jacket.

If you'd become a general, Loren mused for a moment, *perhaps this is how you'd have looked within a few decades.*

That's ridiculous.

You don't see it?

Captain Sailback turned, revealing a yellow set of teeth missing several at the front. When she saw them, she used the gap to give and odd inward whistle, a sound unlike any Litz had heard before. "A little Senice boy!"

Litz was surprised to hear her voice boom out in Jeenobian. Doshni sailors, Litz remembered Kella saying, used a conversational mix of Jeenobian and their own language, but she'd forgotten.

Sailback's smile became lecherous. "What a long way you've had to travel, little Senice boy." A few of her crew at the wide wooden table also looked and whistled. Dramatically, Sailback took two long steps and took her wide, leather hat off her head in a mocking bow, exposing a colourful headscarf beneath.

Evlo looked as though he wanted to seem amused, but everything about his posture came off as defensive. Kella looked jealous enough to burst.

She did say she'd dreamed of living as a pirate. Perhaps she wouldn't mind if you ended up looking like that.

Ha.

Still mocking, Sailback took Evlo's hand and kissed it softly, to more cheers from her crew. Evlo's cheeks reddened, and he seemed to find it hard to swallow for a moment. Litz sympathised. "Uh."

"Uh?"

Finally, he seemed to find his resolve. "I need to go back to Senice. Will you help us?"

"Son, I'm not a transport boat, and I don't take guests on board. And nobody tells me where I should sail."

"Hi," Kella interjected brightly, offering her own hand. "My name's Kella Mabaki. I need to go and slay some dragons in Senice."

Laughter still in her voice but no longer her eyes, Sailback shook her hand. "Mabaki. For Kira?"

"Some still call me Kirasdaughter."

"Hmm. Thought I heard she had a daughter."

Litz narrowed her eyes. Everyone this far east seemed to have heard something about the Mabaki history. Sailback was probably trying to be overly casual, and it seemed to be working: Kella was looking crushed and a little annoyed.

"And I'm Evlo Lindin. May I ask your preferred name?"

"Sailback's fine," she said absently, looking at Litz now. Her eyes lingered on her earrings. "I'd happily have a couple of slayers on my crew. A bunch of mad yins but handy for meeting monsters out there. But I'm not sailing to Senice, and I'm not taking an Aelshian anywhere."

"Why not?" Kella asked.

"They've made themselves unpopular with many of mine. In fact, I'd advise not lingering in my town long either, Aelshian." She smiled at Litz, unpleasantly showing off those gaps in her teeth. "I didn't get your name."

Litz knew she should be wary of saying the wrong thing, but she was exhausted and frustrated that they were entertaining a pirate instead of getting what they wanted already. "Why won't you sail to Senice?"

"Difficult rock formations, monster-infested seas, mean people who hate to trade and can't speak with me. The villages are too poor to raid and the towns too dangerous. Not worth the long journey. Tell me your name, won't you?" As her voice continued to sharpen to an edge, two of her crew moved to stand at her back.

"My name's Litz," she said as Kella interrupted again.

"And if you let us show you what we're transporting, I think you'll want to help us."

Sailback leaned back on one of her boots, considering Kella properly for the first time. "And what are you seeking help for?" She smiled, and it made her seem less, not more, friendly. "Traditionally, me and mine aren't what you'd call helpers. We're not dragon slayers, either. I've got no interest in dragons."

Kella seemed uncharacteristically unsure how to proceed, so Litz stepped forward again. "We suspect you'd want to help grow your legend."

"Lass, if you're aware I have a legend, it doesn't need growing. Now, isn't there a Princess Litz of Aelshia?"

Litz smiled, ignoring that Sailback's height slightly surpassed her own thanks to the boots. "A legend always needs feeding. They must always be outdoing themselves or may as well perish."

The smile turned cold now, warning of consequences to follow if Litz didn't stop talking or at least step back.

"We're going to Senice. And we're going with something only a ship of your size and reputation could manage." Litz smiled wider. "Can we convince you to come and see what it is we're looking to transport?"

❖

Kella suspected the only reason Sailback agreed to follow them was because of the crew beside her. She also suspected that Sailback had every intention of killing them all, possibly ransoming Litz, and taking their "cargo" for herself.

But for whatever reason, Sailback and some ten members of her crew came with them. On the way out of town, Sailback continued to torment Evlo, possibly because meeting a Senice-born Jeenobian speaker was a genuine oddity, perhaps because she found him attractive, or perhaps because he seemed the easiest to fluster between the three of them. She asked incessant questions about the side of Senice he came from, the dragon his family had lived under, what trade he'd grown up learning, all revealing that she had visited Senice enough times to declare it not worth her time.

"Mmm," she said when he told her where he'd grown up. "Heard the rules there were particularly cruel. If ever there was a dragon needing slaying, I'd say that one."

"Thought you didn't care about dragons?" Kella reminded her before the pirate behind her, a broad-shouldered young man around Ker's age, put a boot on her ankle.

"I don't care about 'em here. Senice is different. Doesn't mean I'm taking you there." She huffed out an exaggerated breath, looking at the top of the hillside Loren was hidden behind. "How much farther? If I didn't know better, I'd say I was being led into an ambush." Nastily, she turned a smile on Kella. "But since that's hardly a heroic way to gain my help, I'm assuming the best of you, Kirasdaughter."

No one had called her that in a while, and for some reason, it made something in her squirm and think about Noshi explaining that every girl hated their mother. Her smile thinning, Kella pointed the way with an open palm. "Nearly there."

It was strange meeting someone she'd heard so many stories about. So far, Sailback was frustrating but not disappointing. When she saw Loren, who appeared to be waking from a nap, her steps and her breathing slowed, but unlike the crew accompanying her, she did not cry out or reach for a sword. Kella wondered how she would have reacted had she not had people to keep up an act for.

"This some kind of joke?" she asked eventually. "Slayer and a dragonrider team up and go to the Hidden Isle?"

"Not a joke." Kella crossed her arms as Litz moved casually in front of the weapons now unsheathed to put a hand on Loren, then pull herself into the saddle. It gave the impression she was holding Loren back from something, but Kella suspected she was only trying to warm her hands on the scales. "The dragons I've been fighting all my life aren't right. The key to fixing them is in Senice." She wished she felt as confident about her mission as she sounded.

"Dragons don't belong on boats," Sailback said, eyes still on Loren's feet as though waiting for her to make a move. "Ain't right. Certainly not my boat."

"They sure don't, that's what they say," Kella agreed as she ambled closer, arms still tightly crossed. "And did you become the most feared pirate of the Ninearian Sea by doing what they say?"

Sailback gave her a grin that was almost entirely a snarl. "Don't go baiting what you're not fisher enough to reel in, lass."

"Heh. Who says—"

Sailback cut her off. "You don't know how to sail, or I'd be dead already."

"Maybe I'm a better person than that."

Sailback's glare increased, and Kella wasn't sure what she hoped she'd see or find. "Maybe you are," she said eventually. "But your girl over there wouldn't have bothered with this little display. I'm suspecting if it was up to her—"

"It's not."

"Everything all right down there?" Litz called from her perch, leading Kella to wave.

"I see that," Sailback said slowly. "So she's a soldier, and she's following your orders. That means the dragon's yours to command too."

"No, *no*," Kella started before remembering herself. They were putting on this front together. "But. In a way, sure. You could call me tamer of dragons."

Loren, who had apparently decided to listen, gave an offended huff that frightened the pirates closest to her into jumping back. She followed this by snapping at the jumpers, seemingly just to be nasty.

"You said it yourself," Kella went on. "Slayers are good people to keep aboard for monster-infested waters. Dragons too, believe me. And you say they're hard to talk to for trade? We've got a Senician here who can help with that."

Looking a little uncertain, Evlo gave a short wave.

"In fact, he probably wants some revenge. If you want something valuable from the Hidden Isle, something no one else would be able to bring back, this is your shot. And we'll pay too."

"Not enough, I bet."

"Maybe not. But we'll work." Kella gave up on holding her arms tight and began gesturing again. "Look, if she doesn't fit, we'll figure out something else."

Sailback laughed again, sharp as the bray of a gull, and finally, bravely putting her back to Loren and her hands on her hips. "Oh, if she won't fit, I'm sure a little more care and attention will make it happen. That's been my experience." She sounded jovial and back in control, but Kella suspected that it would be some time before she forgave them for putting her in this position. "Be on the docks by midday tomorrow."

"Aye, Cap'n."

Sailback started walking back down the hill, her crew following with uncertain glances at Loren. "And bring more money than you think you need."

❖

In some ways, travelling with Noshi was reminiscent of travelling with Kella. Except where Kella would start storytelling if the conversation grew quiet, her father would start singing. After a week of travel, this began to wear on Ker, so when they made camp that night, he warned that it might be wise to avoid disturbing any dragons or griffins who might be sleeping nearby.

"Strange we've not seen any," Noshi noted as he polished his drums rather than beating them while Ker found him some of the dried provisions Kella had packed them.

He's right, Ellonya pointed out. *We should have seen dragons by now. I wonder if your king got to them already.*

I don't see how it would be possible, but I don't like it.

Unconcerned with Ker's lack of conversation, Noshi leaned against a rock and looked at the moon, "If we're not singing, let's talk. Tell me a story."

Ker tried for a smile. "Kella's the storyteller in our family."

Noshi clicked his tongue. "Tell me about your father. Or tell me about gremlins."

"Gremlins?" He smiled. He'd rather not talk about his da. "What about them?"

"Where do they come from, how do they work magic, what do they care about, how is it to travel with one?"

Sallvayn turned to Ker unhappily. "He's talking about us, isn't he?"

"He wants to know about gremlins."

"Hmm. We would prefer he go back to drumming."

"Be nice."

Noshi watched them with unabashed excitement. "What's he saying?"

"They." Ker sighed. Maybe playing translator could be fun. "They're saying gremlins want to get dragons back to the way they should be."

"And what is that? Is it in charge like in Aelshia or this Senice?"

"I think just better than now. Not having to worry about dragons burning down villages."

"Why would gremlins want that?"

"They want dragons to think, to be people again."

"Yes, but if those people want to continue burning and destroying, would the gremlins care?"

For a moment, Ker stopped, unable to think of a response. When he spoke, it was not what he'd planned on saying. "Why did you follow our mami around? Did you hate dragons?"

He shrugged. "I'd only seen a dragon once. It flew away before I could get near. But the idea of a woman killing dozens of 'em and walking away unscathed? That was a story." He sighed before hesitating. "Who is your father?"

"A shopkeeper. He sells some books, some herbs."

"Interesting. She chose him, then. He didn't follow her around until she finally spoke to him." There was no jealousy in his tone, no ache. He sounded more like a scientist hearing something new about a creature he'd spent his whole life studying.

Ker supposed grief would always feel a distant emotion regarding someone he hadn't seen in well over two decades, but it still bothered him that Noshi could speak of her that way.

But the grief will always feel fresh to you. You watched it happen.

I made it happen.

You know that's not true, however it still feels.

Slowly, Ker breathed out. "Well, you can meet him when we get there." From what he understood of Noshi, he would not appreciate sleeping in a cave miles from the centre of Malya. And his da would be happy enough to welcome the writer behind his favourite book of songs, even if Ker doubted he'd want him staying long.

"And what's he like?"

"What do you mean?"

"What are his interests, what is his appearance?"

"He likes books, he likes cooking for people." Ker was missing his cooking now. "He looks after a little boy who was originally Narani. He only has one good leg thanks to a dragon attack when he was young. He's about my height, good bit wider, though."

Noshi nodded thoughtfully. "I do love a man with tits."

A little unnerved, Ker stood and made an excuse of finding more firewood. As he wandered past the rocks and jagged bushes, he wondered again at how different the environment felt since he had last travelled up here. There had been the presence of dragons, even if it had taken days to find one. The wildlife was cautious; there was a quiet to the air. It was hard to pinpoint exactly what felt different, but something did.

You can feel what I feel. And I can tell they're not here. Worry gnawed painfully at Ellonya now.

We'll be in Malya soon, Ker tried to soothe her. *If they have been taken somewhere—*

It won't be soon enough if they're gone, will it? With shocking ferocity, Ellonya pushed all her fears, worries, and hopelessness at Ker, overwhelming him. The dragons who should have lived here might be dangerous, but they were people with feelings, and they were as vulnerable to the machinations of shadowy witches as children would be.

In coming to understand the tragedy of the world she'd been born into, Ellonya had sworn to protect these dragons, to fight for them, to win back their reason and standing. But before she'd even had the chance to try, they were in danger. Perhaps she should have stayed to protect them instead of chasing ways to fix them. Perhaps she should have never separated from them to better accommodate her rider.

Shaken, Ker steadied himself on the rockface.

I'm sorry, she said, *but I need you to understand how serious this is to me. It was becoming too big to bear alone, and I have no wish to keep the truth from you. I need this to be your main concern as it is mine.*

It's mine now too. For better or worse, her concerns were his. And especially now that her feelings belonged to him too.

I know normal dragons don't think like this. They barely feel protective over their own offspring. And I don't know if Loren is right, if I've taken too much that's human from you in how I think of my responsibility to them, but I don't care. For whatever reason, it will hurt me greatly if we cannot restore them.

We will help them, Ker assured her but could feel she was no longer able to believe that.

CHAPTER TWENTY-TWO

There was a lot involved in getting a ship ready to set sail Litz hadn't considered. Beyond the gathering of provisions and equipment, a more sober crew needed to be negotiated with. Traditionally, Sailback had more control over her crew than most elected captains, from what Kella said. Her reputation was so ironclad and impressive that those who'd sailed with her would jump to do so again, even if that was as a democratic decision.

But this was sailing with a dragon to a place surrounded by miles of ship-killing rocks. It was a harder sell, with less clear gains. Though Sailback and her kin made up much of the sixty or seventy shifting crewmembers and felt compelled to stick with the boat, the rest of them were less bound to it.

"I've taken this ship to Senice before, but there wasn't much there to rob or trade if we didn't plan on slaying a dragon, and we didn't," she explained to Litz as they walked the length of her ship. Though Sailback still seemed annoyed, Litz suspected she respected her for the virtue of having a dragon to call on. "There's healthy caution from the lads, but enough are convinced. For myself, I'm looking to see a few of these modern contraptions they get their witches building out there. Reckon if we can bring home some boat that can sail on land, we'll be rolling in all the coin we can dream of."

The crew's scepticism worked well for their purposes. Their usual numbers would not function with Loren on board, so all who were not happy with this destination would be left ashore. Sailback left each of them a small sum to live off. There seemed an understanding that they could take work in the duration, but if they took her money and sailed with another ship, they'd be dead the next time she saw them.

Other than talking about their destination and handing over most of their funds, they were not required much for the few days of preparation. However, Kella volunteered them all to work. She cheerfully offered to help in the kitchen, and the ship's cook—a weathered sailor with cut earlobes marking him as someone once enslaved in Aelshia—seemed less than thrilled to have a helper.

He wasn't the only one with sliced lobes, some looking like they might be from forest clans. That had to be what Sailback meant by Aelshians not being welcome in this port. Indentured servitude was becoming more common as a solution to deal with criminals and loud dissidents as the empire continued its expansion east. But it was hard to think of it in such cold terms when she had to walk among them, her intact lobes claiming importance and personhood.

Should I take them off?

It may make them feel you can be intimidated, Loren advised as she lowered herself with comical carefulness onto the ship's deck, daintily using one clawed foot to balance on the side as they tested how the ship would take her. *But it may also make you feel better.*

It would be nice if they forgot who I am.

With me here?

As Loren's weight settled on a good half of the deck, there were a few scattered cheers and whistles. Loren was not enjoying the attention but refused to be embarrassed by it. Though Aelshians were not popular, dragons seemed welcome enough. Litz did wonder if that had to do with the alcohol being consumed while the crew was still ashore.

Maybe you just want a chance to reinvent yourself, Loren suggested, as though nothing was interrupting them. *You can, you know.*

Who should I be?

You don't really want me to tell you that, Loren said gently, and for a moment, things felt normal between them. Litz yearned to slip back into that, as though nothing had come between them, but her buried anger stopped her.

Happily, Sailback interrupted her from having to think on it. "She'll need to land at night," she said thoughtfully. Despite her gruff tone, her keen eyes scanned Loren as though looking at a puzzle that interested her. "She should only be aboard if we can control how much people are moving. When they're back in their bunks is ideal."

"That shouldn't be a problem."

"So long as she's prepared to keep aloft for as long as we have a storm raging, we should be fine. Now," she added, pulling up her belt and resting her thumbs under it. "Speaking of bunks, how will your Senice boy feel about bunking with the rest of the lads?"

Litz had seen enough of Sailback's crew to gather that lads was not intended as a gendered term. "He should be fine. We all will be."

"Well, I was thinking I could give you the room I reserve for my husband whenever he chooses to join me. On the occasion we do have guests, I put 'em there too. How would you and your girl like a real bed so the lads don't forget you're the one with the dragon and the map?"

Litz struggled for a reply. "That's very kind of you."

She made a dismissive noise. "Ain't kind. Don't want 'em all restless if there's an empty cabin for the fighting over." She narrowed her eyes over Litz's hesitance. "Oh, is she not your girl?"

"We are travelling together."

"Heartwarming." Sailback snorted and turned to look at the sea and the horizon. Though scholars had read and studied far more than Litz and confirmed the sailors' claims that the earth was round, its end point had never looked so tantalisingly like an ending. "You act like hers."

Honouring her mother's advice to never answer statements with defensive ones, Litz turned away. "How so?"

"Oh, lass, you don't need me to tell you that. I'll let her know I've given it to both of you. If she'd like to argue, she's welcome to bunk with the rest of 'em." With the mean smile of an overly involved grandmother, Sailback stalked away, her heavy footsteps moving the planks in a pleasant wave to those watery ones beneath.

Are you coming?

It's very difficult to rise from this position. Do not laugh.

Was that a command? Though she'd meant to be teasing, Litz suspected she was coming off as cruel. So she didn't laugh as Loren, with great effort, pushed up and, avoiding the sails, took to the air. Though the ship wobbled, it did not tip. Kella had been right. If there was any ship capable of sustaining a dragon for a long-haul voyage, it was this one, much as Litz had doubted it. It even looked the part: the boat's figurehead was the enraged head of a dragon.

Even as Loren flew over the town, Litz noticed no fear as there would be in Jeenobi, just as there were no walls to keep them out. But these people did not keep animals that might be in danger from dragon interest, and they lived more on the sea than land. Dragons simply weren't creatures that held an interest to Crathmere, and the feeling seemed mutual. Loren hadn't spotted any nearby in the few days they'd spent in town.

With witches too, they seemed odd. Litz overheard something about magic not having a place on ships, implying it might have been tolerated in other situations.

They were rooming above the pub they'd found Sailback in, with Kella reasoning it would be best to keep a close eye on the pirates. Though they didn't suspect Sailback would run without them, they couldn't be sure. The way she had done everything to frame this venture to her "lads" as a quest only made Litz more certain that she did not like being forced and liked appearing forced even less.

"We can't trust her," Kella agreed as they were taking their boots off, facing each other in their three-bed room. In their short time there, Litz's skin had begun to break out in small sores, and she wasn't sure she wanted to know if that was due to bugs in the bed or her skin having a reaction to its course material. It was making her homesick for her own soft bed mats at home that held less secrets. "But that's all right. We just need her to get us where we're going."

"She could hold us hostage," Litz pointed out. "Loren couldn't set the ship on fire with us onboard, and her with nowhere to land."

"They can't stay afloat forever. That'd never work."

"And if she leaves without us tonight?"

"She won't," Kella said certainly. She'd spent this last day purchasing new knives for herself, and the shopping seemed to have both calmed and cheered her.

Behind her, Evlo walked back into the room with the full pail of water and nodded. "It's a challenge to her," he agreed. "That's how she's sold it to everyone. If she leaves us behind now, she looks weak, and she can't afford that."

"I've never left the continent before," Kella said, crossing her legs on her bed and leaning back as Evlo took a seat on his own.

"What about the kraken you took down?" Evlo asked. "Surely, you had to get at least a little offshore for that."

"Heh, that was a weird one. We didn't need to go out to sea. It got trapped in the harbour, and it kept flailing and knocking people off boats. Like, it ate a bunch of people, everyone who made a bad job of going after it, but it wasn't really trying to be there." Kella sighed. "Me and Jev wanted to get it back out to sea, but my mami said it had to die. It had eaten too many people. It might have got a taste for us. Besides, the people wanted to see it dead. That's why we got asked to do it."

"Then you didn't only fight dragons?" Litz asked, smiling. She knew this, but it was nice to hear Kella's stories again.

"No," Kella said as Evlo enthusiastically chorused in with her.

"My first job with them was a wolf," he said flatly.

"Just a normal wolf?"

Kella flopped dramatically on the bed. "We didn't know what it was, okay? It could have been anything. People had been mauled. A kid gave us a description of a monster."

"But it was a normal gold wolf," Evlo confirmed.

"Do you think when we find your wishing devil, it's just going to be, like, a really old witch?" Kella asked, wiping her eyes closed as she continued to face the ceiling.

Evlo's mood soured. "Fucking better not be."

"I've been reading the diary again," Litz said, "and I don't think it could be. The way it's talked about..." Frustrated by her own memory, Litz fished into her satchel for the diary copy and scanned back to where she'd been. "The writer says the dragons didn't like to speak of it, but 'the implications when they do suggest something created beyond powers they could understand but perhaps of their creation.' I think the dragons made this thing, but when they were unable to control or destroy it without risking themselves, they hid it away." She looked at them both, Kella now propped up on her elbows. "Whatever it is we're looking for, I don't think it could be another witch in the walls. Witches..." The word stung but felt most useful here. "Whatever they might be able to make of themselves over time, they're still very human. Whatever this thing is, it's nothing like humans, and it does not use human magic."

"Guess we'll find out when we find it," Kella said and flopped her head back down.

❖

The reasoning behind Noshi's strange insistence to avoid the more populated areas of hill country soon became clear, and as Ker suspected, it was not fear for Ellonya's safety but his own. The giggles in the one town Ker had forced them to pause in were indeed heralding something. Noshi was recognisable in these borderlands, and it wasn't just for the songs he sang.

"She was only his second wife," Noshi explained as they left town that night, travelling back to where they'd left Ellonya. "No need for this fuss. It was only a couple of songs about her feet." He smiled and for a startling moment, looked very like Kella. "And one very good night."

"And what level of fuss do you think awaits if they catch you?"

"Oh, death. Definitely death. But they'd take my cock first," he said, sounding more cheerful with every step they made away from town.

"How did you get away?" Ker asked, feeling the familiar mix of horror and delight that listening to Kella's stories of a long night out usually inspired in him.

"Oh, she helped me, of course. I always charm enough to make allies of 'em, except your mother. I don't believe I ever charmed her," he added fondly.

"And obviously, this chieftain wasn't charmed by you."

A tongue click. "No. And he wasn't really my type anyway. Far too skinny. And he ate this awful root he claimed whitened his teeth. I don't think it worked."

Ker smiled and shook his head. Occasionally, he felt a wave of gratefulness for feeling no interest in pursuing sexual conquests. It seemed to inspire idiocy in even the most sensible and especially among the rarely sensible. And for the millionth time, that made him wonder how Kella might be doing.

It was impossible to untangle how much worry for her was worry for himself. They'd been a pair all his life; it was how he understood himself. How much was he concerned for her, and how much was he concerned for how he might fare without her?

Loren won't let anything happen to Litz, who won't let anything happen to Kella, Ellonya reminded him.

But the dragons there will be far worse than even the Aelshian ones.

Smaller, though. That ought to count for something.

And far from banning magic use, it sounds like they control their witches.

Evlo will help them through that. I think he was coming to not hate me so much, Ellonya said as Ker made up a bed beside her warm scales, creating almost a home from home. Here, so close to the familiar shoreline, they could almost be back in their horrible little cove.

I think that's what freaked him out. He didn't like that he'd stopped being afraid of us.

Afraid of me, Ellonya corrected gently. *We are not a gremlin.*

Their own gremlin raised the alarm shortly after. "The singer has been captured," they explained with some weariness.

Ker, who had almost drifted off, realised that Noshi was indeed nowhere to be seen. "Ugh. Where?"

According to Sallvayn, he'd gone into the bushes an hour ago. Some men who must have followed them from the village had been waiting and dragged him away. "The man was fully exposed at the time," Sallvayn explained.

"And you couldn't help because?"

Sallvayn blinked innocently as Ker grumpily harnessed Ellonya's saddle. He would give the Aelshians this: it was far comfier. "They didn't seem ready to hurt him. And we weren't that close."

"You can move as fast as you blink."

"Yes, but we might not have had much energy left to help."

It didn't take long to find what they were looking for.

"Oh, c'mon, you could have taken three regular guys."

"And what if they'd been your witches?" Sallvayn protested from their position on Ellonya's neck. "That could have been the end of us. It's not like it's your father. I thought Kella didn't even like him."

"It's more complicated than that."

"Hmm. She did tell me."

Ker wrinkled his nose as they started their descent. "How?"

"We talk. Your sister is resourceful. Speaking gradachh is not impossible for a human mouth. It's just not something usually attempted." They smiled, showing their teeth. "Her pronunciation is horrible, but her ways of expressing meaning are creative."

Ker kept his mouth shut. It seemed ridiculous that he was still learning new things about her even after she'd left.

Ellonya landed on the cliff edge with a roar. Dutifully, most of the men began to run. However, the one hauling Noshi, his hands bound and face lit up with gratefulness, was less inclined to give way.

"Release him," Ker ordered, wishing he'd developed a deeper, more commanding voice with age. Fascinatingly, the man was apparently more afraid of whoever had sent him than the current reality of Ellonya, and in moment of admirable boldness, put his knife to Noshi's throat. He yelled something in Nayonan that Ker expected was some variant on, stay back.

Since watching Kella be dragged to what could have been both their deaths, Ker had considered how he'd deal with this situation if it ever arose again. The man screamed as he and Ellonya bent the hand holding the blade back in the wrong direction, and as one, moved their tail to trip him up for emphasis, then blazed a column of fire into the sky.

"*Go*," they said, their voice far more intimidating now it belonged to both of them.

As the man ran, Noshi regarded them for the first time with a little wariness before his face split into a wide smile. "Oh, your mami would love this. Her long in the ground and Mabakis are still saving my life."

Ker smiled and made to dismount. "You really made this guy mad."

Noshi shrugged and brushed the dirt off as he got to his feet. "What can I say? I won't say I ruined his woman for everyone else, but this might be the curse of being memorable."

CHAPTER TWENTY-THREE

King Vikro, Jev's mother, had once kept a parrot, and its knowing cackle when it had caught Kella sneaking into his bedroom haunted her still. They'd called it the second chancellor of the kingdom, and from what Jev had said, it did a killer impression of the old palace sollon.

Even if it was famous and beloved—and it would be mutiny for her to think about wringing its neck the way she wished she'd ended the real second chancellor—Kella still felt no love toward Sailback's harpy. Its awful little red eyes made her feel like it knew everything she was fantasising and mocked her for it.

"How old do you think it is?" Kella asked Evlo, who stood silently by her side. She felt him shrug.

"Feathers look tatty. Must be pretty old. How long do these things live?"

"No clue. Decade, maybe two? You got anything like them in Senice?"

He shook his head. "Nope."

"Finally, you're making the place sound inviting."

He chuckled but stopped when Litz looked over sharply. "She's got a fiercer glare than the harpy," he mumbled after Litz was safely back in conversation with Sailback's first mate. They hadn't set off yet, and Kella suspected Litz, either on behalf of Loren or herself, had some logistics to sort out.

"She does," Kella agreed, a touch proud.

Evlo eyed her with amusement. "Really didn't expect you of all people to fall this hard over a dragon lover."

Kella huffed. "Firmly on my feet, thank you."

"Hmm."

At this point, the pet harpy decided to take a step toward them, and if Evlo hadn't flinched alongside her, Kella wouldn't have known where to look. "I really don't like that thing," she said quietly.

But apparently not quietly enough. "Don't like that thing," the harpy said back at her.

Evlo snickered as Kella scowled, determined not to say another word. The large cowl on its head that so eerily resembled a human face hid a beak and voice just like a parrot's.

"Look alive, lads," Sailback roared as she marched up the deck, ignoring them as she passed. "The waves are speaking to me. They're saying it's going to be a beautiful day for sailing if we see faster feet!"

Evlo frowned. "Should we be doing something?"

"Litz would have told us. Let's just keep out the way."

"And keep hold of our stomachs."

Kella smiled. "I've spent the last year flying about on dragons, and this is not my first time on a boat." Granted, they'd not been successful times, but she was sure she was over that. "Don't worry about me, kid."

Within an hour of them setting off, she bitterly regretted her confidence.

"I've made excuses for you, but they don't seem all that surprised," Litz assured her as she gently pushed her hair back under its scarf and out of the danger zone her face had become.

If Kella wasn't still working through how she felt about Litz being there at all—and if her mouth wasn't covered in vomit—she might have leaned into the touch like a flea-bitten street dog, desperate for comfort and affection.

"And the cook gave me this. I think he said it helps the nausea."

"Gimme," Kella managed, her head still firmly facing the water, the waves that would not stop their incessant movement.

As Litz pressed some leaves into her palms, she laughed softly. "It's a little funny that everyone back home thinks you're some demon sent from the sea. You're not well suited to it."

"Not. Another. Fucking. Word."

More soft laughter. Kella couldn't help feeling warmed, even if it was being enjoyed at her expense.

"Evlo's been put on watch tonight with one of Sailback's nephews. I think it's a kindness. He'll have the hammock quarters almost to himself in the morning."

Kella spat out whatever was still in her mouth, disappointed to find it no more than spittle and phlegm. "No such luck for us, heh?"

Litz went oddly quiet. "Actually, Sailback's giving us a room."

"Us?"

"It's a large bed for important guests. I don't think she wanted to decide who among us was the important one."

Kella listened to someone playing some kind of whistle and stared at the waves that now reflected the moon. It was closing in on Ker's moon now. Gods, she hoped he was safe. "Aelshians don't keep track of birth moons, do they?" she asked, head still down so she didn't have to look at Litz.

"No. That's a very Jeenobian tradition."

"I think you might be a full one." It helped, not only looking away from her but knowing Litz had no idea what she was saying. Full-moon children were what expecting parents prayed for. Said to be blessed by the Moon herself, they would go through life content and wise. And more embarrassingly, they would be the only acceptable mate for a new-moon child, who were always restless, always looking to the horizon.

Kella was, of course, a proud child of the hungry new moon. And the idea of finding someone who would fill her empty, directionless soul was upsettingly captivating.

"Is that what you are?"

Kella felt better in her stomach now. But the idea of speech, or looking Litz in the face, had become far worse.

Litz gave her shoulder a comforting pat. "I'm going to see about getting Loren settled. But when you feel a little more yourself, come to bed." Her voice was so soft that Kella felt a pleasant shudder run through her, almost as physically affecting as the fading nausea had been. Whatever the leaves were, she wished she'd had them hours ago.

"Litz," she started, finally turning. But Litz had already walked away, looking up with a big, tired smile at Loren.

Kella sighed. Now that the pain in her insides was subsiding, she was slowly becoming aware of other discomforts. The wind was good. It was getting them there faster, but it was cold on her bare arms that ached from hours of being slung over the side.

Taking a deep breath, she got to her feet and decided to find the kitchen she had promised to report to hours ago. She didn't like the idea of being called lazy after a lifetime of dreaming of making it onto a pirate ship. Besides, she wasn't brave enough to find out how Litz meant to take things in their shared, private bedroom. No sand, no companions, no excuses beyond perhaps some bad breath on Kella's part. Just the two of them choosing to sleep beside each other.

For now, that was too big a thought. Because it might not happen tonight, but eventually, Litz would realise she'd made a mistake. She'd given up everyone she loved and worked for to save Kella's life, and all it was going to bring her was rough living, danger, and a purposeless street dog of a former dragon slayer. And that would be so much easier to face if they were still nothing to each other.

❖

Life among pirates wasn't so unlike life in the military, Litz decided. People were always trying to catch her off guard, partly to confirm that she was on guard in the first place. People were always busy with their own serious activity, partly to avoid being recruited for a more serious one. But like soldiers, they still knew how to cut loose.

Litz found Kella and Evlo hotly fighting for the rest of their funds in a tense dice game the afternoon after they'd set sail. Thanks to her intervention, they did not lose everything, but they'd lost a considerable enough amount that Kella couldn't look at her after. At least, Litz hoped that was why she couldn't look at her.

There always seemed to be some music too. Their first night aboard, one drummer did her level best to play to Loren, who missed her attendants and was glad of the attention but refused to lower herself and react to it. They were all shockingly comfortable with her, whether she was flying or sleeping on the deck. When she swooped down to the waves with seemingly no warning and scooped a small whale up to feast on, the crew all cheered for her. They might have resented her arrival and mission, but she was one of theirs now. When she deposited half the whale on the deck, it cemented that fondness. They had a dragon on the crew, and she would provide for them.

And whether it was Kella or the ship's cook, the meal crafted from it was the most delicious they'd enjoyed so far. It was also such a task to eat that a party broke out around it that evening.

Litz tried to be subtle in making her way over to Kella but feared she was anything but. The warm, tasty food, the more than generous helping of ale, and the stars above that seemed to dance in time to the quick music made her bold, and she pushed through the embarrassment. Kella had been avoiding her, and she had no intention of allowing that to continue. "Is it everything you hoped for?"

Kella's smile was so slow that Litz felt thrilled by every tiny measurement. She smelled like the food they'd been consuming, and her stance on the gently swaying deck was mercifully steady and sure. "What?"

Litz gestured at the dancers as the musicians began playing a louder tune the whole crew seemed to know. "Piracy. You always dreamed of it. You idolise her. Will you stay here if they let you?"

Snorting softly, Kella looked at her tapping feet. "I got things to get home for."

"Ker?" When Kella said nothing, Litz felt bold enough to press. "And what if he doesn't need you anymore?"

The way Kella looked up sharply, Litz knew she had pushed too far. But to her surprise, Kella didn't snap, though her dark eyes looked like they wanted to. "Doesn't matter."

"What about what you want?"

"I want to fix the dragons. Remember? The quest?"

"Yes, but what do you want for you?"

Kella bit her lip and looked away, uncharacteristically shy. When she did speak, she sounded odd, like she was reciting something she'd rehearsed. "There's never really a good end for people like me."

"People like you?"

"People in stories." She sighed, swaying. "Y'know, when I was a kid, like, before Ker was born, my mami fought this dragon that hadn't hurt many people, but everyone agreed it needed someone to go after it."

"Why?"

"There was a little girl with it," Kella said simply. "I don't know if she was, well, like Ker, if she bonded to it, or if they just…Anyway, my mami killed it, and she took the girl back." Kella's eyes were looking at the dancers but remained distant and faraway. "She had a dirty face, and she screamed and screamed whenever anyone tried to touch it, so we could never get it clean. She was maybe five years older than me."

"What happened to her?"

Kella frowned. "That's the weird part of it all because people in Malya really love this story. Like, I've heard twenty versions of how hers ended if I've heard one. That she turned into some kind of dragon-gremlin creature at night and ate people. That she was actually me, and that's how my mami got me. Some even said she was a very beautiful woman who was so grateful to my mami for rescuing her that she, well, a lot of stories people get embarrassed to tell me. But mami really gave her to a sollon group, who raised her, though she never liked speaking to people. She works in a fish stall in the market, the one I met you in, and she still doesn't talk much. Never married. I thought about going to see her after everything, but…" She paused, and they both listened as a new song had more pirates bouncing the floorboards. Sailback, wherever she was, did not seem to be motivated to stop them, even with a dragon aboard.

"What I mean is, no one ever tried to tell me the real version. People don't like it when the people from stories just go away. They have to go out doing something big."

"And you still think you're in a story?"

"Oh, we're all in stories, Princess." She flashed a quick grin before her expression grew solemn again.

I'm glad I'm in yours, Litz wanted to say, but since Kella seemed newly distracted, she was content to stand beside her quietly as they leaned their backs to the sea.

"*Dragons' sky, witches' earth, But the sea is for the hungry.*" As the singing continued, several of the pirates began to dance in a birdlike strut as they clapped on the beat. Intellectually, Litz knew of sea worship, but growing up in a forest, it hadn't been something she'd seen. Though she was sure no pirate would describe it so, the singing and chanting seemed to transform the boat into a temple of united belief.

The farther north they sailed, the longer the days seemed to become, just a little. Perhaps it was simply the sea air and hard day's work exhausting her, but it felt far too late in the evening for the sun to dip below the sea.

"In the stories, this is when they kiss and turn the sun's light off for privacy," Kella said when Litz mentioned this. "But I grew up and travelled farther and realised the sun will kiss anything."

"It doesn't mean he doesn't still want to kiss the sea," Litz pointed out as the sailors roared, "*The sea is for the free,*" and someone took out a whistle to play.

Summoning her scattered courage, Litz held out a hand to Kella. On Aelshian naval boats, alcohol rations were strictly controlled, but at least this night, it did not seem to be one of the captain or cook's concerns. It wasn't only the sun and sea kissing now. "Would you care to dance?" She risked a smile. "You don't have to stay masked this time."

Kella's fingers twitched, so close to unfurling and taking her hand, before they curled tighter. "No. I should get back to the kitchens. Kinda abandoned my post."

Litz tried to hide her disappointment, but when Kella walked away, Loren opened one eye and stared at her. *I can always feel when something has upset you, beloved.*

Yes, I can hide nothing from you. What she wasn't saying sat uneasily between them, and Litz continued to meet Loren's stare through the dancers.

"*Nothing ever claims the sea, be everchanging and ever free!*"

I truly am sorry this has hurt you, Loren said. *I only wanted to avoid more of that for you.*

I am still angry. Litz paused. *But it would be foolish to try to hold a grudge against the only soul in the world who still loves me.*

I would not be so sure of that. But if it was, I would not allow it to remain so.

Perhaps it was the alcohol, but Litz finally allowed herself to smile. *Oh? What would you do?*

In much the same way we secured passage on this boat, if there is something someone ought to be giving you and they were not, I would remind them you are tied, always, to a vengeful, selfish, magical beast.

So absorbed and soothed to be joking with Loren again, Litz didn't notice Evlo until he gave her arm a tap. "Did I hear you asking for a dance and being rudely, how would you say, spurned?"

Laughing, Litz took his hand. Perhaps she had lost all the humans who loved her, and when she took the time to grieve that, the knowledge would crush her. But perhaps she was making new friends, new loved ones, and they all knew her for exactly what she was. There was no canopy between her and the sky, and perhaps for the first time, she was on her way to doing something good for reasons beyond familial duty. "You did!"

It's Kella's loss if she will not let you lead.

She will.

Loren's amusement warmed Litz as she spun with Evlo, arm in arm. *That's the spirit.*

You'd be pleased for me if she lets me choose her?

I'm just delighted you're making choices, Loren assured her. *And I hope she's worthy of yours.*

❖

Evlo was good at staying still. It was part of the archer thing, about being more sniper than fighter, Kella supposed. He'd often been left waiting for hours while the rest of them baited a dragon into place. Sometimes, they wouldn't even need him; something would go wrong, and they'd kill it early, or it would escape, and nobody would kill anything. Whatever happened, Evlo would have to stay hidden and quiet and still. He was moving now as Kella approached him on the deck but only because the waves were moving the boat more roughly. It gave the impression that he was swaying as he watched the water as though expecting something to break it any second. He was leaning so far over on his crossed arms that when he slowly turned to look at Kella, it showed off just how long his neck was and made it seem strangely shaped, like a python that had eaten well.

"Are the waves speaking to you?" Kella said, imitating Sailback's tone. When that didn't get her a smile, she trained her crossed arms next to his so that she was nudging him. Since learning about the history of those scars on his back, she'd been hesitant about touching him in a way that had started to annoy her. He was her friend, and that wasn't how she acted around those.

"I wish I knew how close we are," he said after they both listened to the waves slap the ship.

"Would it be better if someone told you it was another day? Or another month?"

"If it was another month, I'd be worried we'd run out of food. These pirates can fucking eat."

"You're telling the co-cook."

"Co-cook today? You were kitchen helper yesterday."

She smiled faintly. "How long did it take you the first time?"

He didn't answer for a moment. "I don't know," he said before glancing at her defensively. Like most people, he was taller than her, but it wasn't by much, and right now, he looked even shorter. "I wasn't doing too good," he added, his accent becoming thicker.

She didn't look away. "You never really said how you got out, how you ended up on a Doshni ship. How you escaped."

He tried to frown, but this only succeeded in drawing attention to his wobbling bottom lip that couldn't keep form with the rest of his stern face. "I didn't."

"Like, you mean figuratively, or like…"

"No." He sighed in annoyance, possibly at her and her language, possibly at himself. Maybe both. "I wasn't trying to escape. Not really. I thought I was getting away, but I didn't—"

"Didn't expect to live."

"Yeah."

She wanted to say that she still found it odd to be alive. She'd stopped fighting dragons and not because they'd been the death of her. But that felt like butting in on the moment he was having with himself and besides, was morbid to admit out loud.

"So they rescued you."

He nodded, looking like his head had become ten times heavier. "I remember getting out from where they were holding me but only to the sea." As he spoke, his voice became flatter, and as usual, Kella wasn't sure if this was his accent or a reaction to the emotions the memories drew out. If he recalled events like a list, they might have less ability to hurt him. "The prison was by the shore, so it wasn't all that hard. Used their fishing raft to get away. I was out there three days, I think. A storm took me, and I kept afloat, but I never thought I'd see land or people again. I'd never met a Doshni or anyone not from the island. It was…it was a shock waking up to people who looked and talked so different."

"I'll bet."

"And I wasn't able to walk. And…"

He trailed off, and kindly, she tried to pick up what he couldn't continue with. "You said you were betrayed."

He huffed and turned his eyes away. "I never exactly had it confirmed. But only one of us was never picked up and killed. And they knew everything." He turned to look at her. "I still think all this is stupid. But if anything makes me think the devil is real, it's that they were so keen to get us for even thinking about going after it."

"If you still think it's a stupid idea," Kella said slowly, trying her best to be sincere, "why are you on this boat?"

He leaned his chin on his arms. "Kerali said some things back on your beach."

"You listen to him, huh?"

He narrowed his eyes and smiled a little at last. "You're one to talk. Besides, I was starting to feel like Fin's new plans held little I wanted."

Kella leaned all her weight on one arm and faced him. "How come I'm the one to talk, heh?" She'd decided she would rather face teasing about Litz than talk about Findan.

He only glared, his wobbling lip stable at last. "You know well. I can't believe you haven't slept with her yet."

"Who says I haven't?"

"Ker. The woman herself."

Kella punched him on the arm, an action that made her miss Ker with a keenness that hurt. She hadn't allowed herself to think much about what would happen if something happened to one of them. Or if she never punched Ker's arm to shut him up about something he was right about ever again because he'd become so far from human that he wasn't worth bullying any longer. Without her there to speak to someone human, would he even—

"Why not?" Evlo pressed, and Kella was grateful he seemed oblivious to the odd direction her thoughts had spiralled. "I've known you awhile, and I've never seen you get so hung up on a person before. What gives? She likes you, you're not stupid. And you want her."

She didn't answer, and they went quiet again, before he pointed out a jellyfish in the water larger than a small tree.

"We called them good omens back home," he explained. "Purple is always a lucky colour."

"You guys must go nuts over a purple dragon."

"Yeah, they do."

"Is that all anybody thinks about there? Dragons?"

Seeming moody but not unwilling to talk, Evlo thought for a moment. Kella recognised the look. Sometimes, it was good to think back. Like making yourself throw up after drinking. "People like for things not to change."

"I get that."

"But like, really more than normal. When I think of culture anywhere, I think of this giant pot of soup everyone's proud of."

Kella nodded, wondering what Ballian would think of that. "Is it tasty?"

"I've never tried it."

"What flavour?"

"I don't know. Vegetables, I think."

"Huh. How come everyone's proud of it then?"

"It's, like, a thousand years old."

"Actually?"

"They keep adding to it, so it's never been thrown out. Like I say, they worship things that don't change much."

"Like dragons."

"Yeah." He glanced at the sky to where Loren was flying, apparently unable to help himself. They listened to the wind in companionable silence before he spoke again, sounding choked. "I didn't come here alone just to let everybody down someplace else."

"You won't."

"I've never been needed before."

"You've been on our team for years."

"Yeah, and you never needed an archer before me, did you?"

"Got easier with you."

"Sure. I'm the handy extra. But you guys could have done without me. Now, if something happens to me or I fuck up, you don't have a backup Senician here. Everything's fucked."

"Of course. We'd be fucked if we lost Loren or Litz, the one who can read this fucking map. But we're on a dangerous quest. That's what a godsdamned dangerous quest looks like. We need everyone here, and everyone's in imminent danger." She frowned. "Except for now. The pirates have been shockingly safe so far."

"Speak for yourself. You don't have to sleep with them."

"Sleep with, heh?"

"Y'know what I mean."

"But they're all right?"

"They're all right. Guy above me snores worse than Rall used to, though."

"Fuck, that's bad."

He laughed. "It's why I keep volunteering for the night shift." He half smiled. "I don't mind all that much. Kinda reminds me of home. Both my brothers snored."

"Were you close?" Kella asked eventually. "Before?"

"Normal close, I guess." He glowered at the waves. "I hope Ker's still himself when you get back to him."

Kella felt a familiar chill run through her. "Ellonya's gonna be careful."

"You think a dragon cares about careful? You think she can?" He sounded more curious than angry.

"I think she cares about him." She breathed out slowly. "And I hope she's learned to listen to me."

"You miss him?"

"Fuck off."

He shoved lightly into her. "Yeah, you do."

"Yeah, I do. Glad I got you with me. Need at least one annoying little guy on my team."

"In what universe is Kerali little?"

"Mine."

"And don't be so humble," he said, smiling.

"That's not usually my problem."

"I mean it. You're indispensable too."

A little embarrassed he'd noticed her omitting herself, she smiled. "For my wit? My charm?"

"I wouldn't go if you weren't going." It was said as much like a statement as remarking on the weather.

"Good thing I'm going with you then, heh?"

"Yeah. Good thing."

CHAPTER TWENTY-FOUR

For three weeks now, they had shared a room, and Kella had done her utmost to avoid even looking at Litz. They'd spent so much time together on the road with nothing between them, but now, they had a door to close the world out, and that created a suffocating intimacy demanding to have something done about itself.

The night before, Kella had whimpered in her sleep, and Litz had listened, almost hoping for the chance to comfort her. She could not pass another night like that. Though Litz was loathe to think of other women when thinking of Kella, she had to admit that most of her bedroom experience had been with Nic, who flirted incessantly and annoyed Litz into making a move. She'd assumed that if things moved forward between her and Kella, they might move similarly, since that also seemed like Kella's style.

See? You do have a type.

I don't want to reduce Kella by thinking she's like someone else. She's her own person and a better person than Nic. Or me.

Don't reduce yourself, either, especially not for a relationship you may not be having.

Even if we don't ever move toward each other, we're having a relationship. One that's defined my life more than any other.

Other than one.

More than any human one, Litz corrected herself as she fondly watched Kella wrap her hair for bed with the colourful silk she'd bought from a street merchant at the port. Though trade wasn't common there, she'd convinced him to trade three scarfs for one engraved silver hair bead. Litz had wondered at the time why she'd kept the bead so long now that she no longer had hair of a length to fit it.

"What?" she said as she noticed Litz staring, but even in confrontation, her eyes skittered away to her next task, and she moved to unstring the loose shirt Litz wasn't sure when she'd acquired. Most of the sailors had a similar one.

I'm sick of this.

Hmm. I'll try not to look in on you for now.

"Why can't you look at me?"

Kella flinched as though stung. "I can do what I like, Princess. And maybe I don't feel like it."

"Do you still think you ruined my life?"

"Why? Are you blaming me for ruining it yet?"

Litz shook her head in disbelief. "You self-important…not everything is about you."

For a moment, Kella did look at her with a half-smile hanging from her full lips. "Great. Definitely want to look at you now."

"Not everything is your fault. My decisions certainly aren't."

"Uh-huh." Kella climbed into bed, and Litz felt almost desperate. They likely had another week of being stuck in this room, and something inside her was breaking, like if she didn't act now, she'd lose Kella forever or lose the belief she had any right to try to reach her.

So Litz followed her.

When Kella turned, Litz backed her into the bed. Unable to do anything else, Kella stared, eyes blazing with rage, but Litz had seen enough real anger from her to know this was more show. The real feelings she had were shame and want; Litz could sense that too.

Litz could kiss her now, sure Kella would melt in her touch. And she wanted to get to that, but she was afraid that the ugliness of Kella's guilt would only grow, like an abandoned room in a large home becoming mouldy with neglect.

"I should have stayed where I was," Litz said, holding Kella's shoulders when it seemed she might turn. "I shouldn't have even considered leaving with you. If I had a prayer of finding Eisha, if I wanted to keep any relationship with the family who loves me, if I cared about my career, or doing any good with the position I've done nothing in my life but build. There is a whole clan who might be slaughtered to the last child because I chose to remove myself from the room where decisions on their fate will be made."

Kella's eyes shone with fear and annoyance but hope too.

"But you've never been about making good decisions. You're something I want more than any of those things, Kella Mabaki, Kirasdaughter, and I know that's wrong of me. But I don't regret it. They were about to kill you, and I don't want to live in a world you're not in.

When I'm around you, I feel like my life might be worth something. And I have more fun than I think I've ever had in my life."

Litz paused to rub circles into Kella's scarred and bruised arms with her thumbs, surprised to see Kella's lower lip wobble. "It won't last," she said, her voice softer than Litz had ever heard it. "I'm going to let you down."

"If that's true, you can't avoid it by avoiding me. I'm one of only two people you can trust on this boat. It's not good strategy."

Kella opened her mouth in protest. "Hey—"

And this time, Litz was tired of waiting for the right moment and pressed that beautiful mouth closed.

❖

Kella wasn't used to not making the first move. At home, it didn't matter how prettily she dressed or how tall she was: she was the dragon slayer. Whoever she was spending the night with—except maybe Jev— they expected to be pursued and told what she wanted. Unable to escape being that person, she had always been obliging, even with Litz before they'd learned who the other was, who they might become to each other. Kella had seen something she wanted to taste, something wonderful, and selfishly, she'd reached out to take it. Maybe it was past time she let Litz be selfish too.

Whatever Litz wanted, Kella was eager, feverish to give. Maybe if she kept giving, Litz would stay happy. Maybe she could delay that inevitable moment when Litz realised Kella had ruined her whole life by entering it again. Or maybe she'd leave. Like Jev. For duty or because no matter how fun she was, Kella couldn't hold her interest forever.

But when Litz kissed her and moved her lips below Kella's chin, she wanted to forget that. She moved her mouth in tandem to Litz's long, romantic neck that had always enchanted her, refusing to be left behind. Her whole body felt alight as Litz's teeth grazed her neck to her collarbone, and she hoped that whatever mirroring motions she was making were making Litz feel as good.

When their lantern burned out moments later, it seemed like they might tenderly devour each other in the dark. They had only their hands and mouths to steer them true as the sea rocked them. On a large wave, Kella pulled Litz down by the clothes she still infuriatingly wore and tumbled them both onto the bed.

Overwhelmed by the body she now had permission to touch, Kella's groping hands found only Litz's face. Carefully caressing those cheekbones as Litz's mouth briefly pulled away, Kella let her thumbs stroke over the light sheen of sweat on Litz's nose, the faded scar by her eye. She knew her by sight. Now she wanted to feel her make that smile Kella loved so much, the way her cheeks rose to fit Kella's palms so perfectly.

"I didn't want to start this," Kella said, finding that words came easier in the dark, especially as Litz pulled her closer. She let her hands fall now that the remainder of the clothes Litz wore was unignorable. "The more I'm around you, the more I know I can't give you up." She stroked the curve of Litz's thighs, almost gasping when she felt how much her hand rose. She'd never been this careful, this precious, about anybody she'd taken to bed before. But none of those anybodies were Litz.

"You were scared, dragon slayer?"

Kella grinned and rolled Litz's half-unwrapped form closer so that she almost lay on top of her. "I was being careful."

"Not something you're known for." The knowing, teasing tone was almost more than Kella could bear. This was so domestic and nothing like she knew how to keep. The incessant rocking made it impossible to forget the oddness of their situation, even if it had begun to feel more calming than sickening, especially now. When considering future ends to their roads, it helped to remember that, for now, they were going the same way.

"No. You're different—" She stopped herself from continuing.

"I should hope so. You travelled to Aelshia for me."

"Now who's being self-important." Lightly, Kella dared to tug at her hair. "I came to Aelshia for the books."

"Sure you did. And left the moment something confirmed what you were looking for."

Kella swallowed. Charmed as she was by Litz's attempts at sarcasm, she felt herself sobering. "What if we don't find anything? What if there is nothing that can help, or we get killed looking, or—"

It became Kella's turn to have her face held still. "Then we will have chosen together. And I'm sure we won't make it all the way there, to a different dragon-run society cut off from all our known world, and learn *nothing* of use."

A little cheered, Kella narrowed her eyes. "Is Loren listening in on this?"

A soft, beautiful laugh that Kella was proud to have produced filled the small room. "No. She took herself away earlier when she could tell where my thoughts were moving."

"Ah, so you had designs toward me. This was all your plan, to upset me and then get me into bed."

Kella was still giggling when Litz stopped her mouth again. She was giving, and Kella wanted nothing ever again but to take and take and take.

❖

What a joy it was to finally shut Kella's quick, wicked mouth the way she had so longed to. Just as Litz had suspected during all those lonely months in Verassez, Kella melted perfectly, letting Litz do as she pleased, no hard edges left to her. The soft noises that went with her surrender were just as delicious as the rest of her.

Then, she seemed to remember herself and increased her grip on Litz's back. "Wait," she said, "this isn't right."

"What now?"

"I had a whole plan."

"Oh?"

"I was going to seduce you."

"If you tell me the plan, perhaps we can work on remedying that." Carefully, Litz toyed with Kella's bottom lip, utterly delighted Kella was letting her even as she continued to speak sternly.

"Yes," she said. "First off, you weren't supposed to be wearing all this. I was supposed to have you out of these by now."

"You're halfway there," Litz reminded her encouragingly as she knelt, pinning Kella, and pulled off the rest of her robe.

Almost reverently, Kella groped for Litz's breasts, still hidden by the dark. "Oh."

"Didn't you think I had any?"

"Your uniform always hides everything," Kella said defensively as she started massaging her new finds.

"What were you planning to do next?" Litz asked, her breath hitching as Kella's ministrations became pointed at her nipples.

"I don't remember."

"How anticlimactic."

"There's a lot distracting me."

Shaking her head, Litz got to the task of getting Kella out of the few items of clothing she had left. Though she could barely see, it felt important that they were still on a level. When she was done, she lay on Kella, languorous as a dragon slipping back into the river on a hot day. Their legs fit together neatly, tantalisingly, just as Litz had known they would during all those aching nights lying next to each other.

Slowly, Litz started to angle her body, leaning a hand on the bed, steering them toward the friction that would be there for both of them. She smiled when Kella gasped, feeling the wet slide between them increase. Every now and then, the boat would rock, sometimes frustratingly, sometimes adding a wonderful momentum, and that felt right. They were meant to make each other feel good, but the outside world could not and should not be forgotten. It was part of what had brought them together, what kept them moving forward, chasing a peak and a pace Kella was still obediently letting Litz set.

Litz had dreamed of this. More than shutting Kella up in a fun way or undressing her, she'd longed to make her feel loved and cared for. She hoped Kella felt it now, as clearly as the soft tickle of damp hair between Kella's legs set Litz's whole body alight as it became trapped between them and made her retreat. But not for long, never for long. Facing away and feeling for each other in the dark felt good, but she badly wanted to see what Kella looked like when she made that soft little groan as Litz put more weight on one of her arms to stroke Kella's smooth thigh. The moonlight coming through the cracks in the wood let her watch just how beautifully it was trembling.

That made her wonder if magic could ever be used for sex now that she was finally partnering with someone who knew everything about her. Probably too dangerous. But she would think on it more.

"What are you thinking?" she asked Kella softly.

"Thinking about you." Kella gasped, rough fingers stroking all the parts of Litz she was able to reach.

Moving a little stiltedly, Litz moved down, keeping Kella's legs wide like a river delta, hoping to get closer to everything she'd been so focused on. It was too dark, making the smell of Kella intoxicating, and her fingers deftly guided Litz inside. With gentle strokes, Litz felt Kella rising to meet her when she put her mouth on her.

"Fuck."

Smiling, Litz put her tongue to work, pressing down hard until Kella buried a hand in her hair. At a relentless pace, she moved back and forth over the quivering resistance. She pressed her face still closer as Kella's thighs began to shake and curl possessively around her neck as she gave a cry of complete surrender.

Even as the pressure around her shoulders increased, Litz was enjoying herself far too much to pause. How far would Kella let her push her over the edge? The quaking of Kella's powerful thighs and her disbelieving laughter made Litz change her pace, luxuriously taking her time, just as she might chase the last piece of flavour from a melon that she had all the time in the world to savour. She delved into Kella's folds, using her tongue as surely as her fingers to taste from the source, to open her up to everything Litz wanted to do to her.

Above her, Kella shuddered out a few words, spoken too quick in a Jeenobian accent. Taking that as encouragement, Litz stroked Kella's inner thigh before slipping her fingers back inside, her tongue back to its merciless work above. It didn't take long before Kella was crying out again in a soft gasp that seemed to be wrung from her without permission, as though her body was no longer her own to command.

Slowly, Litz began to stop, removing her damp fingers and only giving a few more teasing licks. She lay there, completely satisfied, breathing through her nose into Kella's curls.

"Okay," Kella said eventually, huffing out a long, satisfied breath. "I'm gonna get my breath back."

"Sure."

"And then we're doing more you. I'm not letting you win this."

Fondly, Litz leant her crossed arms across Kella's pelvis and kicked her feet into the air. Perhaps they wouldn't get a real way to wash for a month, and they would have to smell exactly like this for weeks. Perhaps the traces of Kella's desire would never leave her skin now. She felt branded, changed. "Are we in a competition?"

"Aren't competitions fun?"

"Mmm." Gently, Litz pressed her mouth down, touching the skin just below Kella's belly button. "But as you've tried to tell me before, we make a pretty unbeatable team."

"We're in this together, heh?"

"If you'd like to be." Litz looked up at where Kella's face would be watching her. She wondered what she was looking at. "I'm not going anywhere anytime soon."

❖

Ballian had told Kella that there was a custom in the hill town where his family was from, that when a couple wed, they were sent to a special house kept clean and useful all through the year. This was but half day's walk away and would often be used on a schedule with more than one village. The couple usually spent between one night and three there, but if they had few family or work demands, their community sometime allowed them to stay for a week or two before they returned to their new household together. It was called enjoying Temmas and was said to help the harvest grow.

Those next few days, Kella felt like she'd been on a Temmas retreat. True, there was Evlo and Loren and a bunch of pirates, and they were still expected to work, but it was the break Kella had never had. At home, if she hadn't been working, she'd been waiting, depressed, antsy to get her hands on something to do. But now, with the biggest job of her life still in the distance, she had Litz to get her hands on.

And Litz, dragged away from all her life and problems, would always laugh and oblige, however much she liked to pretend she wouldn't. They might not be about to set up a life together, but they'd been granted a moment away from all the crushing realities and responsibility they'd left behind or were about to arrive at.

And they were in love. Kella wasn't saying it yet because she refused to say something like that first, and she didn't want to spoil how stupidly happy they were with real feelings. In any case, it was too soon. They were sailing toward a quest for something that might not exist, and they might not survive. For now, the life they were making was about learning the right moment to tell Loren to fuck off out of her lover's mind or winking at Sailback or winding Evlo up by how obnoxious they were being to keep his mind off the ever-approaching shore.

Lately, it had also been making Litz tell her every awful thing she considered doing to her using magic. Magic might still be terrible, no matter why, but the idea of introducing something terrible to bedroom play had always thrilled her, so the idea would not let her go.

She was considering those possibilities when the sailor in the crow's nest, Rilva, yelled and pointed out a dark shape in the water. Though it was not fully visible, it made Loren somewhere high in the air seem little. Even those ancient Circle dragons suddenly seemed slim.

"She's not interested in boats," Sailback, who appeared at Kella's side at the edge of the deck, said as quietly as she'd ever spoken. "And this isn't a prize we could ever ferry home. Everyone, stick to your posts and your best behaviour."

The water was still that afternoon. Their journey had been slowing, and as the monster, larger than a whale but looking very much like one, dipped under the boat, it gave them a small wave to ride. Its dorsal fin looked more shark than whale, but its longer nose and wider tail marked it as something different to either.

"What do you call that?" Kella asked, choosing to keep her voice quiet.

"Me?" Sailback folded her arms and laid them on the boat's side. Despite her reassuring words, Kella suspected she was thrilled to still be alive. "Krakeneaters. Only thing I've ever seen take them on. And you don't see them much. They don't like coming to the surface. Something's attracted her." She looked thoughtful, then pointed some way behind Kella's left shoulder. "Look. More of 'em."

They were maybe half a mile away, large enough to inspire nothing but the most confident verification. Only the fins were visible, but since those were almost a quarter of the ship's size, they were easy to count. Maybe eleven of them were bobbing to the surface.

Slowly, Sailback's wide grin began to fade. "Hmm. They're not pack animals. Not usually."

"Why so many, then?"

"Like I said, some'n must have attracted 'em." Sailback was frowning now as she stood back. "I'll get everyone on lookout," she muttered as she marched away.

For what? Kella wondered. Kraken? One might make a move on a boat, but they were also solitary. It seemed unlikely that so many hungry mouths of this size would have congregated for one kraken. And the wind still hadn't returned. They might soon be forced to find out what the krakeneaters were there for.

Evlo joined her, also looking solemn. "I saw one of those big guys on my crossing over here. They don't usually turn up in groups, do they?"

"No," Kella said, trying to sound like she'd heard that information longer ago. She eyed Evlo carefully. "You're on night watch tonight, heh?"

"Sure am, boss."

She grinned. "You wanna see if they'll let you up in that nest? I got a feeling an archer might be handy up there."

He met her with a smile. They were monster hunters, and now they were adrift on a sea of monsters. Something worth hunting would inevitably appear.

"Tell you what," Kella said, daring to lean down instead of running to help in the kitchen. The short break she was taking from it was surely long over now. "Whatever happens next, I bet my mami would have loved it."

❖

They'd taken a boat into Aelshia, an experience Zebenn hadn't expected to enjoy but had found strangely soothing. Though they occasionally had to help row, they were going where the current pushed them, and it was far less taxing than walking or riding. Mostly, all they needed to do was sit back and watch the scenery change.

Aelshia itself was nothing and everything like Zebenn had imagined. Trees stretched taller than the eye, and dragons relaxed everywhere. The humidity was inescapable, with no inclination from the architecture that anyone was even trying to escape it, and the noise of a forest that never truly rested was incessant.

Hallen seemed uncomfortable afloat, and perhaps out of spite, that encouraged Zebenn's ease. Though they'd been assured everyone here would speak Aelshian, a similar enough language to Jeenobian, the pilot of their boat spoke only a few words and in a very heavy accent. That seemed to increase Hallen's discomfort too.

"He'll be from a forest clan," Findan had said knowingly. She knew some of the pilot's language, and Zebenn was able to pick up the basics of manners and greetings. Since he could get by in Aelshian, this wasn't helpful but did make them feel better.

After a week of river travel, they arrived at what appeared to be a city, though not the kind Zebenn understood. It wasn't dusty or overcrowded and didn't seem interested in shutting out dragons or wildlife. Though Findan had explained the dragons were different here, it still felt wrong to walk past them in human spaces, like leaving a baby alone with a sleeping lion.

The centre, as much as there was one, was a wide river basin hugged by cramped buildings on stilts, as well as a cage holding some twenty to thirty people on the central docking area. Most were dressed similarly, but one man, whose eyes looked far past Zebenn and their boat, had very different clothes. They looked expensive, and he stood apart from the rest.

Behind the cage was a dragon.

Zebenn could guess what was about to happen next, even if they didn't want to believe it. The cage was about to be sent into water, and the roof would be lit. The prisoners would be burned on high and drowned below. Though Zebenn had watched countless friends and strangers die by dragon fire, it had never been sanctioned by people. This was truly upsetting in a way they hadn't thought they were still capable of being upset. "We have to do something."

Findan smiled, looking almost girlish. "I suppose we ought to show we've arrived. And let people know who we are." She turned to the pilot and said a few words in his language. He smiled slowly, and Zebenn wondered if they hadn't gotten this boat on purpose. But perhaps the driver's earlier chats with Findan had just been more productive than they'd guessed.

The boat sped up. Hallen was so alarmed, he almost dropped his oar. When they were a little closer to the prison boat, Findan let the boat go and looked at Zebenn. She looked so happy that even here, in a strange place, Zebenn felt at home. "I hear they don't have dragon slayers here. Should we teach them what we do?"

CHAPTER TWENTY-FIVE

You still don't see anything?

A few more krakeneaters following us or going our way. They aren't herd creatures. None of them even noticed when I made a meal of that young one. At least, not until I dropped what was left of it.

They swarmed?

I'm surprised the waves didn't knock the boat over.

Well, they are a little farther away now, Litz reassured them both. *I know Kella's worried, but it seems that if they're after anything, we'll be away before we find out what it's about. The wind's starting to pick up again.*

Not fast enough. I think your little dragon-killing paramour is right to worry. Whatever is big enough to warrant all this attention, we won't be away from it fast enough.

Hmm. Litz was starting to give up her concentration to Kella, who was undressing, revealing a scar Litz had enjoyed kissing and licking the night before as though it was a fresh wound, and she was a scavenger preparing to devour it.

I know you're hardly listening now, but normal sharks are arriving too. I think I saw a kraken. It's pale and shines in the moonlight. But none of this is the prey the krakeneaters wait for.

Mm-hmm.

Fine. Return to your far more urgent fun.

No, I really want to know.

I release you, my silly human, Loren said fondly. *Enjoy your short life to the fullest. The archer and I shall keep eyes to the sea.*

Thank you. I love you. Litz smiled as she felt Loren withdraw and took a few moments to realise Kella was looking at her strangely.

"Loren's keeping watch instead of resting?"

"It's like you hear her words as clearly as I do."

"Thank the Earth, no." Out of her shirt but still with a scarf binding her breasts, she sat on the bed, legs crossed and her face wide with a grin. It felt like a gift to see her like this, no cynicism or responsibilities weighing down the honest joy of her expression. She was happy to be here and because Litz was with her. She seemed younger. "Now," she said, "we were talking about magic."

"All your ideas are too dangerous."

Kella pouted. "I'm a big girl. I should get to decide if I want to risk a hot witch absolutely wrecking my vagina forever."

"Aren't we having a good enough time?"

"Sure. But taking risks with you is kinda what makes life worth living, Princess."

Litz rolled her eyes and approached the bed with a fond smile. "Such poor judgement."

Kella raised her arms, demanding the comfort of Litz's embrace. "That's what you like about me."

"It's true. Your unique brand of foolish heroics has only endeared me to you."

Kella wrapped her arms around Litz's back and pulled her closer. "In that case," she said, rubbing circles on Litz's back. "I'm going to make sure that when I meet the wish demon, I'm going to be incredibly stupid and incredibly heroic."

"Wonderful. What will you ask for?"

Kella made a face. "Oh, I wasn't going to do the asking."

"Why?"

"Not a very good person, that's why."

Litz wished she could take it as the joke Kella was framing it as. "You're a good person, Kella."

"I'm not saying I'm *terrible*, but I have been known to make my share of selfish, foolish decisions," Kella explained, joining her hand with Litz's, threading their fingers like they were supposed to be there. "And if we do find this demon, we have to make sure we ask for something selflessly, or it won't work. It'll bounce back at us so badly, we'll wish we'd never said anything." She frowned as though only just realising something. "I was going to put Ker up to it. He's good in a way that's on purpose." She narrowed her eyes. "You wanna do it? Are you feeling selfless?"

Deciding to relent, Litz gripped her fingers tighter. "What makes Evlo a bad choice?"

"Aw, Evlo's a great guy."

"Okay."

"But we are going to back to this evil place of his childhood nightmares where all his family hates him," Kella explained with some reluctance. "I don't trust him to be making smart decisions, either. Especially not when this is his quest he was never allowed to finish. And he would have wished for something totally different than what we're planning now."

"I can see why that might be a concern."

"But you know what he said the other day?" Kella asked, her mind apparently wandering further from the potential uses of magic in sex.

"What?"

"He said they've got an ancient pot of soup. I have to try it. That's my other quest."

"You want to try an old Senician soup?"

"No, not just old, it's like old, old. Old the way boats or buildings are old and—"

Something was really rocking the boat now. After quickly exchanging glances, they both stood and started getting what few items of clothing they'd taken off back on again.

"Could have just been a big wave," Kella pointed out, not slowing.

Litz shook her head. "I hear shouting."

By the time they made it on deck, they were left in no doubt that they were somewhat under attack. The moonlight shone on the fins of the krakeneaters surfacing alongside them, but they weren't the issue, not yet.

"Fish on deck to the starboard side!"

Remembering belatedly what starboard was, Kella ran toward the speaker and gasped. Fish wouldn't have been the word she'd have gone for. Even the monster catfish back in Verassez looked like house spiders next to the scorpion that had just crashed and broken the deck. Its eyes were staring as hopelessly as any fish out of water, but they were nothing like any eyes Kella had seen before: each was shielded by a material as impenetrable as the rest of its body. It was maybe four metres long, shaped like a sea bass but covered in armoured plates that resembled a rhino's but looked even harder and denser than dragon scales, though nothing like dragon scales. Like a tortoise, this was its body.

As the bashing sounds beneath the ship continued, dread crept into Kella's heart. Sensing Litz watching her, she tried to keep her face from revealing that fear but suspected she wasn't succeeding.

Sure enough, the water kept churning with movement. So many people were watching the rhino fish beneath them that the boat was beginning to tip toward the direction they were swimming from. Behind them, the army of krakeneaters began surrounding the fish. Not pack animals, sure. But neither were dragons, and they would work together for what they wanted.

Slowly, Kella turned to face Litz, watching her reaction. Kella spoke quietly, determined not to cause a panic among the pirates who all spoke Jeenobian. "You remember the catfish?" she asked.

Litz's dark eyes widened. "Oh." She pointed at the still wiggling fish behind her that was still rocking the ship with the sheer weight of it. "You think…"

"Krakeneaters wouldn't come out in force for only a few of these guys. We're getting to the small rocky island areas before Senice. It's practically shallow. This is a migration, and everything around us right now is either part of it or trying to interrupt it." Kella swallowed, terrified but feeling all the more certain this was a night her mami would have loved to see. "And we're in the way."

❖

Despite what felt like a win after rescuing humans again and finishing their long journey, Findan did not seem in a better mood, not even when they settled down for the night. The clan, the Vidan, they had saved had eagerly welcomed them as honoured guests, along with a former palace politician Zebenn wasn't sure of yet. Though he clearly considered himself a friend to the clan he'd been condemned with, they were less sure of him too. But even after everyone had been fed with the best this displaced clan had to offer, Findan seemed lost in a melancholy Zebenn didn't want to follow her into.

But loyal as ever, Zebenn left Hallen and the foppish politician, who had informed them he used to be married to the king, in mutual disgust and went to sit beside Findan by the fire. Quietly, they waited for her to say something. They'd become quieter since Rall's death. Perhaps because it felt someone ought to be, perhaps because their seemingly invincible friend had died. In any case, Zebenn felt aged and pushed into a role where those they considered family relied on their presence.

Silence did not seem to be tempting Findan into explaining herself. So Zebenn spoke up: "Have you met any of this clan before?"

Findan shook her head. "But their language has some overlap with one I know, and I can understand them a little. They wouldn't have called it Aelshia when last I was here. Much has changed."

"What did they call it then?"

She shrugged. "The forest. The river's bounty. It depended, from clan to clan, and the Aelshians had only recently become the most powerful. Magic was shameful, but it was still everywhere. Things weren't quite settled here yet."

"How old are you, Fin?"

Though it would seem a ridiculous question to put to anyone else, if there was one thing Zebenn knew how to do well, it was track and put signs together. And they were sure of at least two things: Findan was not a liar, and she hadn't aged in the whole time Zebenn had known her.

With the dancing fire making playful shadows over her face, her smile was hard to read. "How old do you think I am?"

"I think that the Aelshian Empire has been a formidable force for at least the last two hundred years. Longer, maybe. I'm no historian. But I know my great grandda used to tell stories from his grandmami about battles for the fort above our town, and I do not believe they fought a mere forest tribe."

Though it was a horrific thing to accuse her of using magic for, Zebenn did not feel any great disgust. Rules never seemed to truly apply to Findan in the same way as other people.

"You're right. They were not a forest clan. They never have been. Originally, most Jeenobians and Aelshians came from the same clan far to the south. My mother was one of those who helped move them after great shifts in the earth destroyed the homeland."

"Why tell me this now?"

Findan smiled strangely. "You know, I never intended to hide it. I would have told Kira, had she asked. But she didn't ask much. That was part of what we all loved about her, wasn't it? She met everyone as they were and had no interest in prying deeper." She laughed quietly. "Except for her moon readings. She asked me what moon I'd been born under shortly after we started travelling together, and I just said the first thing that occurred to me. But she smiled and said that made us the missing pieces of a whole, and it was a lucky thing we'd found each other. So I never dreamed of correcting her." She met Zebenn's eyes. "She also noticed I didn't age with her. But she didn't consider it her business to ask." She leaned her arms on her knees, bending as though to beg absolution from the Earth.

"I wanted so badly to keep her children safe. I wanted to see them grow into something she'd be proud of. But I knew from the moment she left us that dragons had already marked Ker, and though I chose to ignore it, that would never truly leave him. But I didn't want to hold that against him. I didn't want to be my mother." She looked a little upset, though in the low light, it was hard to be sure. "Maybe Kella didn't, either. I should have asked."

Zebenn was filled with the awareness that, invincible and ageless and powerful as she might be, Findan was very small. They moved closer in case she needed someone to lean on.

"I just want to stop them needing to fight or make deals with dragons. I'm so tired of it all."

"Is your mother dead?" Again, it felt ridiculous to ask, but nothing really sounded ridiculous anymore.

Findan shook her head wryly. "Hardly. She sits in the bowels of the young king's labyrinth. She enjoys being at their beck and call, waiting for the day they give her permission to make a bigger move." She snorted softly. "I am tired of waiting for permission."

Zebenn blinked, overwhelmed by the new information. "Your mother is the witch in the walls? That's not a myth?"

"No, just not used nearly as often as people claim she is."

Around the fire, music started again. Zebenn worried by how settled these people seemed. Assumedly, they would all be accused of being witches and threats to the empire, but tonight, filled with a sense of victory, they did not seem concerned. Zebenn understood. They had watched many people dance in the ashes of what had been their most important buildings, celebrating the death of the dragon without a plan to rebuild.

"She could get out of there if she truly wished to," Findan went on. "But it's where she wants to be. And if she ever gets her chance, she will do what I plan to do with the dragons. Only, she has the skill and heartlessness to do it with humans as well."

Zebenn heard a level of hurt in that tone. "Did she ever do it to you?" As they asked, a far more uncomfortable thought formed: *and have you ever done it to me?*

She nodded slowly. "I think so. But it's hard to be certain. I was determined not to be like her and so never did it while parenting, and I tried not to teach it to Ker. I didn't teach him much." She paused. "But with other students, I was less careful. One of those I mean to seek out tomorrow."

"Just to see?"

She took a deep breath in. "For good or ill, I'm sure he'll guess I'm here after today. And the issue with not controlling those around me is having to accept they may not always act as I expect or want." Her eyes flicked up to Zebenn, and they wondered if that wasn't something of a plea, begging to have at least one person to depend on.

Feeling a poor prize after hundreds of years of different relationships, Zebenn nodded.

❖

Nic had always been a deep sleeper, except on battlefields, when her body usually stressed itself into staying awake or could be relied on to jolt her awake when needed. Tonight had apparently been one of those times. Xoia had arrived late in her bed after a no doubt disappointing night with her First Mourner, but now, Nic was alone again. And it wasn't morning yet.

It had felt nice that Xoia had come to her. A little intrusive—her space was not her own and never would be—but it felt wonderful to be chosen, to be winning. Not just for fun but comfort too. That felt new. Maybe Nic could get used to consorthood. Especially when so far, it had involved proving herself against her co-consort or being a safe space to bitch about him. She'd tried to be more an encouraging listener than a participant, sensing there was no sense in making her position actively dangerous yet.

He kept pressuring Xoia about his mean little mind-shaping idea. Had he been anyone else, Nic would have thought he had a point. Apparently, the dragons were willing to influence the courtiers to ensure this war restarted, a generous offer they had never extended to the last king.

Nic had never had much interest in dragons, especially after knowing one through Litz. She did not see them with the mystical sheen so many did, whatever their age. Having to account for them in battles had always been frustrating. They might have been a formidable weapon the enemy had no access to, but they did as they pleased, rarely caring about Aelshian casualties and refusing to talk to anyone. And whenever they felt like it, they could read anyone's surface thoughts.

And apparently change them.

Disquieted by the empty bed, Nic stood to wander. She didn't feel confident walking these corridors as if they were her own yet, and only practice would get her there.

Xoia had moved into her mother's rooms but kept her consorts in what had been her mother's attendants' rooms. At first, Nic had assumed this was a nice nod to her mother's living consorts and her brother. There was no need to evict them when things could instead be restructured. But now, she wondered if Xoia was hiding something. Nic knew she hadn't been told all the royal secrets. But considering the old consorts wouldn't do much more than address her politely—and Agsdon actively disliked her—she figured it might be time to find out a few for herself.

When she received no answer to her soft rapping on Xoia's door, she went inside. As she'd suspected, the room was empty, and the theatre it had seemed with Xoia waiting for her, legs spread in an artfully made bed, had gone. Though it was a lovely room, and Nic was nervous to be in it alone, it was only a room. One pine torch still burned, the others having long gone out.

She was sympathetic to the inevitability of a restless night after such a day. A dragon had been murdered by strangers, and Reishann and the

Vidani under suspicion of being associated with witches had escaped. It certainly meant more work for Nic. It meant assuring her officers that until the king knew more, this did not mean war. All visiting traders were ordered to arrive unarmed and expected to find someone to vouch for their character if they meant to spend any time in Verassez.

Nic had spent the day ensuring a Narani caravan would be denied entry. Too many unknowns in so many large families. Though this attack might not have been her fault, any subsequent failures would be. It would be interesting to find how long or well her stint as a consort would last if her appointment to general was rescinded.

Xoia's fears were less personal. The clans had been showing scattered magic use, and just as Xoia tried to punish them for it and set an example, this had happened. A dragon dead, the people gathered for a good execution horrified, and their weak security exposed.

Privately, Nic blamed the dragons. This dead dragon had not requested a human security detail, and no other dragons had been near enough to come to their aid. It was frustrating that one dragon's pride had rendered Nic's army unable to protect people. No human had killed a dragon on Aelshian soil in hundreds, possibly even a thousand years. This was bigger than a tragedy, bigger than the bridge full of people. This was a scandal.

As Nic walked through the dark bedroom, she wondered where the king might have gone. Her chamber for relieving herself was not lit. About to retreat to her own quarters, Nic put a hand to the little brass dragon statue Xoia kept by her bed. The style was far more detailed and lifelike than the modern sculpture style, and the head was smooth and shiny from being stroked over many years. Smiling, Nic followed in the well-worn tradition, but to her surprise, the statue gave way under her hand. Cautiously, she gave it a push, and it dipped back into the table. Behind it, a creak revealed a sliver of dim light.

Nic grinned. Secret passages. Incredible. And Litz had tried to tell her they weren't real. Not even considering turning back, Nic did her best to keep her steps quiet on the narrow spiral stairs lit by a few small torches. Not knowing how far she was about to descend felt daunting, but the longer she walked, the more excited she grew. Joining the royal family had begun to feel like a job, but now, the sheen had returned.

At the bottom of the steps was a wide corridor with a brick floor. It led to one door, and Nic could hear who was inside. Xoia and Agsdon, arguing. Before the door was a small eyehole in the brickwork, allowing her to confirm that.

As she watched, she knew this wasn't meant for her eyes. Though Xoia usually kept a kingly composure, that was gone now, as Nic had only seen when she'd managed to undo her over and over the other night. Agsdon was not rattling her with any methods so delightful. But this hardly felt important when, sitting quietly and politely on the room's single bed mat and glowering was the missing queen of Jeenobi.

"It's all arranged. Please, Xoi, it'll be quick."

"Arranged without me!" Nic hadn't realised how low Xoia kept her voice until hearing it rise. It made her sound almost childish.

He put a hand on her arm. "I didn't want to worry you with it. A king shouldn't have to worry about minor details—"

"My sister's mind is not a minor detail."

Between them, Eisha stared, not looking convinced by either of them. It would seem she'd been living there for a long time. There were books, a fine bed mat, and even flowers on her side table.

Like Eisha, Agsdon did not seem to take much heed of the growing rage in his king's voice. "But if she does not remember or care afterward, surely, it cannot be a major one. The Circle assures me this has been done before, always for the good of the kingdom and dragonkind and that it never has ill-effects. It is never remembered."

"Of course it doesn't have ill-effects to *them*," the sisters said at the same time, using wildly different tones, Eisha's being far more irritated and resigned and in the low register Xoia had long abandoned.

Strange, Nic could not stop thinking it was the dourest the beloved princess of the realm had ever sounded. Famously, she brought good cheer to whoever was in a room, especially her sister. Eisha could enter rooms beside Xoia smiling and—without putting her sister down—could instil trust in any petitioner.

This was not that woman. Though imprisonment did not appear to have treated her too harshly—her hair looked healthy in the half-up style she favoured, and her clothes were fine, likely from Xoia's own wardrobe—she no longer had that lightness in her. Nic had no idea how she'd have felt if one of her siblings had imprisoned her for near on a year. But she also couldn't imagine one of them speaking up for her with the protective certainty that no matter their titles or possessions, nothing mattered to them or belonged to her so much.

In the darkness, Nic's hand slipped from the wall, making Agsdon's head turn sharply. "What was that?" He made to march out of the room.

Nic made her calculations quickly. She did not want to skulk back to her room, never learning what was going on. But being discovered, being forced to apologise, would be more intolerable still. She stepped into the room with her chin up.

At her appearance, Eisha gave her first smile. "Sister-in-law, I believe? Welcome to the family." For a moment, she almost sounded her old self, and Nic felt a pang, remembering Litz's parting words. But in the end, neither Nic nor Eisha had been important enough for Litz to stick around for. Xoia looked unsure of what to do with this new development.

"I told you we had not vetted her enough. She's probably a spy your cousin left here," Agsdon said.

"Litz did not arrange this marriage. I did." Xoia corrected him curtly. "Nic, why did you come down here?"

"To speak to you. When I found your chamber empty, I became concerned." She glanced at Eisha, who half smiled as though daring her to say something. Nic had never been able to resist a dare. "And now I find you threatening the king," she added, turning to Agsdon.

She couldn't be sure, but Eisha seemed a little disappointed. Xoia, however, was pensive. As Nic had hoped, Xoia seemed to be considering her framing of the situation. Nic wondered if Eisha had any idea her father had just rebelled over the mere suspicion that she was held here, that, successful execution or not, he had been sentenced to death. Aelshia might soon be fighting a war on two fronts, all for her. Nic wondered if this was what had hastened Agsdon's treasonous hand.

"How dare you?" he said. "Having just arrived in her majesty's inner court, you have no idea what lengths I go to in her name."

"But not in her knowledge, hmm? What were you about to do here?" Nic kept her voice light. Sentencing important people for mild crimes seemed popular, and the last thing she wanted was to have his accusations return to her spying on them. No, she was here by accident. There was nothing conniving or pre-planned to see.

"He means to have the dragons brand my sister's mind," Xoia explained, her voice strange and her eyes trained coldly on his face. Nic took from this confirmation that Xoia had known her sister was here but hadn't known what her consort planned to do with her. "To change her mind. To mould it to their own purposes."

"To your purposes." He shook his head. "I cannot believe you really mean to wait her out until she is singing your song. A year has proved she will not. For whatever reason, she remains loyal to her dragon-killing husband. She is lost to you, Xoia, and is no reason to further delay war." To Nic's surprise, he turned to her. "I'm sure my fellow consort understands this just as well. With the chaos of Litz's departure and the Jeenobian king's continued resistance, you will not get your war the way you want it without a turn in public opinion. Your sister has the power to do that."

"My sister as she was, not as you would make her!"

As they continued to argue. Nic felt Eisha's eyes on her, wondering just as she was what she meant to do. Because derisive as he might be,

Agsdon had not been able to punish Nic for stumbling in and had appealed to her as though she had become the deciding factor in the room.

"If you find her, if you see her, would you look after her?" Litz had asked before she'd leapt. Nic wasn't sure she wanted to do that. Litz had left her. But Nic certainly didn't want to do what Agsdon wanted. She had no wish to support a plan so obviously abhorrent, though canny.

From what Xoia had said about the technique, this wouldn't be the first time royalty had used it for their own purposes, but it remained rare because it was so uncommon for the Circle to agree that a king's concern would be one for them as well.

"What would you have her say?" Nic asked, curious now.

"He wants me to renounce my husband, claim he harmed me, and that he cares not for the treaty," Eisha answered, keen eyes fixed hard on Nic again. "Nic, how many guards are they keeping upstairs. Any?"

Out of sheer reflex, Nic almost answered, but she suspected the truth was on her face. She knew what Eisha was offering without needing to hear it. If Nic helped Eisha get out of this, she would be well rewarded. But with greater power or position than she already had?

Hopefully, Eisha had not been able to see the other truth: that in her effort to sneak down quietly, Nic had not closed the doors behind her. It wouldn't likely do Eisha any good, but the way upstairs was clear and open.

Nic wondered if Eisha had the same hesitance about turning violently on her sister as Xoia did. Though she was certain that walking into this wild interpersonal scene was an opportunity, it wasn't yet clear how she might use that.

"Don't answer." Agsdon smiled belatedly before returning to looking at Xoia in a pleasing manner that seemed to be working a little. "You can have your sister back, you can have your war, and you will have no dissenters. All I've ever wanted is to give you want."

Thinking of their night in Xoia's bedchamber, of Xoia's outsized gratefulness for the most standard of gestures, Nic doubted that, even if he believed it. But she too was drawn into watching his face.

Eisha sprinted for the door Nic still stood in front of. She could have stopped her. But she hadn't figured out what she wanted to do yet, and Eisha was unexpectedly fast.

"Stop her," Agsdon roared as Xoia cried out her sister's name. As they turned into the corridor, Nic stood against that wall, watching Agsdon glower before producing a bow that he smoothly nocked with an arrow. He must have expected he might need to fight his way out.

Xoia gasped as he cried out, "Not another step, Princess."

Slowly, Eisha, who had just reached the bottom of the stairs, turned. "It's Queen, actually." Though she spoke quietly, her voice echoed clearly along the bare corridor.

From behind Agsdon's tensed back, Nic's eyes lingered on his bow. He wasn't a military man, but she imagined he wouldn't carry something he didn't know how to use, or he would have simply paid someone to be standing beside him. And though the light was dim, his aim looked perfect.

"I don't think you'll do it," Eisha added, smiling a little.

Nic didn't agree, but Xoia seemed heartened by her words, as though they returned some civility to the proceedings. "I command you to put the weapon down," she said, her voice wavering but sure.

His aim remained steady. "If she runs now, she'll be your ruin. If you won't allow the dragons to offer a humane solution, then surely, you can see why this is necessary."

Eisha's soft chin hardened. Though Xoia continued to bluster with shocked indignation, Eisha seemed unsurprised by this side of him. Nic wondered if it was the first time he had come to visit her alone, as he assumedly had today before Xoia had found him.

"Start moving toward us, or I will shoot."

Eisha didn't reply, but her breathing sounded louder. "No."

"I will shoot."

Upper lip curling, Eisha turned, her skirt spinning with her.

Nic didn't give herself time to think. As his fingers got ready to release, the knife she'd placed at his side slashed. He gasped, a terrible guttural noise Nic had become intimately familiar with, and the arrow hit the ceiling, then fell to the ground just like it's master. For good measure, Nic removed her knife and stabbed his chest as Xoia began screaming his name.

Eisha's little footsteps receded up the long staircase. Good. Nic had done as Litz had asked as much as she could. There was no need to concern herself with more worrying about what Litz did or didn't want. And she'd definitely helped herself. Whatever she chose to do next, Xoia was left with one consort, one person to share in her secrets. Though Eisha running free would be a problem, it was one they could tackle together. Besides, the most likely scenario was still that she'd wind up dead somewhere in the forest.

As Xoia's bloodied hands found hers in the dark and she whispered Agsdon's name, Nic's mild anxiety began to fade. This was the right decision for everyone. Not least herself.

CHAPTER TWENTY-SIX

Sailback, Litz could admit, was good at what she did. When Kella and a few others came to her with theories about how much worse it was all about to get, it seemed she expected as much, possibly since they'd first spotted the krakeneaters that afternoon. Just like Kella, she looked uncertain they would all survive and yet strangely thrilled by that fear, like she hadn't believed herself capable of feeling it. Litz had known officers like that. They usually had careers as glorious as they were short, but the fact that Sailback was still standing, her feet planted on the now dramatically tipping deck, looking as grizzled and immovable as one of the barnacles stuck to her ship's hull, was soothing.

Until those fierce pale eyes, now grey as the sea beneath them, fixed on her. "Can your dragon pull a ship?"

We wouldn't be going much faster if I did. It's been some twenty hours since I rested. Not unless you helped.

"I don't think it would help much. And attaching ropes might slow us down more than we have time for."

Sailback nodded grimly. Again, she seemed to have anticipated this and was already moving on to other solutions. As she marched off to give orders about turning the boat and getting the sails out fully, the sailor at the helm tried their best to turn it as quickly as their captain commanded. But despite the rolling sea that made it feel like they were caught in a storm, the sky was completely clear. The danger felt almost dreamlike.

Litz had always struggled to keep herself grounded in situations like this. Ultimately, she knew that she, Kella, and Evlo could escape on Loren. Though they were still a few days' sailing from Senice, that would be far less for Loren to fly, and though she would tire without a break, it would be possible.

But there was no chance they could save everyone, and Kella would not let them leave without trying. And trying might get them all killed, even Loren. If the things in the water could break through the skin of those fish, Loren would be in just as much peril if she came too close to the water, especially if she was dragged into it.

You really would have made a poor general. They need to sacrifice people, I've heard.

Hush, you know Kella would never forgive me if we left.

I think you would also be unable to forgive yourself. You like these pirates. So get thinking.

Loren flew lower over the water, Sailback's pet flapping close behind her, both keeping an eye on the sea. As the harpy got a little too close to the surface, a long, pale tentacle snaked up and almost snatched it out of the air.

I half thought kraken a myth.

The sea is full of myths now.

Loren was right. Between the sharks, kraken, krakeneaters, and these armoured fish that looked capable of plenty damage alone, the sea looked more solid than liquid.

And at least one sailback.

You don't mean the captain.

I do not. And unlike the rest, I suspect it might be prepared to purposefully go after your boat. Be careful.

Finally, the seriousness of the situation began to hit, and a chill ran through her that had nothing to do with the night air that was still and warm. At the same time, something real began to hit the ship again.

The fish that didn't ram the boat as they moved past tried jumping, and they were not good at it. The first was not a large example. Fish that were easily five or six metres long were flopping on deck now, sometimes crashing through the side, and at one point, pinning someone and crushing their leg. They were unpinned just in time for a krakeneater to flop the front of its long, wide mouth onto the deck and pull the fish away. It clamped down with a crack as resonant as thunder, but before it could take another fish or person, it received an arrow to the eye and removed itself from the deck. Evlo's work, Litz assumed, though the crow's nest was too dark to see clearly.

Sensing blood, two more krakeneaters and many small sharks rushed in, though the first seemed to dive for the safety of the depths in time.

Through it all, the armoured fish kept coming. Though maybe one in fifty made a leap attempt on the boat, that was still enough for them to have seven on deck, with something or someone damaged on each arrival, and the combined weight was pulling them to one side.

One of them managed to move all along the deck and crushed its way down to the kitchen, pushing a crewmember off the stairs. Kella ran after them, and Litz was about to follow when a kraken's tentacles did their best to pull a crewmember off the edge, apparently seeing them as easier pickings than the shelled feast in the water.

Litz rushed down the ship, scimitar high, and managed to swipe through some of the tentacle, freeing the man. But panic flooded his face as he failed to catch hold of Litz or what was left of the deck and dropped into the gaping maw of a krakeneater and disappeared beneath the waves with a drowned scream.

Something that could have been driftwood or a limb floated to the surface moments later. Litz couldn't stop staring at it. She was so focused that when she felt a tap on her shoulder, she flinched violently enough to almost drop her sword into the waiting deep.

"You good?" Kella asked, sounding a little out of breath but otherwise unharmed.

"I'm good."

There could be thousands more on their way. It's endless, Loren confirmed in some horror.

No wonder they all arrive in such force. This makes the catfish migration look like a snack.

I've lost sight of the sailback.

At least it's a smaller worry than a thousand heavy fish or dozens of krakeneaters.

Yes, but this one likes to take boats, Loren cautioned. *I'll keep an eye out. You should too.*

A roar of water rushed out of the sea, violently forcing Litz to focus on the noise and chaos and the dark shadow blocking out the moon. *Found it,* she thought with near hysteria as she let Kella pull her toward the stern.

It seemed to take forever to fall. Just as some whales and dolphins, sailbacks enjoyed jumping from the water in a spin to land on their backs. Unlike the krakeneaters, they were only around the size of a large whale, but they more closely resembled dragons, with long reptilian snouts. What they shared with nothing was the huge back piece that gave them their name. It was heavy, it was razor-sharp, and if it landed, it would surely wreck the boat in two, sending all onboard into the hungry sea.

Loren was right. Unlike the rest, though it may have been attracted by the fish, sailbacks liked to hunt boats and loved to consume whatever it found inside.

Without thinking, Litz Pushed it up before it could hit the deck. The mental effort felt so clear and impossible, and it hung in the air for a moment. Beside her, Kella crowed with delight.

The crisis, mercifully, was solved by Sailback the woman leaping onto the deck out of nowhere, a trident firmly in her left hand. Her leap to land on the creature as she pierced it gave Litz the energy to keep Pushing it until it fell back into the water. The crew rushed to the port side to see their captain fall into the black waves. Litz took a deep breath, fighting exhaustion and hoping that no one had noticed her. She was as shocked and delighted as anyone when Sailback's harpy appeared moments later, Sailback held in its exhausted claws.

"Quit staring," she said in Jeenobi before launching into a stream of Doshni that seemed to be more orders.

There were a few scattered cheers in response, but no time to follow up on that or any of the odd looks Litz was receiving. She had been seen, but acknowledging it seemed to be no one's priority. As she heard another fish slam onto the deck, she knew she should be moving, but Litz met Kella's wild smile as she helped pull Sailback to her feet and felt some tension in her ease. Maybe it would be the longest night of their lives, but they could make it through.

They had to have moved away from most of the action now. The rate of fish slamming on the deck had begun to slow. Either they had steered far enough away, or they were beginning to reach the end of the steady migration. Maybe—

Sailback.

She's safe, and we got it. It's fine.

No, it's mother.

Litz looked to the other side of the boat just in time to watch larger, crueller spikes bearing down on them.

This one did not fall so slowly.

"Fuck," she breathed as it crashed into the deck, making a bloody mess of everyone there and cutting Litz off from Kella. She screamed her name but had no time for anything else before her half the boat creaked violently and started to fold in on itself, bound to follow its destroyer into the cold depths below.

❖

Kella had already begun to think that between seasickness and sea monsters, pirating might not be for her after all, but slipping even one leg into the icy sea was enough to decide her. Being surrounded by that would kill her from shock. That cold reality bolstered her into keeping her grip on what was left of the nearest mast and helping Sailback do the same.

"Be nice if your dragon friend could start being useful." Sailback snarled with the effort of holding herself up as their half of the boat began to tip. "Or your witch friend."

Choosing not to answer, Kella got two hands on the beam she'd been clinging to, privately thinking the same when she felt the wood snap.

She made herself keep from screaming as she fell, a wasted performance, considering everyone was too wrapped up in their own battles to stay alive to notice her. Kella had no idea if everyone shared this, but she'd always felt a level of disconnect whenever something bad was about to happen: the feeling of knowing exactly what would happen next and the inability to believe it would really happen. Falling into the cold sea felt like that. Though she could swim, it wasn't something she'd practiced much, and as she splashed, shock immobilised her. Her one thought was that her new aunties were going to be so mad at her.

She remembered herself and made herself as big as she was able. Before coming up for air, she yelled into the depths. Rall had told her years ago to do that with sharks. It probably didn't apply to sailbacks or krakeneaters or most of the other things down here, but the desperate need for air and the saltwater stinging her eyes kept her from finding out how close she might have come to an encounter.

The soft sheen of moonlight draped over the waves guided her to a loose plank of wood, allowing her to see that the ship was slowly sinking and that not everyone had suffered her fate. Above them, Loren had something in her jaws. She took one huge bite out of it before letting its bleeding corpse drop as bait some hundred metres from their wreckage. The "sail" on its back hit the water with a terrible smacking noise.

Just as Kella whimpered at the feeling of something moving past her dangling leg, the plank she was holding began to rise out of the water. Litz was coming to her rescue again.

It didn't occur to her until after she'd already whooped from joy that maybe Litz had wanted to avoid anyone seeing this. But with everyone slowly sinking to their doom, secrecy didn't feel like a great priority. Except, when Litz let her down in the safety of the far shorter crow's nest, Kella realised they were doing a lot less sinking. The pieces were starting to pull themselves out of the water and toward each other, creaking with the strain.

"Good to see you alive, boss," Evlo said as he fired another arrow and made some room without turning to look at her.

"For now. What's she trying to do?"

"Have a guess. She's your girl. Unless this is someone else."

"Doubt it. And don't call her that."

"Would you prefer partner? Lover? What would dragons say, mate?"

"She's nobody's girl. That's my *woman* out there." Kella managed to get out a laugh as their view continued to be pushed to face the sea. And poor as her vision was, she could see Litz and Sailback, with the survivors motioning them to their side of the sinking boat.

Litz looked up, drenched from another armoured fish crashing through the water next to her, and gave a smile that was so real but so strained. She couldn't hold this forever, and Kella had seen what could happen if she stretched herself too far. She had no intention of watching it happen again.

Setting her mouth, she turned to Evlo, whose quick eyes scanned the surf below. "We can't be that far from some kind of land if this is a migration, right?"

He nodded. "I saw things like this growing up. They're smaller and softer in the shallows near my village." He caught her eye, apologetic but not despairing. "I have no idea where they're from, only that they exist."

"Well, that's supposed to be what the pirates are for, right?"

"Do they look like fish experts to you?"

"What's a fish expert look like? Sure, why not?"

❖

Litz hadn't been sure what to expect from Sailback witnessing her impose a little of "witches' earth" out here at sea, but the encouragement surprised her. It might have been gratefulness, the ever-circling presence of Loren, or a lack of judgement over magic at all, but she clapped her hand almost fondly on Litz's shoulder as they watched their abandoned half of boat slip completely beneath the waves. Litz longed to let their half and all the people on it do the same, to let it all go, but Sailback's quiet murmur of, "Keep it up, lass," kept her grounded and focused.

But you can't hold this forever, Loren reminded her as she watched a few scattered survivors, some bleeding heavily, swim to the half of the boat still afloat, making her job a little more difficult with every sailor rescued. *This isn't a real plan.*

I know that. Exhaustion and frustration threatened to bury her as surely as the sea would if she let them, and Litz straightened her arms, her fingers. Though this changed nothing about her control over the breaking pieces of wood, it made her feel a little better. *We just need to think. Could we tie a rope to your tail?*

With that kind of drag, I could barely keep above the sea, even with your help. I would need to know we would arrive somewhere soon.

Seeming to read their minds, Sailback hoisted herself up on the mast and made herself as tall as she was able. The spikes on her shoulders had been flattened by damp, but she still cut a frighteningly impressive figure. "Listen up," she roared over the creaking wood and the yells of her crew. Her harpy flew behind her, taking up a pose that was endearingly like a child hiding behind its mother. "We're going to try to make it to the first of the hidden isles, Berracolmb. It's a barren, useless spit of land, but it's looking like a safe harbour to me now."

"And how do we make it there?" one of her crew dared to ask.

Sailback scoffed. "Use your imagination, and lighten up, boyo. We've got a witch and a dragon. We'll be there in no time." After a few more words in Doshni and a cavalier sneer, she jumped down, admirably keeping her balance without much apparent effort as she approached Litz again. "We'll be there soon, aye? I've lost one nephew and a lot of good crew members in the last ten minutes," she added quietly. "I don't plan on losing any more."

Feeling the ship and all the lives on it weighing her down in every way, Litz nodded tightly. "Get me rope," she said. "And if you can do anything to make what's left of the boat float without me, that would be appreciated."

Something beneath them bashed into the boat again. Though the seas seemed to be clearing, they had covered the area around them with blood, and even the fish that were currently prey were more than capable of tearing a human apart.

Sailback flashed a gold-toothed grin and secured her stolen Aelshian earring. It had a sword and a saddle carved on it, Litz could see now. "Aye," she said, as though trying to convince herself, "I reckon we can manage something like that."

❖

It looked ridiculous, but it was working. Nothing gave Kella a better impression of that than when she made her way down the precariously swinging ropes from the crow's nest. Shapes still circled them in the water, but with Loren now attached to them, they were moving away from the worst of the fray. Sailback was forcing her crew into making whatever adjustments they could to lighten the load and strengthen the front from taking water whenever a wave overtook it, or Litz let it drop a little. Because even with Litz in the centre of everything, looking magnificent and frightening as the sea itself, Kella still feared they would not make it to morning. Her whole body ached, shivering violently. She couldn't even imagine how much more tired Litz had to be.

Carefully, Kella edged her way over. The memory of the last time Litz had so visibly used her powers in front of a group of strangers clung to her mind. Kella eyed the crew carefully, but everyone slipping around with her seemed more concerned with survival. If Litz's actions shocked or disgusted them, they'd put it aside for now.

"Heya, Princess," Kella said while clutching a rope she'd brought for Litz to hold on to. She didn't currently seem to need one. Kella wondered if she had magicked herself into balance along with the ship. In any case, Litz slowly closed her hand around the rope and briefly managed a smile aimed somewhere at the middle distance.

"You're doing great," Kella opened with. "Ya big hero."

"Do I get a badge?"

"What?"

Every word from Litz seemed to require painful effort. "For joining your little guild."

Kella laughed before realising Litz's smile was continuing even as her eyes closed. Terrified of doing the wrong thing but unable to do nothing, Kella shouted her name and slapped lightly at her cheek, but when that seemed to have no effect, she pressed her lips to hers. Sea spray hit at them just as Litz's painfully sincere eyes widened with shock. Kella felt the boat begin to level toward Loren as Litz seemed to get her grip back.

"Stay with me, now," Kella murmured. "Don't you dare quit when we're this close."

"Close," Litz repeated, her voice sounding very small. Then, she gasped out a horrible little scream, and seeing nothing nearby that might have inspired that, Kella looked to Loren, whose wing was now hanging low and seemed to be bleeding.

Litz was gasping for breath, her arms still stuck outstretched. "It's the other sailback," she said with alertness that was startling. "She killed its child. It's come for her."

It didn't take long for the monster to have another go. Agile as Loren usually was in the air, she was tied to the remnants of the boat and had nowhere to fly. Kella suspected that if it hadn't been for Litz watching and able to give a warning, Loren's tail might have been sliced in two just like the ship.

"Okay," Kella said, slow as she might be to reassure a child. "You keep the boat going, and I'll go keep your dragon going, all right?

Protest was in Litz's eyes, but it was weak.

"All right?" Kella repeated.

Litz nodded. "All right."

Taking a deep breath, Kella pulled her way to the mast and found the ropes attached to Loren's tail. It was kind of thrilling. She was back to what she was supposed to be doing, and if she found out this thing could talk later, it had still tried to kill them. That had to be fair game. Especially when she was about to use her dragon bone blade to save a dragon. Not just a dragon but a friend and as much a part of Litz as everything else she'd grown to love.

Kella just wished she was a better swimmer.

Not letting herself think on it any longer because thinking always tripped her up, Kella sheathed her sword again and hoisted both legs up to cross them around the rope like one of the children playing ship rats in the Maya docks. She started climbing, shuffling her way along, the ropes chafing even through her trousers, glad she'd chosen to cut her hair and hoping she wasn't enough of a meal for a sailback to consider jumping after.

"Y'gonna speak to me for this, heh?" Kella muttered to herself and to Loren, who she suspected wasn't listening. Especially as the sailback threw itself from the water toward Loren's throat, but the wall of flame frightened it into retreating into the water. It would be back soon. And though Kella had reached Loren's tail, she didn't know what her play would be when it did.

Usually, when attacking dragons, it was important to keep her mind free of any planning. A mind-skimming dragon might intuit what she would do next if she thought too loud or clearly. But sailbacks, hopefully, had no such ability. With a little luck, even an idiot like Kella, who had lived her entire life as empty-headed as possible—as a point of professionalism— had a chance of outwitting it.

The back might be deadly and strong, but the front had none of the same dangers and seemed almost as smooth as a shark. And it had swam away to Loren's right—

It didn't seem to be smart, but it was learning. It had tried somewhere different every time, so the next would likely be going for Loren's right, somewhere near the middle. Kella made her decision to move just as it launched itself at the right back leg.

She leapt. For a moment, she thought she was going straight into its open jaws, but she had her sword out in time, and when she slipped down the monster's snout and pushed the sword into its eye, she was able to use that as an anchor. Nearly having both shoulders out of their sockets, she was pulled over backward, away from its teeth to drape helplessly down its back when it re-entered the water. It cried out in a ghoulish moan that echoed the sound the ship had made as it broke.

And Kella was back in the cold shock of the ocean, clinging desperately to the worn bone of her sword hilt with both hands.

"Are you sure you still want to cart around a dragon-bone-handled sword on your quest to save dragons? Bit insensitive, heh?"

And Kella had told Jev no because it was a good sword.

She thought about holding on to that good sword and following it and this wounded monster, perhaps the last she would ever be allowed to attack, down into the deep. Everything was moving too fast and was too cold—gods, Kella had never been cold before this—to do anything else. But as she opened her eyes and looked at the terrifying black depths beneath her, she felt a voice in her head:

Let go, Kella.

Without thinking, she obeyed. Didn't she usually? Hadn't that been what her whole career had been built on? Going where Findan told her? Trying desperately to be a more needed version of her mother?

Swim up. Don't you dare abandon her in this mess you've brought her into.

Looking up, Kella saw warm light and swam toward it. The air felt warm too. Dragon fire filled the air, and by the boat, people were cheering like Kella had worried they never would again. Cheering because she'd helped save a dragon.

She felt talons sink into her arm, and her heart sank, ridiculously thinking of her last sight of Rall, carried off by a griffin. But it was the harpy.

"Nothing to it," the harpy crowed. "Nothing to it."

It landed them both on Loren's empty saddle, and following a routine she hadn't realised she'd fallen into, Kella strapped in. Far below was half a boat she was keeping safe with Litz on it, who could now relax a little knowing Loren was safe.

"Keep talking to her," Kella said aloud, trying not to look at the harpy sitting behind her, clearly waiting for a treat she didn't have. "She needs it."

Loren didn't respond, and after her bitchy comments, Kella considered holding a grudge. Hadn't she just saved her life? Then she saw how Loren kept using her energy to breathe out fire, warming her scales and the saddle for Kella. She might be trying to give the boat a better view, but Kella suspected she was trying to keep her warm. And up in the air with wet clothes, Kella appreciated that far more than any words Loren could have offered.

❖

Zebenn had never spent much time in libraries. The Malyan one attached to the university was seemingly very important, but it felt considerably less impressive than this one just for being above ground.

There were not many guards, not enough to stand against Hallen and Zebenn and their few Vidani recruits. The steps were filled with carved images of the Earth and Sun standing strong together. They did not believe the Earth was buried but walked free among them, and after a few days in the expanse of this forest, Zebenn could understand why.

It was cooler down here; the ever-present humidity of the air faded. It felt like descending into a mine or tomb. They were somewhere they were unwelcome, and it had nothing to do with having to fight their way in. Hallen had taken a spear from one of the guards they'd gotten past, and the echoing sound of it hitting each step as he used it to walk filled Zebenn with dread.

"They say there're more books here than in all the known world," they said, keeping their voice low to limit echoes.

"It's true, I think," Findan said. "Most of them are copies, of course, but, yes. The Aelshian empire spurns the spoken tradition of the clans they subjugate."

As someone who'd just spent the day with a clan and seen their mountain village attacked more than once, Zebenn's sympathies were firmly with the subjugated clans. But unnecessary as they personally saw the written word, they still wanted to see what more books than anywhere else in the world looked like. They suspected it would be something special.

It did not disappoint.

"It's like a dragon hoard," Zebenn murmured as they entered the doors at the bottom of the steps. Palaces were not this grand, though it didn't feel particularly decorated or wealthy. The books or scrolls or plates spoke for themselves, like a glittering mound of wealth in a dusty cave. Zebenn wasn't one for reading, but even picking something off the shelf for a moment would feel like a prize.

There were a few shadowy movements around the shelves. Libraries or custodians. All wore dark robes that seemed impractical for spotting each other. Perhaps they all enjoyed their privacy.

"You're looking for a book?" Not everything here would be described as a book, but they were struggling to find the correct words.

"If I can." Findan glanced up. Zebenn wondered if magic could improve the senses. She seemed to be seeing something as yet unrevealed. "Mostly, I want to find a man."

No one approached as they crossed the smooth stone floor. Perhaps the outside skirmish had somehow alerted them. "Who?" Hallen asked. He'd been chewing some kind of bark from their hosts, and it made his breath smell strangely. Zebenn winced away as he came closer.

"An old student of mine."

"In magic?"

Findan nodded, still scanning the balcony. They felt horribly exposed here. Though librarians did not inspire fear, they theoretically had the protection of dragons. "The greatest talent I ever taught."

"Oh, such flattery would have meant something many decades ago."

Findan smiled vaguely as an older, whiskered man wandered out confidently, if a little stiffly, from behind the closest pillar. He wore no Aelshian earrings and did not sound Aelshian, either, yet this building was clearly home to him. "Does it mean nothing now?"

"No. You'll always mean much to me, mandav." He smiled, but his eyes were dull. "You look the same."

"And you very different."

The way they spoke made Zebenn look up, certain that they would soon find themselves threatened from above. But the few figures visible carried books, not weapons. And they became certain that he'd told his people to run, not fight. He viewed them as a threat.

Findan stepped forward slowly but unconcerned. "Are you surprised to see me?"

"Why are you here?"

"I want your help."

"The dragons." His smile flattened into a grimace. "I assume you are not looking for an audience."

"We've passed the chance for dialogue. And I don't believe they would speak to me, do you?"

His eyes glided over them all, making Zebenn realise the others were looking at him defensively. Findan had called him a talented student of magic, but the idea of him being a threat seemed ridiculous. Or maybe it was that they hadn't fought witches in many years. Though magic was distasteful, it had ceased to be something Zebenn considered dangerous to humans.

"Dragons do their best to keep their minds hollow, to do what they can to widen their perspectives. I cannot think they would find yours a particularly open mind."

"You sound admiring." As though sensing some invisible barrier, Findan stopped.

"It is difficult to reside here and not find something to admire about them."

"And yet, I hear you have been opposed to much of their expansion. Their new puppet king allows them much more than the previous did."

"It's easy to admire something while hating what it does, is it not?"

Zebenn was tired even following the tense conversation. They were willing to accept dragons had an intelligence worth wariness, but this sort of dialogue seemed excessive. And confusing for that.

"I want to hurt them. And I hope you'll help me." Before she was able to finish her last word, the man moved.

He was not young, and yet, when he turned his wrist, it was with speed and flexibility. Interestingly, he aimed at Hallen, who was knocked off his feet with a grunt and skidded across the floor.

Coolly, Findan stood her ground. "You're choosing them, then?"

"This is my library," he said, panting slightly. "And I would like you to leave. I don't plan on choosing anyone."

"Ah, the path of neutrality." Findan smiled, and though she did not move, the old man was knocked off his feet. "I thought I forced such cowardice out of you."

"Always useful to keep fear by your side," he managed as she stalked toward him, then stopped in her tracks, clutching at her throat with disbelief. "It would frighten me to do this, and yet, fear might push me to it," he said quietly.

Not having time to think, Zebenn launched two knives at him as Hallen returned to his feet. But though one knife managed to hit his arm, neither they nor Hallen were able to move any closer than ten paces. He was holding them back the way Ker and Findan used to do to dragons.

"We need dragons. It might not be keeping much balance here in Aelshia, but humans need them."

"Don't make me do it, Denone," Findan said as she continued to choke.

He looked confused, then fell back as though she'd kicked him. Releasing her throat, Findan took a shuddering breath and walked over, her short arms outstretched. Though her face was hard, her eyes seemed sad and faraway.

"Hey," Zebenn shouted, watching the old man try to slide away but remain unable to move. "That's enough."

Findan continued to hold her hand out.

"That's enough! We don't kill people, Dani."

"We kill witches," Hallen said quietly, having recovered and walked up behind the old man's head. He tried to meet Findan's eye, who wouldn't look at him. "If they're not with us, heh?"

Zebenn stormed forward, their bad knee flaring painfully. "Don't—"

But Hallen plunged his spear through the old man's eye like he was one more terrible dragon needing slaying and not a man whose home they'd invaded.

"No," Zebenn said, stepping away with disgust curling in their gut.

Findan was forced to take a step back when a hard book block hit her shoulder. From the mezzanine above, a few librarians were throwing whatever weapons they could find. Casually, as though she was swatting flies, Findan flicked her wrist, and two of them were launched out of sight.

She crouched to look at the spasming, bleeding body on the floor. He was still making noises, maybe a last desperate attempt to have his voice heard, or he was dead already, and his mouth was just moving the same way his eyes were still staring. When his movements stopped, Findan hesitantly closed his eyes. She was crying. It was becoming easier to see now that new light was coming from above.

"Ah, Fin, you threw that last one into the torch," Hallen admonished as though she'd just dropped coffee on his clean table. "It's heating up over there."

The two clan members they'd arrived with nodded and gestured toward the exit. Not knowing what else to do, Zebenn moved to help Findan up, but their eyes unbearably focused on the flames above. "We should stop it," they said as they crouched. "They must keep something here to stop fires."

Hallen made a dismissive noise. "Why would we do that?"

When Findan stayed silent, Zebenn reluctantly continued to help her up the stairs. As smoke began to fill the air, they did not turn back.

Findan continued to cry silently as she sat staring at the library entrance. Zebenn felt a stab of anger. She had not cried like that when Kella had been taken away. Perhaps if she had, they would not be here, far removed from their family and purpose.

Zebenn decided they'd had enough of whatever this was. Loyalty was still the most important thing, but even that had a limit, and this no longer looked anything like slaying dragons. They'd been sure they would remain by Findan's side forever, whether or not anyone else stood there with them. She was family and had been for a long time. But just as Zebenn had left home once before, they could again.

It was the saddest thing to not be noticed as they slipped away into the trees to a path that seemed usable.

They knew enough about this forest to be wary, and they tried to make that caution and not the ache in their chest their focus. Hearing the snapping of twigs ahead helped. Something was rushing toward them at a great speed.

Zebenn tensed and slid their sword from their belt. A woman nearly ran into them. She was gasping for breath, her lovely hair falling loose around her face, and her earrings bashed against her cheeks. Even in the dark, Zebenn could see that the clothes she wore would be a novelty outside of a palace; she wasn't even wearing shoes. She seemed frightened, stopping as though waiting to see what Zebenn would do.

As that soft round face looked up, Zebenn took a step back. "Are you the missing queen?" they asked, not knowing or particularly caring how an introduction would be made in the current circumstances.

She gave a soft gasp that sounded like a noise a princess would make. "You're Jeenobian?" Disbelief and hope hung in her voice.

Zebenn leaned back on one foot, sheathing their sword. Perhaps Ballian was right. Perhaps what was admirable about them was not their specific skills or their great loyalty but their willingness to help and be of use. "Are you wanting to go home, Majesty?"

CHAPTER TWENTY-SEVEN

Kella had no idea how long they kept going. She might have slept, though with the wind whipping at her face and anxiety for Loren and all the tired people she towed, she didn't remember relaxing. Nothing else attacked them, and when the sun began to rise behind them, Kella could see only clear blue water around the remains of the boat. At least they seemed safe from monsters.

But not safe. Her first warning sign was when the rope securing the boat to Loren began to strain and dip.

"Hurry, she's losing it," she urged Loren, who snarled out a warning that frightened the harpy from its perch. Kella only frowned and gripped the harness tighter. They were maybe another half mile from the speck of rocky land Sailback had advertised when the boat began to pull them down. Litz wasn't holding it anymore, and it could clearly no longer be dragged without drowning the crew. Kella wondered if the relief of seeing the end in sight had finally made Litz let go.

"Fly lower," Kella yelled. When Loren began to oblige, Kella unstrapped herself and jumped.

Feeling some regret for her newly dry clothes, she recovered quickly enough to remember to keep her body thin as she hit the water. Though the shock affected her less, swimming against the waves after a night like the one she'd had felt near-impossible. Only the thought of Litz needing her kept her on course.

When she made it to the sinking deck, even before looking at Litz, she picked up a half-conscious sailor's knife and cut through the rope pulling Loren down. She roared in response, waking the sleeping sailor, and flew in circles, keeping close as Kella turned to Litz. She hadn't quite passed out, but she didn't seem conscious, either. Sailback and Evlo were at her shoulders, gripping them as Evlo tried to force liquid from a small belt-horn down her throat.

Kella pushed him out the way. "Litz, can you hear me?"

When this got no response, Kella knelt beside her and took her hands. "Don't you dare slip away. You can't leave me in this mess. Loren would kill me." Exhaustion made her want to cry at the energy that joking was taking from her.

Sailback met her eye. "We'll be abandoning ship now, such as is left of it."

"Do it," Kella said. "You can swim from here, right?"

"I'd think less of any that can't," Sailback said, and Kella became aware of all the pirates beginning to jump, some cheering, other fetching bags and stray items. But none of this activity warranted much attention now. Sailback releasing her grip on Litz made her eyes open very briefly before closing. Nothing could distract Kella from that.

"Love you," she mumbled, smiling as her hands went limp in Kella's.

"No, no, *no.*"

As she stared at Litz's face, Kella dimly registered Evlo shaking her. "Kel, we can't stay. The dragon'll come down for her."

Loren, you better get down here right now, Kella thought furiously. "Swim, Evlo," she said aloud. "You can, right?"

He nodded. "You remember what you promised though, heh?"

Kella flinched, unable to think of anything beyond Litz's cold hands and slowing breathing.

"You can't let me go back to that place alone. I know you wouldn't do that, Kel."

She made herself nod, still staring at Litz. His words implied that she wouldn't abandon him because she was a good person, a hero, someone who thought of the greater good, a real friend who was worth looking up to. But what if she couldn't bear to be any of those things if she let Litz die?

Sobbing now she was finally without observers, she wound behind Litz to support her head, trying to pull her out of the water creeping over their legs.

"Not leaving me," she muttered, thinking she didn't care whether or not the world loved her if Litz wasn't part of it. "Can't do that to me. I love you too, you big fucking hero, and I was supposed to tell you first. You can't take this away from me."

Loren swept down and circled low over the waves. Even as she felt the wood beneath her sink deeper, Kella pushed Litz up to safety.

It took a few attempts, and Kella nearly slipped off, but she settled back in the position she'd spent half the night in, only this time, she got to hold Litz close and cry into the growing curls of her hair, mumbling nonsense. "You're supposed to be invincible. You've got a dragon on your team, remember?

"We're going to be there soon, and we're going to fix everything, and we're going to have so much soup.

"I love you, I love you, I love you."

❖

Somewhere in the night, Litz had tried to stop feeling what her body was doing and had succeeded. She had become no longer a body but a force, flowing far stronger than expected through that body and the boat. The gremlins, Ker had tried to tell her, felt that magic wasn't something to be controlled but was natural chaos loose in the world. Connected to every plank beset so harshly by the waves, Litz had come to understand that.

But as she opened her eyes to the new day, she was all too aware of her body. Her eyeballs ached, and her arms felt like they would never click correctly at the elbows again for tensing so long and hard, and even her hair hurt. And yet, still there were something unignorable and wonderful beyond the confines of the body.

"I love you too," she murmured because it was Kella's lovely, worried face looking down at her, and she'd been trying to say the words in her dreams, replaying the worst parts of the night in an endless loop of stress. But now they were away from it: sun licked her salt-splashed skin, and the ground beneath her was solid. She no longer moved with the waves she could still hear.

You're awake. Loren felt exhausted too. *My foolish little hero. Thank you for not shutting me out this time.*

I trusted you would let me take it as far as I needed to.

I'm going to rest now.

Do. Litz smiled, hyperaware of every muscle in her face required to make the motion and watched Kella's lower lip wobble. Odd. She was crying. That was funny.

"Get me something to drink," Kella barked.

Litz forced herself to sit up by her elbows to see who she might be addressing but collapsed immediately.

"You stay down," Kella ordered, but the stress in her voice was beginning to give way to amusement. "You've done enough."

"Aye, let's hear it for the witch," she heard Sailback say as a flask was passed to Kella. Half-hearted cheering dutifully filled the air as Litz took a few long swigs of liquid that burned her throat.

"Have we got any water?" Kella asked, still regarding Litz with concern as she spluttered.

Litz made another attempt at sitting up and succeeded. Where there had been some seventy Doshni pirates and a ship filled with provisions, there was now around forty, including Evlo, with no bags on any of them.

There was some laughter and remarks in Doshni before Sailback asked, "And where would you be picking that up, lass?"

Slowly, Kella's face fell as the reality of being abandoned on a spiky black rock finally seemed to hit her. "Oh," she said.

Litz, who still felt delirious to be alive and moving, smiled at the world and said, "You'd be digging for heaven there."

❖

"I missed this land," Noshi proclaimed the evening they arrived in the mountains overlooking Malya. From here, there was a beautiful view of the palace rock, its salt moat, its maze, and the sea lapping at the edge of the city. A sea Kella was sailing on now if all had gone well for her. Malya itself was built on flat land, and there was no opportunity to get such a perfect view any closer. Inside, it was chaotic and dusty and smelly, but from up here, it looked a calm vision.

Should I tell him this is likely still Nayona?

No. He seems happy.

"I've travelled the hill towns a fair few times, but I haven't been in Malya since travelling with your mother. I expect its changed." He laughed, also transfixed by the sunset on the water. "Though from what you say, they still play my songs."

Ker rolled his eyes and took a seat. *Truly, his brief capture doesn't seem to have fazed him at all. I can understand a little better how he kept up with Mami for years. He's completely unflappable.*

No, he doesn't seem affected.

Feeling Ellonya had something else she needed to express, Ker waited.

Maybe Kella was right.

About what? But he knew because she knew. There was no need for questions between them, but the rhythm, the pretence of conversation helped somehow.

She has your best interests at heart. Just like I'm trying to.

You do.

No, I have your heart. Ellonya's tone was very final, and gradually, he was feeling more distant from what she felt about what she was saying.

Though it was taking clear effort for her, she was trying to hold some of herself back. *She cares for you and who you were and whoever you will be.*

And you don't?

I am you, she said with such simplicity, it was impossible to imagine arguing. *Or I am as close to being you as anyone could be. And maybe no one expected that to be the case for us, and perhaps they are right to worry about what we are becoming together. But that is how it is. I cannot be objective about it any more than you can, but I can judge your sister as worthy a judge as any about when to stop.*

What brought this on?

You know. We almost attacked that man. You were going to use my body to do it like it was one of your limbs to command.

The brief sense of panic Ker had felt was beginning to dull. She was right. Things had begun to get a little stranger. She would speak with his mouth; he would move with her body. She had even helped use magic through him. And after spending a journey with Loren and Litz, he had seen this was not normal behaviour, even for a dragon and rider bonded for well over a decade. *So what?*

I think we should be a little more careful. Finding you has been the great joy of my life. I do not want to lose you inside me. She hesitated. *When Kella said good-bye to me, she asked me to look after you, even if you didn't feel you needed looking after. She was talking about this, I know.*

Feeling a little overcome, a little annoyed at Kella and strangely lonely without her, Ker put a hand on Ellonya's warm scales.

"Am I missing something?" Noshi asked, no longer distracted by the sunset. After a moment, Ker realised he was not joking but very interested. "I was hoping to learn more about dragons and dragonriders, and the two of you seemed like you might be more receptive than the others. You'll make a wonderful song. A perfect irony as well, considering how things ended with your mother."

How things ended. He speaks like she was a performer who stepped off the stage. "But," Ker started, then bit back his next words. *He's supposed to write about Kella.* "We're not a song for you."

Almost smugly, Noshi swung the drums on his belt around to his front. "We'll see. Between whatever happens next with your king and a new war beginning, this could become an epic."

Deeply uncomfortable, Ker walked away with the intention of finding wood for Ellonya to burn before he could say something he'd regret. It wasn't until he'd left them out of sight that he realised Sallvayn was walking with him.

"We should have gone with the others."

Ker frowned, having not expected that. "What?"

"On their journey across the sea. If anyone could have helped them communicate with and understand this different, frightening society of dragons, it would have been us. But we didn't think of this because it didn't occur to us to leave Ellonya or you."

"Sall," Ker said, "when gremlins bond to a dragon, is it emotional? Do you feel like you can't leave them?"

"It can be," Sallvayn said eventually. "It's not as it is for you. But we have great feeling. We often pledge ourselves to dragons who may not choose to stay with us, but we often remain with the same one all our lives, becoming a little more powerful, more beautiful, more like them." Long before, Ker might have wondered at the beautiful comment, but he understood so much more now. Sallvayn did look very different than when he'd first met them: their scales shone bright, and their nose seemed a little longer, a little more like a dragon's. He would even guess them to be taller and heavier than they had been.

"Who was your first dragon?"

"That was too long ago, and we were too many different sorts of people," Sallvayn said dismissively. "But our last dragon…"

"You've been looking for them, haven't you? All your sneaking away at night?"

"We have." But Sallvayn did not elaborate, and Ker chose not to push.

That night, when they camped, Sallvayn disappeared again, but in the morning when they flew to Malya, meaning to land on the king's roof, they were there without comment. Fearing how Noshi would fit into this bold entrance, Ker had insisted on leaving him behind to make his own way into Malya.

It was a very Kella sort of plan, but since Jev had spent half his life indulging Kella plans, Ker didn't think it a bad one. However they announced themselves seemed risky. To do it unignorably and with style felt almost wise.

Almost. Ker felt considerably less bold when they approached the great Malyan wall from its northwestern edge. The wall, while not foolproof, had felled hundreds of dragons through catapults and archers. He did not want Ellonya to be one of their casualties.

But just like the mountains, the walls seemed strangely quiet. Ker would even guess that they were almost unmanned. It was alien and strange flying over them, but he noticed a few catapults, and none of them were ready to fire. Though it was a temporary relief, Ker could not relax. Something was wrong. The city was bound to look different from this angle, but something about the empty walls made it feel unrecognisable.

When they landed, Ellonya roared out a challenge. Though Ker did not share his sister's issue with heights, he would like to think he wasn't a fool, so as Ellonya draped her tail down to the king's bedroom window, Ker did what he could to move slowly and carefully, grateful to be without Noshi's commentary. Falling to his death before even confronting his king would hardly make a good epic.

I won't let you fall.

I know. I know that. He sent her all the love he was able to as he swung through the window that Jev had left open for Kella. Perhaps not everything here would be unfamiliar.

Jev sat up in bed as Ker's feet touched the ground. His chest was bare; all he wore were shorts. He was only just awake, and perhaps that was keeping him in this strange calm. "Ker?"

"Hey." Ker couldn't think of anything to say. Ellonya wasn't standing behind him, and bringing her up from nowhere felt ridiculous, but he should say something. But to who? One of his oldest friends? The king who'd nearly seen him killed not even a year ago? Someone who was also hoping to help the dragons or at least stop them killing humans?

Ker was surprised by how relieved he was when Jev smiled. "I thought you left with Kella."

"I did." Ker stepped forward, and seeming oddly collected, Jev swung his legs down to touch the tiled floor. "I came back," he added uselessly.

"Uh-huh. Did you find Eisha?" He did not sound hopeful, but Ker did not want to be the one to dash any hopes he had left.

"No. I have a dragon on the roof," Ker said in a rush. "She's mine. I mean, I'm her rider. So if you're doing anything about dragons, talk to me, we're your experts."

"Findan taught you how to control them?"

"What?"

Still smiling, Jev stood, rang a bell for his servants, and fetched a long navy robe. "Since you came all this way from Kella's secret mission, let me show you what I've been doing while you've been gone."

It was what Ker had come to ask, but he didn't like how calm Jev was acting, and the Findan comment had thrown him. What did she have to do with anything? Was she the witch Jev was supposed to be in league with? "All right," he said eventually, having nothing to add. When a guard arrived, Ker was patted over for weapons that he hadn't bothered to carry, and he followed Jev down the hallway. Despite Jev having never been fond of mornings and the sun still sitting low in the sky, his steps were quick, and Ker had to make an effort to keep pace.

Everything okay up there?

No one seems to have noticed me yet. It was gratifying to find she also found the lack of dramatics a little worrying. *Should I just pose up here? Yes. But keep your guard up.*

"My mother kept a lot of secrets," Jev was saying. Though Ker had met him in or around the palace many times, he had never been in the residential quarters. "Some she shared with me to keep for myself. But just as I had no interest in continuing her war, not everything she chose to keep hidden was something I agreed with. Do you think your mother would have approved of you learning magic?"

For a moment, the conversational pivot so surprised Ker, he couldn't craft a response. "I have no idea." He'd wondered the same many times, but with dragons always far more prominent in his mind when it came to his mother's opinion of him, it hadn't been high on his list of anxieties. "She didn't hate it in Findan. But I don't think she would have been happy."

"But you don't regret it?"

Ker wasn't sure when it had happened, but the guard behind him was no longer alone. Two more had joined to walk in step with him. "No. Though I guess I've never tried that hard to get good at it, either."

"My mother would despise me for it," Jev said as he turned at the large balcony that overlooked the palace maze. He did not step onto it yet. "Her great secret, as I'm sure you've heard, was keeping a very old and powerful witch imprisoned within the maze, as two generations of kings before her had done. Mostly to deal with dragons if a situation with them on the walls ever became desperate. Occasionally, she was used for other purposes, but mostly, she was kept there as a resource. As one last great weapon we might hold over the Aelshians' heads if we ever were bold enough to use it."

"Are you?"

Jev stayed smiling in a way that almost made Ker jealous. He looked content. "My only regret is how long it's taken to solve the two great issues that have plagued us for hundreds of years. Neither the Aelshian army nor any rogue dragons will threaten us ever again."

"Through one witch?"

Jev stepped onto the balcony, and having no idea what to expect, Ker followed. Below them, the maze was gone, and in its place were rocks and sand. Half of the beach must have been dragged here, not to mention waste from the mines to the north.

And on the sand and rubble and stones were dozens and dozens of dragons.

In Aelshia, Ker had thought he'd seen more dragons than he'd ever seen in his life, but that experience had been nothing like this. That had been a city full of dragons in the same way it had been for people. This was a crowd or a mob.

Or a prison.

A few snapped at each other. One was blowing fire uselessly into the sky. A few slept, curled up like cats under the hot sun. When the comforting sea breeze of home blew past them, a horrible stench hit Ker. They were living in their own filth down there. But even with that, none seemed interested in flying away.

Ker had no idea how he'd done it, but Jev had an army of dragons.

About the Author

Jenna Jarvis grew up in Edinburgh, Scotland, and now lives in Glasgow with her partner. Her degree in literature and history has never helped her find a job, but just like the eclectic mix of jobs she has held, it's definitely helped with writing inspiration. She is happiest in mismatched socks and earrings, enjoys watching horror films with her dog, and thinks karaoke is healing for the soul. *Digging For Destiny* is her third published novel and the second in the Dragon Circle series. She can be found on X @JJnaedrums and on Instagram @jjarvisthefish.

Books Available from Bold Strokes Books

And Then There Was One by Michele Castleman. Plagued by strange memories and drowning in the guilt she tried to leave behind, Lyla Smith escapes her small Ohio town to work as a nanny and becomes trapped with an unknown killer. (978-1-63679-688-8)

Digging For Destiny by Jenna Jarvis. The war between nations forces Litz to make a choice. Her country, career, and family, or the chance of making a better world with the woman she can't forget. (978-1-63679-575-1)

Hot Hires by Nan Campbell, Alaina Erdell, Jesse J. Thoma. In these three romance novellas, when business turns to pleasure, romance ignites. (978-1-63679-651-2)

McCall by Patricia Evans. Sam and Sara found love on the water, but can they build a future amid the ghosts of the past that surround them on dry land? (978-1-63679-769-4)

One and Done by Fredrick Smith. One day can lead to a night of passion… and possibly a chance at love. (978-1-63679-564-5)

Promises to Protect by Jo Hemmingwood. Park ranger Maxine Ward's commitment to protect Tree City is put to the test when social worker Skylar Austen takes a special interest in the commune and in Max. (978-1-63679-626-0)

Sacred Ground by Missouri Vaun. Jordan Price, a conflicted demon hunter, falls for Grace Jameson who has no idea she's been bitten by a vampire. (978-1-63679-485-3)

The Land of Death and Devil's Club by Bailey Bridgewater. Special Liaison to the FBI Louisa Linebach may have defied all odds by identifying the bodies of three missing men in the Kenai Peninsula, but she won't be satisfied until the man she's sure is responsible for their murders is behind bars. (978-1-63679-659-8)

When You Smile by Melissa Brayden. Taryn Ross never thought the babysitter she once crushed on would show up as a grad student at the same university she attends. (978-1-63679-671-0)

A Heart Divided by Angie Williams. Emma is the most beautiful woman Jackson has ever seen, but being a veteran of the Confederate army that killed her husband isn't the only thing keeping them apart. (978-1-63679-537-9)

Adrift by Sam Ledel. Two women whose lives are anchored by guilt and obligation find romance amidst the tumultuous Prohibition movement in 1920s California. (978-1-63679-577-5)

Cabin Fever by Tagan Shepard. The longer Morgan and Shelby are stranded together, the more their feelings grow, but is it real, or just cabin fever? (978-1-63679-632-1)

Clean Kill by Anne Laughlin. When someone starts killing people she knows in the recovery world, former detective Nicky Sullivan must race to stop the killer and keep herself from being arrested for the crimes. (978-1-63679-634-5)

Only a Bridesmaid by Haley Donnell. A fake bridesmaid, a socially anxious bride, and an unexpected love—what could go wrong? (978-1-63679-642-0)

Primal Hunt by L.L. Raand. Anya, a young wolf warrior, finds herself paired with Rafe, one of the most powerful Vampires in the Americas, in an erotic union of blood and sex. (978-1-63679-561-4)

Puzzles Can Be Deadly by David S. Pederson. Skip loves a good puzzle. Little does he know that a simple phone call will lead him and his boyfriend Henry to the deadliest puzzle he's ever encountered. (978-1-63679-615-4)

Snake Charming by Genevieve McCluer. Playgirl vampire Freddie is on the run and a chance encounter with lamia Phoebe makes them both realize that they may have found the love they'd given up on. (978-1-63679-628-4)

Spirits and Sirens by Kelly and Tana Fireside. When rumored ghost whisperer Elena Murphy and very skeptical assistant fire chief Allison Jones have to work together to solve a 70-year-old mystery, sparks fly—will it be enough to melt the ice between them and let love ignite? (978-1-63679-607-9)

A Case for Discretion by Ashley Moore. Will Gwen, a prominent Atlanta attorney, choose Etta, the law student she's clandestinely dating, or is her political future too important to sacrifice? (978-1-63679-617-8)

Aubrey McFadden Is Never Getting Married by Georgia Beers. Aubrey McFadden is never getting married, but she does have five weddings to attend, and she'll be avoiding Monica Wallace, the woman who ruined her happily ever after, at every single one. (978-1-63679-613-0)

Flowers for Dead Girls by Abigail Collins. Isla might be just the right kind of girl to bring Astra out of her shell—and maybe more. The only problem? She's dead. (978-1-63679-584-3)

Good Bones by Aurora Rey. Designer and contractor Logan Barrow can give Kathleen Kenney the house of her dreams, but can she convince the cynical romance writer to take a chance on love? (978-1-63679-589-8)

Leather, Lace, and Locs by Anne Shade. Three friends, each on their own path in life, with one obstacle…finding room in their busy lives for a love that will give them their happily ever afters. (978-1-63679-529-4)

Rainbow Overalls by Maggie Fortuna. Arriving in Vermont for her first year of college, an introverted bookworm forms a friendship with an outgoing artist and finds what comes after the classic coming out story: a being out story. (978-1-63679-606-2)

Revisiting Summer Nights by Ashley Bartlett. PJ Addison and Wylie Parsons have been called back to film the most recent Dangerous Summer Nights installment. Only this time they're not in love and it's going to stay that way. (978-1-63679-551-5)

The Broken Lines of Us by Shia Woods. Charlie Dawson returns to the city she left behind and she meets an unexpected stranger on her first night back, discovering that coming home might not be as hard as she thought. (978-1-63679-585-0)

Triad Magic by 'Nathan Burgoine. Face-to-face against forces set in motion hundreds of years ago, Luc, Anders, and Curtis—vampire, demon, and wizard—must draw on the power of blood, soul, and magic to stop a killer. (978-1-63679-505-8)

All This Time by Sage Donnell. Erin and Jodi share a complicated past, but a very different present. Will they ever be able to make a future together work? (978-1-63679-622-2)

Crossing Bridges by Chelsey Lynford. When a one-night stand between a snowboard instructor and a business executive becomes more, one has to overcome her past, while the other must let go of her planned future. (978-1-63679-646-8)

Dancing Toward Stardust by Julia Underwood. Age has nothing to do with becoming the person you were meant to be, taking a chance, and finding love. (978-1-63679-588-1)

Evacuation to Love by CA Popovich. As a hurricane rips through Florida, so too are Joanne and Shanna's lives upended. It'll take a force of nature to show them the love it takes to rebuild. (978-1-63679-493-8)

Lean in to Love by Catherine Lane. Will badly behaving celebrities, erotic sex tapes, and steamy scandals prevent Rory and Ellis from leaning in to love? (978-1-63679-582-9)

Searching for Someday by Renee Roman. For loner Rayne Thomas, her only goal for working out is to build her confidence, but Maggie Flanders has another idea, and neither are prepared for the outcome. (978-1-63679-568-3)

The Romance Lovers Book Club by MA Binfield and Toni Logan. After their book club reads a romance about an American tourist falling in love with an English princess, Harper and her best friend, Alice, book an impulsive trip to London hoping they'll each fall for the women of their dreams. (978-1-63679-501-0)

Truly Home by J.J. Hale. Ruth and Olivia discover home is more than a four-letter word. (978-1-63679-579-9)

View from the Top by Morgan Adams. When it comes to love, sometimes the higher you climb, the harder you fall. (978-1-63679-604-8)